THE
5K ZONE

COLD WAR BORDER INTRIGUE

www. 5kzone.com

GARY R HALL

outskirtspress

DENVER, COLORADO

The 5K Zone
Cold War Border Intrigue

Outskirts Press, Inc.
http://www.outskirtspress.com

ISBN: 978-1-4787-6386-4

Outskirts Press and the "OP" logo are trademarks belonging to Outskirts Press, Inc.

PRINTED IN THE UNITED STATES OF AMERICA

Dedicated to:

Carolyn — My rock
Theresia — Mähring / Czech connection
Inge —'80s Kella, East Germany mayor
Elena — Russian connection
Nate — Guide to pertinent 5K sites

With heartfelt appreciation

TABLE OF CONTENTS

Author's Note

Ethnic Germans had lived in Czechoslovakia for hundreds of years before 1938. Although their numbers were estimated at over three million they were in the minority and concentrated primarily in the German border area which became known as the Sudetenland. In September of 1938 Adolf Hitler demanded German annexation of the Sudetenland. In what is now recognized as an appeasement to Hitler, the representatives of France, Italy and the United Kingdom granted this demand. No Czechoslovakian representative was present at the signing of the agreement in Munich on September 29, 1938. The Sudetenland was effectively under the control of Germany until the end of World War II. When the Russians liberated the Sudetenland, borders were restored to pre-agreement boundaries and a torrent of animosity toward the German inhabitants was unleashed. The Potsdam Agreement of July, 1945, had mandated an "orderly and humane" expulsion of ethnic Germans from the Sudetenland. In most cases, the expulsions were anything but orderly or humane. The expulsions and other provisions of the Potsdam Agreement, which effectively created an East and West Germany, were the reality of the principal characters in this fictional novel. Beginning in the early fifties, after expulsions were completed, border crossings between the Allied and Soviet zones became strictly controlled and continually improved upon by various means: electrified barbed-wire fences, landmines, guard towers, vehicular patrols, trained canines and other defection-preventive techniques. These techniques were not consistent in time of implementation or over the entire length of the border. The patchwork nature of border fortification by the East Bloc led to inconsistent degrees and methods of security along the border until early in the nineteen seventies. Although the postwar border separated most of Europe into East and West, this novel is concerned with the separation of what became West Germany from the area of Czechoslovakia which had previously been known as the Sudetenland under German control. The terms Soviet and Russian are often used interchangeably in reference to the Soviet Union in that period of history, as are the terms Germany and West or East Germany.

Based on documented history, this novel has referenced no person or persons living or deceased as principals. The author has drawn on his personal experiences, interviews with expellees, research of public documents and his imagination to create this work of fiction.

ONE

THE YOUNGSTERS

From the compact, well-designed patio area in front of his family's home, Peter Ackerman could see beyond the village walls as far as the hillside behind Studánka, almost two kilometers away. He often rested here on one of the comfortable lawn chairs his mother had arranged for the family's relaxation convenience. Normally this was his summer relaxation space after another exhausting day with *Fussball* practice, tending to family tasks, finishing schoolwork, or just hiking and running in the Studánka hills. Today he was confused and feeling anxiety. He was beginning to wonder why his life was changing. *Muti* and *Vati* were often acting nervous and sad rather than like the happy and confident parents he had always known. He was almost sure their behavior was related to concern about the war.

Barely eleven years old, Peter's life had been uncomplicated by politics or war. Now there was an uneasiness in Tachau that seemed war-related. Born in 1933, he was vaguely aware of the annexation of the Sudeten area of Czechoslovakia by Germany. He had heard of Adolph Hitler's triumphant Nazi parade into the Sudetenland in October of 1938 and how happy that entry had made the Sudeten ethnic Germans. He remembered that most school teachers suddenly changed from teaching in the Czech language to teaching in the German language. There had always been a chasm of sorts between the Czech students and the German students, but he never fully understood the reasons for the division. Peter wasn't aware that many areas in the Sudetenland maintained completely separate Czech and German educational systems. Speaking several languages was accepted as normal by most Europeans to whom language capability was never given much thought. This day he didn't dwell on the uneasiness he felt, but it marked his first real awareness and concern for the future. For an eleven-year-old boy he was very mature and perceptive.

There was little talk in the Ackerman home about the war or Nazism. It was as though it was an abstract war, which had no meaning to the family. Armin and Isabella Ackerman attended church regularly and associated socially with neighborhood ethnic Germans. Armin managed the local chemical factory where he employed many well-treated Czechs. Isabella was a traditional German *Hausfrau* who did the cooking, cleaning and organization of family activities. She was more social than Armin; a large part of which was her morning coffee *klatschen* in a German-owned local café. Most of the local German women participated whenever they could. The conduct of the war was taking its toll on the morale of the women and even causing some contentious discussions as the ladies took different stances on Germany, Nazism and the future. This sometimes caused stress for Isabella and carried over to her Ackerman-family life. She had no idea that Armin and Peter could sense her discomfort; but, over the past few months, Peter had become aware that she had changed. He had accepted the problem as temporary because he was young and did not yet know that life can have many negative, as well as positive, twists and turns.

As he relaxed in the early evening sun, he shaded his eyes momentarily with his arm and hand. At this time on a summer evening the temperature always cooled in the Sudetenland, even though the sun was still visible. It was a good time for Peter to run to Studánka for the nature exposure and the exercise. It was uphill going west into the evening sun, but the forested hill provided shade from the sun much of the time. The downhill return was an easy run, which allowed him to quickly attain his top speed. The trail was extremely well maintained, so that baby strollers could roll easily and the elderly would not be hindered by treacherous footing or any otherwise difficult passage inconveniences. When his friend, Trudi Kehle, ran with him, they always stopped and rested at the top. She didn't like to be called Gertrude, her legal name, but he used that often if she was faster than him that day. She always had an inner chuckle when he referred to her as Gertrude. She was aware that he only used Gertrude when she did something he considered praiseworthy; for that reason she took pleasure in hearing him refer to her as Gertrude. She just never let him know how well she understood him. There was a park-like area at the top of the hill with some narrow trails leading into more heavily-wooded stands of trees. One day when he was alone, Peter found an interesting secluded tree he wanted to explore. He decided to surprise Trudi with his discovery on their next trip together to the Studánka hilltop.

Peter and Trudi were ethnic Germans, who were school classmates and members of the village junior sports club. They had become friends while pursuing their mutual interests, although Peter favored soccer, while Trudi was the fastest female sprinter and distance runner—of any age—in the club. She was strong, pretty and an interesting person. Peter enjoyed her company more than any other person in the entire school. Often, she visited him at the Ackerman home to just listen to the family radio and enjoy the camaraderie. One of the stations they enjoyed was the American Armed Forces Network (AFN), which was a recent addition to Tachau listeners. The signal wasn't always strong enough to be received in Tachau but was entertaining when it could be heard. They didn't understand the English-language programs completely, but thoroughly enjoyed the music.

On one particular visit, she asked "Why don't we get the AFN signal all the time, Peter?"

"Papa says it's because of the skip-distance."

"What's that?" asked Trudi

"It has something to do with the signal bouncing off the clouds or just going straight into the atmosphere. If the signal bounces off the right cloud we get it here. Munich is only two-hundred kilometers away by straight line."

"I guess your Papa knows about that. I like the American music . . . Bing Crosby, Frank Sinatra and the Andrews Sisters."

"I like that, also, Trudi, but my favorite is still Marlene Dietrich. Her song *Lili Marlene* is my favorite song. I wish she hadn't gone to America."

Trudi added her agreement. "Her songs are still good for the soldiers, though, even if she is in America. That's what is so confusing. We are fighting a war against America and its Allies at the same time that we listen to Marlene Dietrich, a German lady, on the American radio station. What will happen to us if the Americans are only two-hundred kilometers away?"

Peter added, "I don't know, Trudi, but Papa says we get that station now from Munich because the Americans have advanced and control the city. The programs are for American soldiers in the area."

Trudi Kehle lived near the Ackermans in an area called Chodská. She lived with her mother and her mother's Czech husband. Her biological father had died in the Black Sea Campaigns in 1941. He had been a sailor and a Nazi, but had become a victim of the Soviets who retaliated when the Nazis launched Operation Barbarossa. Her mother had been born in Tachau and lived with Trudi's grandmother until she married. The grandmother was now living with them, but talked often of a desire to return to her childhood home in non-Sudeten Germany, in nearby Bärnau. This talk by her grandmother served to further confuse the twelve-year-old Trudi. Why would her grandmother want to leave the security of family to go to a place where she hadn't lived since she was a child?

This evening Trudi was helping to prepare the evening meal while she was trying to hear her parents muffled conversation from the living room. She couldn't hear everything but could sense that it was a nervous and serious conversation. Something about the war not going well for the Germans and the implication it might have on their dual-nationality family.

It was worrisome to Trudi because she didn't know if she should be afraid, or if this was just another passing irritation. For some time now her mother had been avoiding answering her questions with an uncharacteristic frown on her face. Trudi expected to talk to Peter about her concern when they were together again. Her step-father, named Rudi Jelinek, couldn't afford a hard-to-obtain telephone, so she decided to run over to Peter's home before darkness fell. She wanted to set a time for their meeting the next day, which she always anticipated with a great degree of satisfaction.

As agreed the previous evening, they met early at the Church of St Wenceslas, which was an approximate halfway point between their respective homes. Although they both lived in the Chodská area of Tachau, Trudi lived outside the village wall, while Peter lived inside. The church was located near one of the three cobblestone wall access passages. It was a convenient meeting place for both.

"*Guten Morgen*, Trudi, it's another beautiful day!"

"*Jawohl*, Peter, did you sleep well?"

The formalities created an environment of mutual respect, which had been their norm since the day they met. They were mature, pubescent youngsters full of life and ready to explore whatever life had to offer. They always found interesting activities to satisfy their youthful search for new discoveries. Peter surprised her this morning.

"What is in the backpack, Peter?"

"I brought something to drink and a cheese bread."

"That's nice, but the pack is bulging. What else is in there?"

"That's a surprise for when we get to the park. It's heavy, so I won't be able to race today." It was a good excuse for not racing. It bothered Peter to not be as fast as Trudi although he never let his frustration show.

"OK, we can race another day. I'll carry the pack when you need a rest."

It took about ten minutes to get out of the village built-up area and on the path to the Studánka area. Soon they were in the forested area and could notice the rise in elevation. They would be two-hundred meters higher when they reached the hilltop. Peter was very slow, so they stopped at a bench as they neared their destination.

"*Mein Gott,* Peter, this is heavy." Trudi shouldered the pack as they continued on the path.

"Really? I feel like racing now."

She giggled at his attempted humor and answered quickly, "On the way down, you just wait. The pack won't be so heavy then."

"You're right, Trudi. It will be empty!"

When they reached the park, Peter proceeded to the fir tree that was interesting to him, ceremoniously opened the backpack and removed the contents: bread, then cheese, then *Afri* Cola, then a six-meter length of clothesline rope and finally a heavy metal object that looked like an oversized round screw with a connector loop.

Trudi was only mildly surprised, because Peter was always coming up with ingenious devices and gadgets that would help him satisfy his inquisitiveness and achieve goals. She was always amazed at where his imagination took him. The intrigue of Peter's character ensured that Trudi never lost interest in where he was taking any new set of events. Now she was very curious to find out how these items would be used.

Peter knew she would be puzzled. "If you can figure out what we're going to do with these items, I'll let you win the race on the way back."

"Ha . . . Peter, you are a riot. But give me a clue. What is that metal thing?"

"Oh . . . that came from my father's factory. I think they use it to attach to their equipment wagons so that the work vehicles can connect to the round part and move them around the shop."

"Ok, let's see," she looked at the rope, the apparent weight and realized they were standing before a very large malformed fir tree for a specific reason. She looked up at the huge gnarled branches of the tree and she knew she had it. "I have it! If I'm correct, I'll carry the empty backpack down the hill during the race."

Peter knew it wouldn't take her long. She always got it! Trudi proceeded to tie one end of the rope to the weight, untangled the rope, ensured it had enough slack and threw the weight over one of the huge branches.

"There you go, Peter, now we can climb the tree! But why?"

"Because it could be our place. Let's take a look."

Peter used the rope to pull his body higher and higher as he supported himself with his legs on the fir tree's thick bole. Above the bole the thick branches grew in several directions, sometimes crossing over one another. Trudi pulled herself up effortlessly. The thick branches had grown in such a way that a near perfect bowl was formed that wasn't visible from the ground. Peter noticed several spaces beneath the overlapping branches, leaving hidden, downward openings in the center of the tree's bole. Peter recognized that this could have been caused by decaying heartwood. The youngsters were rather self-satisfied that they had discovered this natural phenomena. Because it was not evident by viewing from below and was in a very isolated area of the park, they claimed the tree as their private place; its location never to be revealed to anyone outside of their families. They had found a remote area with a tall gnarled fir tree that interested both of them. About three meters off the ground several of its branches had grown in different directions. Trudi thought that lightning had caused the deformity sometime in the very distant past. The bole and branches of the tree were huge and the tree appeared to be very old. Over many years the lightening-struck branches re-covered their lives and reached for the sunlight so that their needle-like leaves could continue the process of photosynthe-sis. The thick, healthy, green needles served to provide con-cealment for the youngsters "place," as the branches thrived and bent toward the sun.

They called the tree the *Blitzbaum*. Their normal evening run to the lightning tree became known to them as, "the run to the *Blitzbaum*."

Before departing, they concealed the rope and weight in thick underbrush where they would not be detected acciden-tally by anyone who happened into the area.

After spending the morning and part of the afternoon in the park surroundings, they started back down the hill. This time Peter had no heavy-pack excuse. As fast as he was and with an excellent capacity for endurance, he was seldom a match for Trudi. This day was no exception. It bothered him, but he was more envious of her ability than he was jealous or resentful. She was truly an athletic marvel.

On the *Blitzbaum* hill that day they had discussed the changing disposition of their parents. They couldn't agree on a reason for the change, but both suspected it had something to do with the war. As time passed, their suspicions became reality. The news was reaching Tachau that the war wasn't going well for the Germans. Several injured soldiers had been returned to their homes in Tachau with stories that were guarded but definitely not positive. There was a rumor that one of the returnees was a deserter. Some of the local Czechs were acting-out aggressively in the presence of resident Germans, both verbally and by aggressive actions.

On another day, while sitting in the *Blitzbaum,* Peter and Trudi heard a muffled explosion to the east. Shortly thereafter, an airplane with red stars on its wingtips flew over. The youngsters recognized immediately that the sighting and the explosions could be more than coincidence.

"I think that's a Russian plane, Trudi, we better get out of here."

Peter was correct. The aircraft they saw that day was a Russian Sukhoi Su-2R reconnaissance plane. For many months after that sighting, German-held Tachau was pounded with Russian bombs until the Germans were forced into surrender and the entire Sudetenland was held by the Russians.

That day marked the beginning of an even more drastic change for the youngsters and all the German residents of the Sudetenland.

TWO

HOPELESSNESS

Tachau lay in ruins almost a year after the end of the war. Allied airstrikes and artillery bombardment had leveled the village and left burned-out homes, factories and businesses on both sides of the Mže River. The Soviets had officially occupied Tachau, as well as the entirety of the Sudetenland, at war's end on May 8, 1945. After many frustrating years of war in which the Nazis had turned on their former war-treaty partners and inflicted massive casualties during Operation Barbarossa, the Soviets, under the control of the massive Russian military, were taking their revenge. Pillaging, plundering and raping were words that barely described the conduct of the Soviet occupation. Lip service was paid to the notion that the Czechs were now in control of the Sudetenland, although a certain compromise of control was gaining in practice—as long as the compromise satisfied the goals of the Russians.

The Soviets had no compassion for the ethnic Germans who they believed were complicit in the Nazi effort to invade Russia and subdue the Soviet army. The ethnic Germans were treated by the Soviets and Czechs in much the same manner as the Nazis had treated the Jews and other disfavored ethnic minorities. It mattered not if the Germans pleaded no connection with, or support of, the Nazis. Germans were required to wear an identifying white band on their outer garment sleeve when in public. Control of Tachau was granted to the resident Czechs under the supervision of the liberating Soviets. The Czechs were ecstatic as they began looting and confiscation of German property. The Ackermans were spared some of the initial grief while Armin administratively relinquished his management position in the chemical factory. The Ackermans interpreted the actions of the newly-empowered Czechs as meaning certain disaster for them as soon as the factory transfer was complete. German homes and property were more aggressively confiscated as the official expulsions began. In the eyes of the Soviets, native Germans, who were born and raised in Germany, were no different than the Sudetenland ethnic Germans, who were often born and raised in Czechoslovakia. Relocation of all German residents was to be in the new West Germany or to the Russian controlled area of what was now known as East Germany. The hopelessness of the expulsions was increased by the likelihood of being relocated to East Germany, for fear of poor living conditions and oppressive control of their lives by the Russians. On the few occasions Peter had visited with Trudi after the Soviets arrived, they had reinforced their deep friendship and their desire to do things together again—if and when normalcy was again achieved in Tachau. The *Blitzbaum* was to be their safe "place" for the future that would only be known to them or whomever they wanted to include. Because of his father's plan, Peter told Trudi to check the *Blitzbaum* and all the bowl hidden caverns if he was suddenly to be missing from Tachau. Because of the trust developed between the youngsters, Trudi was told of the planned contents of items he would place there. She was instructed to only confirm the presence of, and safeguard the items from weather and animals. Her judgment could dictate when and to whom the items might be released. The plan for Peter had already been developed by the Ackerman family, but he couldn't tell her anything as his father had emphatically cautioned with foresight that was intuitive and eventually was proven accurate. The plan was high-risk, high-reward. Armin Ackerman had little hope for himself and Isabella; but if Peter could escape, he might one day expose—for the world to see—what had happened in Tachau. Whether the world would care, or whether the world would consider that circumstance a just payback for Nazi atrocities was questionable. Because the future held little hope for the elder Ackermans, Armin considered the plan the best option for Peter. Armin was confident that his healthy, strong and mature young son was fully capable of escaping to the American or British zones.

Trudi, on the other hand, thought she would be safe because she was in a family with a Czech head-of-household. When the Soviet soldiers or the Czech militia arrived on the Jelinek doorstep, Rudi quickly identified himself as Czech. Any other household inhabitants were assumed to also be Czech—or Czech sympathizers—by the greedy, aggressive soldiers with their new-found power. There was some degree of protection protocol when handling Germans with unusual status. Germans in Czech families were allowed to stay as were Germans in critical employment positions. Trudi had dual exempt status as a Czech family member and as a potential world-class athlete whose accomplishments might enhance the image of the Eastern Bloc.

THREE

September 1946

ESCAPE

"Be careful, Peter . . . and please come back safely. We will be together again!"

"I don't want to leave you, *Muti*." Peter was struggling with the reality, but he was aware there was no other option.

"I know, my dearest young son, but now you are a young man soon to be fourteen years old and able to escape to the West. Conditions in the Tachau resettlement camp are so terrible that people die every day, and those that are expelled by train are going to Eger and then on to the northeastern part of Germany under Russian control where life isn't likely to be different than here."

"I know, *Muti*."

His mother continued, "I have been told what it is like in the Tachau expulsion camp. There are over a thousand people in one of the old factories with little food, and only a few stopped-up toilets. Personal belongings, money, bank books and valuables are confiscated. Clothes are taken right off the backs of the men and women. Those who complain are punished severely or even killed."

"But what will I do in the West? What will life be like for a defeated German boy? Will the Americans treat me like a Nazi? What if I get caught trying to escape . . . ?" Peter hardly wanted to talk about that, but it was his greatest fear.

"We will be together again, Peter!" She said the words, but Peter detected her lack of conviction. "I want you to come back when it's safe to retrieve the film. The world must know what happened here. Eyewitness accounts can be supported by the photographic proof of the film. Our family valuables should be kept in the family and away from the soldiers. The valuables can also help us start a new life when this terror has ended." *Frau* Ackerman had heard the rumors of Nazi atrocities and often wondered that, if true, would the world even care about the Sudeten Germans? Her conclusion was that the world's good, compassionate people would one day call to justice the perpetrators of war evils.

"I want to take the film with me now, *Muti.*"

"No! We have discussed that. It's far too dangerous. If the soldiers catch you with the film they will kill you; *Vati* and I know the *Blitzbaum* area where you will hide the film and valuables. We can locate the box with a metal detector. We know Trudi can take us to the *Blitzbaum* if necessary. Maybe we will come back here first or something will happen that prevents your return."

His Mother's sheer terror was apparent in her voice. That terror served to accentuate the fear that Peter already felt. He knew that noise and sudden movement on his escape attempt could end his mission and subject him and his family to the same fate as most of the other three and one-half million ethnic Germans living in Sudeten Czechoslovakia. Many of the local Germans felt no affinity for the Nazis, but that didn't matter now. With Russian support, the native Czechs now had control of the Sudetenland. The Germans in the area who had for many years built up, operated and controlled the area were now being victimized by long-frustrated Czechs who viewed them as Nazi sympathizers. Tachau's resident Czechs had long been aware of the Nazi influence in their village. Many of the village's ethnic German children had joined the Hitler Youth Corps voluntarily because they felt an allegiance to the Nazi movement. To them, Germany was the Fatherland and the Nazis were restoring the pride and power which had been lost in another war. Nonetheless, there were significant numbers of ethnic Germans who would rather have seen the Nazi movement just go away. The Hitler propaganda machine had documented on film the apparent joy of all living in the Sudetenland—including the native Czechs—in October of 1938. Hitler had made a triumphant visit by motorcade into his newly-seized territory. The other untold side of that story was suppressed by widespread terror and intimidation of the Czechs

The immediate future of the Ackermans was terrifyingly uncertain. Their home would soon be confiscated and they were to be relocated somewhere in Germany. Rumors abounded that the trains were going north to the Russian-occupied sector. Where in Germany the expellees were relocated mattered little to the Czechs. Whether the expellees lived long enough to survive the evacuation mattered to them even less.

The Ackerman's had a plan. They felt they had only one option to save their young son, Peter. They knew they did not want to be relocated to the area currently occupied by Russian forces, but that seemed inevitable. They had resigned themselves to that probability, but had devised a plan to enable Peter to escape to the American or British-held areas.

Only thirteen years of age, it was indeed an overwhelming emotional reality for Peter. He would leave his parents likely to never see them again. Armin Ackerman wanted to document the atrocities inflicted on the Sudeten Germans as well as to enable Peter's escape. As manager of the local chemical plant, Armin had access to a camera. He used the camera to photograph murders, inhumane acts of violence and the general conditions under which the Germans were expelled. Secretly capturing these photos was a dangerous and time-consuming endeavor; so that the truth could eventually be known, he felt it was his humane duty to document the barbarism. The photographs would tell the story of the expellees better than any refutable verbal testimony.

On this particular night Peter's mission was to conceal: the film, the jewelry, some small heirlooms and what other easily-hidden valuables the family possessed. He had chosen the *Blitzbaum* for the concealment. His parents were given the general location and description of the fir tree and were told that Trudi Kehle knew of its location. After the concealment he continued in a westerly direction toward the pre-war border. He stopped in the dark every few meters to listen. The wind and a dog in the distance were all that was to be heard. It was cold, but Peter didn't feel the chill. A numbing state of shock had set in to make him feel much the same as in a club soccer match: tense, determined and focused. He was afraid he would make a mistake, but wanted desperately to succeed. There was a curfew, which was strict and would almost certainly be deadly should he be caught. Long ago he had removed the white cloth that all ethnic Germans had been ordered to wear on their sleeve. He worried about the *Blitzbaum* hiding place. Was this the best place to hide the film and valuables? What if there was another lightning strike? Should he believe the oft-told tale about lightning never striking in the same place twice? What if the area was logged? What if somebody found the items by accident? Never mind, he thought, this had been discussed with *Vati* and *Muti*. There was no better option. The local Czechs would dig or sweep the entire area with electronic detectors. They would search everywhere, but maybe not in the park trees.

When he was younger Peter had walked or run with Trudi, many times, from his home to the fir tree in twenty minutes. Tonight it took longer. Every silhouette was potentially a Czech militiaman. Every sound threatened exposure or alerted him to the ubiquitous danger. Walking, crouching and sometimes crawling, was difficult, but necessary. The closely-spaced broadleaf trees with an occasional tall evergreen amid the sometimes thick ground cover were in an area difficult to negotiate noiselessly. Much of the route was off-trail and parallel to a road called Americká. How ironic, thought Peter, that the first night of his journey would be near a road with the same name as his dream destination. When he finally reached the area so familiar to his childhood, he could see the crown of the tall fir silhouetted against the night sky. No militiamen had been in evidence and the area seemed deserted. As he neared the tree, he was thankful he had used it to conceal his water container and scraps of food his mother had given him for the sometimes day-long excursions in the Sudeten countryside near Tachau. As he reached the thick bent branch of the malformed tree he felt safer. Noise was still a concern, but the dense foliage served to conceal his actions. He had only to deposit the container he had fashioned from a large metal box and attached by means of a lightweight chain. How convenient, he had always thought, that nature would form such a useful hiding place. Never had it been more useful than at the present. Carefully, he placed the valuables and the film in the metal container. All items had been carefully wrapped to resist moisture and freeze-thaw cycles. Peter had no way of knowing that he would return one day; returning was a dream at the moment, but he was hopeful. The film, especially, could identify the perpetrators of dastardly deeds inflicted upon the Germans and would vividly reveal the cruelty of the Soviets and the guilty local Czechs.

As he and his father had planned, Peter had the option of continuing on his escape route that night or if weather and security were escape concerns he could hide out a day or two. Peter was studying his maps and reviewing the plan in his mind. He felt mature beyond his years, which was a result of the change of status for the Sudeten Germans. In 1938 the Munich Agreement had ceded the Sudetenland to Germany. That was one of a series of bluffs and intimidations an increasingly aggressive Adolf Hitler had authored prior to the outbreak of World War II. For almost seven years the

Sudeten Germans had been in control of the Sudetenland, named for the nearby Sudeten mountain range. Nazi troops had occupied the land and Czech businesses and industry had come under German control. Now, as the Czechs regained control and the Nazi army was defeated, the tables had been turned. Ethnic Germans were to be "resettled." Property, businesses and government control was being returned to the Czechs. The ethnic Germans became non-persons and were stripped of nearly everything they possessed in preparation for their expulsion. The Soviet Army remained in the area and was typically undisciplined and somewhat out of control. Mistreatment, abuse, torture and even murder were rampant. Peter had matured quickly. He understood the gravity of the situation and he was determined to escape and provide whatever assistance he could in the future of his family and his fellow Germans.

Peter's father, Armin, was the brains behind the escape plan. He knew what Peter would need to do and what material and equipment he would need for a successful escape. Food, binoculars, a sleeping bag, navigating aids and other supplies were assembled. He passed on his considerable knowledge: terrain, weather, troop locations, villages and likely areas of military or civilian activity. Together they had done many map reconnaissance sessions and Peter had made his way secretly to what they called the Tachau release point whenever he felt it was safe. On each ground reconnaissance excursion he had taken food and other items to stockpile for the escape. In the Tachau release-point area, he had now deposited sausage, fruit, water, canned-food items, a flashlight, binoculars, matches, socks and wet-weather gear. The backpack with which to carry all this had remained with him at home until the last departure.

Peter's Tachau release point was located in Herr Schmidt's farmland not far from the *Blitzbaum* on the west side of the Studánka hill. He arrived there immediately after concealing the valuables. It was September 19, 1946. This part of the escape route signaled the beginning of extreme danger. He realized that persons detected on his escape route would likely not be friendly. Most local Germans, who were awaiting expulsion, were in a concentration or internment camp. Those who the Czech militia considered subversive or dangerous because of their leadership potential were placed in the concentration camps, while those awaiting immediate expulsion were placed in the holding or internment camps. Often these facilities were co-located. It was just a matter of degree of security. Some of those held in the concentration camps were eventually released to the internment camp. Others were found guilty of some criminal charge and held indefinitely or murdered unceremoniously. Those remaining in their homes, like Peter's family, were careful not to wander out for unexplained reasons. This left the village and the countryside devoid of humans except the Czech Militia and the Russian conquerors. Peter's primary escape rules, emphasized over and over by his father were, "Assume everybody is an enemy until you are positive about their status," and "Don't enter unfamiliar territory until you know what is there."

Consistent with the plan, Peter had departed the *Blitzbaum,* when he decided it was relatively safe. When he detected no activity and no vehicles he quickly ducked into the thick underbrush which nearly covered a nearby slow-moving stream. From this point it was only a few hundred meters to his pre-established release point. Hidden in a depression in the field, he waited until it was completely dark. He hoped for a very dark night, which would provide additional concealment of his movement. As the evening darkened the countryside, there remained some illumination from the stars when they shined through the cloud cover. The quiet of the evening was reassuring, but ominous at the same time. The solitude engulfed him. He was alone and moving into unknown and uncharted territory. Never before in his young life had he felt so alone. It was dark and quiet. The evening chill was setting in, but his concentration on the task at hand enabled him to ignore it. In the open field his vision was good with illumination from the night sky when the moon and the stars provided just enough light to distinguish a few landmarks. He was aware that the moon was near its perigee and combined with the imminent full moon could influence illumination during the next few nights. He and his father had researched every environmental circumstance that might affect his escape. Armin Ackerman was a chemical engineer who had attended the University in Leipzig, where he had received a comprehensive education; and, by nature, he was a man who was meticulous in his attention to detail. He had learned about the perigee concept which is defined as the time when the moon was at its closest point to the center of the earth. Perigee and a full moon could combine to illuminate the earth considerably more than during normal nights. The cloud cover of this evening rendered perigee a factor he wouldn't have to contend with. His eyes had adjusted as the lighting conditions changed. He was aware that he should avoid looking into any random unexpected light source that might appear in order to preserve his night vision. He visually scanned the area for any sign of movement, light or unidentifiable objects. He listened intently and reflected on his father's rule to not move anywhere until he knew what was there. The night was getting cold with the moisture and lack of sunlight, but he felt warm with anticipation. His backpack and sleeping bag would be burdensome. Food supplies would last four days and he hoped to find water and additional food along the way; perhaps in the form of vegetables from a garden, or an occasional unsuspecting rabbit or chicken that he might subdue quietly and find a safe method of cooking. But the first goal was to get away from the release point and into the forest where he would find marked trails used by hikers in better leisure times. His father had warned that the first night would be difficult because of the open space and the heavy supplies. This was proving to be true. The forest tree line was still in the distance. He was exposed with only the dark of night for cover. Quiet was the operative word. Vigilance of the surroundings was imperative. If he saw or heard anything at all he was prepared to get face down and go motionless in the dirt. At times he would crawl, always aware that the tree line might take all night to reach. Twice he had to leave the sleeping bag as he moved forward about a hundred meters with the backpack, then return unencumbered by the pack to retrieve his sleeping bag. It was an excruciating exercise which his father could not have done. Meter by difficult meter he worked his way to the tree line. He had no concept of time, but he noted the amount of light from time to time. He saw the tree line getting closer and estimated that it would be another hour until he was secured by the darkness within the forested area. He wondered if this amount of diligence was necessary and soon decided that it was. His reasoning was that this was a high-stakes endeavor in which losing was not an option. Maybe the militia was patrolling or observing, and maybe they were not. Peter couldn't take the gamble of exposing himself to the possibility of patrols or observation posts. He continued with the crawl, drag, crouch, walk maneuvers until he had finally reached the tree line. A few hundred meters into the tree line he found a concealed area securely tucked into the underbrush and spread his sleeping bag for some much-needed rest. As his body heat warmed the sleeping bag he was very aware of the discomfort a night in these woods without the bag would have provided.

Peter was awakened when the light crept into his hiding place. Listening first, he heard nothing: no birds, no voices, no dogs, no vehicles and no far-off trains. He seemed to be entirely alone and he was further away from Tachau then he had ever been since the Russians arrived. Opening the backpack he found the items that would have to be eaten right away. Perishables were tasty, but wouldn't keep long, so he bit into the chicken and potato salad his mother had prepared. He began to think about the next phase of the plan. He knew the morning light was coming from the east and that the evening light and sunset would be in the west. His father had told him to look for hiking trails that might still have direction markers that would show directions to the local villages and significant landmarks. According to the map and to his father's information, the American zone was about eight kilometers to the west if he could fly like a bird, but he would have to take a more circuitous route; he would always search for cover and never go into an unfamiliar area until he knew what was there. Bärnau was the goal, but Altglashütte or even Tirschenreuth were acceptable should he be diverted or lose his sense of location for whatever reason. He was aware that he must stay in the forested area for cover, as much as possible, until he came to the dirt road that led to Lesná. He would have to make a dangerous road crossing there and then traverse another open farming area.

Peter found an area away from a nearby trail and away from where he slept where he could relieve himself and bury the chicken bones. He did not want to leave any evidence that a human had been in this area and he did not want animals digging up the bones so he buried them in a hole he dug with his hands and a stick. He then covered the hole with dirt and covered the entire displaced area with fallen leaves and dead branches. He was careful to leave the area with no evidence of his overnight bivouac. Listening again and scanning the area with the binoculars, he saw and heard nothing. Visibility was not good because of the vegetation and leafy trees, but it was possible to view the area in general by changing location several times. Peter searched the trees beside the trail for directional signs, but saw none until he came to a branch in the trail where he saw two signs. Each was pointed at one of the trail forks. A rectangular mildewed sign with yellow printing pointed toward the morning light and read "*Heimbach 4 km.*" The other sign pointed west and read *"Lesná Waldpfad,"* which Peter believed was the direction of the Lesná forest road.

Slowly he moved along the trail always cognizant of what

lay ahead, behind, or anywhere in the area. He could not be
sure if danger was nearby. He didn't know if he would encounter the militia or soldiers of any nationality. He wasn't
even sure if he would find German farmers or Czechs who
were euphoric because their land had been returned to them.
He reminded himself that there was no possibility of trusting anyone until he saw an allied soldier. His father had said
he expected that Peter would find American soldiers in the
area of Altglashütte and north to Bärnau, but that it would be
possible to find the British also. The Czech militia and Russian
soldiers were to be avoided at all costs. That was a sure sign
that he had not yet reached the area controlled by any of the
Western Allies.

It was a slow process moving within the forested area and
using the trail as a guide. The map reconnaissance he had made
with his father in Tachau showed that this leg of the escape
route would be about three kilometers in length. Three kilometers could be traversed under normal conditions in about
thirty minutes, Peter estimated. But, this was not a normal
condition because of the stealth required. Periodically, Peter
would stop to look and listen, always checking behind as well
as ahead with the binoculars. He made it a point to never
crest a hill until he knew what was on the other side. The
sleeping bag and backpack were cumbersome, but necessary
for the success of his escape. He had already experienced
the warmth and comfort of the bag, and the food and water
pools in clean areas would keep his young body in working
order. He tried to keep as quiet as possible, but it was difficult when he had to leave the trail. He thought at times
he might be mistaken for a wild boar charging through the

brush because of his minds imagined amplification of the minimal noise he created.

Peter decided to rest as he thought about his father's words to not wear himself out. His advice had been to always rest and conserve energy when he could. To never let his emotions cause him to do unsafe things. Resting enabled clear thinking. Getting there slowly but safely was better than traveling too fast and carelessly. He found a low area with some high underbrush which was good for concealment. He didn't want to fall asleep and be exposed for a border patrol to see. As he wiggled into the underbrush, he was surprised to find a large round concrete pipe-like structure. It had a metal door which he opened with some difficulty. A culvert, he realized. It must go under the Lesná road. He believed that he was in a dry creek bed. Maybe it was put in to facilitate water flow under the road to prevent washouts. The door contained small openings to allow water to pass, but keep animals and debris out. He saw nothing inside the culvert but darkness. There was no evidence of water flow so the overgrown underbrush concealed the culvert altogether. Water hadn't flowed through this culvert for quite some time in his opinion. Since he was steadily progressing uphill the water flow would have been coming from where he was going. It was large enough for him to crawl through, but he again remembered his father's advice to not enter unknown areas.

Then he heard a noise he knew he hadn't generated. It was a vehicle of a type larger than a moped, he thought, but not a heavy truck. He quickly checked all around to see if there were any sight lines to which he might be exposed. He assured himself that he could not be seen as he crawled up to where he had better vision and listened. The vehicle seemed to be coming from his right side. He determined that this was the next very dangerous point in his journey: the Tachau-Lesná road. With the binoculars he could observe a cleared break in the forest where the road had been constructed. He wanted to be sure he could identify the passengers and determine if they had weapons. He suspected it would be a patrol whose mission was to insure that no unauthorized persons were in the area, but it could be troops moving from Tachau to Lesná for an unknown duty reason. At this time Peter did not know how the border was marked or guarded, or if there was an official border. The war had ended in May, 1945. A year and four months later, how was control organized by the Soviets and the Allies? Rumors in Tachau were that there were serious political and philosophical differences between the Russians and their previous Allies. These differences, if real, could persist. Peter could make no assumptions at this time.

About two hundred-fifty meters to the south the vehicle stopped and some soldiers dismounted. He could see now that it was a light truck with a driver and three passengers. All were armed and dressed in full combat gear. It seemed to be a change of guard that would occur routinely at an observation post. Peter could now see what appeared to be an automatic weapon mounted on a tripod. Low to the ground, something was moving excitedly. It was a dog! A mild fear enveloped Peter as he realized the meaning of this development. If this was a dog trained in pursuit of humans, he could be discovered at any moment. He tried to calm down and analyze. Where should I go from here and how much time do I have? Peter looked through the binoculars at the observation post and confirmed that the number of personnel remaining as the vehicle moved slowly to the south was four. The dog remained, receiving playful pats from the replacements. To the north Peter could see what appeared to be another observation post barely visible in the distance. He could see four soldiers at that post. A field telephone appeared to be in use by one individual. Peter scanned quickly back to the southern post where it appeared a soldier there was using a telephone. They must be talking to each other, Peter concluded. As he scanned the tree line on the soldier's side of the road he caught glimpses of a field telephone wire that had been strung alternately on the ground and through the trees. This was a factor that Peter hadn't considered. Not only were observation posts to his left and right, but they were communicating with each other. That fact, along with the presence of the dog, made his situation even more precarious.

Peter had decided to observe and wait for a more opportune time to cross. Later, as the daylight grew dim, Peter was startled when the dog seemed to be agitated and started down the road toward him. He thought this might be the end of his plan. His palms became sweaty and his heart began beating at an accelerated rate. He wanted to run but knew that would certainly be an exposure of his presence. The dog came closer, appearing to be alerted to the presence of something in the forest. Suddenly, the dog bolted for the woods, chasing and following the sound of something trying to escape. Was it another human? It wasn't Peter the dog had detected! Perhaps it was another escapee or perhaps an animal. Yes! He saw what it was through the semi-darkness. It was a small female roe deer who had attracted the dog's attention. The guards were alerted and frantically made their weapons ready because they didn't know it was a deer. One got on the phone to alert the other observation post which was immediately vacated as the guards there joined the chase for whatever it was the dog was chasing. Hurriedly they passed along the road in front of Peter. Immediately he recognized his opportunity; he secured his gear the best he could, checked once more with the binoculars and made his move to the road. At the road's edge he looked both left and right before entering the open space, quickly moved across the road and found concealment in the underbrush. He wanted to get away from the road, but he also wanted to be sure he had not been detected. From many hours of observing this area, he felt that there was no other soldier's presence in the area. He moved carefully into the forest. The darkness and vegetation had become his ally. "Go, Peter," he told himself. "Away from the road and into the forest as far as you can physically go." It seemed an hour before he began to feel the fatigue. The backpack and sleeping gear were still very cumbersome. How happy he would be when he no longer needed them. Most of the food was gone as he ate out of boredom while observing the soldiers, so he didn't feel hungry. The water supply he had retained was nearly depleted. Finally, he found a place to rest where he was concealed away from a new trail. He saw a trail marker silhouetted on a tree, but couldn't read it in the dark. The quiet gave him a feeling of security and serenity. Never before had he felt so alone. Nobody knew where he was and there was nobody and nothing to look after him now. He knew his mother would tell him that God was always with him. His father was more the pragmatist and didn't seem to have the same degree of faith. In his present isolation he was beginning to understand faith in God. He didn't want to think he was unimportant, forgotten and completely alone. He thought about his mother and father, about his home in Tachau before the war and the subsequent Russian control. He thought about the vindictiveness of the Czechs who had confiscated the property of the Sudeten Germans, and he wondered what lay ahead for him. Were the Americans as forgiving as he had heard? Would they understand that he was not a Nazi? Would he be imprisoned? All these thoughts tormented him until he was overcome by a troubled sleep and his extremely fatigued body began to replenish itself.

Peter opened his eyes but didn't move. He listened but heard nothing. Above him, he could see the faint light. He could see the outline of the tree branches through the underbrush in which he had concealed himself. A squirrel perched on a branch and observed the intruder. Peter's tired brain wandered momentarily as though it needed a rest: a diversion from the constant pressure of his escape attempt. Random thoughts began to dart through his mind as though powered by one nerve synapse after another. He wondered if they had squirrels in America. He would go to America, wouldn't he? He realized that it was what he wanted and he hoped that it was possible. He would find a way. He thought about his mother and father still in Tachau. Their fate in the Russian occupation zone was worrisome. Perhaps they would be lucky enough to find their way west where they could all be reunited one day. Then the reality of his situation brought him back to the present. The immediate danger was still very real. The guard post and the Lesná road were not far away as was the main road from Tachau to Bärnau.

To confirm his navigation, Peter knew to keep the morning light behind him and to keep the Bärnau road parallel to his route. The only real danger lay in the possibility of veering too far to the south in the dense forest, but he had confidence in the old hiking trail signs. When he was convinced there was no one in the area, he carefully rose from the sleeping bag, gathered his things and consumed nearly all the food and water that remained. He thought he must be half way or more to the Bärnau area with the hardest part already behind. Caution was still in order, though, as he remembered "Never get careless or over confident until you are in the hands of the Americans or Brits."

He made his way slowly and carefully toward the hiking trail where he saw a trail marker high on a fir tree. There was more and more daylight permeating the forest floor as the sun rose higher and the sunlight found angles through the tree branches to those areas with which it had clear line of sight. Peter observed the path from several distant locations. When he felt it was safe he placed his gear on the ground and crept silently through the lightly forested area. Finally, he reached an observation point from which he could see the sign through his binoculars. The sign read ALTGLASHÜTTE 5 km. Altglashütte! That is where the Americans are reported to be. Peter remembered his father's words. Bärnau, Hohenthan, Thanhausen or Altglashütte. All of these villages were occupied by the Americans if his father's information was correct. His heart raced rapidly and his mouth felt dry. He knew he had to be more cautious than ever as his excitement overcame him. According to the map there was another road to traverse. This road would be a forested road connecting the Tachau-Bärnau road with an extension of the Lesná road as it made its way to the south. He knew he was now making good time through this lightly forested section. He wondered if he was in fact already in the American sector. His father hadn't had reliable information about the exact location of the border or how it was administered. Peter wasn't sure if the boundaries had been established. He had no way of knowing about the Potsdam conference or that there would soon be definitive borders. He only knew he had to exercise caution until he was in an American or British controlled area.

Soon he saw a clearing ahead, which he couldn't immediately identify. As he neared the area, he saw that it was indeed the forest road. His excitement was hard to control as he realized this could be the last barrier between him and the Americans. Altglashütte was only two kilometers! The same observation and security precautions that got him across the first road were again implemented. This time he found no observation post. He wondered again if he had crossed an impromptu temporary border on the Lesná road. The light of midday made visibility excellent much to Peter's chagrin. Visibility worked two ways he reasoned. If I can see, I can be seen. Peter smiled to himself as he remembered his friend Andre who closed his eyes when he stole the fruit from *Frau* Heigenhauser's apple tree. Andre reasoned that if he couldn't see *Frau* Heigenhauser, she couldn't see him. Obviously that wasn't the case here and Peter waited, watched and listened. The binoculars enabled good distance vision, and he strained to hear any sound as he moved from one location to another.

Hours went by until he decided to cross. He made his way to the edge of the road under cover of some thick-leaved broadleaf trees that had benefited from the sunlight in this cleared area. Quickly he dashed across the road with his sleeping bag under his arm. Again he moved quickly away from the shoulder of the road and into the thick underbrush where he stopped to rest and collect his thoughts. He looked around for the trail which he had estimated was to his left. At that moment a military vehicle came into view, and the soldiers appeared to be Americans! Cautiously he found concealment and observed. He wondered where they were going as they veered to his left. Their ride was bumpy across the open plowed field. They bounced up and down as they crossed the furrowed ruts and alternately hung on to their helmets and their rifles. The passenger was speaking into the radio microphone when he wasn't hanging on. At any other time it would have been hilarious watching this, thought Peter, but not now. What should I do? I'm sure they are American. But, where are they going? The vehicle disappeared over a rise and the engine stopped. Filled with excitement he couldn't contain himself. He ran to the top of the rise to get a better look. There he saw a third soldier. He appeared to be walking along the tree line like a security guard. This must be a change of sentries! Peter now got a better look at the vehicle as it was parked perpendicular to him. He saw the writing. It was exactly what his father had told him to look for: US ARMY! The vehicle started again; Peter ran toward the soldiers while he confidently shouted—
"Hallo, Hallo!"

The vehicle stopped and the passenger jumped out with his rifle at the ready. Peter took his white band out of his pocket, raised both hands high in the air and waved what he hoped would be interpreted as a symbol of surrender. The soldier motioned for him to come closer as he trained his rifle on Peter.

"Hey, Frank, it's just a boy," the soldier nervously related to the driver. "Come over here, boy. Who are you?"

Peter guessed at what he was asking and excitedly shouted, "*Ich bin Peter aus Tachau.*"

The soldier looked him over carefully and told Frank to search him. When they were satisfied Peter had no weapons, the passenger, who was Sergeant (Sgt) Grimes, lowered the rifle, broke into a big grin and said, "Well, welcome to Altglashütte, Peter! Do y'all have anybody with you?"

Peter was surprised by being confronted by the first black man he had ever seen in person. He guessed at the question and replied, "*Nein, ich bin allein.*"

FOUR

THE AMERICANS

Peter did not know what his fate would be with the Americans. His father believed he would be sent to a resettlement camp for expellees. Technically, he wasn't an expellee, he was a refugee. But in these confusing times, categories of displaced persons streaming into the western allied sector were not clearly defined. In August of 1945 the Potsdam Conference had established basic ground rules that were to be expeditiously implemented. In reality, this was easier said than done. Neither the Americans, the British, nor the Germans of the newly-defined zones of occupation wanted the additional burden of the expellees. But it was agreed at Potsdam that Germans residing in the Sudetenland as well as other parts of Eastern Europe would be resettled in Germany. Some would go to the Russian zone, while others would go to the American, British and French zones. Who would go where was not a systematic determination. It was arbitrary and for the most part controlled by the Russian liberators of the Sudetenland.

Few of the expellees wanted to go to the Russian zone. They had witnessed the conduct of Russian soldiers in the

Sudetenland and were well aware of the potential for danger because of the German assault on Stalingrad and other parts of Russia. This was the primary motivation for Peter's escape. His mother and father did not want to take the chance that Peter would be relocated to the Russian sector of Germany with Armin and Isabella. It was a gamble his parents wanted to make so that Peter would have a better chance at a happy and productive life.

The German people were defeated and humiliated. Their big cities were devastated, the economy nonfunctional and people were scrambling to survive from day to day. They feared for their own future and didn't take kindly to the idea of sharing limited resources with expellees or refugees.

American military commanders were ordered to escort all refugees to the resettlement camps for further disposition. Many would be placed with family members—if any existed—but most would be placed with German families with extra room. Extra room under these conditions meant more than one room in which a person or persons could sleep. If the refugee or expellee was lucky, this meant a private room; but usually it meant an additional room previously used for purposes other than sleeping. Owners and residents required to share were quite naturally unhappy about this situation, but most grudgingly accepted the fact that it had to be done. Sharing living space also meant sharing food and clothing. Assigned boarders were expected to take on responsibility for personal and communal upkeep, cooking and other necessary work.

Such was not the immediate case for Peter. The commander of the 472nd Public Affairs Company, to which Peter had surrendered, was tasked with stabilizing his assigned area of the proposed West German/Czech border area. This meant clearing the area of refugees and holdout Nazi groups, like the *Werwolfs,* still in sympathy with the Nazi concept. But Captain Arndt, the commander, had a use for Peter. He liked Peter and recognized the value of Peter's knowledge of conditions in Tachau. On occasion, Peter accompanied Sgt Grimes and other soldiers on reconnaissance patrols to the temporary border as they sought to clear the area and insure no further Russian advance. In the eyes of Harry Truman, the newly-elected US President, the Russians were not to be trusted. He deemed it extremely important that agreed-upon borders be enforced. To this end, Captain Arndt was interested in what the Russians and Czechs were doing on their side of the border. This was valuable intelligence to be transmitted to the command G-2 intelligence office expeditiously. As Peter's English improved, he became increasingly more important to Captain Arndt's intelligence-gathering effort which prolonged his residence with the American unit.

The border reconnaissance missions always brought back memories of what he had seen in Tachau and how his fellow Germans had been treated. The official evacuations, which had been in progress since shortly after the Potsdam Conference, had been anything but orderly or humane. The unofficial evacuations, which had begun almost immediately after the war ended, had been even worse. German homes had been confiscated with little or no advance notice. The Czech militia would arrive and escort the families to holding internment camps near the train station in Tachau. There they remained until they could be transported out of what was again Czechoslovakia.

The lucky ones went to the West and the unlucky ones to the Russian sector of Germany to the North. Armin Ackerman's chemical plant had been confiscated, but only after he assisted in the administrative transfer. German nationals, who were to be evacuated, were required to wear a white band on their arm until they arrived at the internment camp. The sick and weak could not withstand the harsh treatment and many died. Others were murdered out of revenge and pure cruelty. It was no surprise that Armin Ackerman wanted Peter to escape as soon as a plan was devised and an opportunity developed.

Peter had high hopes for his mother and father, but knew this hope to be only a matter of circumstance. If they were lucky enough to be transported to the West, their chances were good. To the Russian zone, their chances were almost certainly not so good. It was during these reconnaissance missions that he became more determined to return to find his parents and to retrieve the film proof of atrocities as well as the concealed family documents and valuables.

He also reflected on his friends from the sports club where he trained and played soccer for the youth team and upon his classmates in the school number five. He thought about his school friend, Juergen. And there were Anton, the *Fussball* player, and Reinhardt. He thought about some girls in his class. Martina, a Czech girl, and especially Trudi he remembered so well. He wondered what would happen to them. Would he ever see them again? He had assured his parents, as well as Trudi, that they would meet again. To fulfill those promises Peter knew he would have to be strong, patient and lucky. He was determined.

There were times on the reconnaissance missions when

he thought he could see parts of the route he had used to escape. His route had been lengthy and time-consuming in order to provide the safest means of escape. The soldiers were constantly asking him about unusual landscape or observed movement across the temporary border. They were ever vigilant for intruders and any other unauthorized persons. They were under instructions to turn refugees back to Czechoslovakia. The typical refugee trying to escape was German, but there were also some Czechs and other eastern Europeans. They were seizing the opportunity to flee to the West. After hearing Peter's stories of the treatment the ethnic Germans received in Tachau, it wasn't unusual for the patrols to pretend they hadn't seen refugees sneaking through the forest. Eventually, these people would reach a western resettlement camp and be better off than if they were turned back to the Tachau area. It was a chaotic period in history in which order and organization were difficult to achieve. There were rules and policies, but each was nearly impossible to enforce. If it hadn't been for this chaos and disorganization, Peter's life would have followed a different path.

There were occasions when Sgt Grimes and Peter went on missions alone. Their duty was generally to patrol the makeshift border and to call for help by radio, if needed, when they observed unexplained activity. They were not to provoke confrontations or use weapons for any purpose other than self-defense. Peter's English was improving rapidly with the help of Sgt Grimes and the other soldiers. On the patrols Peter was the German and Czechoslovakian language interpreter as well as providing local knowledge. On occasion they would let a German refugee continue on into the West if the refugee agreed to avoid Altglashütte. Once they turned back a Czech, although they knew he would just go further to the south and try again. Often, their missions were exercises in making time pass. On the isolated rolling forested hills, the weather was typically central European autumn cold and windy so they found protected areas in the trees or in an abandoned hay shelter. Sgt Grimes always brought along a case of "C" rations which Peter found very tasty and filling. Building a fire to heat the rations became too much trouble because of the wet forest fuel, so they usually just ate them cold. In each case of rations there were twelve individual packs with canned goods and plastic utensils in accessory packs. Peter liked the "Beef Spiced with Sauce," and the "Beefsteak," best. The sergeant liked the "Beans with Frankfurter Chunks in Tomato Sauce." Peter learned that the "P-38" found in the case was necessary to open the cans. Sgt Grimes always took the cigarettes. Peter found some of the chocolate very tasty and quite a treat for a boy who had seldom enjoyed such a luxury.

Sgt Grimes had identified with Peter's situation quickly. As a black man from Alabama, he knew something about oppression, mistreatment and power structures. To Sgt Grimes there were definite similarities in their lives. Only the color of their skin and a separating ocean provided a difference in core life experiences. Peter's English was improving enough that he started asking questions. "Why are you the only black man in Altglashütte, sergeant?"

"I asked for it, Peter. I was in another unit that rotated back to England. Everybody in that unit was black. For the most part the US Army is segregated, but there are exceptions beginning to be made. I wanted to be part of that."

Peter understood and replied, "So that's why you think we have a lot in common? What happened to me in Tachau is like what happens to you in America?"

"Yes, they call me a nigger in America and if you were there they might call you a Nazi. It's a reality you might as well get used to now. Someday it will change, but we have a long way to go."

"You have been a good friend to me, sergeant. You have helped me since the day I came out of the forest."

"In America, we call that 'strange bedfellows.' It means that sometimes you don't know where strong and loyal support is coming from."

The meaning of the conversation that day would stay with Peter and become part of who he was as he matured into manhood. He had been extremely lucky to find a friend with the principles and goals in life of Sgt Grimes.

Peter was developing a great deal of confidence and self-worth with the Americans. In return the Americans were gaining valuable intelligence information about the situation in Tachau. Peter was an intelligent boy and had an understanding of the turmoil involved with the end of the war and the subsequent relocation of the Sudeten Germans. Armin Ackerman had insisted that Peter be kept abreast of daily life, realizing that Peter would eventually need to make his own way in a rapidly changing world.

When the day came, as he knew it would, that the Public Affairs Company received orders to relocate, his security with the unit ended. Captain Arndt could find no way to explain Peter to his superiors. It became necessary to refer Peter to the temporary resettlement facility in Weiden. Sgt Grimes drove him there in the same type of vehicle Peter had first seen as he left the forest near Altglashütte four months earlier. He now knew that type of vehicle was called a "jeep."

Anxiety gripped his psyche as he advanced to yet another unknown. A part of him wanted to be the helpless orphan, but he knew for the sake of his mother and father that he had to be a man. The goal of returning to Tachau was foremost on his mind. The sacrifice of his parents would not be in vain. He was well aware that much of the world would consider him a Nazi because he was German. The truth of the matter was that his family had not been political; they felt removed from the Nazis, and had contributed through the chemical factory to the well-being of both Germans and Czechs. It was with mixed emotions that the Ackerman family had experienced the Nazi takeover of the Sudetenland in 1938. The Ackerman family felt displaced from the Nazis, but also estranged from the Czechs. Living in the Sudetenland had been a double-edged sword. The family had experienced the resentment of the Czechs after the Munich Agreement allowed the annexation of the Sudetenland to Nazi interests. They were appalled at the behavior of some Germans who lived in Tachau, by the conduct of the Nazis and by German visitor's boisterous superiority behavior.

The countryside was devoid of activity as they made their way toward Weiden. Although the sun was warm, dormant flowers were in evidence, and nature was on its best behavior, and there was a feeling of dismay in the air. "How can this be," thought Peter. "How can nature be aware of human circumstance? Or is it my perception because I understand reality? Is it my presence in the here and now that's playing tricks on my mind?"

Peter was curious about this new environment. He had never been far away from the 472nd bivouac area except with the patrols along the border. It didn't appear to be much different than the area around Tachau. Peter had envisioned a completely different appearance, even though this was only a short distance from Tachau. Having been born in the Sudetenland, it was all he knew. Soon they approached a dirty yellow and black road sign that was leaning away from the road proclaiming that they were entering Flossenburg. Sgt Grimes seemed to be looking for a place to pull off the road and soon found an old farm road that must have given access to the fields for the local farmers. From this slightly elevated vantage point Peter could see what looked like a makeshift prison. Some bare buildings in rows seemed to be mounted on rectangular cement foundations. A high barbed-wire fence surrounded the area. Several wooden observation towers were visible inside the barbed-wire fence. There was no vegetation near the fence or between the vehicle and the fenced-in compound, although there were many recently-felled trees spread all around.

"What is this place?" a confused Peter asked.

"This is the Flossenburg Concentration Camp," Sgt Grimes replied. The Sgt had a very serious look on his face. Peter sensed that he had something to say and could only hope this wasn't the resettlement camp.

"Peter, Captain Arndt chose me for this job because he knows you and I have had a good relationship since the day you came out of the forest from Tachau."

Sgt Grimes looked nervous and squirmed uneasily in the driver's seat. "The captain felt that I should have a talk with you to help prepare you for your future. We appreciate the help you have given the 472nd and we really are sad that you can't remain with us. Unfortunately, that isn't possible; so here we are. Your life will change again in the resettlement camp. It might be difficult for you there and you are going to have to be very strong. You are German. Nazi Germany lost the war. In the eyes of much of the world, all Germans were Nazis. This is the stigma you must deal with and overcome."

Peter wasn't totally unaware of this concept, but with the American military it hadn't become an issue. At this point he couldn't fully grasp the long range implication on his life that this fact could bring.

Sgt Grimes paused and then continued. "In this and many other concentration camps the Nazis' prisoners were held under inhumane conditions. Some prisoners spent years here and many died or were murdered. Most of the prisoners were Jewish, but there were many others who were considered a threat to the Nazi regime or who were considered unworthy to live in the new Germany. There were gypsies, thieves, deserters from the Nazi Army, homosexuals and even resisters. Resisters were Germans who didn't support the Nazi ideology and actively tried to sabotage the Nazi effort. One of these resisters was Dietrich Bonhoeffer, who was hung here in April of 1945. There were others, but the Bonhoeffer case is the most well-known."

Peter had seen the atrocities inflicted upon the German expellees in Tachau, but he had only heard stories from the soldiers in Altglashütte about the Nazi concentration camps. He trusted Sgt Grimes, who was now explaining a real camp he could actually see. Can this be possible? It was a shock to hear this and he hoped it wasn't true, but the evidence was beginning to mesh with hearsay. Peter felt numb. He had troubling questions on his mind. Will I be punished in some way? Am I on my way to a prison? Is this really true?

Sgt Grimes continued, "Another reason the Captain gave me the job of transporting you to Weiden is because he knows what my war experience has been. I didn't come to Germany with the 472nd. I was transferred here from the 97th Quartermaster Company when the unit was transferred back to England. I asked to stay in Germany to help clear the aftermath of a brutal and devastating war. But, back in April, 1945, the Quartermaster Company I was assigned to was conducting operations in this area. Most Nazi units had retreated to Berlin and many units were suffering mass desertion. We met minimal resistance in this area even without the infantry to clear the way. What we found, was this camp. Flossenburg! The camp guards tried to evacuate the prisoners to avoid detection of the conditions here. It was too late, but they didn't have any other alternative. They ran, but they couldn't hide. Prisoners were physically unable to walk. The evacuation was a failure and when we approached, the guards shot the prisoners on the road to try to block it. Their last ditch effort was to gather the remaining prisoners on the road and execute them. They used small arms and an MG 34 *Maschinengewehr*. When that didn't work, they broke ranks and ran for the hills. We captured or killed nearly all of them. They were Germans, Peter, like you. Later, we found that Germans were also killed at Flossenburg. One of them was the resister, Dietrich Bonhoeffer. He was a German, like you! I'm telling you this, Peter, because you are about to enter a different world. A world filled with confusion, sorrow, helplessness, hunger, displacement and grief.

Like you, there are boys and girls who are alone and very frightened. They fend for themselves. It's nearly a dog-eat-dog world except for whatever control the Allies can maintain. There is no functioning Germany and there is no German government. You will have to be strong and you will have to be smart. Nobody will look out for you as well as you look out for yourself."

Finding it difficult to hold back his emotion as he looked in Peter's now tearful eyes, he continued, "The captain and the rest of us really wanted to keep you with the unit, but it is impossible. This seems to be the best alternative for you, Peter. The resettlement camp could be difficult, but it is a place for you to start. The war is over and your new life is beginning. The captain gave me a letter for you. It has his title, *Altglashütte Area Public Affairs Officer,* and is notarized by the Judge Advocate General in Regensburg. It is written in both English and German. The letter emphasizes the value you have contributed to the unit mission and asks for special consideration in your rapid resettlement. Hopefully this letter will assist in whatever the future has in store for you. Any American soldier you contact at the resettlement camp will take notice of this letter. Guard it with your life and use it wherever you can!"

Back on the road again, Peter was terrified. Sgt Grimes was preparing him for the unknown in his future. His words were soothing, but the message was very clear and very terrifying at the same time. Trying times could lie ahead. Passing through Flossenburg he couldn't help but notice the quiet dreariness. The buildings where people lived were cold and gray-looking. Few people were to be seen. No cars, no mopeds and only a few bicycles. In the center of the village the buildings were so close to the road only one vehicle could go through at one time. Leaving the village, they had to pass a farm vehicle with a load of manure fertilizer attached. The old tractor driver didn't look up at them as they rapidly passed.

Along the route they passed many American military vehicles and a few farming vehicles interspersed with the occasional bicyclist. Soon they came upon a sign marking the entrance to Weiden. It proclaimed this city as *Weiden i. d. Opf*. Peter remembered his father referring to Weiden in den Oberpfalz. Was this to be his new home? If not, how long would he be here? Sgt Grimes followed the "Resettlement Camp" signs until the facility came into view. Peter gathered his thoughts, ignored the shock and fear and prepared for what he had accepted as inevitable. What he didn't know at that point, was how his life would change.

FIVE

THE HOPS FARM

Peter was surprised by his relatively short stay in Weiden. Living there was depressing with the constant stream of mentally and physically weakened occupants. There was a mix of expellees from the Sudetenland and other parts of Eastern Europe, displaced German citizens, gypsies and even Jewish survivors of the concentration camps. Most were weak from lack of nourishment and had only scant tattered clothing. The women and children were pitiful-looking; they were always near the breaking point. The younger women were hardened by repeated instances of rape and other severe abuse. Nobody trusted the strange mix of local Germans and Allied military who were administering the camp. Nights were spent in wooden frame cubicles with straw, tattered cloth, or anything that could be found to soften the sleeping area and cover the body from the cold winter and chilly spring evenings. Food consisted mostly of potatoes and apples. Occasionally there was a watery broth containing tiny bits of sausage. Peter thought he weighed about thirty-nine kilograms (eighty-five pounds) on his five foot four inch frame. He had been fed fresh rations—when they were available—by the Americans for many months. He had grown and gained weight even when only "C" rations were available, but he was slowly losing that gained weight in Weiden.

Peter was elated, but with a touch of suspicion, when he was called into the commandant's office after several months. He anticipated news about his disposition, but was aware that it could be bad news as easily as good news. Sitting in a chair near the commandant's desk was a man dressed like a local farmer. He didn't appear to be a displaced person.

"Peter, this is Herr Waldbau, from Nandlstadt." The commandant was speaking. "He is looking for an orphan boy to help him on his hops farm. If we can arrange this, we will be sending you with him today. You will be temporarily under the control of Herr Waldbau. He will feed you and provide a place to sleep for you in exchange for your work."

Peter was alternately shocked and relieved. On the one hand, there was the mystery of what lay ahead. On the other hand was the overwhelming desire to leave the camp and start something new. It could be a long and twisting road for him to achieve his goal of a return to Tachau, but the effort had to move him along and the camp was nothing more than a stumbling block and an impediment.

"Your documents are in order, so it seems there is no problem with releasing you to Herr Waldbau. According to your personal documents you are Peter Ackerman, born February 4, 1933, in Tachau (Tachov), Czechoslovakia, to Armin Ackerman and Isabella Bergstum Ackerman. You also have a letter of recommendation and a request for expeditious handling from Captain Jessee Arndt, the Chief of Public Affairs for the Altglashütte area. The primary reason for this letter is because you are separated from these parents and have been of extraordinary value to the mission of the Altglashütte Public Affairs Officer. This speaks well for you. Herr Waldbau has been impressed."

Peter knew the decision had been made for him and he would be going whether he agreed or not, but it was kind of the commandant to make it appear that he had a choice. He was happy with this decision. He had heard the stories about orphans being shipped to places like Rumania or Yugoslavia, where they were forcefully resented. He had long ago developed a desire for America—where opportunity abounded— or the American sector of West Germany, where he could develop a plan to return to Tachau after maturing and becoming stable. Always first and foremost in his mind was reuniting with his family and providing for their safety. He hoped that Nandlstadt would be the next stop on his journey!

"You are advised that your records will be forwarded to the joint American/German command in Munich until your case becomes permanently resolved. Herr Waldbau could return you to Munich or you could be permanently assigned to Herr Waldbau. If this is acceptable to all, you will need to sign this document and you can be on your way to Nandlstadt."

The Weiden-Freising train route was one of the first to be completely restored in West Germany that year. The crowded train made many stops. Most passengers were either traveling to keep contact with relatives or traveling to look for work.

Some were just opportunists. If they saw an opportunity to steal or otherwise take advantage of exploitable situations they did so. Charles Darwin could have used this scenario as an example of his "survival of the fittest" theory. As Peter looked around, it was apparent to him that every person on the train was left to their own devices and their survival skills were being tested. Peter had long ago come to realize that survival was the father of pragmatism; exactly as he was leading his own uncertain life. They passed through villages with strange names like Luhe and Pfreimd. A change of trains in Regensburg was necessary, which made the trip even longer. Peter had never been this far away from Tachau and even though this was his country, it was strange to him. Only the language was similar. Peter's exposure to accents and new slang was limited. The Bavarian accent was certainly different enough to make understanding everything he heard somewhat difficult. The many years of separation between the Bavarians and Sudeten Germans had been cause for subtle variations in the pronunciation of certain words and introduction of new slang and other mainstream words. As Peter and Herr Waldbau passed through Ergoldsbach, and Landshut, they talked.

"This is a difficult time in Germany, Peter," Herr Waldbau spoke first. "We are all doing what we must to recover from the war. My *Frau* and I don't have much, but we are luckier than most because we have a hops farm. Do you know what hops are?"

"Isn't that something that goes into beer?"

"Actually, it is one of the ingredients of good beer. Water and barley are the only other ingredients in German beer in accordance with the Bavarian Purity Law of 1487 *(Reinheitsgebot)*.

Hops give the beer flavor with a slight bitterness. I have been involved in growing hops since I was your age. That's over 30 years. My father had the farm before me, but he died in an air raid during the war. He died in a building near the center of Munich when the building was leveled by a British bomb."

Peter was curious, "Why are you growing hops, now? Why not food that people can eat?"

"That's a good question, Peter, and the answer is morale. The German people value their beer as much as art, music, or opera. We want to rebuild our country. It will be easier with beer. You might say the West German rebuilding process is a formula process of work ethic, skill, building material, determination . . . and beer!"

Peter and *Herr* Waldbau—Fritz was his first name Peter learned—exchanged information and achieved a level of relaxation with each other during the nearly two hours before they reached their destination of Moosburg. The train was crowded because it was one of a limited number of transportation means available. A formal West German government had yet to be developed or authorized. Day-to-day functioning of West German life was administered by the occupying forces. In the American zone the US Constabulary was assuming many responsibilities as a police force and administrative agency. As Peter and Fritz arrived in Moosburg and exited the train onto the station platform by means of a metal step at the rear of the coach, Peter knew he would be working hard but he felt comfortable with *Herr* Waldbau.

"We must walk to Nandlstadt from here, Peter. It will take about two hours, but we might catch a ride on a farmer's cart if we are lucky."

They started walking along a country road that was part gravel and part blacktop. Secondary roads had been neglected by the Nazis as they directed their pre-war resources to building the *Autobahn,* and then to the war effort. No vehicles were in sight, but Peter could hear an engine in the distance. As the sound grew louder, they could see the vehicle behind them. Fritz waved his right arm in an up and down sidearm motion in the European hitchhike style. Peter could see, as the vehicle approached, that it was a US Military jeep. It was the same vehicle type that he had first encountered as he left the forest in Altglashütte. Remembering what Sgt Grimes had told him about hitchhiking in America, he raised his arm, clenched his fist and pointed his thumb in the direction they wanted to go. Surprisingly, the jeep slowed enabling the driver to look them over as it passed by and then stopped a few meters ahead of them. The driver was alone and was watching them intently as they approached the vehicle.

"Where are you guys headed?" the driver asked.

Fritz didn't understand, so Peter answered, "Nandlstadt."

"Well, OK, I'm going through that village. Hop in."

"Thank you, thank you, Corporal Mays." Peter was reading the insignia and name tag of the driver. He raised and tilted the passenger seat forward which allowed Fritz to climb into the back seat and then he occupied the front passenger seat. Corporal Mays slowly re-entered the smooth driving part of the road and accelerated to a safe driving speed.

"What's your name?" the Corporal asked.

"Peter is my name, and this man is Fritz. I will be working for Fritz on his hops farm."

"OK, I am Corporal Mays, as you noticed. You speak

English very well, Peter, and you know how to hitchhike like an American. Where have you learned that?"

"I worked with the Americans in Altglashütte. But when they left, I was assigned to the resettlement camp in Weiden. I am still assigned there, but I will work with Fritz temporarily. My records are being transferred to Munich. I am now considered a refugee."

The jeep was moving along at only thirty mph, but they seemed to be making good time. Corporal Mays was on a duty messenger mission, but couldn't tell Peter anything about that for security reasons. There was still plenty of caution by the US Forces because of lingering Nazi sympathy, so Peter was surprised that the Corporal had stopped. The hitchhiking signal was probably a big reason he stopped and then the language capability helped, while his experience with the US Army was the clincher. The Corporal did offer the information that McGraw *Kaserne* in Munich was his home base. He stated that McGraw was about thirty kilometers away. A certain rapport between Corporal Mays and Peter was developed during that trip. Their obvious curiosity about each other insured that they got along well. When they reached the village of Nandlstadt, Corporal Mays gave them each a small rectangular shaped brown box which Peter recognized immediately as "C" rations. Peter had a box marked "Beans and Frankfurter Chunks," while the box Fritz had was marked "Ham and Lima Beans." Peter was familiar with both.

"Good luck, fellas! Maybe we will meet again sometime! Where is the farm, Peter? Maybe I can come by with some "C" rations to trade for hops sometime. I have friends who brew their own beer. I'm sure they would appreciate some flavorful hops to work with."

Corporal Mays knew of the current struggles of life in West Germany. He was the type of person who just wanted to be helpful. The hops request was to mollify the sense of inferiority the passengers might feel from a gift not reciprocated.

"One kilometer on *Altstrasse*," answered Herr Waldbau as he guessed what the question was. It was an easy sentence for Fritz to say in English. "*Komm freilich vorbei!*" He invited the corporal to visit; the information was passed along to the corporal.

"Yes, and I thank you for the ride and the "C" rations. *Auf wiedersehen,* Corporal Mays." Peter was quick to show off his English language skill.

Gudrun Waldbau was a pleasant German *Frau* of the era. Short, somewhat sad-looking, and always dressed with loose-fitting, plain and practical clothing. Peter assumed that her sadness was from worrying and not enough to eat since the Allies took control of the war. She was hard-working and attentive to the needs of her husband and the household. Confusion about the future was apparent in her eyes. She and Fritz had married long ago and soon thereafter they had two sons. Both had died in the battle for Stalingrad. She hadn't recovered from the trauma. Joining the Hitler Youth Corps seemed the prudent thing to do for the boys under the circumstances, but she and Fritz had always had reservations about the reasons for the war. As humble people just trying to get along with their hops farm, they did what everybody was doing. They kept their mouths shut and sent their sons to the Hitler Youth Corps. That the boys ended up dead in Russia was a fact from which they felt guilt and would never recover.

Peter's small unheated room had one small window which gave him a view of *Altstrasse*. The one toilet in the house was further down a narrow unlighted hallway from his room. This was fine since once he got in his bed and was warm he didn't see any reason to get up again until the morning. His room provided him the only comfortable privacy on the hops farm. Inevitably, in his private time, his thoughts turned to his mother and father. He had no way of knowing where they were or if they were safe. He never thought about his parents without reflecting on the instructions they had given him. He was to do what it took to get to America where they felt he would be safe until he matured and could return to his home in Czechoslovakia. They never expressed their belief that he might never see them again if they came under Russian control. In their minds, the primary purpose for Peter to return was to retrieve the photographs and other evidence of Czech and Russian atrocities in Tachau. The money and valuables were less important, but could be useful to him in his new life. But who really knew? Would the currency retain any value? Probably not, but keeping it out of the hands of the new power structure in Czechoslovakia would provide them some measure of satisfaction.

Peter's days were long and the work was hard. He had to learn how to grow and harvest hops. Fritz had few tools, but managed to produce enough of the coveted hops to sustain his farm and the three of them. Peter had arrived at the farm just in time to harvest the yearly crop. Fritz had contacted the resettlement agency because he needed inexpensive labor.

Harvesting hops was time dependent and he could have used twenty men if he wanted to harvest in a short period of time. Unfortunately, he had no money to pay for labor and there was a labor shortage after the war anyway. The war had taken a severe toll on the German people and especially the males who had been part of the failed Nazi objectives.

During harvesting Peter used a ladder and a knife to cut the hop flowers from the tall perennial plants. He collected them in a basket he wore around his neck until it was full. Fritz sometimes used stilts since he had only one ladder. Eventually Peter would learn to walk and work on the stilts, but this first year he wasn't strong or steady enough. With experience he would gain that ability. He was sure of that and very determined to make it happen. It was one of the intangibles of human character that competitive people, like Peter, view difficult tasks as a challenge. Peter first displayed this competitive fire of personality on the soccer field and it carried over to how he viewed other challenges in life. He still remembered Trudi's constant encouragement, even when she won most of their races to the *Blitzbaum*. She said her parents always told her she might lose a race, but she would never lose her future as long as she never gave up. The wisdom of that advice was one reason he was able to cope and thrive in the months and years since he left his home in Tachau.

Every evening during the harvest season, a Volkswagen van would arrive to load whatever hops were available from the day's harvest. The van would collect hops from several small farms in the area and transport them to the Weihenstephaner brewery in Freising. Peter saw the cash changing hands between the driver and Fritz, but he never knew how many *Marks* (referring to the Deutsche Mark) were being exchanged. The Waldbau family always found a way to get by with the money they were making. It was an unquestionably meager existence and not anything like before the war, even though pre-war Germany was barely recovering from poverty then, also. Peter assumed, from observing present conditions on the farm, that his family in Tachau had had a better life than the Waldbaus. His father's position as manager of the chemical factory had served them well. He wished those days could return, but now realized that that was not to be.

During that first year Peter became very close to the Waldbaus. He worked hard and they treated him well. They were sharing what food and clothing they had. Occasionally the hops truck driver would bring a case of beer and a case of *Afri* Cola. No doubt it was part of the payment for the hops since nothing was free. On special days there was a chicken to eat. Gudrun would bake it in her wood stove. At dinner time they would sit around a table with nothing but a plate and a fork. The chicken was picked clean until there was nothing left but bone.

One day when Fritz had walked to Nandlstadt in search of potatoes and any other vegetables and fruit he might find, Peter and Gudrun began to talk. She was in her usual sad and melancholy mood. They had never before talked about her boys, or her life before the war. This was the day that would change.

"Fritz is very happy with your work." She turned to face him with just a hint of a tear in her eye. "And I am, also," she continued, "You remind me very much of my boys. I remember when they were your age."

"I'm so sorry they didn't come back from the war," Peter answered, "Do you know what happened?"

"They were very proud to be a part of the Youth Corps. They were handsome and strong boys. I was happy for them, but I worried when they went away."

Peter began to be uneasy as the tears became more evident. He sensed that she wanted to talk but he just didn't know what to say. For the first time he realized that her feelings about losing her sons, were no different than his feelings about losing his parents. The only difference was he had hope; she did not.

"They had been allowed to serve together in the same unit only because they volunteered for the infantry. They were killed when the Russians overran their unit near Stalingrad. I love Germany, Peter, but do I love it more than I did the boys?" The tears began to run down her cheeks. Peter couldn't hold back his tears. They embraced and cried. This was the moment they bonded like mother and son.

"Can I call you *Muti?*"

"Yes, Peter, you are like my son."

They cried together until they went limp. It was a cathartic moment which was to bond them for the rest of their lives. They were as close as orphan and mother who had been united by circumstance and the reality of life could possibly be. Neither understood or supported the war. Neither provoked war, nor had any desire for *Lebensraum* or lingering animosity over the results of a long-ago war. Nonetheless, they were victims of the ideology and greed of others. That they didn't understand egos, power, drugs and mental illness, didn't matter. They were victims who must learn to cope. It would be a strange and challenging world that lay ahead for them and all other victims of the tragic war event. At that moment they had no idea what the future would bring, but Peter knew that he had a mission and would remember the Waldbaus and all those that helped him in pursuit of his goal.

SIX

OUT PROCESSING

Most days on the Waldbau farm were long and strenuous for Peter. He had quickly become a capable and reliable worker for Fritz and Gudrun. Almost two years after arriving at the Waldbau farm he was experienced in maintaining, harvesting and packaging the hop flowers for sale to the local breweries. As a handyman for odd jobs around the farm he became a valuable asset to the Waldbaus. Fritz and Gudrun appreciated his attitude toward learning and accomplishing what needed to be done. Their symbiotic relationship worked well as Peter matured and developed physically. There were always some additional duties for which he was needed. Sometimes he had to gather, chop and stack wood for heating the house in the winter and sometimes it was nothing more than helping Gudrun preserve berries and fruit that they gathered in the nearby forest. Gudrun had a vegetable garden which always seemed to need attention. Peter was busy most of the time, but it was a small price to pay for the security and the affection he felt as part of the Waldbau farm. It was, however, frustrating to not know what the immediate future held for him. He knew that one day he would find a way to America. That was what his parents had encouraged him to do and that was his goal. Frustration stemmed from the fact that he didn't know how—at the moment—to get it done. In the back of his mind, he wondered if he would have to wait five years until he was old enough to apply for immigration. The closeness he felt to the Waldbau family was also a factor. He and Gudrun had a mother-son relationship in which the bond became ever stronger. He thought of the prospects of leaving the farm as a bittersweet reality which was an example of a turning point in the lives of humans. When the time came, he knew that the bond would make parting extremely difficult.

One diversion from Peter's daily routine was when Corporal Mays visited while on his messenger route. He always brought some "C" rations and occasionally a pack of cigarettes for Fritz. In return the corporal always loaded a few bundles of hops to take back to McGraw *Kaserne* in Munich. Peter talked often with the corporal about life in general and specifically the situation in West Germany and Peter's plans for the future. The corporal actually knew more about his desire to go to America than did the Waldbaus. Peter didn't want the Waldbaus to feel he was unhappy, because he was not, but he knew he would take the first opportunity to move on to America where he could be on his own to mature, become fiscally solvent and make plans. That would be significant progress toward his goal of returning to Tachau.

Today Corporal Mays seemed to be in an especially good mood. When the time was right and the two of them had some privacy, Corporal Mays told Peter about some new legislation just approved in America. It was called the "Displaced Person Act" and was signed by President Truman in July of that year.

"What does that mean?" asked Peter. ·

"It means that you have a chance to immigrate to America as a displaced person. Displaced persons are defined as families and orphans who cannot return to their homeland for specific reasons. With your situation, I think you are qualified"

Peter was nearly numb as the news became clear in his mind. He wasn't sure he understood, but his heart was pounding. "Are you sure that could mean me?" he asked hopefully.

"Yes, Peter, it does mean you. I have a friend who works in the resettlement office. He found your name in the records and has already had a letter sent out to the Waldbaus."

Peter was astounded. Even though he had hoped for something like this since the day he left his parents in Tachau, he wasn't prepared for the reality. His mind was racing. Will this happen? What will the Waldbaus do? Can they ignore or deny the letter? Where do I go and what should I do? What is America really like? Are the streets lined with gold as I've been told? Will I be treated like a Nazi? All these questions and so many more were racing through his mind.

Corporal Mays continued, "The letter requests that you appear before the screening committee with your documents. They will want to hear your story in your own words. They will want to ensure that you are not a threat to the United States and that you have the potential of becoming a productive citizen. I'm sure you will be accepted!"

It was with a great deal of excitement—and fear—that he appeared for his interview. McGraw *Kaserne* had been used by the Nazis during the war. Now it was occupied by the American Constabulary with the mission of organizing, policing and governing the West German population until such time as the Nazi influence could be purged and the government could be reorganized with leaders from the German resistance or from among the many Germans who could be verified as having not been active in the Nazi party. This wasn't always accomplished perfectly because of the fine lines of the German war psyche. Germans were conscripted into the forces without regard to their beliefs. To escape conscription one had to flee the country, be working in a war-related industry, hide, or become invisible.

McGraw *Kaserne* was unlike the 472nd Public Affairs Company in Altglashütte. The 472nd was a temporary field unit working out of tents and trucks. McGraw had more permanency. After clearing the gate security with the help of Corporal Mays and the interview letter, Peter saw a permanent American facility for the first time. It was not a large area, and was surrounded by a wall/fence combination. It was designed in a huge square with an open grassless field in the middle. A flagpole displayed the American flag prominently at the distant end of the field. Later he would learn that the grassless field was used primarily for military formations such as reveille, retreat, or parades and for multiple other uses. The buildings were elongated three story structures with many windows on each floor. They appeared to be constructed with a composite mortar, sand and stone material. Two buildings were on each side of the field and one at each end. A cobblestone road separated the buildings from the grassless field. There were several small military combat vehicles like he had been a passenger in so often (jeeps). There were also some olive-drab colored sedans with white stars on each front door. Most of the vehicles sat idly before what appeared to be a primary entrance to building seven.

Corporal Mays stopped in a small parking lot near building seven. "This is it, Peter, we have to go to room two-thirteen. That's the displaced person (DP) processing office. Your appointment is at 1430 hours, but first we have to go to the dispensary so you can take your physical. The results will be hand-carried to the DP Officer before your interview."

Peter remembered the words of his mother and father. "Have no fear, Peter, and do what you need to do to get to America. That will be the safest place for you and will provide an excellent opportunity for you to get educated and develop a better life for yourself. One day you will come back and be reunited with us."

Peter had no concept of how that would happen, but he felt sure that his parents had sent him on a journey that was best for him under the circumstances in the Sudetenland at this time in history. He drew strength from their words and resolved to make the words a reality. Today was a major step for him. He took a deep breath, gathered his documents and followed the corporal into building five where the dispensary was located. It was 1225 hours on October 20, 1949. It was to be one of the most important days in the life of Peter Ackerman, the displaced orphan from the Sudetenland area of what was once again a part of Czechoslovakia.

Promptly at 1430 in the waiting room of the DP Office,

a private first class came in and called his name. Peter followed the private through a door marked "Captain Russell, DP Interviews."

"Sit down, Peter," said the captain, "I just want to ask you a few questions and verify the information I have in your records. Do you understand everything I have said?"

"Yes, sir." Peter was somewhat familiar with American military courtesy that he had learned while working in Altglashütte and from friends like Sgt Grimes and Corporal Mays. Familiarity with the military may or may not be necessary, Peter thought, but it can't hurt and he wanted to put his best foot forward.

"You are sixteen years old and the whereabouts of your parents is unknown—is that correct?"

"Yes, sir," replied Peter.

"When did you last see them and what were the circumstances?"

"I last saw them in Tachau, Sudetenland. They were expecting to be expelled to the Russian zone of Germany. They sent me away in hopes that I wouldn't have to go with them. I made my way to the American sector and never saw them again. That was over three years ago in September of 1946."

The captain nodded in acknowledgement and offered some surprising information. "We sent an inquiry through Allied forces diplomatic channels to determine their status. The reply was that your parents had vacated their residence and there was no record of their disposition. Peter, this can be very bad news. The US Forces will do everything in their power to try to locate them, but experience tells us this may be difficult. It is important for you to understand this as we process your application for evacuation to America. Do you understand, Peter?"

The reality of the captain's words was a shock, even though he knew what the army had found was a probability. Peter had come to the conclusion that his parents had sent him away precisely because this scenario might play itself out. After recovering from the captain's words, he managed a barely perceptible, "Yes, sir."

"OK, Peter, I am going to schedule you for transportation to Ellis Island, New York. You will appear here on December 14, at 0900 hours with no more than twenty kilograms of baggage and all your personal documents. You will receive a packet of documents from us that morning to take with you and your official packet will be sent in care of the ship's captain. Your transport vessel will be the USS *General Harry Taylor*. Congratulations Peter! My staff will assist you in completing the necessary documentation. We will notify the Waldbaus of our decision. I hope your life will be enjoyable and productive in the United States."

Peter felt light-headed but ecstatic as he left the building. Corporal Mays greeted him with a big smile and a knowing look of success on his face. "Are you going?" he asked. "Did you make it?"

"*Ja, Jawohl, Ich fahre mit Schiff nach Amerika!*" Peter reverted to his native German in his euphoric state of excitement.

"You are going to America by ship. You will be in America before me. That is wonderful news! I am so happy for you, kid!"

Corporal Mays took him on a tour of the *Kaserne* while they both settled emotionally. He pointed out building nineteen, which had been the only building on the *Kaserne* to be damaged during an allied air raid. Peter hardly remembered what he saw and little did he realize that one day he would return to West Germany and make use of the Post Exchange (PX), the bank, the laundry, the snack bar and all the other facilities the corporal was now showing him. He saw some well-dressed and obviously well-fed juveniles that were identified as American by Corporal Mays. American dependents were already in West Germany supporting their active duty sponsors. It was indeed a great day, which suddenly held more promise for the future than at any time since the day he crawled through the fields to escape Tachau.

SEVEN

THE *HAUPTBAHNHOF*

Gudrun and Fritz were aware that the day would come when Peter would leave them. The three of them had been good for each other. Peter worked hard, learned fast and became like a son to the Waldbaus. They had fed him and provided for him as best they could with the limited resources of post-war West Germany. With ration cards, bartering, black-marketing, the gifts from Corporal Mays and the vegetables they were able to grow in the short summers, they survived quite well. Country living was easier than living in the cities where resources were extremely scarce. The Marshall plan was beginning to work with additional goods coming from North America mostly, but also from anywhere they could be purchased. During the physical examination at McGraw Kaserne, Peter learned that he was now five feet seven inches tall, and weighed 125 pounds. He was growing and gaining weight. The weight was now considerably more than other German boys he had seen in the DP camp. He felt as strong and healthy as the physical examination determined he was.

Gudrun was especially sad about Peter's departure. He had

become her surrogate son replacement for the two sons she lost in the war. Peter thought of her as a mother figure. They had become the classic "accidental family." Gudrun often thought of life as an accident, even though her belief in God remained strong. She didn't always know the reasons why, but was positive there were reasons, even for the death of her sons. Her observations of life were the basis for her determination that her new family was an accident with a purpose, but without explanation. She asked Peter to promise a return to Nandlstadt when life was better in West Germany. He promised to do so and it was a sincere promise that he intended to keep.

Fritz was also very sorry to see Peter leave. He too, thought of Peter as family and respected the boy for being mentally and physically strong and for being a loyal and responsible worker who learned fast. Losing Peter's labor was only a minor problem. He had recently accepted two former French prisoners who had been released from the nearby Freising internment camp and had chosen to remain in West Germany. The hops farm was doing well enough that two men were now needed. The Marshall Plan and the change of currency from the *Reichsmark* to the *Deutschmark* (DM) was slowing inflation and pumping a small token of life into the West German economy. Fritz was no longer worried about survival. Peter could be replaced as an employee, but not as a surrogate son. Peter would be missed as a family member, but like all children, eventually they leave the nest.

December 14, 1949 . . . Corporal Mays had become a familiar figure at the Waldbau farm, so it was no surprise when he arrived early in the morning with the familiar jeep in order to load Peter and his weight allowance of baggage. The good-byes were difficult. Gudrun kept repeating, "Come back, Peter, don't forget us!" Both Gudrun and Fritz had trouble holding back the tears. Peter was crying like a baby for only the second time since he left his mother, but now it was time to go. Corporal Mays started the jeep engine, Peter hesitantly climbed aboard, and the corporal drove slowly toward the main road. Peter wondered if he would really ever see the Waldbaus again.

Corporal Mays was very familiar with the route to McGraw *Kaserne* located on the south side of Munich. His messenger route between McGraw and Ingolstadt took him through Nandlstadt two to three times every week. This morning was special because it might be the last time the two ever saw each other. The corporal knew it would take over an hour to drive to Munich even if the unforeseen didn't happen. Farm vehicles pulled by cattle, were appearing back on the sometimes crude roads. Through the numerous villages along the way bicyclists were often moving along as a primary means of transportation for many people. Occasionally a civilian truck or Volkswagen "bug," a common name for the Volkswagen Beetle, would be seen. Caution was in order when passing through narrow openings at exits and entrances to several walled villages along the route.

The corporal had thought often about advice he should give to this boy who was on his way to America. He knew Peter would soon have to become a tough young man in order to endure until he was settled and established. "Are you excited, Peter?" He was searching for an opening to begin a serious conversation.

"Yes," Peter replied, "excited and afraid."

"I understand and I want to tell you about some things you can expect. What have you heard about America?"

"Sgt Grimes and the Americans at Altglashütte told me I would like it. They said there is plenty of food and that there are really good schools, but that I will have to study and work hard in order to develop a new home and lifestyle. Germans tell me the streets are paved with gold. I don't believe them, but I understand the analogy."

"It's good that you are realistic with your expectations. It will not be easy for you. There will be the language problems, a new foster family with which to integrate, meeting new friends and almost every area of your life will be different. We don't know where you will go, but America is very large and there are differences between the parts of the country."

"I want to be a cowboy!"

The corporal smiled and replied, "That is possible Peter, but cowboys today aren't fighting with Indians or robbing banks on horseback."

"I saw that in the movies."

"Some boys you go to school with might call you a Nazi. They don't know any better. They only know what they have heard at home and from radio broadcasts that they didn't understand. Most Americans think all Germans are Nazis. You will hear words like *Kraut, Heine, or Herman*. Don't be intimidated by that. Find a way to deal with it until you have gained respect. Some might even ask how many Jews you killed. I'm telling you this so you can be prepared. A strong personality and lots of patience will see you through the hard times. I have no doubt you will overcome the difficulties and become a valuable American citizen. Just be tough and in control of yourself."

Peter had heard this advice and variations thereof so often that he no longer doubted its veracity. The corporal's reminder served to cement the thoughts in his mind and prepared him to be mentally tough if any of these situations arose in the future.

Time seemed to fly as they continued through the backroads and tiny villages of this part of Bavaria. Peter had too many questions in his mind. He had enough fear of the unknown that he couldn't think of everything he wanted to ask. Eventually they reached McGraw. Before entering the staging area Peter was given the name and addresses of the corporal's parents and sister in Ohio. In the envelope was also the Army Post Office (APO) address where he could contact Corporal Mays at his current address. Peter was to contact Corporal Mays by mail as soon as he was settled.

In the staging area Peter was immediately processed and assigned an identification number. He was surprised that there were so few Germans being processed. Two families with children and another boy and an unrelated girl—who had been expelled from Poland—were the only ethnic Germans. Most of the displaced persons were from the Ukraine, Poland, Greece or Czechoslovakia. All were equally confused and frightened by the unknown and by their minimal English-language ability.

When processing was complete they were loaded on busses for transport to the *Hauptbahnhof*, which was the main train station in Munich. Those speaking a common language quickly befriended one another. In what seemed like thirty minutes they arrived at the train station. Only then did they get briefed by interpreters and a group leader who was an American military policeman (MP). Fortunately the damaged rail lines had been repaired after the war and no delays were expected. They were to travel from Munich to Frankfurt, where they would transfer to the Bremerhaven duty train where the USS *General Harry Taylor* was docked. The MP would escort the group and ensure a smooth transfer in Frankfurt.

Peter had some time to look around the *Hauptbahnhof*. It was a very large area with about twenty separate rail lines ending in a boarding area. The roof canopy which would normally protect passengers from bad weather was severely damaged. Glass skylights were seemingly hanging by a thread and the wind was noticeable as it was funneled into the boarding area. There were many people moving quickly from train to train and separate groups were apparently traveling together to some unknown destination. Everybody appeared to be in some degree of mild shock or confusion. Only the American soldiers appeared confident and in control. This image of the Americans was consistent with every other American contact he had experienced and was a lasting one for Peter. He had no doubt that his parents had made the correct decision when they directed him to escape to the American zone.

Since the beginning of the war, Munich had been subjected to over seventy allied bombing raids. The city, which included the *Hauptbahnhof* area, had been devastated by the persistent allied raids. At least half of the buildings were either totally destroyed or rendered uninhabitable. Fire-charred skeletons of buildings stood as a testament to the raids. Clean up had begun to the extent that the original street grid system was restored as the rubble was mostly just moved out of the street so bicycles, pedestrians, military vehicles and various civilian motorized transport apparatus might pass through. Removal of debris was a slow process at this time. Women bore the brunt of the work because so many men had been killed or severely injured in the war. Many areas were marked with signs which read, *Gefahrlich: Eintritt Verboten,* because of known or suspected unexploded munitions. Other areas were identified as condemned because of unstable buildings.

Restoring the rail system had been a priority. The Allies immediately saw the need to reopen supply lines and for overall management of the rebuilding process. By the end of 1945 most of the rail lines were operational. The War Crimes Trials had begun in Nürnberg that same year. The Marshall Plan, which served as the catalyst to invigorate the West German economy was beginning just as Peter prepared to leave for America. He knew little of these political maneuvers and wouldn't have fully understood their implications if he had. He listened and he observed, but it was not to be until many years later that he fully understood what had happened to Europe in general and in Germany and his home in the Sudetenland specifically. At the moment, he was focused on his evacuation to America as a displaced person. His parents had gambled—as he was beginning to understand—hoping that he could stabilize his life in America and return to Tachau when conditions improved. Neither his parents nor Peter himself could have known what difficulties lie ahead that would make the success of that plan very difficult to realize.

As he waited to board the train destined for Frankfurt and a subsequent transfer to Bremerhaven, he was struck by the obvious stresses of the people in the *Hauptbahnhof.* The dearth of males was evident. So many losses in the war had depleted the

European and German male population to an extreme. Most males were older or younger, like him. Everybody looked undernourished and wore odd arrays of old, dirty and sometimes tattered clothing. Body odor was a fact of life, although the people hardly realized that circumstance since everyone suffered from some degree of uncleanliness. Many of the women were alone or with younger children. All had shocked, deadpan looks on their faces. Peter couldn't remember when he last saw a smile on the face of a non-American. It has been four years since the end of the war. Peter was stunned by the ruinous effect on the people he was observing.

The group leader finally gave instructions that they were to board the train on track five. The cold wind through the boarding area had a bite so the group was happy to be boarding. Peter and the other Germans followed one another closely, as they boarded. The familiarity of language was the binding factor as they all searched for some degree of camaraderie and mutual security for the uncertain journey ahead. Peter learned that the girl's name was Hannelore and the boy was Dieter. He was aware that her name was the same as Trudi's mother. Dieter and Hannelore had not been as fortunate as Peter. They had been living in the displaced person camp in Lenggries, which was far south of Munich. Independently, they had found their way to West Germany by teaming up with refugee groups for short periods, stealing westward under the cover of darkness and using advice from local Poles on the best way to get to West Germany. After finally entering West Germany they were detained by an American patrol and escorted to the camp in Lenggries.

On this day they again depended upon strangers for

support and understanding of their circumstance. The train was crowded and cold. In compartments meant to accommodate six people, six to ten people huddled for warmth. The group leader moved from one compartment to another counting the number of people and reassuring when questions arose. Everybody had been told to bring their own food and water and that there would be nothing to eat until they reached the duty train staging area in Frankfurt. Toilet facilities were located at the ends of a few of the coaches, but were small and unclean. To find the toilet, he followed the *WC* signs. The cold was distracting until the train suddenly jolted forward with a loud staccato chain reaction as each coach reacted to the forward thrust. To Peter it sounded like the artillery barrages that he had heard occasionally outside Tachau just before the Russians entered.

They huddled together so they could be warmed by the body heat each person was generating. The ride to Frankfurt took seven hours but seemed much longer. There were many stops and delays because of the not yet efficient management of the rail system. Few passengers were getting on or off because this was a dedicated US Army train bound for Frankfurt. At one stop he saw a sign that identified the station as Augsburg, and another as Mannheim. Peter tried to sleep or snacked on hard cured meat and drank some of *Frau* Waldbaus cold tea. Like in a dream he heard the voice of the group leader. "Frankfurt station, get ready to disembark."

Everybody came alert with a start. One leg of the journey was about to end. Gathering their meager belongings, the group followed the soldier group-leader off the train and on to a platform which led them to a US Army transportation-processing area. This was the duty train area. They were counted again and each had to produce their identification number. The waiting train was under the control of the Allies and was dedicated to the transportation of refugees, and others authorized by the military, for travel to Bremerhaven. The boarding confusion was less than in Munich. The refugees were given a brown bag lunch, a seat number and sufficient time to go to the toilets. On the relatively comfortable train Peter found his seat quickly with his German friends nearby. A different group leader identified himself and told them to expect an overnight trip of about ten hours.

The group relaxed as they enjoyed the warmer and roomier coach. It would be a long overnight trip. Soon the *clackity-clack*, *clackity-clack* of the train moving over the tracks became hypnotically monotonous. They were very fatigued and relaxed enough to get some sleep. Peter reflected on his adventure since he left Tachau. With each passing day he understood more about why his life was evolving in such an uncertain manner. His family had been notified that they were to move out of their home. Eviction was a mild word for what was to happen to them. They were to be expelled from the Sudetenland. His parents were very fearful that they would be expelled to the Russian-controlled sector of Germany, although it was possible they could go to the American or British sector. When the Russians came into Tachau, it was dangerous to be a German. Revenge by out-of-control Russian soldiers was the fear of the Sudeten Germans. Peter saw first-hand how the Germans were treated. They were physically abused and their valuables were confiscated. Women and girls were raped and beaten. Peter witnessed, and his father photographed, murders committed by the Russian soldiers and the Czechs who now felt empowered after many years of German dominance. It was the photographs—now hidden away in the forest west of Tachau—which Peter hoped to retrieve one day.

It was in this atmosphere of fear that Peter had been directed by his family to abandon them and escape to the West. Three years ago, he had succeeded in stealing through the fields and forests until he found the Americans in Altglashütte. It had been challenging; now, America was his next destination. Fatigue overcame him and he slept.

In 1938, before the Nazi invasion of Poland to start WW II, Adolph Hitler had bullied and bluffed his way in order to become more powerful in Europe. One of his principles was the concept of *Lebensraum*, or room for Germany's expansion. To this end he had intimidated his country of birth and caused the annexation of Austria. The *Anschluss*, defined as "the connection," was accomplished with no resistance from Austria. Emboldened by that success, he shifted his desire for *Lebensraum* to Peter's home, the Sudetenland. The Sudetenland was the area of Czechoslovakia that immediately bordered Germany. Germans had lived there for hundreds of years, but always under Czech rule. Shortly after the annexation of Austria, Hitler threatened to invade Czechoslovakia if the Sudetenland was not ceded to Germany. In the early-morning hours of September 30, 1938, the Munich Agreement was signed by the heads of state of Italy, France and England. For this act of appeasement to Hitler and the Nazis, no Czechoslovakian representative was present. The Czechs later referred to it as the Munich Dictate.

It was ironic that the Sudeten Germans were suffering a

fate similar to that of the Jews, Gypsies, soldiers and people of conquered lands—or any other group deemed to be of undesirable genetic stock by the Nazis. The Sudetenland belonged to Germany for less than seven years, but in that time Czech resentment had seeded itself deep within their collective consciousness. After Czech power was reestablished, severe reprisals were not unusual. The Sudeten Germans were generally not involved with the Nazis. They were sympathetic to their homeland, but more indifferent to the Nazi cause than aggressively open activists. Some of the young German males had enlisted or been conscripted into the German Army. Their conversion to Nazism took place slowly but methodically under Nazi Party and military leadership.

When the Sudetenland fell to the Russians, the ethnic Germans became captives who were essentially unimportant and undesirable persons. They had no rights; they were in limbo until the Allies could mandate their fate. The Russians were the first into the Sudetenland so they wielded the most authority. Under Russian control and with the pseudo authority of the Potsdam agreements, the Sudeten Germans were expelled under the cruelest of circumstances. Many never lived long enough to be comfortably resettled. The Ackermans of Tachau were among the many, as Peter would discover many years later.

EIGHT

BREMERHAVEN

Through his fitful sleep Peter was not always aware of his surroundings. Occasionally he would drift into a deep sleep induced by overwhelming fatigue only to be awakened by the *clackity-clack* noise of the train coaches grinding relentlessly on the northbound route. Flashes of light were dancing in and out of his sub-consciousness as they passed through stations along the way or received sporadic flashing lights from the infrequent automobile or dimly-lighted village structure. His neck was sore from lack of support as he alternately leaned against the headrest on his right and then the headrest on his left. The cloud cover insured darkness; the night was bordering on pitch blackness in the long stretches between stations. A light cold rain pattered on the coach windows with a soothing effect on Peter's interrupted sleep pattern. That the weather was very much like in Tachau—or even Nandlstadt—was a thought flitting through his grogginess. He thought he saw a series of station-identifying signs that read Gottingen, but he wasn't really sure and that didn't much interest him anyway.

During the time he was awake, he thought about the

significant people in his life. He wondered where his mother and father were and if they had been safely resettled. He was aware that they may not be safely relocated, but he was hopeful. It had now been over three years since he had seen them or heard anything about their well-being. It was a function of his youth to have these parental thoughts at every period of relaxation in his daily life.

The Waldbaus and the hops farm were often in his thoughts. He could still remember Corporal Mays with his ever-present smile and he recalled the positive attitude that was such an inspiration for him. He still remembered Sgt Grimes from Altglashütte. In the depths of his memory, he remembered his school in Tachau. Trudi, who was always so capable and confident, was fresh in his mind; as was Anton, the soccer player. He remembered how it became difficult to be as friendly with Martina because of the changing relationship between the Czechs and the ethnic Germans. Then he drifted back into a few moments of sleep. Hours were passing as the train made its way to the north. In Hannover the train stopped for what seemed to be a routine scheduling stop. Managing hundreds of trains on a limited number of rail lines was something the Germans had done well before the war and were continuing that legacy after the war. Even though the Allies were in control of the country to include rail transportation, the hands-on, everyday management was locally controlled by the West Germans.

After a short coordination pause the train began to move again. The next stop was Bremen. Peter assumed that Bremen must be near Bremerhaven because of the similarity of names. The American group leader soon came through and confirmed

Peter's assumption. He alerted passengers that they would arrive in Bremerhaven in less than two hours and that they should be prepared to exit the train quickly. They would be taken by bus from the train station to the dock on the Weser River where the USS *General Harry Taylor* was available and waiting for them to board.

The busses were waiting—as promised—in a huge parking lot just outside of the train station. The busses were olive-drab in color with the familiar large white star visible along the side panels. Corporal Mays had once told him that olive-drab was the same color as the greenish-looking poop that babies left in their diapers when they were sick. That wasn't as funny to Peter at the moment as it was when first related by Corporal Mays. He was in a state of numb semi-shock. It was overwhelming to be sixteen years old and leaving your homeland without your family or any other personal support. Not knowing the whereabouts or condition of his parents added to the shock. He asked himself if this was the right thing to do, but ultimately trusted the wisdom of his parent's decision to encourage him along this course of action. It was the seriousness of their decision that gave him the strength to continue. It was the seriousness of his determination to be reunited with them that reinforced that strength.

Peter saw the reason for the need to quickly exit the train and get organized. There weren't enough busses for everybody so the busses had to make several trips. There had been hundreds of passengers on the train in differing categories. Not all were refugees or displaced persons, as the Truman legislation defined him. Some were military men or women returning to the United States after completion of their tour of duty in

Europe. Many of the passengers were dependent family members of active-duty military personnel. Peter could see that the families were loading on the busses first, then unaccompanied military personnel—the refugees waited.

Processing stations were set up on the docks. Documents were checked, identification verified, baggage weighed and a final cursory physical examination was conducted. Peter and his new German friends were directed to a ship gangplank. As he leaned forward to overcome the slant of the gangplank, he felt no need to look back at Germany. Peter realized his future was straight ahead on the USS *General Harry Taylor*, bound for America.

Peter and Dieter were led by a merchant marine to a lower steerage deck down several flights of steep metal steps. The crewman advised them to drop their bags to the next level and lower themselves carefully. Families and females were quartered above in more private and comfortable compartments. It would be some time before he was to see Hannelore again. The boys were given bunks above and below each other. Peter took the top bunk which was very much like a miniature hammock. They placed their bags in a small group storage section. The crewman guided them around the area they would be authorized to occupy. They were shown the latrine, as the toilet area was called, and the mess, for dining. Between the sleeping area and the mess area there was a common area landing space for the narrow steel steps which lead to the top deck. In this area there were also several large metal garbage containers which puzzled Peter somewhat.

They were asked to volunteer for work in the mess. They could choose to work one of three different shifts beginning immediately. Dieter started to volunteer thinking about working with the food. Peter stepped on his foot to get his attention and declined for both of them. Corporal Mays had advised against working in the mess. Finding volunteers was not a priority for the crewman, apparently because other refugees—thinking like Dieter—had already volunteered. Peter and Dieter's duty, became sweeping and mopping the living area and to be available for any other maintenance as needed.

In the dining area they found long steel tables and benches, with low rails along the edges of the tables. These rails kept the food trays from sliding off the table during rough seas. There were windows called portholes—several feet above the tables which allowed some light from outside to brighten the area. Peter observed the kitchen area where several cooks were busily preparing for the next meal. Peter and Dieter were informed that they would be in mess group "Bravo," since not everybody living in steerage could be fed at the same time. Peter was hungry even though the mess area smelled rather unappetizing. The odor was most likely the effect of cooking smells clinging to the metal frame of the ship with little ventilation in such a cramped area. Other nearby areas were marked "off-limits." They were told those were crew only areas that were used for the routine operation of the ship. To complete the tour the merchant marine alerted them to the ship's public address system. This system was used to notify the passengers when a mess group was ready to be served. It was also used to announce the times that accessing the main deck were allowed. To conclude the orientation the boys were advised that life jackets and lifeboats were located on the main deck and that before sailing an evacuation drill would be conducted.

Not so difficult, Peter thought. Maybe the length of the trip will be the most difficult part.

It was expected that the trip to the New York harbor, where Ellis Island was located, would take approximately ten days depending on weather. Peter had heard about the Statue of Liberty's significance and its effect on those who saw it for the first time. The green lady of peace, prosperity and freedom lie ahead. In ten days it could be his reality and no longer just a dream. Each new day presented a different set of challenges which served to distant him from his past ever more. Little-by-little, each passing day became a step in the direction of a new life for Peter.

That afternoon the USS *General Harry Taylor* was maneuvered away from the Bremerhaven dock and into the Weser River by several tugboats. There was an announcement on the public address system authorizing all passengers to go to the main deck to have a last view of Europe before the beginning of the long journey. When Peter arrived on the main deck, land was still in sight as they made their way toward the North Sea. The refugees were silent as they surveyed the landscape and contemplated this life-changing event. Tears were visible on the cheeks of many of the women while the men just looked stone-faced, as if in a trance. Refugee children just looked confused. Peter and Dieter managed a weak smile as their eyes met, but neither spoke. They saw Hannelore with the grouping of refugee women and families. Tough and resilient as her life had demanded of her for survival, she waved at them with a confident look on her face.

The American dependents and their soldier sponsors were in a festive mood. They were on their way home, Peter thought, but so am I. They know where they are going in America. I don't. The crew went about their business with an air of indifference. This was routine for them and barely mattered emotionally.

The sight of land slipped away as evening fell. They were both exhausted and very hungry, so the announcement for dinner was welcomed. They hurried down the narrow metal steps to the mess area. They were familiar with most of the American food, but there were some pleasant surprises as well. Peter was given two fried chicken legs, some green beans, mashed potatoes and a green salad. The surprises were an orange, a glass of fresh milk and ice cream! It had been two years since he had even seen some of these items. It wasn't much food in reality, but he found it difficult to eat everything because of his severely shrunken stomach.

After dinner they quickly made their way to the sleeping area for some much-needed rest. Peter took off his shoes, climbed into his top hammock-like sleeping area and wrapped a thin blanket around his body. He fell into a deep untroubled sleep.

Many hours later his deep, restful sleep turned into a dream world. After a series of nonsensical eclectic dreams his subconscious fantasy became clearer. He was in his father's chemical-business building and was riding the small one-person elevator. His attention had always been directed to the elevator when he visited the plant. It was the only elevator he had ever seen and—as boys will—he rode up and down between the first and third floor, which was the top floor in the building. It was not long until his father or some other adult stopped his joyriding. Now he was dreaming about the elevator. In his dream he was riding to the third floor slowly and then the elevator rapidly fell back to the first floor. This process repeated itself until his stomach began to feel uneasy in his dreamy trance. Up slowly, sudden fall—again and again. Peter awoke with a start and realized the sudden panic of not knowing where he was or what was happening. From the common area where the metal garbage cans were placed he heard the sound of vomiting. *"Raaalllppphhh!"*

He sat up in his hammock-bed to get a better look. His mental orientation soon returned him to the reality of the ship and the beginning of his voyage to America. He reasoned that the dream was induced by the movement of the ship as it reacted to the forces of the sea. He didn't want to be sick. Not only was sickness unpleasant, but it could be interpreted as a sign of weakness. Peter had long ago decided that he needed to be tough—even assuming a touch of machismo—in order to develop an aura of strength. Vomiting in a garbage can at the first exposure to rough seas wasn't going to enhance that image.

The dream had left him with an uneasy stomach, which he was trying to ignore. He heard the public address announcement that breakfast was to be served for group "Bravo" in five minutes. He had to pass the garbage cans to get to the mess. He put his shoes on and quickly walked toward the mess. There were now several pale-looking refugees around the can. There was a reason they were staying close. As Peter neared the can he saw somebody bend over the can and empty his stomach with another sickly *"Baaarrrfff."*

The sound of sickness and the smell emanating from the can were more than Peter's stomach could resist. *"Buuuwwwaaa,"* was his involuntary response. All he could think about was:

no more orange, no more ice cream and no more dinner. He lingered near the can until he was sure his stomach was empty, then moved to the toilet area where he could wash and gargle with water. He passed by the mess dining area where he saw only five people sitting with food in front of them. He decided to skip breakfast that day.

Dieter had felt ill also, but claimed he didn't vomit. Peter was skeptical, mostly because the truth might damage the machismo image that Dieter, also, was trying to develop. They cleaned their assigned area with difficulty because some of the refugees hadn't made it to the cans soon enough. Peter assumed that they were on the Atlantic Ocean but wondered about their exact location.

"Dieter, do you think every day will be rough like this?" The ship was rolling from side to side and lifting, then rapidly falling. Sometimes the movement was more severe than others. They couldn't see the ocean from where they were except from the portholes in the mess area and even then it was mostly just waves breaking against the ship.

Dieter responded, "The crewman said we weren't in the Atlantic yet. It might be worse when we get there."

Puzzled, Peter asked, "Well, where are we then?"

"When we fell asleep, we were still on the Weser River. The river took us to the North Sea and then we sailed west to the English Channel. I believe we are still in the English Channel."

"I don't understand all of this. I wish we could go above."

"It wouldn't matter. The English Channel looks like the ocean. He said you can't see land from the channel on foggy days anyway."

"Do you think the ocean will be even rougher than the channel?"

"This is December, Peter, we will be lucky if we don't go through a storm or two, but I didn't know the channel could be so rough."

Neither of the boys knew about the weather problems on the English Channel that plagued the Allied invasion of mainland Europe immediately before and on June 6, 1944. It was ironic that these two German boys were being evacuated from the very country that the invasion was designed to destroy and that they were now making their way over the body of water that had given access to the invading forces.

Fortunately, the ocean was relatively calm when they entered the open water later that first full day. As time went by, they gained some strength from the regular meals and they adapted to the constant rolling of the ship. Their "sea legs" enabled them to negotiate the narrow passageways of the ship without fear of falling or being thrown into metal structures and being injured. The tedium was difficult to deal with, but occasionally they were allowed above for some cold fresh ocean air. There wasn't much to see except open-ocean, but the turbulence and whitecaps were frightening in their size and potential. At times the seawater seemed to completely engulf the ship at one end or the other. In the center of the ship it wasn't as bad, but he wasn't going to wander far from his safe vantage point. It wasn't difficult to imagine the reason for the constant movement he felt when below. On those few occasions when the sea was in extreme chaos, he didn't linger long on the main deck.

Periodically movies were shown for the steerage passengers.

There was a "theater" on the second deck. The theater was a small auditorium-like room with folding wooden chairs all askance around the seating area. Peter didn't always understand everything in the English-language movies and it was even more difficult for Dieter. They both knew they had to learn the language so they tried to concentrate on the dialogue. One evening the movie featured a John Wayne western. They were both familiar with John Wayne having seen some of his movies in their villages during better times. John Wayne was Peter's movie hero and was the reason he had decided he wanted to be a cowboy. This was the first of the John Wayne movies he had seen in the English language.

When they discussed the movie at its conclusion, Dieter remarked, "I didn't know John Wayne could speak English."

Peter smiled, having figured that one out already. "John Wayne can do everything. That's why I want to be like him in America. I hope I go to Texas."

"Why is he always chasing the Indians?"

"Not always," said Peter, "Sometimes he chases the bad guys who steal the cattle."

"I understand that," replied Dieter, "but the Indians didn't do anything."

Peter thought about that for a moment. He was searching in his mind for some defense of John Wayne." I think they are fighting over the same land. The Cowboys want to have room for their cattle."

Dieter had a look of doubt on his face. "You mean like the Czechs, Poles and Russians moved us away from our homes so they could have more land?"

Peter was shocked at Dieter's insight. His own depth of

thinking had never reached such a serious level. He was surprised that this statement came from Dieter, whom he had
considered rather shallow and passive. This development made
him reflect momentarily on his father's advice to never ignore
another point of view no matter the source. Peter didn't want
to reveal his confusion, so he tried to spin the mood without
appearing to evade Dieter's question. "Remember what John
Wayne called his friends? You know, the ones who were good
but maybe not as strong or capable as he was?"

Dieter thought about that a moment and answered,
"Pilgrim!"

"Yes, and I will call you Pilgrim. We are both Pilgrims. In
the John Wayne sense of the word and as refugees to America,
we are Pilgrims!"

"OK, Pilgrim Peter! Let's go down and get some sleep if
we can. It will be just a few days until we reach America."

"Don't forget it will soon be Christmas. We may see the
Statue of Liberty on the first Christmas day."

When they were below and in their hammock-beds,
Peter's mind was still affected by Dieter's land-possession
question. The question steered his thoughts toward another
question. What about Sgt Grimes's stories about the treatment and status of blacks in America? Sgt Grimes never mentioned land-grabbing. He only referred to being a different
color and having no power. Surely there is more to it than that,
he thought, and realized that he had so much to learn about
America. One more ominous thought crossed his mind before
he dozed off. He wasn't an Indian and he wasn't black, but he
was different. He was a German who might be thought of as a
Nazi. Mercifully, sleep overtook his thoughts.

NINE

Ellis Island

Christmas music made the morning quite pleasant. Peter recognized most of the soft melancholy songs that he had heard in Tachau; only the language was different. Usually the words couldn't be directly translated, but the message was the same. There was often a religious reference to the events surrounding the birth of Jesus Christ. Other songs were meant to reflect on good times with family for the festive holiday season such as *White Christmas*. Peter recognized some of the words sung by Bing Crosby so he hummed the tune silently to himself as he readied for the day.

A public address announcement alerted the refugees and displaced persons in steerage that they could go on the main deck, if they wished, to view the Statue of Liberty and the surrounding New York/New Jersey coastal landscape. Peter hurried and checked to see if Dieter was getting ready. All the refugees were excited about their first sight of the statue. They crowded the narrow metal ladder as they ascended to the main deck where it was cold, slightly windy and with a hint of

snow in the air. Excitement permeated the passenger groups:
refugees, military passengers and dependents, as well as the
crew members. From the area authorized for single male refugees, he could see the lines of passengers crowding to the railing on the starboard side of the ship. Not far away were the
two German families in a group which included Hannelore.
They waved excitedly as the Christmas music was audibly con-
tributing to the excitement and satisfaction of everyone. The
cold was a non-factor because of the minds and bodies flush
with anticipation of their first glimpse of the Statue of Liberty.
Suddenly, as if the curtain were opening in a stage play, the fog
lifted and the statue appeared. Tugboats began guiding the USS
General Harry Taylor toward the New York harbor providing an
even closer look at the statue as it grew larger and larger before them. Peter was aware of the symbolism of the statue. A
female wearing a seven-pointed crown with a torch raised high
above her head with her right arm. To him she was a symbol of
freedom from oppression and an opportunity to make a good
life. Many of the older refugees were in tears and some were
weakened to the point of near collapse. They sat on the deck or
just supported themselves on the railing. Peter was elated that
this part of the journey was ending. The statue was impressive,
but he hadn't forgotten John Wayne and the Indians or his conversations with Sgt Grimes. The symbolism was inspiring and
he shared the excitement of the newcomers to America, but
his excitement wasn't restricted to the current euphoria. The
uncertainty of his future was foremost on his mind.

The ship was bearing to the starboard so that the statue
was on the port side as the land became clearly visible. The
last thing he saw, before his exit from the ship sometime later,

was the tugboats escorting the USS *General Harry Taylor* to the Hudson River pier on the New Jersey side of the river.

To Peter it seemed an eternity as impatience set in while the steerage passengers waited to disembark. The maneuvering, docking and securing of the ship was accomplished in a skillful step-by-step procedure by the tugboat and docking crews. When the ship was securely in place the military and dependent passengers began their processing: check ID's and orders for active duty personnel and passports for dependents. These two groups were then spirited off to US customs and immigration for their official authorization to enter the United States. After they were cleared, they were free to continue their journeys on the dry land of America to wherever their destinations would take them.

This was not the case for the immigrants, refugees and displaced persons. When the dock was finally cleared of the military and dependent personnel, the steerage class passengers were called to the main deck. They had to show their number identification and their visa or other official paperwork allowing entry to America. In Peter's case it was a document allowing him permanent residence in the United States under the provisions of the Displaced Persons Act of 1948. They were all under the watchful eye of the many immigration officers and other security personnel as they were directed to a waiting ferry for transportation to Ellis Island. Peter and Dieter were again side by side, like brothers, in order to gain some much-needed mutual security. Hannelore and the German families were also nearby. All had believed that the USS *General Harry Taylor* would be docking at Ellis Island, but could see now that that wasn't the case. The ferry ride was a short one until they docked and disembarked onto Ellis Island. Peter could read the sign which identified this location as their official American in-processing center. It read: "Welcome to Ellis Island," and below that: "Gateway to America."

They were all relieved that the long ocean voyage was over. Traveling in the cramped and foul-smelling steerage-class area was somewhat depressing. The air was stale and the washroom facilities were without showers and were otherwise inadequate. Later, Peter learned that as difficult as his steerage-class living conditions were, they were actually much better than historical steerage-class passengers before him had been provided.

As they entered the processing building, Peter could see the Statue of Liberty to the south on what he would learn was Liberty Island.

The Statue of Liberty was large enough to dominate the surroundings and served to reassure the group that everything was going to be fine for them in America. Security personnel were not as visibly numerous on the island because the only unauthorized exit from the island was to swim.

Their numbers were checked again and they were directed to sit in specific areas of the processing center. Hannelore and Peter were sent to the same area, but they were separated from Dieter. Periodically, a door would open on the right side of Peter's waiting area. He could see some officials at processing desks and a group of civilians, with no apparent purpose, standing idly by. Each time the door opened an immigration official would call out a number and a name. The person that responded was told to bring his or her baggage into the processing room. The persons called gathered their bags, as directed, and never returned. There had been little activity on the side of the room where Dieter was sitting. Peter had considered some possible scenarios by now. He told Hannelore that he thought they were going somewhere soon and that Dieter would be staying behind. When the door to Peter's right opened again, an official called out, "Hannelore Schmidt, 88215."

Hannelore rose and looked sadly at Peter. Peter stood and hugged her. He whispered in her ear, "A*uf wiedersehen, Hannelore, und alles gute.*" They made no attempt to hide their tears.

Peter assumed that she was going with one of the persons waiting in the other room and that he would be going with one of them also, as soon as they called for him. It appeared that Dieter and the others were staying in the processing center for some unknown reason. Eventually the door opened and the same official called his name and number. He looked over at Dieter as he gathered his bag and belongings, turned to face in Dieter's direction and said, "*Auf wiedersehen*, Pilgrim."

Dieter looked frightened, but managed to reply, "*Auf wiedersehen*, John Wayne."

In the adjoining well-lighted room there were several desks positioned along the perimeter walls. Serious, but tired-looking men in crumpled long sleeved white shirts sat at each. Peter was directed to a desk where a distinguished-looking gentleman sat smiling on one side of the cluttered officer's desk. On the desk was a nameplate which read, "Toby Randall, Processing Officer."

"Number," the serious official asked, looking at Peter as though he wasn't sure he would be understood.

"88212, Mr Randall," replied Peter. He wanted to erase any doubt about his understanding of the proceedings on the chance the processing would be completed more quickly and accurately. The words were the first English-language words he had spoken in America. That was significant in Peter's mind because it signified the placement of the first brick in his new life's foundation.

"Name," asked the official, who seemed to be pleased by Peter's comprehension.

"Peter Ackerman."

"Good, Peter, I have your records. I will process you to be released to Dr Swanson if everything is in order. This is Dr Swanson from the state of Washington. Dr Swanson is your sponsor and you will be in his care until you are released by the Department of Immigration or until you become a US citizen."

The doctor rose, still smiling, and offered his hand in greeting. Peter offered his hand still very confused, but with a favorable first impression of the doctor. He managed to say, "Pleased to meet you, sir," as he had learned from contact with the Americans.

The official was examining Peter's documents intently, seldom looking up. All documentation was found to be in order as he extracted some documents and seemed to stamp every page. Peter had to sign some of the documents as did Dr Swanson.

A packet of documents was being assembled for Peter and his sponsor. When the processing was complete, the official offered the packet to Peter and explained the contents. The most important was the authority to enter the United States for the purpose of permanent residency under the provisions of the

Displaced Person Act. This document was signed by President Harry S Truman and certified as a true copy by the processing official. Peter was elated as he slowly understood the meaning of the moment.

The official continued, "You are to make contact with the immigration office in Seattle within two weeks in order to schedule an appointment. That office will be your initial controlling facility. In order to achieve citizenship you must establish a good record in terms of behavior and allegiance to America. This can include a clean police record, and an understanding of American history and current government policies. Your educational advancement and your service to country and community are also important factors." He paused as if to insure that he was understood. Peter did understand because he and the other displaced persons had been briefed on this information many times.

"Are there any questions, Peter?"

"No, sir."

"Do you have any questions, Dr Swanson?"

"Not at all, but Peter and I have a lot to talk about."

"That's very well, doctor, you are free to go. Congratulations, good luck and Merry Christmas!"

Peter felt helpless, but confident at the same time. He was sure the American government would do the right thing for him and that he would be safe.

Outside of the processing center there were other people waiting. Many sponsors had friends and family with them that were not allowed inside. Dr Swanson had been accompanied by his son.

"Peter, this is my son, Danny. He is sixteen, just like you"

Peter was somewhat relieved at this news. A boy his age would be easier to talk to at this time and could become his new best friend. They greeted each other with friendly smiles and a handshake. Danny's grip was firm but not aggressive as he used this opportunity to establish his own identity. Danny was much taller than he and very well-dressed and appeared to be strong and healthy. Peter felt inferior and embarrassed in his dirty, tattered clothes and his generally unkempt condition.

Dr Swanson suggested Peter go to a group men's shower, which was provided at Ellis Island. "Danny brought some clothes for you. He can go in with you and watch your things while you shower. I know you must be very tired, but you will feel better with a shower and some fresh clothes."

This sounded like a good idea to Peter. He was already realizing how fortunate he was to have the Swansons guiding him. He was becoming less tense and more trusting. After the shower and teeth brushing he nearly forgot how tired he was. He wanted to just throw away his dirty clothes, but he stuffed them in his bag with the other things he was sure he would just dispose of eventually.

"Hurry along, boys, we have to catch the ferry to the Liberty Park train station." Dr Swanson was assuming a lesser relationship role so that the boys could bond. Peter appreciated that, but was surprised at the need for another boat ride. He wondered if you have to ride a ferry to go anywhere in America.

The reality was that this ferry would get them off of Ellis Island and within walking distance of the Central New Jersey Railroad (CNJRR) station. An afternoon train would take them to Chicago with arrival in the morning, according to Danny.

In his mind, Peter questioned the geography of that route and asked Danny, "Isn't Chicago west of Washington? And what is Seattle?"

"We are going to the other Washington. I mean Washington State, on the West coast, where Seattle is the largest city. We live in Snoqualmish, not far away from Seattle. It will take nearly four days to get there on the train. We will change trains in Chicago."

Four days! Peter thought incredulously. I know America is big, but four more days? I've been traveling for almost two weeks already. "I thought we were going to Washington, where the President lives. I remember now about the state of Washington. On the map it is above California with borders on the Pacific Ocean and Canada."

"Yes," answered Danny, "The President lives in Washington DC. Our first train is called the *Columbian* and will take us right through Washington DC. We stopped there on the trip out here to meet you."

The *Columbian* was the name of the route in the Baltimore and Ohio train system. The *Columbian* route would take them through or near major cities: Philadelphia, Baltimore, Washington DC, Pittsburgh, Cleveland and Detroit. Peter had heard of some of these cities, but he had little knowledge of their actual location. When they entered the *Columbian*, Dr Swanson led them to their reserved seats. He and Danny sat side-by-side in what he hoped was a forward-facing direction. Danny said the trip to Chicago would take almost a full twenty-four hours and that they would have to sleep as best they could in these seats. Peter was no stranger to that circumstance. He was delighted to hear that in Chicago they would transfer to

the *Hiawatha* and have a sleeping space for the next two over-
nights. Danny called the sleeping space a "Pullman" berth.

While the train sped them toward Chicago they had time to
talk. Peter tried to explain the USS *General Harry Taylor* experience from Bremerhaven, but couldn't get very detailed about
his life since departing Tachau. He wasn't yet sure how much
detail he wanted to divulge until he knew the Swansons better. He trusted them to this point, but everything was still very
confusing for him. Tentatively, he had decided to not express his
desire and motivation for a return to Tachau. He was very interested in how they had known about him and why they were accepting responsibility for his welfare. Dr Swanson explained the
family's interest as humanitarian. They were well aware of the
consequences of the war on people like Peter, who had slipped
through the cracks during end-of-war confusion. When they
volunteered to take a male displaced person under seventeen
with the assistance of a local church group, they were quickly
accepted. A background check on the Swansons and an in-home
inspection by the responsible government agencies was routine
and approved expeditiously. The Swansons had been notified of
the approximate date of Peter's arrival along with all the information contained in his records. It was their choice to meet him
on Ellis Island or wait until he could be transported to Seattle.
Peter was happy they had made the trip to Ellis Island. It grew
dark, as time went by, and the *clackity-clack* grew monotonous. The last thought in Peter's mind before dozing was that
American trains *clackity-clack* was exactly like the *clackity-clack*
of West German trains. The boys awoke in Chicago having slept
some, but not fully rested.

They barely had time to eat and stretch their legs until it was time to board the Milwaukee Road *Olympian Hiawatha*. This was a beautiful train equipped with sleeping cars, dining cars, lounges and a domed car for sightseeing. Such luxury, Peter thought. They had two air-conditioned seating areas with adjustable seats. At night the areas could be closed off for privacy and converted to sleepers. The two areas were adjacent to each other and connected by a narrow access door. Peter wanted to test the sleepers, but decided to wait until it got dark. Time was unimportant to him until he realized it was the second German Christmas day. This was the only Christmas day observed in America. Was there any divine significance in the fact that he finally felt secure on the American Christmas day?

They had found their seats easily, but the conductors in their red caps and black front-buttoned uniforms were still moving through the coaches checking tickets. Just like Germany, Peter noticed, some passengers can never find their assigned seat. While they waited, the doctor and Danny were explaining the trip. Danny asked, "Do you know about the forty-eight states of the United States?"

Peter thought this was a rather patronizing question, but he also understood that they didn't know anything about each other at this point. "Yes, I know, but I don't know where they are. Chicago is in Illinois, isn't it?"

"Yes, and just north of here is Lake Michigan. Lake Michigan has many times more surface area and volume than Germany's Lake Constance."

Peter assumed he was referring to the *Bodensee* but wasn't sure if this was bordering on bragging about America. "I've never seen a lake that big before. Is it as big as the Atlantic Ocean?" Peter was beginning to engage in a battle of wits with Danny.

"No, but you think you are on an ocean from the middle of Lake Michigan. But that's not all, Peter . . . there are four more huge lakes in this same area."

"Really? Would that be Lake Superior, Lake Ontario, Lake Erie and Lake Huron?"

Danny was astounded that Peter could recite these names so readily. "You are correct, Peter, how did you learn about them?"

"My father taught me many things about America. He always said the day would come that the information would be useful to me. Also, my American friends in West Germany talked about their homes and places they were familiar with. I remember some of those conversations. I haven't been in school much for over two years, though, and I miss learning new things."

Peter looked out the window and sensed that his coach was moving, but he had noticed no physical sensation of movement. He quickly realized it was that relativity phenomenon that his father had taught him. It was a nearby train that was moving and providing the relativity. At that moment they were not moving, but a few seconds later he felt the thrust of the coach as the coupling devices engaged. Slowly, but consistently, they gained speed and were on their way to northern Illinois and then southern Wisconsin.

"Shall we go to the Super Dome? We don't have too much daylight left for today." The doctor was speaking to the boys.

"OK, Dad, we can look around the train and then view the countryside from the dome if it is not too crowded."

Danny wanted Peter to see the countryside but he remembered that it was difficult to find room when they traveled east a few days earlier. Difficult at the beginning of the trip, but more room as the novelty of the Super Dome wore off with most other passengers. Peter was just following along as he familiarized himself with his new environment. Other than being familiar with some of the names he heard he had no knowledge of where they were or where they were going. On this Christmas day there was snow on the ground in some places which was esthetically pleasing, but covered much of the normally snow-free landscape.

Dr Swanson pointed out the Wisconsin River as they crossed over and then not long after that the mighty Mississippi. Peter had heard of the Mississippi River and was impressed by its size. Darkness was setting in, so the doctor said it was time to go to the dining car before they tried to get some sleep. The dining car was just like a restaurant on wheels thought Peter. Restaurants in Tachau were not this fancy even before the Russians came. He saw delicious-looking meat, gravy and vegetables on the other tables as they were being seated. Quality food like what he saw here had been difficult to find for Peter over the past few weeks, so this food was capturing his attention completely. The aromas and the attractive presentations ignited his salivary glands immediately, but he tried to not outwardly show his hunger. He didn't want to act like a hungry wild dog even though he felt like one. Dr Swanson sensed his hunger and quickly ordered a steak and baked potato for Peter.

When his meal was served by the waiter, he ate quickly. He hardly talked, but at one point he made reference to the extremely large potato.

"That potato comes from Idaho," stated Danny. "It is a Russet potato and just delicious when served with plenty of butter or sour cream. We will pass through Idaho on this trip."

"I've never seen a potato this large," replied Peter. "At home we put *Schmalz* on our potatoes."

"What is *Schmalz?*" asked Danny.

"It's what you get from pork drippings after it hardens."

"Yuck!" Danny grimaced. "That sounds like lard."

Dr Swanson chuckled and remarked, "That is exactly what it is. I think there will be other differences between German and American food preferences and eating habits."

"May I have some *Eis* before we go?"

"OK, you mean ice cream, I think."

"Yes, that's correct. Sometimes I forget my English."

"Milk, also?"

"No, thanks, I'll just have some ice water when we get back to our compartment."

They converted their compartments into sleepers and laid down for some much-needed rest. Danny and Peter were in one compartment adjoined by Dr Swanson's Pullman berth. It was the most comfortable sleeping environment Peter had experienced since leaving Nandlstadt. There was some bumping and shaking, and lights flickering through the shaded window from outside, but Peter hardly noticed. In this bed he was able to stretch and even roll over. He never knew that they crossed the Missouri River near Mobridge, South Dakota, or that they passed through a tiny corner of North Dakota. He slept soundly and restfully the entire night until Danny woke him up sometime after daylight.

"Hey, Pete! Can I call you Pete? Everybody in Snoqualmish will call you Pete anyway."

"Yes, OK."

"OK, dad has been up for a while. We just passed through Three Forks, Montana. You could have seen Yellowstone National Park but I didn't wake you out of your obviously peaceful sleep."

"I've heard of Yellowstone."

"It was the first National Park ever in the world. It's huge."

"Is that where the hot water shoots out of the ground at predictable times?"

Danny was again surprised at the knowledge of Peter. "Yes, this is the place. I've heard that the geysers shoot 120 feet into the air. In this park you might also see many animals. There are bears, buffalo, deer and mountain goats as well as many animals I've only heard about."

"Buffalo?" asked Peter incredulously. "Are there cowboys here, too?"

"Yes, there are cowboys here and all over the West."

"I thought they were only in Texas."

"Pete, we do have a lot to talk about." Danny smiled and suggested breakfast.

Peter thought it was very soon to eat again after the big meal the previous evening, but he wasn't going to argue. He had a lot of catching up to do nutritionally.

When they returned to the compartment they quickly tidied up. Dr Swanson took them to the domed coach again so they could go to the observation deck for some morning viewing. Dr Swanson related some information about where they were that he remembered from his outbound trip.

"We are approaching Butte, Montana and the Bitterroot Mountains. The Bitterroots are one of the many sub-ranges of the Rocky Mountains. The summit of the Bitterroots, as well as the entire length of the Rockies, is called the Continental Divide, or the Great Divide. It is given these names because it separates the East and Midwest of the United States from the West. The Continental Divide stretches all the way from central New Mexico to Canada and even north into Canada."

"I have heard of the Rocky Mountains, but not the Continental Divide." Peter wanted to be sure they knew he was paying attention.

"As a general rule, water draining from the eastern slopes of the divide eventually empties into the Atlantic Ocean or the Gulf of Mexico, although some makes its way to the Arctic Ocean. Any water draining to the west empties eventually into the Pacific Ocean."

This was all very interesting to Peter as his knowledge of places on the earth had been restricted to the Sudetenland, West Germany and books. He was beginning to realize how big America and the world really were in comparison to the little village of Tachau.

Dr Swanson was continuing, "Just past Butte, we start up into the Bitterroots. This is when the train switches to an electrification system. Only the Milwaukee Road trains do that in this area. It is much more cost effective to electrify, but isn't done often because its startup costs are prohibitive. It's much cheaper, but provides service of less quality than diesel power or even steam power. So, instead of diesel power we are on electricity for the next 440 miles. There will be another part of our route in Washington that is electric."

"Isn't Washington where we are going?"

"Yes, but it's almost 400 miles from the Washington

border near Spokane to where we are going in western Washington."

Peter thought all train systems in Germany were diesel powered, but he wasn't sure. Some of this information was coming very fast and he struggled to keep up. He was very tired and asked to sleep again.

"Where will we be when it gets light again? I think I may want to sleep until then if I can eat again and then sleep. That bed is so comfortable."

"We should be in Washington, near Spokane."

"Please wake me up in Washington. I want to see everything in my new home state."

Peter was beginning to feel fully rested when they arrived in Spokane. There was a short stop for passengers, another breakfast and they were on their way. Peter saw that eastern Washington wasn't different than the state of Montana. It was gray, cold and rather dreary looking. Some rolling hills were in the distance with scrubby grass bunches in clusters along the flanks of the hills. A wood frame building could be seen occasionally. Cattle and horses were in fenced areas, and then to his surprise, riding out of one of the buildings was a cowboy! He could see a sign on the building that said "Dude Ranch."

Peter asked excitedly, "Is that a cowboy?"

"Yes!" Danny joined in Peter's excitement.

What is a "Dude Ranch," Danny?

"It's a vacation area where city people come to ride horses and have a western ranch experience."

"I don't see many people here."

Danny explained that "dude" is what the vacationers were called and that they came mostly in the summer.

"This is Christmas Day," said Danny, "in the middle of the winter. People are at home with their families enjoying their Christmas presents, or they are in church."

"So, if I wanted to learn how to be a cowboy, I could come here in the summer?" It was a statement presented as a question as new information was processed and stored in Peter's memory bank.

"Yes, if you have an inclination for that sort of thing, it can be done."

"Where are all the Indians?" Every exposure to something new raised new questions in Peter's mind.

"They are part of everyday society now. They can live on reservation land that the government has set aside for them or they can live in the community like everyone else."

Peter thought about that for a moment, then asked, "If they were here before the cowboys, why does the government control where the reservations will be?"

For the first time, Danny felt some frustration with the difficulty of Peter's questions.

"Ask my dad, Pete. I can't answer that one."

Danny didn't understand why matters such as this interested Peter. He had little knowledge of the German annexation of the Sudetenland or the subsequent expulsion of those same Germans six years later by the Allied mandate. The possession of land, it seemed to Peter, is what people and countries covet enough to give reason for war.

The further west of Spokane they traveled, the more the

landscape changed. Dr Swanson pointed out a huge rock sitting in the middle of a field.

"That's what they call a glacial erratic, Peter. How do you think it got there?"

Peter had no idea, but he was sure Dr Swanson was going to tell him.

"If I told you that that boulder was made out of minerals not found within 200 miles of here, what would you think?"

"Somebody brought it here on a big truck, or on the train?"

Dr Swanson smiled, almost expecting an answer like this. "Well, we really don't have equipment that can lift boulders that size, nor do we have trucks or trains large enough to carry them."

"I don't know, then."

"Think about the term 'glacial erratic.' "

"It sounds like it comes from the word *glacier*. Glaciers like in the European Alps. Were there glaciers here?" asked Peter.

"Yes! Scientists are sure of that, but there is another theory of how they got here. There is some evidence that they were brought here by rapidly-moving flood water."

Peter had never heard of anything like this, but he had no reason not to believe Dr Swanson. He was sure he would learn more about this in his new school.

Dr Swanson wanted to make some further points as if to make the theory more plausible.

"Harlen Bretz, at the University of Washington, first made this theory public in the 1920's. But he could never explain where the water came from until he got support from a fellow scientist named Joseph Pardee just a few years ago. Pardee theorized that the water came from Glacial Lake Missoula. You were sleeping when we passed through Missoula, Montana, so you missed the huge bowl-like feature where the city sits. Pardee thinks this bowl was filled with water because the Clark Fork River was dammed by a glacier. When the glacier dam weakened the water was released into Washington. The flooded area is now called the *Scablands* because the land was stripped bare—right down to volcanic basalt—by the fast-moving water. The water left plenty of other evidence, also, such as coulees, ripple marks, gravel bars, potholes and hanging valleys."

"When did all this happen," asked Peter?

"Over ten-thousand years ago," was the doctor's answer.

"Can that happen again?" asked Peter

The doctor reflected pensively on Peter's question, but soon answered affirmatively.

"Any natural phenomena that occurred on earth in the past can happen again."

Peter wondered if that statement applied equally to natural phenomena and to a myriad of differences that countries, and even individuals, found with one another.

Peter thought Danny was hearing this for the first time. He wondered if Dr Swanson had found some intellectual connection with him that he didn't have with his son. It hardly mattered, though; Peter was receiving so much information that—combined with anticipation of a new home—he was hardly retaining everything he was hearing.

"Were there Indians here then?" He had been taught in school that the Europeans didn't come to America until about five hundred years ago.

"That is possible, but anthropologists don't agree about that."

Peter was constantly looking for answers as to who has the right to land. It was one of those questions that puzzle people for their entire lives without ever being answered. Because of experiences in Peter's life, it was a question that commanded his attention. He would soon find that most of his peers in America had no such knowledge or interest.

Soon they were in Othello, Washington. Dr Swanson mentioned that they would connect to another electrification system for the remainder of the trip to Seattle. He stated they were getting close and could be in Seattle in a matter of hours. They still had to cross the Cascade Mountain Range which was one of the reasons for the electrification. Practicality dictated the change, since electrification was much more efficient in the mountains. Peter was happy with the news that they were close; the stomach butterflies started to act up again.

There was another river crossing, this time the Columbia, and then the train followed the slowly rising tracks into the Cascades. There had been snow along the route from Chicago, but since he slept through the Bitterroots, the Cascades snow depth was the extreme of what he had seen. Gradually, trees started to appear. Pines, he thought, and then other types of cone-bearing evergreens. He didn't know their names, but they were hemlocks, cedars, true firs and the mighty Douglas fir. Near the summit he saw some ski areas and two men walking toward a lodge. He could see a ski lift in the background. Just as suddenly as the skiers had appeared they were gone. The pull of the engine eased and the train settled into a controlled descent to the west side of the mountains. Danny told him they had just gone by the summit of Stevens Pass where the highway ran parallel to the train route.

"I can hardly wait to see my mom," said Danny, "She is very excited about having you live with us. I'm sure you will like her."

"I am excited to see her, also. I can see that you have missed her."

"We are going through Monroe now, next comes Snohomish and then we pass right through Snoqualmish but the train doesn't stop there. We have to go twenty-five more miles to Seattle. She will pick us up there in our new car."

Darlene Swanson hurried toward her husband and the two boys. She was smiling and her eyes sparkled even in the dimness of the cold damp day. Peter was not quite over the fact that everybody in America was smiling all the time. That was just one of many curiosities he would need to adapt to as he adjusted to a new home in a strange land. She gave Peter a glance before hugging Dr Swanson and her son. After they exchanged greetings and the quick questions about the trip, Dr Swanson introduced Peter to Darlene.

"This is Mrs. Swanson, Peter, but you can call her Darlene and you can call me Philip since we are going to become family."

Peter smiled like an American and made himself available for a hug if that was what she wanted. It seemed appropriate and she seized the opportunity.

"You are a handsome boy, Peter. We are so happy to have you stay with us. How do you like America?"

Even though he anticipated that question, he found appropriate words difficult to find at the moment.

"It's wonderful! Philip and Danny have been so good to me. I think I've seen the entire country on that train trip."

"Indeed, you have seen a lot. Now let's get on the road to Snoqualmish. We can talk on the way."

TEN

ENIGMATIC AMERICA

Snoqualmish was nearly twenty-five miles north of the King Street train station in Seattle. Through parts of the city and along Highway 99, Peter got his first look at his new home. Strange-looking cars, he thought, and everybody seems to have one. Dr Swanson was very proud of his 1948 Buick Sedanet which he had purchased only a few months earlier. It was a little uncomfortable for Peter riding in this roomy four-door sedan because he felt that only the president should be afforded such luxury. Most of the people he saw were well-dressed and appeared to be confidently busy with their lives. He began to understand the metaphor of *streets lined with gold* that so many adults in West Germany seemed to believe. The streets were not actually lined with gold, but people acted like their pockets were.

They made their way to Snoqualmish without ever leaving Highway 99. In his new city they drove through some residential areas until they stopped in front of a large white two-story house with pillars that supported an ornate canopy over the entrance area.

"This is it, Peter," said Dr Swanson. "Danny will help with your bag and take you to your room upstairs."

"Thank you very much. You are all so kind to me. I can hardly wait to see the city and get settled in here. Everything is perfect!"

It was Monday, December 27, 1949. Peter had completed the long trip to his new home in America. Darlene had prepared a very welcome meal of roast beef and potatoes, which Peter devoured hungrily. It was cool and there was a light mist in the air. Later he would learn that this was normal for northwest Washington at this time of the year. He showered and got some much-needed sleep.

School was not in session because of the Christmas holidays, but Dr Swanson had been in contact with school district officials and the principal of Snoqualmish High School. It was determined, that because of Peter's somewhat-limited English language capability and the fact that his formal schooling had been minimal for three years, that he should be placed in the sophomore class. School would begin again the following Monday which gave the family time to familiarize Peter with the neighborhood and the city.

Snoqualmish had about 30,000 residents, Peter learned, and was dependent upon the Boeing Aircraft Company, the shingle mills, the timber industry and fishing as the primary means of employment and economic vitality. Darlene was driving Peter and Danny around the city while Dr Swanson was busy with his medical practice. She stated that the local economy was getting stronger every day after surviving the

Great Depression and World War II. It was surprising to Peter that the family was so detached from the war and its aftermath. He had been a part of those days in Europe and was here because of them, while she and Danny talked about the war in the abstract. To them, it was something that happened far, far away to some people to whom they didn't relate. Sometimes Peter was tempted to go into detail about his experiences, but thought better because of his need to keep his ultimate plan to himself until such time that he understood everything that was going on around him. Because of his experiences in Tachau and the knowledge he gained about the war after he was gone from Tachau, he had decided to trust no one with his plans for the time being.

On several other occasions Darlene took the boys on trips through the city so that Peter could quickly be acquainted with its parameters. He learned about the Snoqualmish waterfront and the Puget Sound inlet of the Pacific Ocean. She said that many of the fishermen used piers in Snoqualmish to sell their catches to the processing plants. He also saw several shingle mills which converted timber from the nearby mountains into various-sized lumber planks and pieces for building, roofing and other construction uses. Not far from the Swanson home in the north end of Snoqualmish there was a park overlooking most of the waterfront. Peter could see that Puget Sound wasn't the ocean because the Olympic Mountains were directly to the west, effectively serving as a land block between the ocean and Puget Sound. This was interesting for a boy who had never lived near an ocean or any other large body of water.

Forest Park was an interesting city park on a hill in the southwest section of the city. At the entrance Peter saw his first live bear. Several of them were in a cage which had a pond and a cave that provided shelter from inclement weather. They probably used it to escape people also, thought Peter. More animals were in a small zoo on the main, elevated section of the park. Grassy areas and picnic tables were all around as well as tennis courts. It was very different and surprising to Peter to see the relaxed atmosphere and carefree lifestyle of the people in the park. On the way out of the park they saw a few peacocks with their long, colorful feathers spread linearly away from their bodies. They strutted proudly and looked at the automobile in an aloof manner as if to ask what people in cars thought they were doing in their park.

Danny asked his mom to drive by the golf course. Many of the north end boys played golf at the city golf course during their summer school vacation. Peter knew what golf was but thought that it was a game only the rich Englishmen played. It didn't seem like much fun to him to hit a little white ball with a metal or wooden club and then go hunt for it so you could hit it again. Danny said a couple of the boys got good enough to play in state tournaments and that there was some talk with the school coaches that they might organize a school golf team. Peter already knew what the answer would be when he asked about his favorite sport of soccer. He was surprised when he found that Danny was familiar with soccer. He said they played it at recess in primary school. He said they had a lop-sided brown ball with a thin skin that they kicked around until it went over the sidewalk at either end of the playground. The sidewalk was the goal. If it went out in the street to the west of the playground or onto the blacktop where the basketball hoop and the bicycle rack were located, it was out-of-bounds. *Hmm,*

Peter thought, they don't know that soccer is a very challenging sport. Do they really think hunting for a little white ball in the weeds is better than soccer?

One day Danny invited Peter to go with him to basketball practice. He was on the school team whose season had started before Christmas. The coach had arranged for practice during the Christmas break. Danny wanted to show Peter the school gymnasium and promised to teach him a little about basketball. Basketball was another sport not played in school in the Sudetenland, but Peter thought it more interesting than golf. At least it was played with a big ball and there was a goal to try to put it in. The players even had to run! They got to the gym an hour before practice started. Danny, acting like a coach, picked up a basketball and demonstrated a two-hand chest pass by throwing the ball to Peter. Instinctively Peter threw out his chest and knocked the ball to the ground where he controlled it with his feet and started moving it toward Danny. Danny was shocked momentarily, and then laughed uncontrollably as he recognized the well-executed soccer move. Peter laughed with him before he picked up the ball and threw it in the basket. What an easy game, he thought, nobody was standing in front of the goal trying to knock it away! They laughed again as the ball rested momentarily in the net before gently falling to the floor. Peter scored two on his first attempt ever. They were becoming genuinely good friends.

Peter's life normalized quickly when he started school. He made some friends in his classes and learned to remember the names that were strange to him. There was a Bill and a Mike and a Larry among the boys and a Marlene, Janice and Barbara among the girls. Some of the names were spelled the same as in Germany, but not pronounced the same. Danny was busy with his basketball team and social activities. He tried to integrate Peter into his circle of friends, but that was a slow process because of the dissimilar backgrounds. His fellow students and teachers seldom asked about his life or how he came to be in America. They only knew him as Pete from a German section of Czechoslovakia. Peter had decided to use Czechoslovakia as his home in order to minimize the potential questions that might arise from being known as a former citizen of Nazi-controlled Germany. The Swansons had agreed that this would answer questions without straying from the truth.

Peter did struggle with his English classes. He found that conversational English, with which he had become proficient, was only a part of total fluency. He progressed well, after a slow start, in his typing class and in classes which required extensive reading. In math classes such as Algebra and Geometry he was ahead of most students. There was a German language class which he considered in order to help maintain his proficiency, but no Czechoslovakian class, which he felt he would need as part of his long range plan.

Peter enjoyed the physical education classes because he was getting stronger and more physically aggressive with every new day. The instructor had developed games that were meant to let students of all physical capabilities enjoy and that were not competitive. When they played basketball it helped Peter gain some skill. He could see that he was as good as any of the boys in his physical education class. He had a long way to go to be competitive with the varsity players who were not required to take physical education. At home with the Swansons, he played a game called *horse* with Danny where a basket had been installed on the garage. Peter could never win, but he did improve his basketball skill as Danny gave him technical pointers about ball-handling and the finer points of defense and rebounding.

Living with the Swansons was as good as it could get for Peter. Danny was a friend who was very helpful to him in his daily life and especially at school. Very often they were not in the same circle of social friends, but they were one-on-one friends nonetheless. Dr Swanson had his medical practice to attend to during the day, but was more interested in Peter's background than Darlene or Danny. He recognized the academic potential of Peter almost immediately. It had started with the *Scablands* discussion and continued to develop over time. Peter was interested in the sciences as a result of his father's encouragement, but was also a very perceptive philosopher for a teen-age boy. His knowledge and interests, together with his life's experiences, made Peter an interesting conversationalist for the doctor. Danny was too much the school star-athlete type to be extremely interested in academics. Philip appreciated that, but secretly wished Danny would show more interest in academics. Darlene was a strong mother figure for him. She expected his help around the house and let him know in firm but kind words and confident body language what she expected from him. Peter complied willingly and tried to help beyond what she required. It was little different than working with the Waldbaus in Nandlstadt.

One evening Darlene and Peter were cleaning up in the kitchen after dinner when she asked rhetorically, "It's your birthday soon, isn't it?"

"Yes, on February 4," answered Peter.

"We would like to give you a birthday present in celebration of becoming seventeen. What would you like?"

The question surprised Peter enough that he had to think about an answer for a moment, but then answered, "You shouldn't give me a special present because you already do so much for me. More than I could have dreamed of three years ago."

"I knew you would say something like that, Peter, but we insist. We are very pleased with how this has worked out for us with you here. We just want to do it."

Peter thought about that for another moment and answered, "Well, I would like a map of the Sudetenland and German-border area that I came from. I never want to forget my roots."

The "roots" reference was only part of the reason he requested the map. The map could be the first step in formulating a plan for his return to Tachau. On his birthday the family presented him with a very detailed topographic map of the Tachau area. They had mounted it on a cork board so that it could be hung on his bedroom wall. For his years with the Swansons it served as a constant reminder of what he hoped his destiny would be.

As the years passed Peter became Americanized. That first summer Danny had introduced him to golf. Chasing a little white ball around an open field became a thinking man's game which required much self-control, patience and discipline, as well as some athletic ability. Walking the seven to ten miles around the Snoqualmish Municipal Golf Course kept him in good physical condition for the summers. The boys did this twice every weekday. Peter's skill level improved dramatically the second year during which he became a golf addict. His intramural basketball during the winter and his golfing summers served to keep him in good physical condition. Golf tournaments taught him self-control, patience, stick-to-itiveness and a healthy respect for rules in an individual sport. He knew it would be important to maintain good physical condition. He didn't know the circumstances and conditions under which he would return to Tachau, but he still remembered the physical and emotional demands of his escape.

Maintaining, and even improving, his German-language capability wasn't too difficult. That was his primary language for well over fifteen years. At the high school he had developed a rapport with the German teacher through casual conversations, but Peter was a little leery of questions about his background, so he kept the relationship on a formal basis. The improvement of his Czech-language capability proved to be problematic. There were some courses offered in Seattle, but the transportation issue was more than he wanted to deal with. Eventually he found a refugee family in Snoqualmish that was willing to befriend him and help with the language.

Dr Swanson always kept abreast of what Peter was doing so it was only natural that he was curious about Peter's Czech language interest. The subject came up one evening at dinner.

"Peter, you already speak two languages, so it's hard to understand why you want a third. Americans hardly have an interest in foreign languages. Foreign languages were dirty words when I went to school, because that usually meant Latin."

"Why Latin," asked Peter, "I know most of the high school students at Snoqualmish take Latin instead of German or Norwegian."

"It's because education administrators have decided that

students who want to go on to medical or legal professions will need to be familiar with formal Latin names and phrases so common to their potential careers."

Danny chimed in with a common student reaction to Latin. "I hate Latin."

"Danny, you never saw an academic subject you didn't hate," replied Dr Swanson

Defending her son Darlene said, "Well school isn't as easy for everybody as it was for you, dear."

"I understand, sweetie, and I could never score twenty points in a basketball game."

With a smile on his face, he continued, "We are not all alike. We just need to give our best effort at whatever we do."

There was a nodding agreement at the table as nobody chose to add to the conversation. As if to lighten the mood, Dr Swanson offered a rather strange question which the others didn't immediately recognize as bait for a joke.

"On the subject of languages . . . what do they call a person who speaks three languages?"

Everybody was a little puzzled, but Darlene spoke up and said, "trilingual."

"Correct," Philip responded, "And what do they call a person who speaks two languages?"

Danny was quick to jump on that one as if to prove his level of intelligence.

"Bilingual, I'll bet."

"Correct," stated Philip again, "So what do they call a person who only speaks one language?"

There was silence and quizzical stares around the table as Philip smiled while contemplating the punch line.

Peter recognized the lightheartedness of this conversation and because he was beginning to understand Philip's sense of humor, he answered, "American!"

Philip laughed out loud, which made everybody laugh at him and at the joke.

"Correct, again. Nobody can fool this family!"

Peter noted his inclusion in the term "this family," which reinforced the feeling of inclusion and security that he had developed.

Darlene had been exploring channels of information about Peter's parents. She had active searches going with the American Red Cross and a local refugee group which was in its infancy. She had made some inroads into obtaining information from refugee search agencies in Europe. These agencies, overwhelmed as they were, had provided little information about any of the Sudetenland East Germany expellees. Peter was thankful for her interest and the work she was doing, but he was aware of the difficulty involved in finding meaningful information.

During his days at Snoqualmish High School Peter worked hard developing an excellent command of the English language. His accent, although slight, was noticeable, but certainly not distracting. He became one of the better students in the school, mostly through sheer effort. He was accepted by the mainstream of the students and found that his fears of being labeled "Nazi" were mostly false fears. Few of the students had more than a rudimentary knowledge of the extent of the war. Most of their parents had not been called into the military because of their age and the fact that they had families. Peter learned that a few parents had been called up toward the end of the war, but had been returned to their homes when the war ended before they completed basic training.

In Peter's mind, he never became exactly like the collective student body. His own background wouldn't allow that. In his view, they were mostly unaware of anything that happened outside of their little Snoqualmish closed environment. School functions and sports events were their primary interest at this stage of their lives. There was no chance that any of his peers could relate to his life or his future plans even if he had wished to confide. He had his map and his memories to remind him of who he was, but not much else.

Snoqualmish High School Peter and Tachau Peter were two different people, but he did a good job of separating the two. Dating, dancing, following Danny and the sports teams was fulfilling and enabled him to become a socially mainstream student. Darlene and Danny taught him to drive the family car and he was licensed after passing the driver's test. The family gave him lots of space to pursue his own interests and friends; space in which he could mature physically and mentally while becoming an independent man. As the time for high school graduation drew closer, he began to think seriously about his future after school. In the immediate future, he had the option of getting a job or going on to higher education. He knew he wasn't ready to return to Europe at eighteen years of age. He didn't have the money or resources—or confidence, for that matter.

He followed events in Europe as best he could through newspapers and radio news reports. Occasionally he found a West German newspaper in Seattle. These papers didn't provide much useful information, but there were some references to the deteriorating conditions between the Russians and their former Allies. He was aware of how Berlin had been isolated because of political and social system philosophical differences between the East and the West. Germans were fleeing from East Berlin to West Berlin and from other parts of the new East along the Czech border. He learned that there was difficulty in crossing the borders, and that former residents of the Sudetenland were being denied re-entry. Peter thought this was to keep the former residents from reclaiming their property. This news made Peter aware that he might have to enter Czechoslovakia illegally in some manner. He had no idea how that might be, but it was a probability that he had to seriously consider.

Peter wanted to pay back the Swansons for providing a loving and comfortable home for him. He was beginning to develop a depth of responsibility as he perceived it. First, he needed to gather information and plan for his return to Tachau. Then he needed to mature a little more, become more educated and acquire the funds to carry out his plan—as well as repay the Swansons in some form or another. He was sure they weren't expecting that, but it was something he now felt obligated to do. But how? That was the question as Peter graduated from Snoqualmish High School in June of 1952.

Any matter concerning Peter's future was best discussed with Philip Swanson, who had both experiences in life and the adult male perspective. After a series of discussions with Philip, Peter decided to attend the local Junior College and try to find a job at the same time. Peter still withheld his end plan because he thought Philip might not be supportive. The warnings about trying to do too much were forthcoming as

Peter expected. Peter was somewhat naive in this respect, but thought that no one could understand what hardships he had already endured in his life; that humans were capable of much more than they were usually expected to do. And what if he couldn't handle it all? Back off and try again! That's the worst that can happen.

School started at the junior college and Peter was lucky enough to find a job as a longshoreman at the local port. It was strenuous, but inconsistent work. No ships—no work. Because of this it was treated more like day labor. Once you qualified and joined the longshoremen's union it was an on-call job. He could show up every day to check for work or go to the college library when he needed to study. When the union didn't have enough people to load a ship they would call your home. Miss work too many times and you lost your union accreditation and couldn't work anymore. In this case you had been fired! Still, this provided more study opportunities than working at the local Boeing aircraft plant where you had a full-time scheduled shift.

Two years went by with this schedule. Danny didn't understand why Peter would choose such a life, but even he realized that all people were not alike and, for sure, he and Peter were not alike. Danny had moved along to play basketball at the University of Washington and basically had a completely different lifestyle than Peter. They maintained their friendship even though they hardly crossed paths with each other. Danny now lived in housing offered by the University's athletic department.

Danny's absence from the Swanson home left a void for

the Swansons which Peter readily filled. Philip was very interested in Peter's history to the point that he knew everything about Peter except his desire to return to Tachau. Peter
learned about the war from an American point of view and
Philip learned from a boy who had been very close to the
war. They had some philosophical differences which more often than not led to unanswered questions or to conclusions
that developed through exchange of ideas. The one question
that neither could answer, nor even develop a theory for, was
that of how so many Germans could have supported the Nazi
philosophy. This question bothered them both enough that it
came up repeatedly during their discussions.

When Peter finally moved on to the University of Washington
as a student, he had accumulated enough money to pay his own
tuition and buy a car. Finances were going to be his biggest problem in getting back to Europe. It was clear now: he wasn't a boy
anymore and he couldn't expect the Swansons to provide his
room and board forever, even though they seemed willing to do
so. It looked like he was going to be able to graduate from the
University in June of 1956.

One day as he exited the undergraduate library he saw a
military man in a dress uniform which he had never seen before. This brought back memories of his time with the military, which influenced him to approach the sergeant.

"Good morning, sergeant! What are you doing here on
campus?"

"Good morning, sir. I represent the US Army and I talk to
students about their future and what the army has to offer."

"That is interesting," replied Peter, "I've never seen you here before."

"OK, I am Sergeant First Class (SFC) Dawson. I work out of the Recruiting Main Station in Seattle. I have an on-campus office over in Suzzallo. I'm usually there on Tuesdays and Thursdays."

"I see," said Peter as an epiphany danced through his mind. "I worked with the Army in West Germany right after the end of the war. I was a displaced person who was lucky enough to be resettled here in Washington. My name is Peter Ackerman."

Sergeant Dawson offered his hand for a handshake which Peter accepted.

"Do you have plans for the future?"

"Not exactly," was Peter's reply.

"OK, would you like to come in and talk on Thursday?"

"Yes, I can make it after my political science class. How about 1100?"

"Sure, I can do that. I am in room 105 on the first floor in Suzzallo."

"See you then, sergeant."

"I'll see you, Peter . . . nice to meet you."

ELEVEN

THE RECRUITER

Dr Philip Swanson sensed Peter's slight nervousness as they engaged in yet another conversation about life in general, or about Peter's war and post-war experiences specifically. There had been an unusual circumstance in western Washington which had captured the attention of the populace and was the feature item in the print media and on radio news programs, but Philip doubted that Peter could be upset by this story. It had been reported that mysterious pitting was appearing in automobile windshields over the past few days. Reports of the pitting came first from the north near the Canadian border and were spreading rapidly in a southerly direction. In Seattle, two police officers had reportedly seen the pits suddenly appear as they sat in their police sedan. Reports of strange vapors wafting off the pits were also received by police and news agencies. Speculation was rampant. Many people believed it was the result of alien action, while others attributed it to vandals with pellet guns. Everybody had a theory which led some of them to near panic. It was an issue for the general population because reports were coming from reputable sources, the pitting was observable by anyone and was given widespread media attention. It was an issue, at a relative moment in time, until cooler heads, logic and science intervened.

Peter was aware of this circumstance and had given it some thought. When the reality of this incident began to surface, it was determined that the pits were mostly pre-existing but fueled by stories that just spontaneously grew in enormity. As the stories spread, more and more people started looking at their windshields and noticed pre-existing pits for the first time. That caused them to enhance the credibility of the story. The stories grew and grew until they became commonplace, and accepted because "everybody" knew what was happening. Logic took over when it was noted that these pits were appearing almost exclusively in the front windshields of older vehicles. Very few pits were found in newer vehicles or in any other types of glass windows. Eventually the hysteria was overcome and the incident became a non-issue. It was a non-issue for most people, but not for Peter.

Peter could relate this incident to a question that he and Philip often pondered. That was the question of how so many Germans could have embraced Nazism. Through his high school studies, cursory as they were, and discussions with Philip, he was able to connect his own experiences with the reality of Nazism. Nazism had always been extremely puzzling to Peter until the pitting incident.

He related his theory to Philip by explaining that the German people were told stories favoring Nazism by "credible" government officials; citizens made observations in the improvement of their lives, and eventually bought in because "everybody" knew it was the right thing to do. Nobody wanted to be cast as an outsider by not accepting what "everybody" knew to be correct. Add in the German reputation of guilty lower-class losing underdog, which resulted from the adjudication against Germany by the Treaty of Versailles in 1919, and it became easier to understand the collective consciousness of the German people. Not only were they told by "credible" sources that Nazi principles were good for Germans, the improvements in German society were visible, and the German people wanted Nazism to be their destiny.

Philip hesitated as if deep in thought before he said, "You know, that is an interesting theory. I think sociologists and psychiatrists would call that 'collective delusion' or some fancy name like that. If you integrate 'collective delusion' with the fear of the possible deleterious results of nonconformance with Nazi principles, you begin to have a more complete picture."

"Yes, and we already talked about the bully effect. I saw bullying, even in my school in Tachau. First it was by the German kids until the Russians came in and then it was the Czech kids who bullied with their new-found power. Bullies get their way by use of intimidation, the power structure and physical force."

These discussions were always difficult for Peter because—as a German—he still felt some guilt about Nazi history. He thought it was probable that the German "collective delusion" had now turned into "collective guilt." His memory of what happened to the ethnic Germans in Tachau was his proof that any group of people could become guilty of dastardly crimes against another group of people given what they considered a plausible justification. Validity or non-validity of justification was unimportant. This thinking served as further motivation to retrieve the photographic evidence he had hidden in the

Blitzbaum, in order to show the world what had happened in Tachau. He thought of those photos, in part, as further warning to those who think that Nazism was an anomaly.

This wasn't Peter's reason for nervousness this day, however. He wanted to talk to Philip before his appointment with the army recruiter on Thursday, but was apprehensive about the reaction he might receive. Though unspoken, the family was aware that Peter would soon choose his own direction in life; however, parting would be difficult. He might have felt the same apprehension if he wanted to leave for a job in Oklahoma, or Connecticut, or wherever. After all, it was just talk with the recruiter, right? Peter was trying to rationalize and justify his actions to himself.

"You know I will graduate next year," Peter began, "so I have been thinking a lot about where I will go and what I will do after graduation."

"Yes, this is true. You need to be thinking about that. With a degree in international relations you should be easily employable, especially with your background in Europe and your language capabilities."

"I am definitely considering that with the advice of professors and the employment placement office at the university. There are other possibilities also. I made an appointment to talk to an army recruiter tomorrow."

Philip was very surprised to hear that, but realized he was no longer a controlling factor in Peter's life. He was confident that Peter had a great deal of trust in him and was sure that the reason for this discussion was a courtesy as well as to solicit advice.

Peter continued, "I just want to explore the options. I

didn't join the Reserve Officers Training Corps (ROTC) at the university, as you know, but I've heard that with a college degree I am eligible for Officer Candidate School (OCS). I'm certain there will be other options. Now that the Korean War is over, there seems to be a real need for troops in Europe. I think I would like to go back."

"I have every confidence that you will do whatever is the right thing for you. I don't know a lot about the army or any of the other military services, but you will have my support in whatever you choose. Just be sure you investigate all your civilian options very closely, and don't be in a rush."

Peter was surprised by both the variety of options presented by SFC Dawson and the varying qualifications for each. He learned quickly that it was a good decision to come for the talk. The citizenship issue came up right away. That was something he had to get started on immediately for many jobs he might pursue whether they were military or civilian. His five-year threshold had been passed so he was now eligible for citizenship. Another issue was that of his ability to obtain a security clearance. SFC Dawson thought that wouldn't be a problem since none of his family had been members of the Nazi Party or had participated in the war. He had a clean police record, which was a requirement, and he had to pass a physical exam. For some of the options such as OCS, Rangers and Special Forces (SF), he would have to pass a physical endurance test before the enlistment contract could be guaranteed. He was surprised to learn that he couldn't be an infantryman without what the sergeant called a "picket fence" physical profile, which amounted to excellent function of all primary physical systems, such as vision and hearing.

As a result of this talk, Peter had already identified the options of OCS and Special Forces as requiring more consideration. He promised to return for more information and said that he wanted to talk specifically about combining his college education and language capabilities with an assignment to West Germany or somewhere in Europe. The sergeant promised to research this, but also stated that the preliminary screening and the physical examination would need to be accomplished in order to establish eligibility for enlistment and for specific options. He also made it very clear that citizenship was required for OCS, Rangers and Special Forces.

Peter walked out of the recruiting office with an air of excitement. It was almost as though the army was a gift for him, by which he could return to West Germany and be gainfully employed at the same time. He had work to do in the next year—beginning immediately. He hurried across the grass field to his next class.

TWELVE

TACHAU, CZECHOSLOVAKIA: JUNE 1955

TRUDI'S DILEMMA

Trudi Kehle sat down on a park bench on the north bank of the Mže River where she rested on most summer Saturday afternoons. This part of central Europe was typically warm in June, with the occasional windless rain shower. She sat on this particular bench because she was suspicious of her surroundings. She often had the feeling that someone was watching her. Not every day and not always the same person. One week it would be the classic male spy figure, the next week it might be a lady pushing a baby carriage. Whether it was real or just a figment of her imagination, she wasn't sure, but awareness of her surroundings had become a way of life for Trudi and her German friends who had remained in Tachau during the ethnic German expulsions. Some of the Germans stayed for family reasons; for others it was a matter of economic security or just intimidation. Some Germans were needed by the Czechs for specialized labor tasks or expertise in maintaining infrastructure. These people had swallowed their pride and closed their eyes to the reality of the expulsions. In every case they justified their decision to stay as the best course of action for them under the circumstances surrounding an unpredictable future. As a young girl, Trudi stayed with her mother who was married to a Czech.

Like most Germans who had remained, she was unhappy with the conditions and the way that Tachau had developed under Russian influence. It was no secret that many Czechs were also unhappy with suffocating Russian control. As early as 1948 the Russians had stanched the desire of the Czechs to develop a free-market economic system and a democratic political system. That year the Russians effectively took control of Czechoslovakia with a bloodless coup.

The result of the coup was a deterioration of living conditions for all in Tachau. There were constant promises of improvement, but nothing ever improved. The reality was that life was getting slowly worse for most residents of the new Czechoslovakia. Border controls were tightened to the point that now she had to obtain a pass to cross over to West Germany to visit her grandmother who had been granted a former West German resident exit authorization. Exit from, and entry into Czechoslovakia was controlled through designated crossing points. Attempts to travel between the two countries by unauthorized means and unauthorized routes subjected violators to harsh discipline by the Czech/Russian government.

The bench where Trudi chose to sit was by design. From this bench she could observe everyone that wasn't hiding or didn't want to be seen. In addition to the fields of vision this bench provided, it was placed conveniently under a lonesome linden tree for shade from the warm summer sun. Her suspicion had made her even more aware of her surroundings on days that she planned to visit her grandmother in Thanhausen because it seemed to her that she was being followed more often on those days. The more she thought about her crossings to West Germany the less surprising it became that she, as an ethnic German crossing often to West Germany, would be a subject of surveillance. It was frightening to worry about being watched and not completely understand the reason for the surveillance, or her possible fate if found violating some fabricated rule.

Today she was just relaxing and trying to pass another uneventful day in Tachau. She hadn't noticed surveillance, but that didn't mean it wasn't there. The warm sun made her a little drowsy and encouraged reflection on the past. The end of the war and the arrival of the Red Army had been traumatic for her and her family. There was that period of uncertainty of the immediate future and fear of the present. To be a German was reason enough to fear the wrath of the new Czech/Russian power structure. Most of her German friends had fled or been expelled to places unknown. Losing friends like Peter Ackerman was emotionally unsettling for a young girl whose best friend had just suddenly disappeared. After witnessing the treatment of Peter's mother and father before they were evicted from their home and moved to the expulsion holding area, she assumed, and was happy for his escape. She had no knowledge of what had happened to him, but felt confident he had made a surreptitious exit from Czechoslovakia and was safe somewhere in West Germany.

Finishing her education in the local school had gone by quickly, even though it was a difficult adjustment to suddenly be a student in a Czech controlled school without most of her best friends. She knew little about the 1948 coup, but since that time life was more difficult In Tachau. Getting a job with the Russian colonel with her stepfather's help and her athletic ability gave her a certain degree of independence and assisted in her pass procurement for visits with her grandmother in West Germany. *Oma* had been fortunate to finally move back to her childhood home in Thanhausen as part of the expulsion program. Trudi's visits to the West German border area served to illustrate the differences between the Czech and the rapidly-recovering West German lifestyles. She felt sure she was being watched, in part, because she knew the difference and the fact that she worked for Colonel Gochcnko. It was tempting to just stay with grandmother, but what about mom and what about her own good job? They were making progress in West Germany, but jobs were still hard to find at this time. Each successive trip to Thanhausen made her more envious of the West German lifestyle. Young women her age dressed with attractive clothes that actually fit. Makeup and hairstyles gave them a fresh, confident look and helped build their self-confidence. She often felt the stares of inferiority at the *Gasthof Zur Post* in Bärnau, when grandmother took her there for dinner and entertainment. Thoughts of her future were on her mind today like every other tedious Tachau day. She worried often about the border restrictions, which were becoming tighter and tighter. People were being moved away from the border so that only the military and the border police were allowed within one kilometer of the fortified border. She heard that some entire villages were being evacuated and buildings boarded up and placed off-limits. Escape rumors persisted so she knew she wasn't the only one thinking about getting out.

A year ago the border crossing point at Broumov/Mähring was closed. Fortunately the Tachau/Bärnau crossing was still open, but searches and document scrutiny were increasingly thorough upon exit from or entry into Czechoslovakia. A visa was needed to cross the border into Czechoslovakia if travelers didn't have the temporary pass which was issued only to permanent residents of the Tachau area. Among her German friends there was more frequent talk of getting out by escaping to West Germany because most of them couldn't get even a temporary pass. She had heard whispers of clandestine border crossings, but she had ignored the talk for reasons of her own security. As long as she could get a pass she wasn't going to worry about it, but who knew how long that would last?

Inevitably, on days like this, she reflected on the conversation she had with Ursula Kuhn on her last trip to Thanhausen. Ursula had been a classmate in Tachau until she and her family were expelled. The family had been arrested and robbed when Czech locals, accompanied by an official from the Czech gendarmerie, arrived at their home without notice and forcefully moved them to the Tachau resettlement camp. They lived there in small unheated rooms with no bedding or change of clothes. Their food consisted of ersatz coffee twice a day and a thin meatless soup in the afternoon. Occasionally they were given a cold potato and enough clean water to keep them alive. After two weeks they were moved to a farm where they worked in fields harvesting turnips and potatoes or were assigned other hard labor jobs. One day they could be loading or unloading goods to or from farm vehicles or cargo trucks, and the next day they could be working on road construction. The women were on twelve to fourteen hour shifts or until they collapsed.

Many of the women died from starvation, disease, or during childbirth. Where she worked, only five people survived until they were eventually expelled to the American Zone of West Germany in 1947. Like Peter Ackerman's parents, Ursula's parents did not survive.

The warm summer afternoon and tranquility of the moment didn't dull the rage she felt about the situation in which she and the other Tachau Germans found themselves. The Russians and the Czechs had made it very clear that they considered all Germans to be Nazis—even though they knew it wasn't true—and that Germans were only receiving payback for what they gave the Jews and other "undesirables" under the Nazi doctrine. Trudi was having thoughts of joining the underground to enable escape with her mother and stepfather. The unfortunate death of Rudi Jelinek made life for Hannelore Jelinek and her daughter, Gertrude Kehle, more difficult. Trudi's athletic prowess and her job with Colonel Gochenko were the last bits of leverage they had to provide for a livable life in Czechoslovakia.

THIRTEEN

SEATTLE, WASHINGTON: MAY 1956

GRADUATION

Everybody was there: Philip, Darlene and Danny Swanson as well as many of the friends Peter had made during his nearly seven years in Washington. Danny had graduated the year before, so this was a second commencement in two years for the Swansons. Commencement at the university was proving to be a happy festival of relaxed students who had attained a goal in life, accompanied by their most loyal lifelong supporters. Clarence S "Hec" Edmundson pavilion was packed to capacity with celebrating spectators. It was a day in which all could be proud of student accomplishments. Peter shared their joy as he reflected on the endless hours he had spent in classrooms, writing term papers, agonizing over finals and all the other scholastic requirements he had dispatched. He felt a deep sense of satisfaction over his educational accomplishments and felt deeply indebted to the Swansons who had treated him like a son for all these years. As he sat listening to the guest speakers he mentally reinforced his resolve to repay them in some way, some day.

There was a nagging emptiness in his life; however, he was as motivated as ever to solve the mystery of his parent's status and to realize his reentry into what he would always consider his Sudetenland home.

Through ongoing discussions with SFC Dawson, the army recruiter, Peter had finally decided to enlist for the Special Forces option. He had completed his citizenship processing and taken the oath of allegiance. The naturalization ceremony was an emotional experience for the fifty-some new Americans that day. He had taken the oath seriously and still remembered parts of it:

> . . . that I will support and defend the Constitution and laws of the United States of America against all enemies, foreign and domestic, that I will bear true faith and allegiance to the same; that I will bear arms on behalf of the United States when required by law; that I will perform noncombatant service in the armed forces of the United States when required by law, that I will perform work of national importance under civilian direction when required by the law, and that I take this obligation freely without any mental reservation or purpose of evasion; so help me God.

This was powerful dogma for Peter and required some soul searching. In the end it was the fact that the Germany he remembered no longer existed and the fact that the United States had given him an opportunity to have a free and unencumbered life. In exchange, it was the allegiance contained in the words of the oath that was required of all citizens—native-born or naturalized. To Peter it was a fair exchange for which he intended to uphold the intent of the oath.

Peter was fortunate to be an Ackerman on this day. Hundreds of students were to graduate and receive diplomas in the pavilion. Alphabetically, he was one of the first. It would be an hour or more before they reached the end of the alphabet. He strode proudly to the speaker's platform when he was called.

"Peter Ackerman . . . Bachelor of Arts, International Relations," was his cue. He strode nervously across the platform, hoping he wouldn't trip on his long black gown or that his hats tassel wouldn't hit him in the eye. Governor Langlie was presenting the diplomas and shaking hands with the graduates. Peter was glad he didn't have to shake hands all afternoon like the governor, but he thought it a privilege to be recognized by Governor Langlie at this moment in time.

After the hugs and handshakes from his family and friends his thoughts quickly turned to the future. He was enjoying the present, but the past and the future still defined who he was. After weighing all the options presented by SFC Dawson, Peter had reasoned that the Special Forces option was best for what he had planned. A big plus for Peter was the Lodge-Philbin Act of 1950. This Act provided for the expeditious procurement of personnel who had extensive knowledge of the eastern European landscape and topography as well as language capabilities. He had chosen Special Forces Engineer Sergeant as a career path. In these so-called "Cold War" days he felt confident that he would be assigned to the only Special Forces unit in West Germany which was stationed at Bad Tölz. The Czech language was his ace in the hole. He didn't think they were going to send him to Korea or Panama to utilize his Czech language skills, although there were jokes that this was the typical method of operation for the army. The Lodge-Philbin Act seemed to insure his assignment to West Germany.

He was scheduled to enlist on June 29, 1956. He expected to be sent to Ft Ord, California, for his basic training. He would actually be in the army for six months before he even started Special Forces training. It would be two years before he could be assigned to West Germany. He also had the option of OCS before applying for Special Forces training, but that made his Germany assignment more uncertain and extended the training time frame. He definitely didn't want a desk job in the Pentagon examining maps of Eastern Europe and translating documents. He knew the Special Forces training would be tough and that there was no guarantee he would qualify to wear the Green Beret; successfully completing the training was a near-term goal.

After basic combat training and advanced infantry training, he would begin his SF phase one training at Ft Bragg, North Carolina. Phase one was basic SF indoctrination and training; Phase two was his specialized engineer training which consisted of construction, munitions and explosives as the primary subjects. There was a survival course following the two phases and then finally the language course. Even though he felt he was proficient in the Czech language, he would be required to attend the language training until such time that he graduated or was recommended to challenge the final exam. Even the army understood there was little need to teach students something in which they were already proficient. His native German language was never a factor because it was a language skill possessed by many soldiers who were native-born Germans. Peter saw a use for his German-language skill in his personal goals, however, and was satisfied that his German-language skills would serve him well. The preparation phase was moving along as planned, but he was aware of the long road ahead.

Qualification for guaranteed Special Forces training had involved physical and mental testing above and beyond that routinely administered for mainstream enlistees. He had scored eighty-five on the Armed Forces Qualification Test which was sufficiently over the requirement of seventy-five. SFC Dawson had escorted him to Ft Lewis for the physical testing on one of the base athletic fields. Even though he had prepared for weeks, the test was difficult. Much to his surprise the most difficult part was the requirement to run five miles with an average time of eight minutes per mile. It was only after this testing and his formal background checks that he was able to sign his enlistment contract for a minimum of four years. Even then, the contract had its caveats. He must successfully complete each phase of training. It was a gamble because he was obligated for the four years should he not complete the Special Forces training for whatever reason. Because of this clause in the contract he was determined to not let failure be an option. The draftees were obligated for two years and the typical enlistee for at least three years. Peter had no problem with a four-year enlistment. He knew his training would take two years, after which his anticipated assignment to West Germany would leave him another two years to formulate a plan and complete his personal mission. He was concerned about balancing his personal plan with the oath of enlistment in which he pledged to be loyal to America and the United States Army. Neglecting his army duties in order to accomplish personal goals would not be loyalty as he saw it. Tentatively his ideas of how to handle that centered on his leave, or off-duty time. There was also the possibility of being discharged in West Germany after completing his army enlistment. Because numerous options existed, he was confident he would find a solution. Overcoming problems was what gave him a great deal of personal satisfaction; it was his strongest attribute and would be tested to its limit in future years.

FOURTEEN

FT BRAGG, NORTH CAROLINA: SEPTEMBER 1957

SPECIAL FORCES

Peter felt like an animal and was beginning to act like one. During a temporary hallucination he was asking himself what animal he would like to be. Before he could answer, he shook his head and took another deep breath. In the second week of survival training, he was trying to avoid a simulated enemy in the far reaches of the two-hundred fifty-one square miles of the Fort Bragg, North Carolina, training area. He and twenty other students had been forced to abandon their simulated mission and return to friendly territory. This was the nature of SERE (Survive, Evade, Resist, Escape) training. He had completed airborne training at Ft Benning, Georgia, and had been training at Ft Bragg since February.

Living off the land and sleeping in concealed, makeshift beds of pine branches wasn't easy. Special Forces training was the most difficult set of challenges he had ever faced in his lifetime. The realism of this exercise was surprising. He felt nearly as much stress the past two weeks as he had felt during his escape from the Sudetenland. Physically, this was tougher because it lasted longer and included the prisoner of war (POW) training, which he had yet to experience. Conversations with previous students and hints from the cadre of instructors had made clear what he would face during this exercise. With his compass and map he was making progress, but the exercise instructions had dictated that the trainees should be in a pre-designated location at a given time. This is where he expected to be captured. The POW experience and the escape opportunities would end the primary field exercises of his training. All that would remain would be the Czech language phase, which he felt capable of completing easily. He might choose to challenge that training, but that decision was still in the future.

When the New Year arrived, Peter received his orders for Germany. It was common for soldiers to refer to West Germany as just "Germany." The assumption was that US soldiers were not being assigned to East Germany. Having been promoted from Private, then Private First Class, he was now a Specialist Third Class (SP/3). It would be just a matter of time until he reached the rank of sergeant, the same rank as Sgt Grimes from his Altglashütte experience. The orders directed SP/3 Peter Ackerman to report to McGuire Air Force Base (AFB), New Jersey, on April 10, 1958, for transport to Rhein-Main Air Force Base, Germany, and subsequent assignment to the 1st Battalion, Tenth Special Forces Group, at Bad Tölz, Germany.

A visit to Washington to see the Swansons was an obligation in Peter's mind, but one that he had no problem fulfilling even though it took some time away from his plan in the form of used "leave." Every soldier was allotted thirty days of "leave" every year. He didn't want to use any of that time unnecessarily, but felt that he wanted to see the Swansons before he departed for an undetermined destiny. He fully understood that he wouldn't be without the assistance of the Swansons, if needed, and wanted to maintain contact with all who had helped him. Maintaining contact and advising them of his whereabouts and well-being was a part of his promise to himself to repay their years of support and kindness.

He had decided to complete the entire language course, even though he could have challenged. Because he was thinking of the future, he recognized that building long-term friendship with his classmates was a good thing that might prove to be of value. As he suspected, two of his fellow students were assigned to Bad Tölz also. The Czech language course was excellent and he now felt fluent with only the slang, idioms and accent to perfect. Peter had finished first in his class and received honor graduate recognition at the course completion ceremony. A commendation letter was included in his 201 personnel file. That letter would be helpful should he be considered for promotion or special assignment in the future.

The flight from McGuire AFB, New Jersey, to Rhein-Main AFB, Germany via Gander AFB, Newfoundland, took almost twenty actual elapsed hours. Because of the six hour time zone change it would be well into the next calendar day upon arrival in Germany. It was a chartered *Trans World Airlines* piston-engine aircraft with a passenger load of near three hundred in Peter's estimation. He wondered if this aircraft had been built in Snoqualmish where one of the Boeing Aircraft plants was located. Most passengers were fellow unaccompanied military personnel, but there were several career men with dependents. The children and most of the adults nodded off or slept soundly as soon as darkness set in and the dinner meal was completed. Some slept through the brief refueling stop in Gander much to Peter's surprise. He didn't sleep much at all as he anticipated his return to Germany.

Processing at Rhein-Main Air Force Base (AFB) went quickly for Peter. The Green Beret that he wore had a respect effect on the in-processing personnel so he was hurried through the necessary paperwork with little fanfare. He had the option to stay overnight in the transient barracks, but opted to move right along. The Rhein-Main air base had a joint runway-usage agreement with the newly-formed West German government, but no military aircraft were readily apparent to Peter. Another surprise was that after processing and being issued a train ticket, a military bus took him to the *Hauptbahnhof* where he was on his own with advice from the bus driver that his train was "over there."

Peter was confident with his own German language ability, but wondered how difficult this procedure would be for a first-timer that spoke only English. At the Rhein-Main processing center he had exchanged all his greenback dollars for *Deutsche Mark* (DM) and Military Payment Certificates (MPC's, also known as script). He was a little surprised at the dollar/DM exchange rate of approximately four DM to one dollar. He had been informed where he could find the train scheduled to depart for Munich at 1700 hours. *Gleis 17*, from which his train

would depart was well marked and finding it was not a problem. He fought to overcome jet-lag with the help of his adren-
aline-secreting internal system. His trip would take ten hours,
including the waiting period to change trains in Munich.

The first few days at Flint *Kaserne* were spent in-processing, orienting himself to his surroundings, and recovering
from jet-lag. Sgt Willie Kyles had been assigned as his sponsor whose job was to assist with the transition into the unit
and with Peter's personal needs. This was a change, thought
Peter, from the long, hard training routine he had experienced
in his first two years in the army. Draftees that entered the
army at the same time as he were now completing their active duty, while Peter was just getting started with his first
permanent assignment after basic army and then an extended
specialized SF training period. At the personnel in-processing
office, he had been told he would be assigned to a team after
they reviewed his records and verified his security clearance.
He would be scheduled for an interview with the battalion
commander who also served as the post commander since he
was the ranking officer on the *Kaserne*. Colonel William Watts
had a reputation for being as tough as nails and demanding of
strict military discipline.

Also housed on the post, but not yet operational, was the
Seventh Army Non-Commissioned Officer (NCO) Academy
and various support personnel organized under the 210th
United States Army, Europe (USAREUR), Support Company.
This unit consisted of the *Kaserne* medical and dental person-
nel, a few military policemen, the mess personnel and had
responsibility for supervising the civilian building engineers.
Anything not directly related to the missions of the Special

Forces or the NCO Academy fell under the responsibility of the support company. The NCO Academy, being moved from Jensen Barracks in Munich, was due to open in October.

Flint *Kaserne* had been built for the German Army for the purpose of training junior officer conscripts beginning in 1936. It had served various functions during the war in addition to training, until it was captured and occupied by US Forces. General George S Patton made his Third Army Headquarters at Flint in May of 1945. Flint was laid out somewhat as Peter remembered McGraw *Kaserne* in Munich. A chapel was immediately on the right before passing through the brick and mortar archway which was flanked by short conical-shaped buttresses. The main area of Flint was a huge parade ground surrounded by one continuous quadrangular-shaped, three-floor building with numerous entrances. In one corner of the building Peter found the mess hall and a snack bar. The northeast corner provided entry to the NCO club and the medical/dental offices. Spaced all around the building were barracks for troops, mostly on the second and third floors. Other facilities found in the main area were a movie theatre, an Armed Forces European Exchange System (AFEES) laundry shop, a Post Office, a PX and an American Express Bank

On the east side of Flint was a row of junior and transient officer quarters, which separated the built-up area from the golf course, a softball field and the rod and gun club. Peter was happy to see that there was a golf course at Flint, although it turned out to be a very short practice-like course. To the southeast, but still bordering the golf course was the staff-officer quarters. Directly across from the main entrance to Flint were two housing areas separated by a secondary road. These

housing areas consisted of typical German three-story apart-
ment buildings and were for enlisted soldiers with families.
Peter was told that there was another small US Army *Kaserne*
thirteen miles to the south in Lenggries, which was a combined USAREUR communication and quartermaster school.
The closest "big" PX was located in Munich about twenty-five
miles to the north. Peter remembered that Lenggries was
where his refugee friend, Hannelore, was detained temporarily after her escape from Poland.

Orientation completed quickly so Peter could begin his
life as a US Army Special Forces engineer specialist. Progress
toward his personal mission was on schedule. The next step
was undetermined, but the plan foundation was solid at this
point. He was gainfully employed and he was living closer to
Tachau than he could have previously expected.

"Double time . . . March!" SFC Thompson was leading
the physical training (PT). SP/3 Peter Ackerman wasn't surprised. He knew the unit would do PT every day, sometimes
for up to three hours. PT was an important part of Special
Forces readiness. If you weren't physically fit, your specialized
expertise was useless for the varied missions you might be assigned. He expected to be doing this PT routine often. Today
SFC Thompson took them out a back gate to a wide alpine forest trail. Bad Tölz was located near the forested foothills of the
German Alps. Peter expected to be doing some team training
in these same hills, but the exact routine was still quite unknown to him. During short breaks there was a lot of kidding
and innuendo ranging from fantasy missions, to sabotaging

the Soviet Union, to competitive runs to the top of Blomberg Mountain which was sixteen kilometers to the southwest.

"Quick time . . . Huh," bellowed SFC Thompson.

Peter estimated they had run in double time for about thirty minutes. After a short rest pause there was a command to "Fall in!"

Long-time members of the group seemed to anticipate what was coming next as SFC Thompson continued with a command of "At ease!" He continued with instructions. "First one back to the parade ground doesn't have to run tomorrow, last one back owes me fifty pushups."

There was some milling around while Peter processed the words in his mind.

"OK, line up by rank on the footbridge five abreast. That means you are last, Ackerman."

"Yes, sergeant!"

They are testing me, thought Peter, as the competitive juices began to flow through his body.

"Line up . . . go!"

Peter was estimating how he should run this race. He figured it was about three miles, mostly downhill, to the parade ground. Did he want to try to take the lead right away or just wait until the group developed some spacing? He felt he could take this group because he was always among the leaders during runs at Ft Bragg. The trail had somewhat uneven footing, some loose gravel and was a little slippery. He had to be careful not to fall if he didn't want to finish last and be the object of ridicule back at the parade ground.

Two "rabbits" took off as if they could sprint the entire distance. This may have been to tempt runners to burn themselves out too soon. Peter didn't take the bait. He passed several runners who looked like they were struggling already. He could see he wasn't going to be last unless he fell, but just finishing in the middle of the pack wasn't good enough for him. He wanted to win. Footing down the hill was still treacherous, so even though he felt fresh he stayed under control within sprinting distance of the "rabbits," who were now slowing. As soon as he reached flat ground, he sped up in order to catch the leaders. One of the sergeants he passed encouraged him with a "go, rookie!"

Adrenaline was flowing enough that he didn't feel fatigued. He passed the "rabbits" as he saw the back gate of the *Kaserne* for the first time. Three strong-looking runners passed through the gate ahead of him, but two of them lost time trying to get through the gate at the same time.

Peter stretched it out a little knowing he still had something left for a final sprint. This wasn't about avoiding fifty pushups; for Peter this was about winning and gaining some respect as "the new guy." As they passed the golf course and the rod and gun club, Peter realized there was only a few hundred meters left. He passed the gate strugglers and took aim at the lone runner ahead of him. He could see now that it was his sponsor, Sgt Kyles. He closed the distance with a slight burst of speed until he was three steps behind with about a hundred meters between them and the parade ground flag pole. At fifty yards he gave it all he had. With each stride he closed the separation between himself and Sgt Kyles. For the first time he felt his muscles strain and he controlled the urge to gasp for more air. His training had taught him how to run with strength and wisdom. Sgt Kyles never wavered, but Peter was too much for him as he reached for the flag pole. He touched a mere second before his sponsor. He had won on his first running test as the newest member of the Tenth Special Forces Group at Bad Tölz! His reward was the self-satisfaction that only driven competitors feel.

"You are something, Ackerman! That's the first race I've lost in six months. My congratulations, rookie"

"Thank you, thank you," muttered Peter between gasps for air, "that was all I had." It was a common occurrence for Peter to have strange thoughts at unexpected times. This time he smiled to himself as he resisted the urge to say, "You ought to meet Trudi!"

The parade ground was filling with the other runners, most of whom were equally exhausted. Some asked who was first, but most were just happy the run was over. Staff Sergeant Jones was last and owed fifty pushups. That was to come later, apparently, as SFC Thompson called for a daily dozen PT formation.

Peter's afternoon was to be spent at a post orientation meeting. This meeting was conducted by the administrative section of the post (post and *Kaserne* are interchangeable with the troops even though post is more strictly US military terminology). Some of it was pretty dry so he had enough time to let his mind wander. To this point his plan was working to perfection. What was needed now was his in-country plan. It was early, however, because he had no idea what the Special Forces had in store for him. He would first have to establish a routine in which he could begin planning for the future. Although

he was getting general information from the orientation—
and that information applied to all soldiers on the post—he
found some of the information new and interesting. There was
an explanation of exactly what was meant by the term "Cold
War," and how it affected military personnel in Europe. The
Soviet Military Liaison Mission (SMLM) was emphasized and
instructions outlined as to what actions should be taken if one
of the authorized Soviet vehicles was observed

The 5K zone was the most interesting to Peter. The 5K,
short for five kilometer, was the zone which was five kilometers from within West Germany to the East German or
Czechoslovakian border. US personnel were not allowed in this
zone unless they were on a duty mission, or they had special
authorization from USAREUR. This special authorization was
to allow visits to relatives or for other approved personal business. The speaker had never been aware of one of these special
authorizations actually being allowed, so his advice was to just
stay out of the 5K zone. In the past, there had been a few deliberate defections by US personnel and some accidental crossings into the Soviet Zone. To enforce this restriction the US
Second and Fourteenth Armored Cavalry (AC) Regiments and
the *Bundes Grenzschutz* (BGS), which was the German federal
border agency were required to detain any US Military personnel not authorized in the area. The *Bayerische Grenz Polizei*
(BGP) also had some overlapping border duties with the BGS.
Detained personnel were usually taken to Coburg or other US
facilities and held until their units could retrieve them. There
was also information about dependents evacuation called
NEO (Noncombatant Evacuation Operation), which didn't
affect Peter since he had no dependents. The SOFA (Status of

Forces Agreement) was interesting because it dealt primarily with financial and legal considerations while dealing with West Germans and other Western Europeans. Because the US military was no longer an occupation force, the German government could specify the terms under which US personnel lived and worked outside the military environment.

At the conclusion of the briefing Peter returned to his barracks room and found Sgt Kyles waiting for him.

"What's up, Speedy?"

"Speedy who?" Peter answered, but not quite sure what was on the mind of the sergeant.

"Speedy Ackerman, of course. You know . . . the speedy guy that is so fast he can turn his bedroom wall light switch off and be in bed and covered up before the room gets dark!"

Obviously this was a reference to the morning's run. Peter was relieved that this was a light-hearted conversation, but was still not sure where it was going.

"Did you bring any civvies with you?

He was referring to civilian clothes, Peter assumed, and answered in the negative.

"That's OK, kid, get your class A's on after chow and we'll go to town. I have something to talk to you about and I can show you around Tölz at the same time."

Peter was anxious to get off the post and curious about what was on Sgt Kyle's mind, so he answered right away. "OK, see you here right after chow!"

FIFTEEN

EVENING: APRIL 16, 1958

WILLIE KYLES

As a non-commissioned officer, Sgt Kyles was authorized to possess his own privately-owned vehicle. The short
ride from Flint *Kaserne* to the business district of Bad Tölz reminded Peter of Tachau. The cobblestone streets were slightly
rough, but appeared to be well constructed and long lasting.
Each stone appeared to be hand laid with great care in order to endure and not need constant maintenance. The driving lanes were not as wide as in the US. Peter knew from his
memories of Tachau that this meant trucks and oversized vehicles would pass each other with difficulty and with great
care. Strategically mounted mirrors sometimes helped determine safe right-of-way at particularly difficult road merging
or narrow passageways. Buildings and architecture were much
different than in America, most dating hundreds of years longer than those he was recently familiar with in any part of
America. Many half-timbered houses, built with fitted heavy
wooden beams that were filled in with replaceable composite
material, were apparent in the residential areas. Only a few

four-wheeled vehicles were on the streets, but bicycles and mopeds gave reason for Willie to drive carefully.

Willie was dressed in a suit coat and tie, which Peter had already learned was mandatory for US military personnel who were off the military *Kaserne* and not in military dress uniform. Soon, they parked in front of a building with a single sign above the door identifying the establishment as the *Lido Bar*. Several other vehicles nearby bore the green and white license plates which identified them as being registered to US Forces personnel.

"This is where the Green Berets hang out, Peter, when they go to town. The NCO club is also popular since you don't need to change clothes to go there after work."

Peter noticed that they were now on a first-name familiarity, and that fact sparked his curiosity even more about what it was that Willie had to discuss with him.

Willie continued, "One beer is my limit when I'm driving. You need to be aware of the drinking and driving policy. Colonel Watts will have you on a fast train to Baumholder with a slick sleeve if you get involved with the German police. You don't want to go to Baumholder, believe me."

They took a quick look inside where Peter saw several rustic tables with troopers in civvies drinking beer and flirting with several waitresses. The short haircuts and the loud talk were a sure clue that they were American soldiers. They quickly exited and started walking along the nearby Isar River. The Isar separated the old and new sections of Bad Tölz. As Willie explained, Bad Tölz was a vacation spa town with curative baths. As West Germany recovered from the war, more and more Europeans were coming to the town to take the "cure," as they called bathing in the spa. The spas were located on the west side of the river which was more modern. The *Altstadt,* was on the east side and consisted of mostly older half-timbered buildings.

After the introduction to the village, Willie changed his mood and the talk became more serious.

"You didn't get to the Tenth Special Forces Group by accident, Peter. Colonel Watts and our operations officer have been tracking you ever since they discovered your existence with the help of Department of the Army (DA) personnel files."

"What? I don't understand." Peter was confused by this statement.

"You are perfect for a mission the group commander has been assigned. The Commanding Officer (CO), Colonel Watts and Captain Wilcox, the S3 Operations Officer asked to have you assigned here because of your Czech language ability and your familiarity with the area around Tachau."

Peter was shocked. All the effort he had put into getting assigned to Germany and Bad Tölz had been unnecessary. Other factors had influenced his destiny without his knowledge. He wondered if they suspected his personal agenda. He would need to be careful as this discussion continued.

"What kind of mission is it?" Peter asked.

"I can't tell you much right now, Peter, but it does involve Czechoslovakia. If this mission is a go, we will be working together. You and I are the only two Czech speakers in the group at the moment, although there are two of your classmates from Ft Bragg on the way. They may be useful at some point as our planning progresses, but neither has the Tachau connection that you have. I was assigned as your sponsor in order to get to understand your personality. I have to report to the S3 about my impression of your suitability for the mission and our mutual compatibility. The mission is highly classified and considered dangerous."

Excitement was coursing through Peter's body. The need for more information was overwhelming. "Tell me everything you can! How did they know I lived in Tachau?"

"Captain Wilcox will be talking to you after I report to him on my impressions. Your security clearance should be verified soon. I assume the information about Tachau was in your personnel file. For sure it would have turned up during your security clearance investigation. The mission will have a Top Secret classification, if not higher. I can't say any more until you are approved and the mission is authorized to proceed to the next phase. We will be briefed by Captain Wilcox. The CO has the final approval. All I can say right now is . . . let your hair grow!"

Peter was aware of the coolness of the evening as the sun set in the West. His mind was racing with curiosity, but he knew he would have to wait for more information. He was aware of, and surprised by, the lack of outside lighting on the street as darkness arrived, but then he remembered that West Germany was still recovering from the war and the infrastructure was far from complete. His home village of Tachau had never been lighted as well as in the US even under peaceful conditions. He assumed that Germany was no different. Germany . . . he hadn't yet come to grips with the fact that now there was a *West* Germany and an *East* Germany. In his mind it was often still just Germany.

Willie interrupted his thoughts with a buddy-like invitation to, "Have a beer at the *Lido*."

Willie seemed to relax as they grew a little closer. It would soon become apparent that they would need a closeness and a good partnership for the proposed mission. The night ended after one beer, small talk and a little flirting with the pretty *Fräuleins*.

SIXTEEN

THE MISSION

Daily training with his motivated and capable team members was interesting and demanding. All were in excellent physical condition and had specialization in weapons, engineering and communications, in addition to their individual language expertise. Willie was the only other Czech speaker with SF experience, but others were fluent in European languages such as Greek and Italian. Peter learned that two of the team members were away on assignment. Their missions were classified which meant that no reference was ever made to their whereabouts. It was an unspoken reality of the Cold War Green Beret that security was an unquestioned consideration. The team was indeed a team and could work together effectively when required, but individual members could be, and were, assigned specialized missions depending on need and their particular area of expertise.

This morning, as anticipated, Peter and Willie were summoned to the S3 office to see Captain Wilcox. Thomas Wilcox was a classic Special Forces Officer who was alert and friendly with impeccable military bearing. His office was neat and appeared to be highly functional. Maps adorned the walls and Peter could see that many were of Eastern Europe. They reported and saluted as military protocol required.

Captain Wilcox gave the "at ease" command and asked them to sit down in chairs near a map board. He began, "Welcome to the Group, Specialist Ackerman. Are you settled in and ready to go to work?"

"Yes, sir." Peter answered enthusiastically, but he hoped not with a contrived image. His curiosity was almost unnerving. He had no idea what was to come and was a little worried that he might be questioned about his adolescence in Tachau. Willie had only told him that the mission involved Czechoslovakia and that he had been targeted for this job. He assumed that his familiarity with the Tachau area and his Czech language expertise were factors.

Captain Wilcox began, "First and foremost, I want to declare security considerations for what we are about to discuss. This is a Top Secret mission, and as such you will not talk about anything that could be mission sensitive with anyone other than myself, Colonel Watts and some of my staff. You will not compromise any of this information with your team members, or any other military members and certainly not with civilians. Sgt Kyles has been involved in mission planning for quite some time and can bring you up to date on certain particulars, but you are not to have discussions in unsecured areas. Is that clear?" The captain's eye contact indicated that the instructions were directed at both of them.

"Yes, sir," they answered in unison.

"Good, then we can get down to the nitty-gritty. This

mission has been assigned the code words "es corial" after a particularly potent alcoholic drink found locally. Progress reports, support requests and mission-related personnel and administrative correspondence will always refer to the code words in all lower case letters for reasons of attention to detail and security."

Peter could barely contain his curiosity. The plot was about to unfold.

The captain continued, "Ivan (referencing the Russians), is to our east and cannot be trusted. We're not sure what they have on their minds, but it probably isn't good. At a minimum, we have to be aware of what they are doing and what the possibilities are. This is what the Cold War is all about. A different form of government—Communism—is their dogma. An objective of controlling all of Europe is a probability. We can't let that happen! Soviet military action against the West is a concern. Our intelligence sources must track the activities of the Soviets. That is where you are needed." It was again evident that the captain was addressing both of them.

"We have been, and still are, researching methods of gathering intelligence in the western sector of Czechoslovakia. Generally in what used to be the Sudetenland, and specifically the Tachau area, where you once lived, Specialist Ackerman. Is that correct, Specialist?"

"Yes, sir." Peter was totally shocked that the captain knew so much about him and shocked about what was unfolding. Was it possible that this mission, and he himself, had similar goals? Could he kill two birds with one stone?

The captain continued, "For intelligence purposes, we need to know about any military activity, weapons, vehicles and any other information we can gather about daily life in Tachau. How strong is the Czech militia, how many Russians are there in the area. What is their military potential? Are there any construction projects underway? Is there military activity on the Mže River? To gain this information we are researching a clandestine intrusion. Precise details will be forthcoming as you prepare for this mission, but I'm sure you get the big picture. Preparation for the mission will take some time. You will begin your planning immediately. Sgt Kyles is the team leader of your two-man team. We do not plan on adding team members; however, we are dealing with a fluid situation. I want at least a weekly planning report, sergeant, but my door is open anytime you need help. Are there any questions?"

Peter had many questions, but hardly knew where to start. His primary question at the moment was one of entry into Czechoslovakia. Peter asked, "Sir, I've heard about the guarded border, and in the arrival briefing I was told about the 5K zone. How will we get across undetected?" Peter recalled the explanation and warning about the 5K zone that he had received at the post briefing.

The 5K zone was the area within the western five kilometers of the official border. No unauthorized US or Western allied personnel were allowed in this area. This restriction was a safeguard against accidental border incidents or deliberate defection attempts. During the arrival briefing he learned that both situations had occurred in the past. There was also the possibility that an accidental crossing could be considered provocative by the Warsaw Pact authorities.

"Sgt Kyles has some ideas about that which he will be discussing with you. One of the reasons you were singled out for this job is because you may have some local knowledge ideas. I fully expect that you will make some reconnaissance trips to the area near the Tachau border area. You will be authorized a civilian clothing allowance for this purpose, and you will be billeted in private rooms at the bachelor officer quarters temporarily with a cover identity of DA civilians. Group personnel that may recognize you know better than to ask questions. There is a promising border-crossing option being developed in the Tachau area, but that will remain unknown to you at the present. It is considered a viable option but we want to explore all possibilities through your team efforts. Your reconnaissance missions might turn up something to consider."

Peter considered relating his personal goal of information about his parents, the film and the family valuables hidden in the malformed fir tree near his old home, but decided to keep quiet at least until he knew more about the planned border breach.

"You have some obstacles to overcome in order to achieve success in this dangerous and complex mission. You both speak the Czech language, which will be helpful, but you both know, it is practically impossible to conceal accents. Ackerman's German-language knowledge will be necessary on recon; however, Sgt Kyles, being black and not speaking fluent German could be a problem. You will need to devise cover stories and plan carefully to avoid exposure of the mission objective. Just don't forget that the Special Forces Group has resources. Ask, and you shall receive!"

SEVENTEEN

IDENTIFYING OPTIONS

When Peter's hold baggage arrived from Ft Bragg he finally had his civilian clothes. In order to assume the DA civilian identity charade, it was necessary to move into the BOQ in civilian clothes. In his mind, Peter questioned the need for such security, but reasoned that his superiors were much more qualified than him to make that decision and there was the possibility that this was an attempt to impress upon him the total need for security in every aspect of the mission. He reminded himself of the chaotic days and cruelty he had observed in Tachau under Russian/Czech control. It was possible that he had become soft in his thinking because of the relatively safe and casual lifestyle in America. He was adjusting his mental approach to his last memory of Tachau and was accepting security considerations, whatever the reason.

Peter and Willie had adjoining rooms in the southernmost BOQ building. Most of their planning would occur here. They seldom encountered the other officer residents who seemed rather disinterested in what they assumed were a couple of nerdy DA civilians. This circumstance was exactly what they were striving for. Their rooms were secure for planning sessions, but not for storage of classified material.

Willie had long ago procured pertinent maps, documents and the secure office space with the equipment they would need to formulate a plan. A safe had been provided for their dedicated use. Willie and Peter spent their days planning. Willie had completed several reconnaissance missions in the border area in the vicinity of Bärnau, which was a scant two kilometers from the border, well within the 5K zone. As cover, Willie had a German driver's license and a rental Volkswagen with German license plates. Because of the increased suspicion he might create as a black man near the border his story would be that he was a former soldier looking for a woman he believed was the mother of his child. The German border patrols and the US Army border patrol units were instructed not to ask further questions if they encountered Americans with this story. The woman's name they would recognize would be "Brigitte Berg." Willie was careful to not attract attention, but they had to account for all possibilities. Documentation for the "rental" was in order, although the car was actually owned by USAREUR with headquarters in Heidelberg.

They discussed the general situation in Bärnau and surrounding villages. Willie related that people were poor, but happy they were separated and relatively safe from the Czechs and Russians across the border. Most were farming families who subsisted with the fruits of their labor and by bartering for other necessities. Morale had not completely recovered from the psychological and physical damage of the war. Some of the households were still shared with German expellees from the Sudetenland and other parts of Eastern Europe. This sharing was hardly ever voluntary and often a cause of friction and outright hate because of the cramped quarters and mandatory sharing of scarce resources. Working days were long and time for relaxation was short. There was a dearth of males in the area because many had never returned from the war. Hard labor tasks were the responsibility of women who often had the additional burden of care for children and aging parents. The Marshall Plan was a distant memory having ended in 1952. Much of West Germany and Europe had surpassed pre-war economic conditions, but remote and border areas still struggled. Willie had observed few automobiles, but had encountered a few mopeds and many bicycles. All means of transportation were rigged to carry the maximum amount of cargo. It was not unusual to see old women in long ragged dresses peddling a bicycle with a box of apples, potatoes, asparagus, or even a ten-bottle case of beer strapped to the frame. Peter was aware of Willie's descriptions from his youth in Tachau, but listened intently.

Willie continued with details about farm animals on the roads: many pulling carts loaded with harvested goods, feed for the animals, or even manure for use as fertilizer. Often these were driven by women with their forlorn-looking children, who were sharing the work, riding in the cargo bed or wherever they could hold on. He had seldom seen people engaged in pleasant conversation or smiling about anything. He did see a fueling station, which offered gasoline and diesel fuel, a small grocery store and a building with a sign identifying it as a *Gasthaus*, or a guest house. Peter was aware that a *Gasthaus,* was a country-style combination restaurant-tavern usually with very tidy rooms to rent. Near the center of Bärnau, Willie had noticed that the *Gasthof Zur Post* was the hub of leisure activity and offered overnight accommodations. Willie thought it was ironic that the *Gasthof Zur Post* was located on *Bahnhofstrasse*, but the *Bahnhof* (train station) was no longer operational for passengers.

Willie said he hadn't approached the border, but had seen the signs warning that he was fifty meters from the border and that closer than fifty meters was a restricted area for all residents. Because he didn't want to attract attention and because of his limited language capability he hadn't attempted to talk to anyone.

They spent many hours studying their maps. Willie related information he had been provided by the S3 (operations) and S2 (intelligence), such as location and construction of barriers, suspected heavily guarded areas and observation/listening posts. Known location of buildings, roads and trails and suspected mined areas were discussed and studied. Other pertinent intelligence, such as weather, types of wild and domestic animals in the area and likely festivities on local holidays were all important items for consideration. Adjusting planning for weather conditions would not be a problem for Peter because of his local knowledge and the similarities between forty-seven degree latitude Seattle and the forty-nine degree latitude locally. The amount of detail already collected by Willie was both informative and reassuring. Peter was tempted to approach the subject of his personal motivation for entry into his former home territory, but decided to wait until he understood the plan in more detail. The biggest question in his mind, at the moment, was whether or not two entries into what was now Czechoslovakia would be required. He fully understood his responsibility to Willie, the SF Group and to America, for that matter; however, he also felt responsibility for his parents and all the Sudeten Germans for whom he felt a need for redemption.

When Willie felt that Peter had sufficient background they started their map reconnaissance and the exchange of ideas. Willie had made it clear that he wanted to discuss and explore all possibilities no matter how extreme. Pros and cons would be weighed and options systematically eliminated. Willie had done some study previously and developed some ideas which he wanted to discuss, but he also wanted to entertain new ideas that Peter might develop with his experience in the former Sudetenland. The end result of their collaborative efforts would be offered to the S3. They knew they must work quickly, but intelligently, but felt no pressure for haste at the present. They were aware that there was an option being held by the S3 for a more propitious time—probably for reason of security. Apparently they were tasked to identify a better plan, if one could be found. The next step would be some ground reconnaissance which Peter was anticipating with excitement. Controlling emotions was a common theme in Special Forces training so Peter was able to resist the open display of churning he felt throughout his body. He had no doubt that Willie was experiencing similar emotions, albeit for not exactly the same reasons.

They discussed possibilities as simple as a direct breach of the barbed-wire barricades to something as improbable as a night parachute jump when wind conditions would enable drift from West German airspace to a touchdown on Czech soil. Some of their ideas were laughable and they did laugh, but it served to emphasize that they were truly considering all options. Complicating their planning was the fact that whoever gained entry would also have to have an undetectable return route. It hadn't been discussed at this point, but there was an implication and unspoken assumption that Peter would be the one to make the entry, if only one of them was to go. Because he was white and had a more advanced language capability and accent nuances to go with some local knowledge, the issue was obviously a no-brainer.

Peter had offered the possibility of merely applying for entry with the Czech government as a former resident. He found that that option had been explored long ago. When Willie had been informed of Peter's pending involvement with the mission, the S3 had made it clear that former residents were not being granted access and that information about current residents and disposition of expellees was sketchy at best. The Czechs certainly did not want former residents, who had had their property confiscated and were unceremoniously expelled from Czechoslovakia, returning to make claims of property and to make accusations of expellee mistreatment and murder. Peter knew this, but it was just another no-stone unturned consideration to get sent to their planning cut-list.

EIGHTEEN

MAY 1958

RETURN TO NANDLSTADT

Although most of the team's operational planning consumed their lives in entirety, they also had to maintain a normal life with its personal problems and personal business. They also had a need for rest and recuperation. The S3 was well aware that the mind, like the body, needed to be rested and replenished. One day Willie had a dental appointment with the base dentist. "Base," like "Post," and "*Kaserne*"were often interchanged in the minds of the soldiers in West Germany who never completely abandoned their stateside military jargon.

They decided to take this day away from their planning; a break would provide an opportunity for Peter to visit the village in search of clothing and boots that might help identify him as a Czech peasant. He remembered the common dress of the poor citizens and had learned through the team's research that Czech dress standards hadn't changed. Clothing wasn't difficult to find in the *alt Kleider* second-hand store. This was one of his first opportunities to speak German with a native since his return to West Germany. He found the transition smooth,

180 ✳

although the Tölzer Bavarian dialect differed somewhat from
the Bavarian German used in Tachau. Most Germans were able
to converse in High German *(Hoch Deutsch)*, when conflicts of
dialects arose. Peter made a mental note to discuss the dialect
subject with Willie during a training and planning session.

The *Frau* tending the store was pleasant enough but not
overly enthusiastic about doing business. Peter reasoned that
attitudes among West Germans would have taken a serious hit
because of the war experience. There was no way to quickly
ascertain and understand the history of an individual's war al-
legiances. Women were usually—in some way—connected to
former Nazi soldiers, whether it was to unwilling conscripts,
or to those who were dedicated Nazis. Non-support—in any
form usually had to be done secretly or by telling lies. Many
who supported their Nazi friends and relatives did so with
reservations that they did not express. Others claimed they
knew nothing and claimed they were shocked when the truth
of Nazi atrocities became known. Peter had his story, the *Frau*
had hers and millions of other Europeans had their stories.
It would be some time before Peter began to understand the
reality of this fact, even though he himself was one of them.
He left the store without having found boots that would fit,
but with some clothes in hand. He was confused about the
woman, but not passing judgment on her. He was sure he still
had a lot to learn as he attempted to determine the fate of his
parents and to expose the atrocities committed **against** the
Sudeten Germans.

Peter was learning and beginning to understand the mac-
ro European situation. At this time in 1958 post-war borders
had been established and a West German government was

functioning. American and other NATO (North Atlantic Treaty Organization) forces were omnipresent in many sections of the new West Germany even though the occupation of the three western zones by the French, English and Americans had officially ended on May 5, 1955. West Germany was allowed limited rearmament and joined NATO on May 9 that same year. Many of the people living in West Germany in 1958 were not residents before the war. Many were refugees from Eastern Europe or displaced persons from other parts of Western Europe. Some were ethnic Germans, like Peter, some were not. It was a hodgepodge of accidental residents intermixed with pre-war ethnic Germans. Determining who belonged in West Germany and who did not was not extremely important. West Germany needed manpower to rebuild. They allowed thousands upon thousands of *Gastarbeiter* from countries like Italy, Greece and Turkey, to help rebuild the country. Many became citizens and never again left the country permanently. Recovery was under way with the *Deutschmark* serving as the new currency and valued at four DM for one dollar. Almost everybody who wanted a bicycle had one. Mopeds were commonplace, and a few Volkswagen bugs were in evidence. Surprisingly, the taxi stands contained many diesel-powered Mercedes automobiles. If a person had more than one set of clothes for everyday wear they were fortunate. Clean drinking water was not always found and running hot water was a luxury. Hot water for kitchen, laundry and bathing was heated only for immediate usage. Electricity for lighting was used sparingly. Only one room was heated and lighted when needed. Destitute as it was, living conditions in the late fifties were a luxury compared to the years toward the end and immediately after the war.

He was now familiar with terms like "Cold War" and "Iron Curtain" which originated right after the war ended to describe the tension between the US/NATO alliance and the Soviets with their Warsaw Pact. The United States had a huge force of ground, air and sea power at the ready, while on the other side of the Iron Curtain the Soviets were also ready for war. The constant threat perceived by each was the essence of the Cold War. NATO forces trained intensely in places like Grafenwoehr, Vilscck, Hohenfels, Wildflecken, and Baumholder. Practice alerts were conducted monthly and communication systems were tested routinely through "Handicap Black" drills. Security was emphasized continuously all the way down to the lowest-ranking soldiers. Duty-related talk about troop strength, equipment, deployments or maneuvers was not allowed in earshot of civilians. Civilian dependents were required to conduct practice evacuation trips to deployment ports in France and other emergency evacuation sites. The major army command was designated USAREUR, while the air force was organized under USAFE (United States Air Force, Europe).

Ground troops were concerned with border security and the possibility of a surprise invasion in places like the Fulda Gap. The armored cavalry had the primary responsibility for border patrol and for first contact to slow an invasion attempt. The Second Armored Cavalry (AC) had a responsibility along part of the East German border and all of the Czechoslovakian borders that stretched over 730 kilometers. The Fourteenth AC was responsible to the north. The Second AC would be informed of team es corial's presence and conduct of operations in the area of Bärnau. The code word "Brigitte Berg," Peter remembered, was the key to dealing with the Second AC patrols if that became necessary.

On a Thursday in May, Peter and Willie were summoned to the S3 to see Captain Wilcox. Willie had been reporting periodically on team progress, but this was the first time Peter had been directed to appear along with his team leader. Willie reported new events and some suggestions about the planning and execution of the es corial operation. The captain acknowledged the report and commended them for the work they had done and then changed the direction of the conversation. Peter sensed that something new and important was forthcoming

"Your team has done well. I am impressed with your diligence and attention to detail. It is clear to me that you understand the importance of your planned mission and that you take it seriously. Obviously, you understand the danger and the reason for strict security."

Thoughts of his personal mission were dancing through Peter's mind as the Captain spoke. He suppressed the urge to bring up the fir tree and its hidden contents. It wasn't yet the optimal opportunity.

The captain continued. "So today I have some good news for you and some new news."

Peter hoped the captain's choice of words was an attempt to be crafty and not an attempt to disguise what was bad news.

"I'm authorizing a three-day leisure pass for you in reward of a plan progressing well. I recommend that you get away from Tölz and relax. Always keep security in mind and don't let the good German *Bier* play tricks on you."

The captain was smiling, but Peter was sure that Willie had reported on this type of potential character weakness if he had detected any.

"Use the passport we've provided in the case of any contact with the US Forces Military Police or the German authorities. With that long hair and the way you dress there shouldn't be a problem. But, if there is, you know what to do. Military personnel stationed in the European Theater have no need for a passport so the fact that you have one is good cover."

The expression on Captain Wilcox's face changed noticeably as he shifted to the "new" news subject.

"The new news is that you will be leaving Tölz for the duration of the mission."

Peter was shocked at this news, but attempted to not show an obvious reaction.

"The team is being placed on temporary duty (TDY) with the sixty-sixth Military Intelligence (MI) Detachment "L" in Mähring, on the Czech border. You will be closer to your potential intrusion point so that you can do reconnaissance more efficiently and you will be perceived as part of the community more easily. An Army Security Agency (ASA) detachment from Herzo Base has a listening post on nearby Mt *Schneeberg*. Their mission is to eavesdrop electronically and conduct visual surveillance on military activities across the border. The MI detachment is a general intelligence-gathering unit that is kept informed of all intelligence gathered by the ASA. You will be under the operational control of Major Taylor, who is the MI detachment commander. Major Taylor has been a part of the es corial team operational plan from its activation. Neither of you have had a need to know any of this until now. Your

transfer, and all other information discussed here this morning is classified, of course. Enjoy your weekend. Monday you
can pack your gear and everything you have been working
with and will be transported to Mähring by military sedan on
Tuesday. The driver and one guard will be armed and charged
with getting you to the sixty-sixth MI. There you will be under
the control of Major Taylor. Nothing changes related to your
mission planning except that now it is time to begin reconnaissance and come up with your best plan. I can tell you at
this point that there is a plan which may be implemented if
you don't find something better. Work hard, but keep this in
mind. The alternate plan is solid, but we hope you can develop
something better. No stone unturned, as they say. Do you have
any questions?"

Willie and Peter looked at each other quizzically. They
both had a thousand questions but nothing that seemed mission related at the moment.

"No, sir," Willie stated, as he established and maintained
eye contact with his superior. It was a trait that the captain noted and approved of in Willie and noticed increasingly in Peter.

"Peter?"

"No, sir, let's get it on, sir!" Peter spoke confidently as he
sensed that this turn of events was approval of his work and was
acceptance by the captain as a friend and trusted subordinate.

The three-day pass provided Peter with the opportunity
he needed to go to Nandlstadt to reunite with the Waldbaus.
Not only did he feel obligated to return as he promised, but
he missed the family and his surrogate mother. The work

ethic and sense of responsibility passed on to Peter by the example of Fritz and Gudrun Waldbau had served him well. He was also confident that he had learned what the true German psyche was at that stage of their recovery. That experience had been his foundation rock during all the years in America that he had endured occasional uneducated and biased behavior directed at the German people. He had quickly noted that "Nazi" and "German" were interchangeable by many Americans. The Waldbaus were very much like his own family and had no resemblance to hard-core Nazis. Nazis were the product of events following World War I. Appalling treatment of the Germans following the loss of that war, their loss of territory and the abject poverty of the people had slowly but surely caused the evolution toward Nazism. Adolph Hitler had masterfully exploited an opportunity. Peter had observed little of that, but had been somewhat aware through the teachings of his parents and the actions of so many arrogant ethnic Germans in Tachau.

Willie had decided to take his time off to go to Garmisch-Partenkirchen. "Garmisch," as it was referred to by the soldiers at Tölz, was a US Military rest and recuperation (R&R) area located at the interface between the German Alps and the lowland to the north. Germany's highest mountain at over 9000 feet, the *Zugspitze,* was the dominant feature in the area. US Military-controlled hotels for the troops were spread around the village. Many activities were available depending on the time of year. The soldiers and dependents could partake in all common winter sports or they could golf, hike, boat and play tennis among other activities when the weather was cooperative. The night life was lively and very appealing to the soldiers. Peter had heard about the good times in Garmisch and knew Willie would enjoy himself.

Peter had used the pretense of needing to find the right boots and shoes for the mission and for a desire to see some of Munich outside of the *Hauptbahnhof* where he had boarded a train so many years ago. Nandlstadt, and the home of the Waldbaus, had been his destination of choice as soon as he realized it was a possibility with the three-day pass.

The train ride on the *Deutsches Bundesbahn* (DB) took about an hour from *Tölz* to Munich. Peter had purchased a second class round-trip ticket for twenty *Marks* which was a bargain for military personnel whose pay was much higher than the average West German wage. The second class compartments on this train accommodated six people comfortably and had sliding glass doors for comfort and a degree of privacy. He took advantage of the close proximity to other passengers to further test his German. He hadn't used much German for quite some time and was curious how his accent would be accepted. The conversations went well for him and he had complete confidence in his ability to communicate. The isolation he detected in most passengers was a little surprising, but he reasoned it was a carryover from the years after the war when Germans lived in an isolated, fend-for-yourself world. Many feared they might be questioned about their wartime allegiance. They would rather not discuss that subject because of how they feared it might be interpreted—good or bad.

At several stops Peter noticed passengers with bicycles boarding on one of the coaches toward the rear of the train. He estimated there were about eight coaches in total. One of the passengers was unwrapping a sandwich he took from a bag.

It appeared to be made of a light brown bread called *Bauernbrot,* or "farmer's bread." Peter was familiar with this bread and was not surprised that it enclosed thin slices of *Wurst,* which was much like American cold cuts. This made Peter aware of his hunger and he decided to search for a *Doener Kebab* when he arrived in Munich. The *Doener* food idea had been introduced in Germany by the *Gastarbeiter* from Turkey and had become very popular. Gudrun Waldbau had first introduced him to the *Doener Kebab* on a trip to the city so many years ago.

The trip from Tölz to Munich took about an hour, as expected. He would have an hour before he had to catch a bus to Nandlstadt. Upon arrival in Munich, he recognized the general layout of the *Hauptbahnhof* and noted the improvement in cleanliness and signage. Several shops selling a few clothing items, souvenirs, candy, cigarettes and even magazines and newspapers were in evidence. He soon found what he was looking for: the hanging rotisserie with beef, lamb, chicken, or other available portions of meat which were thinly sliced and served with available vegetables and a creamy white sauce. All these ingredients were served in a cone-shaped thin, flat-bread wrapping. Peter smiled as he recalled Gudrun telling him no one knew what the sauce was made of and they didn't always believe the vendor when he told them what the meat was. She did agree with Peter though that the *Doener* was always tasty.

Outside the train station he found the bus stop for the Landshut destination. Nandlstadt was an intermediate stop for the bus en route to Landshut. It would take less than an hour to arrive at Nandlstadt. As he boarded the bus for route number 4732 he felt the excitement coursing through his body. It had been ten years since he left the Waldbaus and began his journey to America. He wondered if they would recognize him. He was now nearly six feet tall and had a healthy, chiseled body as a result of his demanding military training. He had never been weak or fat, but never as strong as he felt now. He carried an old used rucksack he had found at the *alt Kleider* shop in *Tölz*. They might confuse him with one of the ubiquitous wanderers found in the Munich area. The Waldbaus were two of the many people who had helped him along his way from Tachau to America. He remembered Gudrun fondly and the pseudo mother-son relationship they had developed. He now had an even more profound understanding of the emotions she displayed upon learning of the loss of her two sons. Peter was positive that their bond had its roots in Gudrun's real loss and the probable loss of parents that Peter had always feared. He had always been hopeful in his thoughts about his parent's welfare, but was realistic and prepared for the worst should the worst become reality..

His thoughts were interrupted when the bus stopped on the *Marktstrasse* in Nandlstadt. From the bus stop to *Altstrasse* was a short walk, then another kilometer to the Waldbau farm. As he approached the farm Peter noticed that the fields contained more hops plants—in the industry they were called bines—than when he was working there and that there were now vehicles in the fields. Two men seemed to be inspecting plants, but he didn't see Fritz so he turned to walk toward his old home. He saw movement in the window of what he knew to be the kitchen. He assumed it was Gudrun as he walked slowly down the narrow road toward the house. The movement stopped as the now distinguishable woman's face stared with a quizzical look. Peter smiled as he recognized the plump rosy cheeks of Gudrun. She quickly left the window and came to the door. Peter stopped, but continued smiling.

"PETER!" she practically shouted.

"*Muti,*"he almost whispered.

She fell slowly to her knees beginning to sob. He approached, went to his knees and embraced her. They were overcome with emotion. They had been on different paths since their separation, and there had been hard work and uncertainty for both. For Gudrun there had been her part in the West German war recovery effort. She had had to deal with the loss of her boys who were loyal to Germany, the poverty conditions of a war-torn country whose cities had been reduced to smoldering rubble and the personal shame she felt for Germany as the reality of what the Nazis had done became clear. Peter had been displaced into a world of which he knew little with a personal agenda that his new friends could not fully understand. It had been ten years. It was a reunion, which allowed both to appreciate their bond and be thankful that their daily lives had improved.

Fritz soon returned from the fields and was equally as shocked and happy with the return of Peter. The three of them had a lot to talk about which they did over a generous supply of *Augustiner Brau* and *Schwartze Katz Wein* from the Mosel vineyards. Peter learned that the Waldbau hops farm was doing well enough to hire more people and to purchase a work vehicle. A hops clearing house had been established in Freising where Fritz sold his crop. Fritz wasn't happy with the distance he had to travel to market his hops, but it was less expensive than paying to have them retrieved at his farm by clearing house van. Gudrun was visibly older, but happier. Consumer goods were more plentiful now and sufficient basic food and staples were available. Social activities were beginning to be reestablished in their community. Gudrun regularly met with the women of the village at the *Bäckerei* for coffee, cake and conversation. Many of the women's stories were similar to her own. Families had lost their men to the war while some men were still unaccounted for. The missing were assumed dead or continued to be held by the Russians.

Saturday nights there was a routine gathering at the local *Gasthaus*. The *Gasthaus zum Sternen* was the meeting place for good food, *Schnapps,Wein,* or *Bier,* as well as social interaction. The meeting and activities of the evening was their primary collective method of psychological recovery. Peter was invited to accompany the Waldbaus the following evening. He would return to Tölz on Sunday. Because he had Saturday night free, he readily accepted.

Peter only spoke of his army assignment in Tölz but never the specific plan. The Waldbaus were in awe of his journey and experiences in America. Gudrun expressed her firm belief that Peter would return one day, as he had promised.

The invitation to the *zum Sternen* was welcomed by Peter primarily to serve as another platform to test his accent recognition and get a little better feel for the mental state of the Nandlstadt populace at this point in time. He knew he would have to become attuned to the details in life that came naturally to the native Germans.

In addition to thoroughly enjoying the evening, his mind was working hard to put his situation, and what he was observing, into perspective. He was no longer the Special Forces candidate at Ft Bragg. He had been quickly and unexpectedly transformed into an important player in the intelligence endeavor of the US Army. That the army mission he had been assigned and his personal mission had so closely paralleled each other was a strange coincidence indeed, but he had accepted the coincidence and was thankful for it. He was satisfied, at the moment, with his idea of two penetrations into the forbidden Czech territory. His loyalty to the army and to America had become equally as important as his loyalty to family. Each of the two concerns would get his undivided attention and complete effort as situations allowed.

As he met people throughout the evening and observed their individual personalities he began a series of mental visions about some of them and how they had come to be who they are. The absence of military-aged men was noticeable. Those that had returned from the war were often disabled or had been obviously mentally destabilized. Peter questioned the mental stability of some whether they were, or were not, Nazi army veterans. The damage that had been done to the people was enormous. The question in Peter's mind was whether or not they had brought it upon themselves.

He realized that in this room there were probably ex-Nazis, Nazi sympathizers and passive supporters of Nazism. Some were too young to be any of those things, while some were passive non-supporters, and others were outright members of, or supporters of, resistance groups. Peter could see the folly of categorizing all Germans as Nazis. But here were all; they were attempting to regain a communal solid ground on which to rebuild. None of them wanted to relive the past in memory or reality. Some had war backgrounds they wanted to hide. They felt the shame, but were thankful nobody talked about the war years or asked questions publicly. Many had photographic evidence of friends or relatives in compromising situations or in actual Nazi uniform. This evidence was secreted away for posterity and never publicly displayed. People knew Nazi hunters were active. They also knew that culpability was ambiguous. They just wanted the memory of the war years to go away. In most cases, they got their wish, but had years of anxiety and sweat until that happened.

Peter felt that he knew some answers as to who and what, but in his mind the answers as to why were difficult. He had experiences in life that most West Germans and Americans didn't have. He had lived first within an environment of Nazi-influenced German power, and then a position of Russian-influenced Czech power. He had experienced post-war West Germany with the Waldbaus and then he was almost magically immersed in an American culture that knew little about the war and could not possibly understand life from his perspective. His experiences were indelibly etched in his young mind. The evening activities had re-enforced opinions and conclusions he had developed. The Nazis were people; the Germans, Czechs, Soviets and Americans were all people. Collectively, none had a genetic disposition for evil, but powerful individuals and specific circumstances could have and did develop evil. The evil that became Nazism was set in motion at the conclusion of World War I by the standards imposed on the Germans by the victors. The resentment felt by the Germans became a lightning rod for Nazism. Hitler's promises were embraced by many, not because they were true, but because people wanted them to be true. His short-term successes fueled the flames of discontent through nationalistic doctrine and a goal of revenge. People bought it, and the collective psyche changed for the masses. Eventually, followers bought in for self-preservation or because of indifference. He had seen his own family's desire to be invisible for self-preservation and knew the Waldbaus to be followers in support of their sons.

There were personality types that were easily influenced by Hitler. Aggressive, greedy, emotionless and loyal minions of Nazism were handsomely rewarded. These were the people that wielded power and influenced behavior at the highest leadership level. Their teachings and aggressive discipline enabled the growth of Nazism.

Peter was also aware that many Germans were not believers or followers. They were the resisters. They were men and women who risked or actually gave their lives in order to defy the Nazi doctrine. He recalled Sgt Grimes's words about Dieter Bonhoeffer in Flossenburg. There were thousands and thousands of escapees that fled Germany both to avoid persecution and to be non-participants in Nazi doctrine. A part of him wanted to hold the masses blameless, but charge individuals. There had to be minimum standards for human behavior below which were intolerable, of course, but are there excuses in some cases? Or are there never any acceptable excuses?

Peter enjoyed the evening and felt it had been productive in terms of his own assimilation into the local mainstream. People just didn't want to ask questions that might lead to the past. His accent was a non-issue among this melding of post-war local citizens and displaced people from all over Europe. Peter did attract the attention of several of the *Fräuleins*. Young, healthy, German men were at a premium. The young ladies were especially attentive to him when they found out he was an American soldier. A young, good-looking American soldier was a prize to be pursued! Peter was impressed by several of the ladies. Under different circumstances, he was sure he would have returned the flirtatious innuendo, but tomorrow he had to go back to Tölz and prepare for the move to Mähring. He did exchange information with Gisela, one of the pretty ladies, and promised to look her up if he returned to Nandlstadt. For security reasons he did not inform the Waldbaus of his move. Bad Tölz was his home base and he had no way of knowing how long he would be on TDY to Mähring. He did promise to visit them when he could.

Gudrun had found a pair of old boots for Peter that he could use as proof that he had been shopping in Munich. Involving Willie with the Waldbaus seemed unimportant and could lead to unanswerable questions that he didn't want to entertain. On the Sunday return trip Peter used the time between transfer from bus to the Bad Tölz train to do a quick visit to the *Marienplatz,* the *Hofbrauhaus,* and the *Viktualienmarkt.* He was getting quite proficient with the busses, trams and trains. Although he hadn't seen the devastated city for comparison when he was in Munich in 1948, Munich now looked like the old European city he had envisioned. Restoration was under way with some buildings already looking like no damage had occurred. City leaders had chosen to restore the city to what it once was. They used photographs that had been meticulously produced and accumulated by the Nazis. The choice of restoring the old city was in direct contrast to what was done in Frankfurt, where that city had been effectively demolished and rebuilt from the ground up with modern architecture. Peter hoped that one day he would be able to spend more time in Munich. He enjoyed what he saw and was sure it would be a wonderful city in which to live or visit.

NINETEEN

TDY MÄHRING

The monotony of his *Bundesbahn* coach as it relentlessly moved along the track en route to Tölz gave Peter time to contemplate the events of the last few days in Nandlstadt. Reuniting with the Waldbaus had been rewarding. On this Sunday morning they had planned to attend the Catholic Church in Nandlstadt as had been their habit as long as he had known them. Historically, Europe had had some contentious religious disagreements dating to Martin Luther's Reformation in the sixteenth century. As time passed, Luther's Protestants and the mainstream Catholics had learned to coexistent much the same as Germany was now learning to coexist with the Jewish people. If only it hadn't taken a world war to establish a foundation upon which the coexistence could germinate. Peter saw parallels between the war and other catastrophic events around the world. One example was the issue of slavery in his new country of allegiance. He didn't understand how Americans could be so judgmental about the Nazis while overlooking their own history of treatment of the Native Americans and the Negroes. Partly, he surmised, because contemporary

Americans, especially in the West, were so far removed from those days that the reality of the memory had faded. He had heard so many deny responsibility because they weren't a part of it. But what if they had been a part of it? Would they have acted differently? Again the "people are people" principle came to mind with the supporting belief that it's only the conditions of a person's existence that determines who they are and how they act.

When not distracted by noise and activity the mind has a chance to try to sort out the input it has received. Sometimes events of years past are triggered by the input of current information. Sometimes the mind just dances from memory to memory. Peter reflected on the obvious appreciation of the Waldbaus when he offered the gifts he had taken them. The American Chesterfield cigarettes for Fritz and the nylon stockings for Gudrun were coveted by the Germans, but very expensive on the West German economy—or not available at all. Thoughts of the move to Mähring and the projected mission were ever present on his mind. Tomorrow the team would begin a new phase of its preparation. Willie would have returned from his Garmisch vacation and they would begin working again toward their common goal. But for now his mind was still darting from memory to memory and from one experience to another. He remembered how important religion was to both his family and to the Waldbaus. He was taught that God created, controlled and urged preparation for the afterlife. Peter listened and had no reason to doubt until science came into his life. At the University of Washington he had been introduced to the work of Charles Darwin. *The Voyage of the Beagle* had been the basis for Darwin's theory of evolution and caused Peter to reconsider his religious teachings. Despite the dichotomy of conviction, he recognized value in life for both.

The trip seemed longer between Munich and Tölz on the return trip, but eventually he arrived in Bad Tölz. He found a taxi waiting and was taken back to Flint *Kaserne*. His first extended time off was complete and he was looking forward to his move on Tuesday—but, first things first. He needed a good night's sleep.

Peter and Willie were refreshed. For the better part of a month they had concentrated on map study and preparation for the es corial mission. Willie had his Armed Forces Recreation Center (AFRC) experience to talk about with extreme excitement and animated examples. From the *Zugspitze* to the *Partnachklamm* he had enjoyed every moment. He was especially excited about the *Partnachklamm* as an awe-inspiring experience. The *Partnach* River had forged a passageway from the nearby steep alpine mountains through an ancient narrow *muschelkalk* rock formation on its relentless journey to the Loisach River, then to the Danube and eventually the Black Sea. When Peter mentioned that the Black Sea had shores in Soviet Union territory, Willie, with tongue in cheek, stated that if he had been Cyrillic-language capable, he would have sent the Soviets some words of wisdom via a message in a bottle. Willie had a knack for providing levity for their mostly serious mission-related discussions, which Peter appreciated.

Peter was purposely vague about his trip. He hadn't found the right time or situation to talk about his West German acquaintances or his personal mission. He had decided that the duty mission came first and that, if need be, he would find a way to gain access to Czechoslovakia and the material hidden away in the *Blitzbaum* on another occasion.

At 0800 on Tuesday the sedan with driver and guard arrived at their quarters. Both escorts carried a sidearm in holsters worn around their midriff. The team loaded personal gear and were driven to the Special Forces Headquarters to take possession of required classified material and to receive final instructions from Captain Wilcox.

"Good luck and Godspeed," offered the captain.

They saluted and replied almost in unison, "Thank you, sir."

Soon they were on the road to Mähring. The trip was expected to take about five to six hours via Munich, Regensburg and Weiden. They couldn't discuss the mission in the presence of the armed escorts so they mostly took in the scenery, engaged in small talk, or experienced personal thoughts about what lay ahead. It was ironic that as they entered *Bundesautobahn* 93 they were so close to Nandlstadt where he had met with the Waldbaus just two days earlier, and that they soon passed through Weiden where he had been detained for a short period of time after his escape from Czechoslovakia. He noted that activity in the countryside had increased considerably since his trip so many years ago. Farmers were busy in the fields and on the secondary roads with their farming vehicles. Most of the vehicles were powered by cattle, but there was the occasional barely serviceable tractor. At times, the sedan was slowed until a safe passing area could be found. Peter was surprised to see so many women working in the fields. He was surprised until he remembered that this was because so many men had died in the war or had been displaced or detained by the Axis powers. He wondered if his own mother had been put to work on a work farm in East Germany.

They exited the A93 *Autobahn* at Weiden and soon passed through Tirschenreuth which was the last city of sizeable population before they reached Mähring. The couriers had been directed to meet the sixty-sixth MI personnel at *Buchenwegstrasse,* number one, near the center of the village. Waiting there was Staff Sergeant Martinez in another US Army sedan. After exchanging identification information Sergeant Martinez directed them to follow him for a short drive to what he referred to as the "facility." The facility was a gated area that could previously have been the residence of a well-to-do Nazi, Peter thought. It was fenced all around with an eight-foot-high brick and mortar wall. Broadleaf trees within the facility provided shade and security from nearby line-of-sight observation. There were five buildings within the facility. The area appeared to be about five thousand square meters in size. The largest building had parking spaces provided and appeared to be the headquarters although it was unmarked.

Sgt Martinez directed them to follow him and bring any classified material with them. The classified material was then signed over to a clerk who was attending a vault. The couriers were released and told to wait outside with their vehicle. Only then were Peter and Willie formally introduced to the executive officer: First Lieutenant (1Lt) Adamson. This meeting was to accept the two Special Forces specialists as working partners and to settle them in with their temporary unit. A meeting with the sixty-sixth MI Detachment "L" Commander was scheduled for the next day, and they were released to Sgt

Martinez for billeting assignment. The building they were assigned for quarters was a small, two bedroom, fully furnished
house. They inspected the house for damage, inventoried the
contents and signed for possession. After unloading the van
filled with their personal equipment the couriers were released. It had been a long day. Neither Willie nor Peter wanted
to even think about the couriers and their return trip. But that
wasn't their business and they reasoned that the couriers could
easily find transient lodging at a US facility in Regensburg, if
necessary. Now what they wanted was to rest and prepare
for their next day meeting with the detachment commander.
Mission preparation was moving right along, although they
still didn't understand the full ramifications of what was in
their future.

The morning briefing was conducted by the commander
himself. Major Taylor was a tall man of around thirty. A West
Point graduate, he could have easily fit the image of a gung-ho
Special Forces officer. Peter expected a stern disciplinarian,
but was surprised by the major's easy-going attitude. He put
the two of them at ease quickly and got right down to business.

"I'm fully aware of your mission, men," the major was
speaking. "You will receive all the support you need from us
here at the sixty-sixth. Everybody here is cleared to include
Top Secret, but only Lieutenant Adamson, Sergeant Martinez
and I will be monitoring your activities. You will be provided
with a civilian car registered to the detachment with locally-
recognized German license plates. You will not draw attention because of the car you are driving, but I realize that you,

Specialist Ackerman, still need some German traffic drivers training. You can handle that, Sgt Kyles."

"Yes, sir!"

"Let me begin by clarifying assets and responsibilities of the sixty-sixth MI Detachment "L." The battalion headquarters is located in Frankfurt. That is our parent unit, but its mission is fractured all over Europe. You might call them an administrator and a supplier of necessities, but for what we do here, our chain of command is directly to USAREUR. We may or may not have several missions or instances of inquiry going on at the same time. You need not be concerned with any of that unless you have a need to know. You concentrate on your mission and keep me informed."

Peter was happy with what he was hearing at the moment. Team es corial would have a great deal of autonomy, at least during early planning.

"Several of our responsibilities will have a definite overlap with your mission. We take first possession of defectors from Czechoslovakia. After interrogation you may be granted access to them for questions about the current situation where they came from. Then I dispatch them to the Germans for disposition or I have them sent to Frankfurt or Heidelberg for further questioning."

They were both a little surprised at the detail and preparation necessary to find intelligence information at every opportunity. What they were hearing added a little pressure to their mission in terms of efficiency expectations. They would have to be good, and felt a growing pride that they had been selected for this mission.

The major continued, "We also get support from Army

Security Agency detachments in the area. In fact, we are located here to be central for the listening posts on Hoherbogen, Mt Schneeberg and another very near Mähring. These units do electronic surveillance of radio communications from across the border as well as visual surveillance. They report to us so that we can evaluate and forward pertinent intelligence to USAREUR. You will be provided with any information the listening posts pass on to us if there is any chance it could be pertinent to your mission. Any questions?"

Willie asked, "Will we have a secure working area and what about weapons when we need them?"

"Good question, Sgt Kyles. Sgt Martinez will brief you in detail on those subjects, but rest assured you will have every bit of support you need. Sgt Martinez is your contact for messing, clothing, pay, mail, vehicle concerns and any other problems. I'll turn you over to the Sgt now, but I do have one more item of interest to you, Specialist Ackerman. I just received a copy of orders from your unit in Bad Tölz. You have been promoted to sergeant E-5. Congratulations, sergeant!"

Handshakes and pats on Peter's back followed. Everybody congratulated the new sergeant and took turns addressing him as "Sgt Ackerman!"

They spent the remainder of the day familiarizing with everything they would need for their mission and for personal needs. They were on separate rations, which meant that an allowance for meals was part of their pay. They could utilize the mess facilities on Mt Schneeberg, or at the listening post in Mähring on a pay-per-meal basis or purchase meals and food anywhere on the German economy that was convenient for them. Greenback dollars were not authorized for use at military facilities in order to keep the dollars out of the civilian black market. It was necessary to travel to a US Facility that had an American Express bank in order to exchange their payroll script currency for local DM. Sgt Martinez recommended Bayreuth or Grafenwoehr for banking and all other American military-provided conveniences. They were shown their secure working area and briefed on signing out and returning classified material to the secure storage area. Weapons were stored in a small armory in the basement and could be signed out from Sgt Martinez himself, if needed. A quartermaster van came by once a week to pick-up and deliver laundry. Mail was sometimes delivered by the van driver, but delivery could be inconsistent. Probably the most important item, at the moment, was to take possession of their automobile. This was to be a 1956 Volkswagen Beetle, commonly referred to as a bug, with a TIR license plate reflecting that it was registered in Tirschenreuth. This vehicle would provide them a degree of anonymity wherever they needed to go, but especially in the local area. They were also provided with—and signed for—a large metal key to unlock the entry gate.

Sgt Martinez had an office adjacent to the Commanders office and across the hall from 1Lt Adamson. The three of them were the team's operational contacts. There were others they interacted with for administrative reasons, but they discussed their mission concerns with nobody else in the detachment; they asked no questions about the duties of the other men.

As the orientation was drawing to a close, Sgt Martinez had one more item on his agenda.

"You will have every asset and all the support possible of the sixty-sixth MI. Our assets include the ASA people at

Hoherbogen, Mt Schneeberg and here in Mähring. We will begin to visit those facilities tomorrow. I'll take care of identification by authorizing your access as USAREUR mission-planners. You will be placed on each facilities entry list so that you can gain entry should you desire to visit without me."

Sgt Kyles and the new Sgt Ackerman were getting the picture. Much detailed planning for their mission had preceded their involvement. Willie was learning his involvement in Bad Tölz had been minimal. The scenario was beginning to look like the scope of their mission was not only important, it was critical.

TWENTY

HOHERBOGEN

Sgt Martinez lived outside the compound with his wife and their three-year-old baby girl. Many of the Mähring-area personnel lived in nearby Tirschenreuth as did the sergeant. None of these families had children of school age because there were no American schools for military dependents in close proximity to Mähring. The single or unaccompanied soldiers lived on the compound in quarters in another building near Willie and Peter. Dependents were not authorized to be in the 5K zone where the compound was located. Signage was placed on roads warning of entry into the 5K zone, but these signs were sometimes knocked down, stolen, or just obscured by mud and road debris. The Second AC patrolled the area to ensure unauthorized American personnel had not entered the 5K zone. Sgt Martinez explained en route to Hoherbogen that this was primarily to prevent accidental border incidents, or possible voluntary defections. If the Second AC detained unauthorized American military or dependent personnel in the 5K zone they were obligated to escort the intruders to Coburg—if it was a case of accidental intrusion—where their units would pick them up. Disciplinary action may or may not result depending on the circumstances surrounding the incident; regardless of circumstance, it was never good to be detained in the 5K zone.

The trip to Hoherbogen was going to take about two hours in a tactical quarter ton truck (jeep) equipped with mounted frequency-modulated (FM) radio. They were talking business with a few personal stories to break the serious nature and pass the time. Sgt Martinez told a story about a soldier in his privately-owned vehicle who was out for a Sunday morning drive with his pregnant wife. It was a warming morning after a hard freeze the night before. The thaw caused some muddy spots along the route, one of which had caused the 5K zone warning sign to be unreadable. The US Forces license plates and the American-make automobile identified the Americans immediately to some young Germans, dressed for and on their way to church, who waved their arms to alert the car occupants. The driver, a staff sergeant from Erlangen, realized the mistake and pulled off the road in order to turn around. When he did so, his vehicle sunk to its axle in the soft ground. The sergeant was well aware of the problem he might have if the border patrol checked the area so he was very grateful for the help the young West Germans were giving. In their finest clothing they started digging to free the car from the mud. Even the young ladies pitched in or went for shovels or other helpful tools.

It was inevitable: the border patrol arrived just as the car was back on the road. The sergeant knew he was in trouble and his wife was visibly upset. Her pregnant condition didn't help matters. The sergeant walked over to the border patrol vehicle and immediately recognized a redheaded SFC from an NCO academy he had attended a few years earlier. When the door of the five-ton truck was opened, a flip-top beer bottle fell out at the feet of the 5K zone offending sergeant. As the story goes, the redheaded border patrol team supervisor told the sergeant, he wasn't supposed to be in this area. The offending sergeant agreed, but pointed out that he thought the border patrol wasn't supposed to be drinking beer on duty. The situation was pretty much a wash.

"Ha-ha," Peter and Willie both laughed." So what happened?" Willie asked.

"The sergeant and his wife were told to get in their car and get out of the 5K zone immediately. And everybody continued along their merry way!"

"That's funny! Has your wife ever had a problem with the 5K zone?" asked Sergeant Ackerman.

"Not on your life! She would never be so careless."

Eventually they reached a little village called Rimbach, which would be the last village they would pass through on their way to Hoherbogen. Sgt Martinez began explaining the Hoherbogen situation and its relevance to the es corial mission.

"Last summer the Warsaw Pact, led by the Soviets and Czechs, had training exercises in Czechoslovakia and East Germany in the area of the Fulda Gap, but also south into the area which can be observed from Hoherbogen. The Fulda Gap was long ago identified as a potential invasion route for Warsaw Pact armies into West Germany. This entry point would give easy access to the militarily strategic Rhein River. Those maneuvers have made our intelligence experts extremely nervous when considered with our deteriorating relations with the Soviet Union. We especially want to know what's going on

over there with the Soviets. That's why Hoherbogen and es corial have become part of our intelligence plans."

The words of the sergeant were like a light bulb illuminating Peter's inquisitive consciousness. Although he had toyed
with many scenarios previous to this day, Sergeant Martinez's
words were lending more credibility to what was in store for
es corial.

They had continued to the east and were entering what
looked like a crude access road probably used by foresters
or loggers. Ruts and mud pools had recently been gouged by
heavy vehicles. Peter assumed this orientation indoctrination
was part of the overall mission plan for team es corial.

"Hang on, men, this could get rough. We're going up another two kilometers or so. This is Mt Eckstein, which is part
of the Hoherbogen range. Our ASA team from Herzo Base is
in the process of establishing a permanent listening post. As
you have been told their mission will be to conduct visual and
electronic surveillance of military activity. The surveillance
site is about 1100 meters in elevation and provides excellent
vision of the Czech countryside on clear days. The border is
five kilometers away; the Hoherbogen site coincidentally happens to be on the boundary of the 5K zone."

They bounced along the forested mountain road gaining
altitude until reaching a level clearing. A uniformed guard with
an M-1 Carbine rifle slung over his shoulder, was stationed at
a makeshift shack. For the guard, a US Army jeep driven by a
soldier in uniform was not unusual. He was alert to Willie and
Peter in civilian clothes, however. He was signaling their vehicle to stop. Sgt Martinez presented his identification which
the guard checked against his access list.

"OK, sergeant, you are good to go. Are you sponsoring these two men?"

"Yes, and I need to get them on the access list. They are working with the sixty-sixth MI. Is the lieutenant available?"

Summoning the ASA detachment commander by field phone soon brought Lieutenant Cornwell, who recognized Sgt Martinez immediately. The lieutenant had been informed that the sixty-sixth MI would be requiring access to the Hoherbogen site for personnel not on the access list. After producing identification Willie and Peter were entered on both the master and the working access lists. ASA personnel knew that they were not to ask questions of MI personnel. They were only to cooperate with reasonable requests after establishing valid identification. Rank was unimportant in conducting business, but the customary standards of protocol, discipline and bearing were always observed.

Sgt Martinez explained that this site might eventually provide information that es corial could use in planning. The end objective of the Hoherbogen site activity and es corial was the same. They were both tasked to gather information about Warsaw Pact: activities, equipment, manpower and plans. They were working together, but for security reasons, they knew only specific information was to be exchanged; they just didn't know why. Es corial would get necessary information from the sixty-sixth MI, so the detailed operations of each group hardly mattered.

Microwave telephone links were being set up by signal corps personnel which would connect Hoherbogen to the MI unit in Mähring and to USAREUR headquarters in Heidelberg. There would be both secure and unsecure links as well as a link to the West German telephone system.

The ASA men were obviously very busy preparing the site. Sgt Martinez said they had occupied this site only recently and were nowhere near fully functional. Three field tents, which accommodated ten men each, had been erected for the troops and NCOs—a smaller tent for officers. On the perimeter of the area was a two seat wooden commode with cutoff metal barrels to capture the bodily eliminations. A urine tube was dug into the ground and had been directed to an exit on the side of the steep nearby cliff. A wind-breaking and privacy-providing canvas wall had been put up around the entire latrine area. They walked over to the cliff so that Peter and Willie could get their first look at the Czech countryside from Hoherbogen. Peter was looking at what was formerly his Sudetenland home. The sight gave him pause and delivered mixed emotions. Gone were feelings of homesickness, but recurring were thoughts of his parents and what had happened to them. He still had memory of his soccer club teammates and the good times with family. He remembered Trudi who had been his closest friend at the school. They were young and not mature enough to have feelings of love or permanent togetherness; they did talk, laugh, study, explore, train athletically and had often sought each other's leisure-time companionship.

Sgt Martinez was cautioning about getting too close to the sheer rock outcropping in front of them. His voice jolted Peter out of his temporary state of nostalgia.

"That's over a thousand feet almost straight down," he was saying, "you don't want to walk out here at night if you're not sure exactly where you are!" Jokingly he commented that the ASA already had to replace two sleep-walkers.

Peter could see the evergreen trees below, but those trees

were still high above the valley floor. At the base of Mt Eckstein and the entire Hoherbogen range, the valley floor leveled off nearly as far as he could see into Czechoslovakia. The actual border was located so that part of the valley was in West Germany, but the vast flat land he could see to the east was all Czechoslovakia. The actual border fortifications weren't visible with the naked eye, but Peter was sure he would get his chance to view them with the ASA surveillance equipment as their planning progressed. Today was merely part of the orientation to, and information-gathering about, their support assets before they got down to serious work.

Willie asked about the Second AC and the *Bundesgrenzschutz,* which was the federal West German border patrol.

"They work together and exchange information, often patrolling right up to the actual border. The primary concern of the BGS is defectors from Czechoslovakia. Any defector would be screened to determine their intelligence value and then turned over to us in Mähring or to the West German immigration authorities, as appropriate. The Second AC is primarily a watchdog for any potential Warsaw Pact aggression. I know what you are thinking; the answer is yes . . . we can coordinate any of your activities with the border patrols. Should there ever be a problematic situation, just use the 'Brigitte Berg' code word. Tell them you are looking for Brigitte Berg."

Peter hadn't forgotten the code word, but the use by Sgt Martinez brought attention to the reality of what es corial was planning. Little by little, Peter could see the development of the plan and the fact that at this point in time, the es corial plan had only begun to materialize.

"We have at least two more stops to make on the way back

to Mähring. In the MI, we have our eyes and ears open for intelligence at all times. You two need to integrate that principle into your thinking. When dealing with the locals, your persona is casual and friendly, but always attentive. You'll meet people who seem honest and trustworthy, who must nevertheless be treated with caution. Our first stop will be at the *Gasthaus Schoenblick* which is run by just such a family. If useful information is exchanged, we want to be sure it is a one-way exchange. . . from them to us!"

Peter was sure the stop had a twofold purpose. They would eat lunch and be introduced to a potential information asset at the same time. *Herr* Reichelberger and his wife were indeed friendly and accommodating. Peter soon became the center of the conversation because of his language capability. The Reichelbergers spoke English adequately, but more accurate information could be exchanged quickly in German. There was an air of polite curiosity probably because the Eckstein site and the Americans working there were still new kids on the block. Interaction with black men was relatively new to these West Germans, so Willie commanded extra attention. The food was good and the hospitality accommodating. The Reichelbergers asked no duty-related questions, but acknowledged the work being done by the Americans only one kilometer away.

"One more stop, men: The *Pension* Hoherbogen." The sergeant was navigating the crude road carefully, and continued, "There is a requisition in with the engineers to come up here and pave this road. Hopefully that will be soon, but it has to be coordinated with the local government because of cattle, farm vehicles, and their forestry agents also using this trail."

The *Pension* Hoherbogen was located closer to the center

of Rimbach and was under consideration for housing the un-accompanied troops who would work the Eckstein site. The *Pension* provided several rooms, a convenient location and could serve some meals for the troops. Transportation to and from the work site would be eased if the majority of the men lived at a central location. One work crew could be taken to the site to relieve another for return to the *Pension*. This plan was for the future, however, while the site was being prepared for permanent occupation. After a quick stop at the *Pension*, Sgt Martinez took them on a tour through the little village for as much familiarization as possible. If es corial returned it would undoubtedly be without Sgt Martinez. Rimbach and Mt Eckstein had been identified as the southernmost of the es corial target area. Willie and Peter had done plenty of map re-connaissance of the border area from Hoherbogen to northerly Waldsassen. Peter was inwardly elated to finally be doing some ground reconnaissance. Memories of Tachau were returning often with the familiarity of the environment all around him. Weather, ecosystems and the totality of the West German sur-roundings served to remind Peter of the difference between America and this part of Europe. Weather and vegetation were as similar to Snoqualmish as they were dissimilar to Ft Bragg, North Carolina. Many old buildings in disrepair, lack of neon lighting and road signs with funny pictures and German print, accentuated the differences as well. There was always a bit of nostalgia for Peter, but the seriousness of the reason for his presence here and now was the primary thought in his mind. An inner tenseness of anticipation, coupled with a touch of fear, were his constant companions. This inner tenseness grew as each progressive item of mission-planning developed. Peter equated the feeling to that of preparing for a championship soccer game in Tachau; each day closer to the game increased the inner tension. Unlike soccer, however, Peter realized that he was no longer engaged in playing youthful games.

His thoughts were interrupted when Sgt Martinez began to exit the *Autobahn* at the US Forces gas station. This stop would give them a chance to use the restroom and purchase some snacks. This rest stop was strategically placed to serve US military personnel from Grafenwoehr, Hohenfels, Amberg, Regensburg and any other US Forces personnel that might be on-duty or in an off-duty status. Basically, a series of US *Autobahn* rest stops throughout the American sector provided gasoline and snacks so that personnel wouldn't need to find an American military facility in order to refuel. Quartermaster and Esso gasoline was rationed to cut down on the black market operation. Esso coupons were available for personnel traveling to areas where US Forces gasoline stations were not available. These coupons were available at less than European-economy prices under the Status of Forces Agreement (SOFA) which had been negotiated with the new West German government in the early fifties. All three of them purchased a *Bratwurst* and coke and Sgt Martinez signed for the quartermaster fuel. No coupons were needed, but the sergeant had to provide his unit and vehicle designation along with his military identification. Peter assumed that the fuel accounting system was different for military vehicles than it was for privately-owned vehicles.

The *Autobahn* exit at Weiden took them through part of the city and then through Tirschenreuth and a number of small villages before they reached Mähring. Their previous map study and trips through this area served to make the route more familiar. Sgt Martinez wouldn't be available for the next few days, so the es corial plan was to do their first ground reconnaissance the next day. Mt Schneeberg and the Mähring ASA sites would have to wait.

TWENTY ONE

WHERE IS BRIGITTE?

After making another map inspection the team decided to go north on St 2175 which was a Bavarian State road. They found themselves consulting their road map for their initial navigation. They also had military topographic maps which contained detailed elevation and relief information. The topographic maps were classified Top Secret when in association with mission activities, but would probably not be needed until interesting locations were identified. St 2175 was generally parallel to the border but could be very near, or somewhat remote from the border proper depending on where the landscape had provided ease in road construction. At times they could see border barrier devices; at other times there were hills, buildings or vegetation blocking the view. This was not a surprise for the team since it was consistent with their map studies. They were aware that there can be considerable difference between map study visualization and what is actually seen on the ground. That was the primary purpose of the reconnaissance excursions. Willie was driving the VW Beetle while

Peter took notes. Occasionally they stopped to discuss unusual or interesting areas that could be pertinent to the es corial mission. They passed over and took note of bridges, as well as the volume and direction of water flow. Vegetation of all types was noted. Density of vehicular traffic, number of pedestrians and type of vehicles were meticulously noted. The only activity seen on the Czech side was in the occasional occupied observation tower. Prominent elevation changes were recorded for later comparison to their topographic maps. They passed through little villages with names like Altmuhl and larger cities like Neualbenreuth. Neualbenreuth was interesting because the eastern sector was isolated farmland continuing right up to the border. They agreed to drive out to the Neualbenreuth border and take a look on their return trip. Along the route they passed several signs which were warning about proximity to the border. They were passing signs with such warnings as: *Achtung Landesgrenze 1 KM,* and the oft-encountered warning of only fifty meters to the border.

The Czech-side barrier construction itself was mostly double rolls of barbed wire on the ground with a third apparently electrified roll on top. Directly behind the barbed-wire barrier and across a security-inspection road was a strip of cleared and raked soft soil which would show evidence of intrusion. It was well known that this cleared area could contain pressure release landmines. Exactly where the landmines were located was the unknown factor. Ivan and the Czechs weren't telling. As a SF trained engineer sergeant, Peter had some knowledge of disarming landmines, but it wasn't his favorite duty activity. Guard towers were strategically placed to provide overlapping fire power coverage. Some towers had trained attack dogs to assist in their area security. Whether the *Caucasian Ovcharka* was trained to avoid landmines was probably a factor to consider. Peter recognized the breed from previous planning sessions and knew them to be Russian bred and trained..

Peter, being the consummate thinker, wondered why these barriers were necessary. From his experience in life he certainly understood how it had come to be, but, wasn't this now peacetime? Why is there a Cold War? Of course, he knew the usual answer the Warsaw Pact nations were giving. Some form of not wanting to pollute their politics with democracy and capitalism. Keeping westerners out was the solution, they said. The reality was that no one wanted in, anyway, so the barriers were nothing more than a means of keeping their own people confined. Restricting their own people with their brain power, became known as the Eastern Bloc solution to the "brain drain."

Peter was well aware of Soviet and Czech brutality as the native German expulsions from the Sudetenland were implemented. He was well aware of the stories and increasing evidence of the Nazi murder of millions of Jews and any other minorities they felt stood between them and their goal of racial purity and superiority. The Nazis were apparently guilty of mass murder of millions of people over an extended period of time. The Russians and Czechs stood unquestionably guilty of the murder and inhumane treatment of the Sudeten Germans, but over a shorter and lesser-known period of time. The world has judged by the volume of atrocity and overlooked the same behavior by others on a lesser scale, and just maybe because the world's collective human psyche didn't want to deal with it anymore. As some Nazis paid the price for their deeds, so should the Soviets who invaded his home, and the Czechs who murdered, looted and confiscated from the fleeing or expelled Germans. He still hoped for the best for his parents who had sacrificed for him, but he was realistic about their chances. He had devoted his life to—and was making progress toward—finding his parents and exposing atrocities.

Willie suggested taking a break for lunch, which Peter thought was a good idea. From local map study Willie had identified a *Gasthaus* west of the state road they were using as a primary exploration route. An advantage would be that they were more likely to find local customers there than they would closer to the main thoroughfare. They weren't going to be asking revealing questions of the locals, at this point, but being ever vigilant was an important part of their information gathering. The somewhat remote location would also reduce the chances of exposure to the border patrol and the associated questioning that could occur. A black man not in uniform and not working with the US border patrol—in this part of West Germany—was unusual enough that it was sure to draw the curiosity of the patrols and the locals. Willie had long ago learned that the Germans couldn't resist testing his tight curly hair and sometimes inspecting him like a zoo animal. German friends that he knew in Tölz had explained the German curiosity, and that there was no degrading or ominous intent. Willie had accepted the explanation and moved on without any unsettling emotions. He found many things about the Germans unusual, also, so it was a normal, unimportant circumstance that was no longer a surprise to him.

"We need to get to the *Kranz,* before 1400 in case they stop serving warm food until the evening meal as is often the case." Willie was alluding to the *Gasthaus Zum Grünen Kranz*, which was located a few kilometers to the west in a little village called Schachten on road number TIR 25. It was not unusual for a country *Gasthaus* to discontinue warm food during the afternoon. They usually did stay open for *Bier* drinking and card playing, however. The afternoon card games usually took place at the *Stammtisch,* which was marked and reserved for regulars and their guests.

They found the *Kranz* easily and were pleasantly surprised by the ambiance. Well lighted with attractive, sturdy, wooden tables. The tables were covered with two layers of cloths. One large permanent table cloth which covered the entire table and another smaller, more attractively designed cloth, laid over the permanent so that the underlying cloth was exposed at the corners of the table. The designer temporary cloth was removed and replaced for each new customer. A *Skat* card game was in progress at the *Stammtisch.* The team could see shot glasses of *Schnapps* and *Cognac* and a few *Bier* mugs with overflowing heads of foam. The *Stammtisch* table was uncovered to facilitate the *Skat* game. Care had to be taken to prevent wet cards from the mug overflows. Smoke from cigars, pipes and cigarettes formed a thick cloud floating upward only to be trapped by an ornate ceiling. Some of the men sitting or standing around the table were dressed in working *Lederhosen* with thick, heavy suspenders and a *Trachten* hat with *Gamsbart* and decorative pins attached. Loud conversation and pounding of the table as tricks were turned in the *Skat* game could be heard throughout the *Gasthaus*.

There had been a momentary silence when they entered. Stares were directed at Willie, but he acted like he had been there before. That served to lessen a confused, defensive situation that might have otherwise developed.

The *Gruß Gott* greeting offered by Peter seemed to relieve the tension even more. The card players now knew the new customers weren't complete strangers to Bavaria, but they did create a certain curiosity.

This was the first of many potential outings to West German establishments the team was planning. It was important that they become familiar with local customs and conduct so that they would be more relaxed, confident and accepted by the locals wherever they visited. They had agreed to be vague about their business and would identify themselves as American tourists. Willie was to be an ex-soldier previously stationed in Bad Tölz and Peter was to be a native German born in Lenggries. The story was that they had met in Bad Tölz and kept in touch even after Peter immigrated to America. That story would satisfy most of the Germans for a while.

Willie ordered the *Wienerschnitzel, which* was the favorite of most Americans and many Germans. The *Fräulein* understood Peter's *Hoch Deutsch* perfectly for which he was grateful. He knew that *Bayrisch,* the Bavarian dialect of German, was the standard in Lenggries, but was not exactly the same in their current east Bavarian forest location. Peter ordered the *Sauerbraten mit Bratkartoffeln. A* very attractive salad accompanied the meals. They ordered a *Bier, helles* style, so as to not cause further doubt about their status by ordering *Cola* or some non-traditional European drink. They wanted to project a persona of familiarity with the area and the local culture.

One of the men who had been observing the card game seemed especially interested in Peter and Willie. When Peter smiled and Willie also appeared approachable, the man came over and asked, in English, if he could sit down with them. Peter granted the request with a friendly *"Bitte schön."* They exchanged pleasantries in small talk. The two Americans were cautious, but it turned out that the friendly German just wanted to talk about his brother's war experience. He introduced himself as Karl-Heinz. His brother had been captured by the Americans in the Battle of the Bulge and sent to a POW camp in Texas. To his amazement, as his story developed, his brother was treated well and simply released in Texas after the war ended. His brother had made no attempt to return to Germany because he said he didn't want to be a part of the post-war Nazi image. This conversation was getting very interesting just as it was interrupted by the entry of two American border patrol soldiers. A lieutenant and a specialist third class from the Second AC, as they were identified by their uniform insignia, came into the *Gasthaus.* The lieutenant was obviously as shocked to see Willie as the escorial team was to see him. Peter panicked for a moment, but then realized this was a chance encounter. Their car had German plates on it and there was no other reason to suspect that American military members were inside. This must be a regular stop for them, Peter reasoned. Maybe they are on their break, or maybe they are on an unauthorized *Bier* stop. Neither happenstance concerned Willie or Peter. They just wanted to see how they would manage this first of many potential unexpected situations.

Peter could tell by the familiarity the *Gasthaus* personnel had with the lieutenant and the driver that the two border patrol agents had been there before. Without appearing anxious the team paid their bill, excused themselves and exited the

Gasthaus. The lieutenant followed and confronted them in the parking lot.

"Are you American?" asked the lieutenant.

"Yes," replied Willie.

"What are you doing here in the 5K zone?"

"We're looking for Brigitte Berg," answered Willie.

The lieutenant's face expressed surprise momentarily— then understanding. Before abruptly turning toward his vehicle and driver, he displayed his acceptance of the explanation by stating, "Carry on, men, and good hunting."

Karl-Heinz was watching from the *Kranz*. He was disappointed that the Americans had departed so abruptly when the border patrol arrived. He observed the short conversation in the parking lot, but did not see the patrol check identification. Karl-Heinz thought it was a strange contact between the American civilians and the border patrol. He couldn't visualize an alternate scenario for the Americans, he had spoken with, but if he were to guess at real scenarios, a planned border intrusion would not have been on the list. He would talk about the Americans, with some of the card players. The locals were still aware of the decade-long intrigue along the Czech border. Karl-Heinz would remember the Americans he had met that day.

TWENTY TWO

THE *TREPPENSTEINER*

It was time for Peter to get behind the wheel. Willie was cautiously nervous. "Ever drive a stick, Peter?"

"Yes, but not with a four-on-the-floor gearshift."

"I can tell. When you shift gears, it's like you are grinding out a pound of hamburger!"

"Just can the wisecracks, sergeant. I'm doing fine. I'm pulling off the road at the next rest stop."

"For what? You weren't paying attention on the way up. On these minor state roads you may never see a rest stop. You have to pee?"

"No, I just want to see if I can find reverse."

Peter pulled off the road in a clearing and struggled with the gears.

Willie laughed and said, "Put it in neutral, depress the knob and move the gearshift up and to the left."

When Peter finally found reverse, he commented that only a German would make driving a car so difficult.

"You are a German . . . one of your engineer relatives probably designed that transmission system."

They both broke into a laugh. It was their way of relieving the tenseness they felt in the *Gasthaus*. Peter did need the training both on the VW Beetle and with the roads and road signs. Peter was fiddling with the radio and eventually found AFN being broadcast from Amberg. They were talking about the anniversary of the Allied invasion of France at Normandy.

"D-Day, June 6, 1944," remarked Willie, "We wouldn't be here now and we would be speaking German if that hadn't happened."

"I do speak German, sergeant, so I can't take any credit for supporting the invasion. I was living in Tachau, playing soccer and chasing Trudi. I was a German citizen."

"Who, my friend, is Trudi?"

"A girl I knew in school. We got along very well. I remember her as a good person and very, very athletic. My mom liked her, too."

"Do you think you will ever see her again?"

"About as much chance as seeing my mother and father." Peter didn't like where this conversation was going and decided to change the subject.

The discussion returned to more immediate concerns. They talked about the day's reconnaissance and the meeting with the border patrol at the *Kranz*. Willie lamented the fact that they had to leave Karl-Heinz so quickly. He thought Karl-Heinz might eventually provide information about the border situation in the local area.

Peter asked if there would be a day soon when he could go to a PX and the American Express bank. He also wanted to send some letters to the Swansons in Snoqualmish, Sgt Grimes from Altglashütte and Corporal Mays. He wanted to

THE 5K ZONE ✸ 229

remember the people who had been so helpful in enabling his secure lifestyle.

Willie said he would check with Sgt Martinez and ask for a day soon to do that. He stated that he also had business of his own. D-Day would not be a good day since some facilities would be closed to honor the veterans. Sgt Martinez was busy with another mission and wouldn't be back until after the D-Day anniversary. They agreed that day that there was no agreement among historians as to what the "D" in D-Day stood for. "D" as a code for day similar to "H" as a code for hour in H-Hour seemed to be the consensus. It was their nature to test each other's knowledge of military trivia.

The team explored the Mähring local area while Sgt Martinez was away, but had scheduled a visit to Mt Schneeberg the next day. The Mähring ASA site was on the highest point in the area at Poppenreuth Hiltershof. Although only 781 meters at the summit, it gave the best view of Czechoslovakia east of Mähring and Bärnau. Observation of Czechoslovakia was not as useful to them to the north and south. They had been tasked with gaining intelligence information from the Tachau area and surroundings, whether by observation from West Germany or by actual on-ground intrusion into that part of Bohemia. Hoherbogen, Mähring and Mt Schneeberg were expected to provide useful surveillance information for their final report. The Mähring officer-in-charge (OIC) had been informed of their visit, as the team expected. The tour was extremely helpful with the equipment display and explanations of the types of radio communications that they could intercept and interpret.

They were treated like inspectors because the site personnel had no idea of the purpose for their visit. They had only been identified as "mission planners," which was very vague indeed.

A look around the Mähring village area took up the rest of the day. Peter recognized the *Haus Resi* on *Buchenweg* where they had met Sgt Martinez for the first time. The village was quiet with few people in sight. Willie laughed at the old lady driving a tractor through the village. She must have been eighty or more. They watched her drive that tractor until she stopped in front of a small grocery store, left it running while she climbed down like a teenager, went quickly inside, made a purchase and then drove away like this was routine. Peter said it was routine in a small village like this with very little traffic. It was Peter's opinion that she went in for a flip-top of the local *Bier* to get her through the remainder of the day.

Zollstrasse was a nearly straight-line street heading east to the border. It was only two kilometers to the border, so they followed the *Strasse, right* up to the border where they were confronted with a warning sign that declared fifty meters to the border. A single strand of chest high barbed wire didn't seem formidable, but about one hundred meters further ahead was another barrier of triple-stranded barbed wire. The top strand had insulators that were either part of an electrical system or meant to give the illusion of electrification. This was the dilemma they faced. Getting into Czechoslovakia might not be nearly as difficult as getting out. If this street were not blocked, you could follow it to the little Czech village of Broumov and on to the larger city of Marienbad. There were visible armed Czech Militia guards visible on the Czech side who were interested in what they were doing. Willie and Peter had read intelligence reports stating that persons from the West had crossed over at the invitation of the Czech guards. Whether they were drunk, crazy, or just plain stupid couldn't be verified since they were never seen again. The 5K zone for American and Allied military personnel was established, in part, for just such a possibility. Whether intentional or accidental, unauthorized military crossings into Czechoslovakia were to be prevented.

Access to the border from Mähring was also possible on a street nearly parallel to *Zollstrasse*, named *Treppensteinerstrasse*. Along the *Treppensteiner*, behind a sturdy wire fence was a bevy of roe deer. Neither of them knew the purpose of the bevy, but they were obviously restrained and not fearful of humans. At the end of the street, only meters from the border, was the *Gasthaus Treppensteiner*. The same border fence combination as on *Zollstrasse* was in view, but no guards were visible. The area surrounding the *Gasthaus* was rather unkempt and appeared to be a small rendering operation. Willie and Peter were putting two and two together. Roe deer in captivity with a rendering operation nearby! Was it a coincidence to have a *Gasthaus* serving venison meals with their overnight accommodations? The interior of the *Gasthaus* was rustic, with well-worn wooden tables and chairs. A wooden floor was divided into three small seating areas created by the presence of sturdy wooden support beams. They took a table in the middle area where they found condiments, snacks and a round plastic container marked *Tischabfälle*, or literally "table waste." They each ordered a *Radler*, which was half *Bier* and half lemon soda. The menu featured several fish dishes, the standard *Wienerschnitzel* and some *Wild* dishes, such as wild boar, rabbit and venison.

Peter thought he knew where the venison came from. They both ordered *Forellen Blau,* which was boiled trout.

The proprietor and his wife ran this *Gasthaus* by themselves as far as they could determine. Herr Hary, the owner, warmed up a little after getting over the shock of having a black stranger in his remotely-located *Gasthaus.* He turned out to be dead-pan funny when he finally decided to talk. Peter asked how the delicious gravy for the *Spätzle* was made. With a smile *Herr* Hary said it was a *"Betreibs Geheimnis,"* or business secret. Peter tried to be casual when he asked how far it was to the border. D*er Herr* smiled again and said it was close enough to kick a soccer ball into Czechoslovakia. Willie understood and asked if he had ever kicked a ball over the border. Peter translated. This time his dead-pan answer was an animated *Nein!* He didn't want to set off any Czech landmines when it hit the ground. Then he laughed, which served to further lighten his disposition and the light-hearted mood in the *Gasthaus.*

Peter asked about the World Cup soccer tournament being played in Sweden.

"Ja,"Der Herr answered, "West Germany defeated Northern Ireland 3-1, and they tied with the boys from across the fence in *Koruna* land." *Herr* Hary made a facetious reference to Czechoslovakia. "The German boys drank too much *Schnapps* the night before the game. But they made it to the quarterfinals and will play Yugoslavia on the nineteenth."

In the name of mirth and the ever-present intelligence agenda, Peter asked if any defectors had come across the nearby border fence seeking refuge in his *Gasthaus. Herr* Hary answered in the affirmative, but stated he didn't rent to them because they couldn't get their wheelbarrow full of *Koruna* through the barbed wire. The team was learning about the love the two countries had for each other. *Koruna* was the Czech currency and apparently not worth much to the Germans.

"But I did let one stay. He told me some stories." *Der Herr* was warming up very well.

"It seems that one night a young man from Broumov tried to cross carrying nothing but a new pair of jeans he had bargained for in Prague."

"What happened," Peter asked?

"He threw his jeans over the fence just before the border guards saw him; then he had to run"

"Did he get away?" Peter was translating for Willie and keeping the conversation alive.

"Yes, but they found the jeans and retrieved them."

"Did they ever catch the guy?"

Smiling again, *Herr* Hary answered in the affirmative without explaining. He was adept at telling stories and building suspense. Peter was entertained but still withholding judgment on the veracity of the story.

"How did they catch him?"

Matter-of-factly, *Herr* Hary replied, "That same night they rounded up every young man in Broumov that fit somewhere near the description of the man they had seen. Then they made them one-by-one try on the jeans until they found a person that they fit. They narrowed it down to three people. It wasn't difficult after that."

Peter and Willie thought it was funny for a moment. They might never know if it was true, but now they had developed rapport with *Der Herr*.

"Whatever happened to the guy?" asked Peter.

"They put him in prison in Prague for a year and banned him from ever coming back to Broumov."

"Ach, Du Liebe." Willie threw in his appreciation of the story so as to also be befriended by *Herr* Hary. "Did the defector ever talk about the Russians?"

"He only said that the Russians came to Marienbad for the bathhouses, but they were usually from Tachau or Prague. They did build a church in Marienbad even though they claim to be an atheistic nation."

Although the team was already aware of this, it was important to them to sharpen their contact-building skills. There was always the chance that they would learn by the sheer volume of input. Sometimes, isolated bits of information seem unimportant until combined with other stand-alone, apparently unimportant, data.

As their training had taught them, they stopped the questioning. They didn't want to appear overly interested in all things Czechoslovak until they knew more about *Herr* and *Frau* Hary. Willie asked if the deer belonged to the Harys.

Der Herr said they did and that he raised and sold them to restaurants and large rendering establishments in the *Ost Bayern Wald* in addition to serving venison in his *Gasthaus*. It was an appropriate time to get on their way, so they paid their bill and promised to return if they were in the area. They both knew that the *Treppensteiner* area would be worth another visit.

TWENTY THREE

MT SCHNEEBERG

Es corial had no schedule or routine working hours. They were to take advantage of opportunities as they appeared and to explore the advantages of odd day or odd hour occurrences in their border area of interest. During the week the team had continued their "settle-in" and enhancement of their familiarity with the MI detachment administration. They did map study after each reconnaissance and worked on their weekly progress report for Major Taylor. The trip to the PX had been helpful. Script dollars were exchanged for DM, letters were mailed at the APO and non-perishable personal items were purchased. Peter assumed the mission would run for six months or longer, so he purchased accordingly not knowing when he would get another chance to return. With proper registration documents for the vehicle and a valid military ID card, entry was allowed at most US Facilities even with West German license plates on the car.

Sunday, June 15 . . . Sgt Martinez had returned on Friday from his involvement in a separate MI mission that he was supervising. On Sunday morning he and the team departed early for the ASA site at Mt Schneeberg. They paralleled the border as far as Neualbenreuth in order to take advantage of a Sunday morning view along the border, before they headed west. Passing through several of the villages they heard the church bells calling the devoted to church. All were dressed in their finest, which was sometimes their only clothing.

The westerly drive was pleasant with a subdued contented mood apparent for the churchgoers. Peter thought this was an indisputable example of a healing nation. What was going through any of their minds fifteen years after the end of the war couldn't be known by Peter, but he could surmise that it wasn't completely dissimilar from his own thoughts. It was a cool but clear morning that found most people in the villages walking. Peter was a little uncomfortable riding in the cramped jeep for such a long period of time. It was taking more than the two hours they had projected because of unscheduled stops and detours. The frequency-modulated radio mounted in the rear of the jeep was taking up space, but did provide communications with both Mt Schneeberg and the MI facility in Mähring. A sedan hadn't been available for them; Peter was getting some practice as the radio operator, but just routine radio checks for the most part. Peter thought it was doubtful that Mt Schneeberg could communicate with Hoherbogen even though they were both elevated and had an excellent line-of-sight. He didn't yet know if the two facilities had any other direct communication method. The communication system for the four facilities the team would be using for support was something they would have to learn more about. It would be helpful, Peter thought, to know what all three listening posts could observe at any given time. Later, he would learn that the MI detachment in Mähring did indeed have both telephone and radio communication with all three listening posts.

Sgt Martinez explained the current situation at Mt Schneeberg as they grew closer. The facility had been in operation for several years. The site had duties similar to the duties of Hoherbogen, but was further developed and had a more advanced capability. High frequency radio intercept was their primary mission. They had partial visual observation of the Fulda Gap, which was especially useful in clear weather. This was the northernmost location that the team had been assigned to reconnoiter but it didn't mean the US and NATO interests stopped here. The sergeant explained that other positions were located to the north; Point Alpha was the closest. The Fourteenth Armored Cavalry had a defensive responsibility in that area. Point Alpha also had a partial view of the Fulda Gap. They did electronic surveillance and were charged with early-warning responsibility. In the event of a Warsaw Pact invasion they were to abandon Point Alpha and fall back to prepared defensive positions. These positions were located where they had more than a fighting chance to slow the invaders before serious damage was done. That the Fulda Gap provided a clear shot to Frankfurt and the Rhein River was a major concern to those responsible for the defense of western Europe. The Schneeberg facility was enclosed by a fence with trained dogs and German guards. Many of the guards were former German soldiers who had been screened and cleared for loyalty. Czech interpreters were scheduled to be assigned but hadn't yet arrived. Peter thought it would be interesting to speak Czech with someone other than Willie. He knew that neither of them

could pass for a native Czech because of their accents and because of the fluency that identifies a native language speaker.
Improvement over time could be expected with continual usage, but perfect fluency was not likely.

There was a mess hall on the site which they would visit
for lunch. An operations building also housed some of the ra-
dio-intercept equipment. The families of most accompanied
soldiers lived in Bischofsgrün at the base of the mountain. Mt
Schneeberg was at an elevation of 1051 meters, slightly lower
than Hoherbogen. Bischofsgrün was outside the 5K zone, so
the US personnel in the area need only be careful to not enter unwittingly. It was possible to get an entry pass for rare
personal business, but justifications for that were difficult and
seldom requested.

Around the Bischofsgrün area you could always find vacationers as the economy improved. In the winter the nearby
ski-jump at Ochsenkopf was popular. In the summer the area
was frequented by dog-walkers, hikers, mountain-bikers and
other nature lovers. Summer ski-jumping was also popular by
using a combination of porcelain, fiberglass and wet plastic
grass for a take-off and landing slope.

The single guys had found several places, like the *Tanz
Café Reismann*, to meet some *Fräuleins* and have a *Bier* after
their work trick. German-American friendship was thriving,
which was a testament to the resiliency of the German people.
Fifteen years ago some of them wanted to kill Americans. Now
they want to be America's best friends by inviting the families
to their annual summer solstice celebration and other local
events. The Germans find a way to celebrate anything and everything. Reasons abound—from commemorating historical

events to celebrating natural events. It's all good reason to do things like ignite huge bonfires and drink *Bier,* as in the solstice celebration. Bischofsgrün was a wonderful little village of half-timbered buildings and a laid-back way of life. It was changing, however, as more and more tourist money found its way to the local economy. The US dependent wives were ecstatic when they arrived in Bischofsgrün. Their husbands had to find a place for the family to live before they could get authority to bring them from their permanent homes at government expense; however, that wasn't hard to do at the present because the soldiers had more money to pay for rent than the typical West German citizen. The American families tended to get some of the best rentals in this scenic vacation village. The wives were happy even though the jobs of the soldiers provided an ominous reality in their lives. They all knew they wouldn't have been here if there wasn't a threat. They realized the border was close and that they could be vulnerable in the event of an invasion attempt.

The tour that day was similar to what they had accomplished at Hoherbogen; time had enabled more advanced development and site proficiency. Some construction was still in progress, but the team understood the site's relevance to their mission. Every time Peter looked out over the Czech countryside, thoughts of his parents and his friends, like Trudi Kehle, recurred. It was difficult for him to adjust to the reality of being so close to "home," but still so far away. The fact that he may have to go into Czechoslovakia twice, with life-threatening implications both times, always brought back that familiar knot in his stomach. Today was no exception, but he was handling it well once again.

TWENTY FOUR

FRAU DREXLER

Tuesday, June 17, 1958 . . . The team orientation was complete. They had toured the primary es corial support sites in their area of operation from Hoherbogen in the south to Mt Schneeberg in the north. They knew they would obtain needed equipment and up-to-date intelligence data from the MI detachment in Mähring. Their mission was to seek out possible clandestine entry points or other methods of entry into the Tachau area for the purpose of intelligence gathering. If the Warsaw Pact conducted training exercises in the Fulda Gap area, the US Forces wanted to know every possible detail about their intentions and capability. Information concerning Pact participants, types of equipment and numbers of personnel was extremely important to US Forces intelligence. Willie and Peter had decided that if only one of them would make the attempt to enter and gather information, it would be Peter. Willie would be his first level of security and mission support.

The team decided to make an extended reconnaissance to the south of Mähring because they hadn't yet explored that area in detail. Willie requested and received a per diem authorization for the team for four days. They departed in the VW Beetle and were due to return on Friday.

First on the agenda was to drive along the border as close as they could with occasional stops in select villages for visual inspections. The first night would be at the southernmost boundary of their target area near Rimbach. Passing Second AC vehicles on the road was normal, but relatively infrequent. For the most part these border patrol vehicles were wheeled jeeps or heavy trucks. There was the occasional tracked armored personnel carrier (APC) with a fifty caliber machine gun mounted. On one occasion they saw an M48A2 Patton tank nestled in an opening in the forest. These encounters were not surprising to the team. But what was surprising was the number of non-Second AC US military vehicles in the area south of Bärnau. They hadn't been informed about the cargo vehicles they encountered. Willie made a note on his daily log. The German border patrol was also in evidence examining maps and exchanging information with the American patrols. Civilians seemed to take all this in stride. The team had been told that the civilians were not much of a problem because they knew the military and border patrol activity was necessary to maintain stability for them in the border area.

Peter wanted to go through Altglashütte for the sake of nostalgia, if nothing else. He remembered vividly escaping from Czechoslovakia and being rescued by the Americans. That was twelve years ago but seemed like yesterday. Sgt Grimes had been a partner on many reconnaissance missions in the Altglashütte border area. Peter felt that his familiarity with the area would be a definite advantage for their local Altglashütte reconnaissance.

The former 472nd Public Affairs company bivouac area was barely recognizable. If it hadn't been for two white birch trees standing on a slight rise where the headquarters tent had been located, he wouldn't have recognized the past bivouac area at all. He reminded Willie of the stories he had related about his time with the Americans on this location. He reflected on his fear and insecurity of those times. Intimidating would be the most descriptive word he could use now. Minimal English language capability, strange-looking soldiers and the uncertainty of his future made those times frightening and overwhelming for a thirteen-year-old boy.

Peter remembered the culvert he had encountered just before crossing over the Lesná road while the outpost guards were distracted by their dog chasing the roe deer. They searched briefly for the upslope end of the culvert, hoping to get lucky. Since water obviously would have been flowing down the hillside, they searched for small valley inclinations, but found nothing. Peter wasn't sure the culvert would be useful even if they found it, but it was a matter of leaving no possibilities untested, as they had been instructed. Logic dictated that there was a beginning and an end to the culvert, but where the beginning might be was difficult to imagine without having access to the end. Peter's guess was that the end he had stumbled upon was across the border in Czechoslovakia. They decided to give it up for the moment and enter that information on their after action report for Major Taylor. The 472nd had occupied an area a short distance from the Schützhaus on the southwest of the very small community. Peter had never ventured into the village built-up area and saw no need to look around there now. There was a *Gasthaus* called the *Blei* where they might find some useful information at a later time.

Following along state routes they sometimes paralleled the border and other times the road again distanced them from the border. When their maps showed secondary roads to the east that looked interesting, they took secondary road exploratory excursions. Many times these roads just ended abruptly at the fifty meter zone warnings and at other times a road would semi-circle back to the state road. It was evident to them that there were many potential intrusion points. The worry was twofold: what about mines, dogs and guards on the other side, and once penetrated, how is return possible?

The only authorized border checkpoint was located in Bärnau, as they had been briefed. This checkpoint was established to allow controlled movement back and forth across the border. Movement from east to west was seldom allowed and usually only for older persons. West zone and East zone administrators and security guards checked authorization papers from stations a few hundred meters apart. In between was a no-man's land that was usually technically controlled and used by the East as a buffer zone. Passage was allowed for official business and sometimes family reasons. The crossing checks were used primarily as a deterrent to defectors and spies. Neither side trusted the other, but like many processes emanating from the East, there was a certain favoritism in the granting of passes—for no apparent reason. This fact kept both sides on the alert. The simple question always was, "If this person has no apparent reason to cross, why has this person been provided with an exit/entry permit?"

The team made an early decision that the area of interest

would have to be reduced. That was what the reconnaissance was all about, they agreed. The similarity of access potential and the increased distance from entry to the Tachau area influenced that decision. They didn't want to leave so much distance, from entry point to Tachau, that it increased the chance of detection. They knew they were not under any unreasonable time deadline and could expand their search in the future if it became necessary. The reentry problem would be the most difficult phase of the mission for which they needed to find a solution. They decided to concentrate on the border area between Waidhaus in the south to Mähring as a northern end point. Bärnau provided the shortest distance to Tachau, had the interesting authorized border crossing stations and seemed to always gain their attention for one reason or another. They were still puzzled about the unexplained US Forces vehicles in that area that they had observed.

On the first night they would get rooms in Waidhaus. From *Bundestrasse* fourteen, they turned east just before reaching Waidhaus. Very close to the border they found the *Gasthof Frölich* and a nearby *Zimmer Frei* (bed and breakfast). It seemed to be perfect for a meal at the *Gasthof* and inexpensive rooms at the private residence *Zimmer Frei*. If they were lucky they might find a talkative proprietor in the breakfast nook the next morning.

A *Zimmer Frei* often provides a hearty breakfast for the guests. Frau Drexler served a standard, but very appetizing breakfast: *Brötchen, Wurst and Käse,* with *Kaffee* or *Tee* for the main offerings, with *Butter, Marmelade, Joghurt* and a soft-boiled *Ei,* if desired. Peter was familiar with the food: the bread roll, quality cold cuts, cheese and coffee or tea as well as the butter, marmalade and egg served at a typical Bavarian breakfast. Willie had limited experience with this type of breakfast, but thoroughly enjoyed the quality and variety. *Frau* Drexler was quite curious about the American "tourists." This was good for the team because a conversation ensued without the appearance of unusual interest by the team.

"What are you doing here in Waidhaus," she asked. Her English was good, even though she had stated she hadn't used it much since school days. She said the American border patrol had stayed with her once.

"We are just curious about life along the border. We weren't in the war, but Willie was stationed in Bad Tölz a few years ago."

"Life here is getting better. We had some bad times during the war and right after when the expellees and refugees came across. The rooms you stayed in last night were occupied by a family that fled the Sudetenland. It was tough for us because we didn't have much and they had nothing, but we still had to share. The last days of the war are still vivid in my memory."

Frau Drexler seemed to be searching her memory with a slight fear in her eyes. "The Americans were the first to come to Waidhaus. . . I think it was May 5, 1945."

Willie asked, "Were you happy to see them?"

"No, it was war. We didn't know what to expect. The Americans had been bombing us with artillery, mostly at night. I was a young mother who had to feed and protect my five-year-old daughter. During the daylight hours we would hunt for food in the village and then at night we went to the cellar at the *Gasthaus* for protection."

"The *Gasthaus Frölich?*"Willie asked.

"Yes, almost everybody stayed there at night for protection . . . mostly women and children."

Frau Drexler continued, "One evening after the bombing stopped, we heard someone speaking English and trying to open the cellar door which was above some steep stairs. When it opened, we thought we were going to die. A big black man was pointing his gun at us and shouting *'Alle Raus! Alle Raus!'* My daughter, Barbara, and all the other children were crying and sobbing 'mama, mama.' "

Her description brought back some memories of wartime Tachau for Peter. His empathy for *Frau* Drexler was overwhelming. Peter tried to control his emotions with a question. "The war was ending. Why were the Americans so aggressive?"

"We later found out that our *Burgermeister* was a Nazi and was still fighting. He wouldn't give up. He and his sympathizers were killed that same day. We were treated well by the Americans after they took control. Then the Russians came in for a short time until the new border was established. We still have the same border."

Difficult as it was to hear this story, the team had to maintain the tourist charade. The team knew the difference between expellee, and refugee, but Willie asked for clarification so they would appear to have more of a tourist curiosity.

"Expellees were forced out of the Sudetenland by the Czechs. Refugees fled on their own without the knowledge of the Czechs. It was just a matter of semantics. The Czechs wanted to control those exiting for security and for their own feeling of power, I suppose. The expellees went to designated locations in the Russian-controlled area of Germany. The fortunate expellees were shipped to the West. Almost all of the refugees tried to get to the West."

She didn't know that Peter was a 1946 refugee.

Peter asked, "If you had nothing, why did you take in the refugees?"

"Because the Americans forced us to do that. It was either make room for as many as possible or risk losing your house entirely. Most refugees were first moved to camps that were available and then later relocated further west."

Because the conversation seemed to evolve without specific intent, Peter's questions penetrated a little deeper into the border situation. "Do people still come across the border?"

"Yes, but not as often as a few years ago. Security on the border is tighter all the time. Just recently they installed floodlights. At first they were on all night so some of my neighbors shot them out. Now they only turn them on when they are looking for someone or just to test them."

"How do the refugees get across," asked Willie?

"They just find the right location. Landmines and electrified barbed wire are not everywhere and can sometimes be disabled. Guards in towers can't see everything in valley depressions or in foggy weather. Usually escape attempts come after months, or even years, of studying a specific location. And, of course, fewer and fewer people make it across these days. Many are captured or killed during their attempt."

"Why don't they make a mass assault on a weak border security area?"

"That's because not everyone wants to come across. Some are secure enough where they are and some have bought into the communist doctrine. From what I've heard, escape attempts have to be planned clandestinely. Neighbors don't trust neighbors."

The team was finding this conversation very informative, but didn't want it to continue into disinterest, so Willie took the exchange in another direction.

"Do people ever cross from west to east," he asked.

"Yes," Frau Drexler smiled: "criminals, people running from a bad marriage, people escaping debts and even some who want to test the communist lifestyle. There are many reasons. Some have family members that can't get out and some think they can hide their Nazi past more easily in the East. We've even had cases of border breaches to the East and then back to the West by the same disillusioned people. They say life can be very bad in the East for people not valuable to the communists."

Conversation with Frau Drexler was indeed informative. The team had plenty to digest already and they were just getting started.

TWENTY FIVE

THE CULVERT

June 18, 1958 . . . From the Drexler *Zimmer Frei* the team drove north in search of the road that most closely paralleled the border. Secondary roads took them through little villages like Pfälzerhof and Frankenreuth as they tried to hug the border. The border in this area was the Rohlingbach stream. It appeared to be easy to swim across or maybe even walk across in some spots. That wouldn't get you into Czechoslovakia, however, because some type of barrier would need to be breached even after crossing the stream.

Often they found themselves the object of a farmer's curiosity. They were strangers and obviously spending a lot of time visually surveying the area. The fact that they drove down some dead-end roads and then circled back into the village created some suspicious curiosity, although the people of the villages were more curious than suspicious. Curiosity was the inevitable result of enduring many years of border intrigue and escape attempts, omnipresent border patrols and inquisitive border sightseers. They stopped in the village of Reichenau for a rest break and map study. Near a small kettle lake they found a picnic table to use for spreading their maps. They were busily engaged in map study when a middle-aged farmer approached.

"*Grüß Gott*," he offered, which was a common Bavarian greeting term. Peter soon discovered that he spoke no English but was curious about their activities. He identified himself as the administrator of fishing regulations locally. He had authority over the kettle lake and a defined area of the Rohlingbach stream. He wanted to help them with fishing questions, he said. Peter was sure he was curious if they had anything other than fishing on their minds.

"No, we don't fish. We are American tourists just exploring. We're not sure where we want to explore next, so we were looking over the maps."

The man was familiar with border-curious people, and not unfamiliar with people assisting with planned escapes. Americans involved in that would be unusual, but over the years he had learned that nothing was out of the question when it came to the border.

"We know we are close to the border and are being careful not to get too close. How far is it from here?" inquired Peter.

"About a hundred meters. You don't want to go any closer. That's another reason I came to talk to you. It's easy to make a mistake."

"I thought so. We saw a fifty meter warning sign earlier. So what is in the hills west of here? It looks very heavily forested on the map."

"You can drive most of the way to the top. There are some hiking trails through the cattle grazing area and a few benches where you can rest and have a great view of Czechoslovakia."

"That's funny, you can look at, but not touch Czechoslovakia!"

"You can see all the way to Tachau on clear days. It's about fifteen kilometers."

Peter couldn't resist asking, "Do you ever get bothered by the Czech border guards with lights or explosions or anything like that."

"Not lately . . . but a few years ago, yes. There are no lights in this area yet, but I won't be surprised when the Czechs install them."

"OK, thanks. I think we will take a drive up in the hills. Thanks for everything."

On the west side of the village, they found a dirt and gravel road leading up a moderately-inclined hill. Peter noted in the after-action report notebook what they had found in Reichenau. Near the top of the hill they found a parking place. There was a bench with a great view in the direction of Tachau. They walked around the area without letting their vehicle get out of sight. The equipment and classified material it contained had to be safeguarded. They passed through a cattle-securing electrified gate area which could be opened with insulated grips for the convenience of hikers. Embedded in the earth directly under the gate was a *Weiderost* which was a device with raised parallel metal strips separated by just enough space to not allow the cattle to get firm footing. The cattle had learned through years of experience to not even attempt a crossing if they didn't want a broken leg. The *Weiderost* was installed as a safeguard in case the gate was left open by hikers or vandals.

The view was the main interest for the team. This could be used to supplement the information they received from Mt

Schneeberg, Hoherbogen and Mähring. Willie had a great view with the binoculars and commented that it looked like peaceful farm and forest country. He didn't notice any moving or stationary vehicles.

Peter took a look with the binoculars as far north as the trees would allow and noticed an unoccupied guard tower apparently on the Czech side of the border. Like Willie, Peter saw nothing else unusual.

Their interest in Reichenau was basically a function of its proximity to Tachau. Only ten kilometers because of how the border snaked out and formed a bubble-looking map feature toward Tachau; it was only one kilometer more than from the border at Bärnau by their preliminary estimate. The farmer/fishing supervisor had apparently given his best estimate of fifteen kilometers. At this point they favored a crossing at Bärnau, for distance reason, if nothing better was found. It still depended on the return from Czechoslovakia; nothing would be more important than the return route.

State route 2154 was the closest primary north-south highway along the border when they resumed their northerly route, but again, didn't always afford the views of the border that they wanted. It was time-consuming because of the detours and frequent dead-ends. It did, however, give some excellent opportunities to inspect the border barriers without local citizen observation. Often there was a guard tower on the east side with armed soldiers watching over their assigned section of the border. The team almost always found at least two rolls of barbed wire; sometimes they found the standard three with electrical insulators on the top roll. There was a smoothed road on the Czech side of the border barriers that would allow a small vehicle to pass within meters of the barbed wire. Apparently this was for the use of motor-powered patrols. The road was laid in two strips with perforated concrete blocks to accommodate the wheels of a small vehicle. The concrete blocks were inexpensive to use for construction and would help disperse wet weather runoff. Across the road was a smooth raked area meant to show footprints of intruders. This strip of soft, raked earth was about ten to fifteen meters wide. Team briefings had emphasized that this raked strip was often mined, although Peter and Willie could not identify mines in this area with their binoculars. The towers were located in areas meant to provide maximum overlapping visibility of the border. Generally the towers were about twenty-five to fifty meters from the soft strip. No lights were visible here, but they did notice the ladder-like steps at the rear of the tower platform. Rope, or some kind of lifting device, was seen hanging over the back of the tower. Presumably this was used to lift weapons, ammunition and other equipment to the platform. The west side of the border was not much more than a single roll of barbed wire and warning signs. They took some pictures and noted precise locations. Between Neudorf and Altglashütte there were several similar locations. This area deserved further consideration, in their opinion, and was duly noted in the log.

As they approached the Altglashütte area Peter was again reminded of the culvert he had encountered near the Lesná road. He knew that the opening he had found was in Czechoslovakia. If they could find the other end in West German territory it could be a promising lead for follow-up. That might be a very long culvert; however, the culvert was a long shot worth investigating. But that was what this reconnaissance was all about—exploring all possibilities. How the culvert could have been overlooked by both the Czechs and the Allies was puzzling—adding to the mystery. Never lacking in imagination, Peter imagined the possibility of a long ago buried culvert to allow for the construction of a farming road that wouldn't flood over. It was possible that after that time the stream dried up when German farmers dammed it on higher ground to provide irrigation water for their crops.

Willie was sure that if the culvert existed, it would be in a slight depression or valley to which the water would be directed by gravity. They concentrated on finding these features when they reached possible areas. Peter remembered the area somewhat from his escape and his days as a reconnaissance assistant with Sgt Grimes. They couldn't find anything by following probable water flow paths. All leads ended in flat dispersion zones before they even got near the border. As one last-ditch effort, Peter suggested finding ponds or water retention areas on the flat land above and searching for evidence of old run-off routes.

Fortunately, no curious farmers were to be seen as they searched for, and found, two water-retention ponds. One appeared to be man-made with no input source or need for damming. The other, however, had a water source from the hills to the west and was dammed on the east side. They got excited and quickly followed the dry stream bed downhill. Near the border in a deep debris-covered depression, they found a raised, rounded rock outcrop. Willie was curious and slid down to the outcrop. He dug with his hands at the edge of the outcrop until he found something solid.

"Come here, Peter, I have something." Peter joined in the digging. Eventually they uncovered a large drainage pipe.

"Would you believe? This is incredible," Peter exclaimed excitedly, "This could go right under the border barriers!"

"Yes, but we don't know how far it goes."

"What should we do? We can't go in there without knowing where it goes or if we can even pass through."

They calmed down and explored the area trying to ascertain exactly where they were and where the border was. They decided they were close enough to list this culvert as an item for further investigation. They returned to the culvert entrance and gave it a thorough inspection. It was large enough in diameter on the inside to allow a human to crawl through, but with difficulty. It was dark a few meters into the aperture and contained forest-floor debris. They covered the opening with the debris they had dislodged and some dead tree branches. They wanted to disguise the exposed earth and any evidence of their digging. The location was noted and entered into their log. They studied the area carefully so they could find it again, if necessary. Willie thought it would be no problem to find if they followed the retention pond's old creek bed, like they did this time. What a surprise for Peter that this discovery was so close to where he had spent his first days in the American zone of Germany after escape from the former Sudetenland.

Further north, on the Bärnau southern perimeter, they found access to the border blocked by closed roads. The state highway was the only way to get from Altglashütte to Bärnau because all the secondary roads leading to the east were closed with *Sprengstoff* (explosives) signs posted. The mystery was getting deeper. First, they had seen unidentified US Forces vehicles and now a warning of explosives in the same restricted area. That they had not been informed of the activity here was especially perplexing. They would get answers back in Mähring, but for now it was evident that a closer look around Bärnau was warranted. They drove in a westerly direction through Thanhausen and turned toward Bärnau in Hohenthan. They passed through an under-construction *Geschictspark* which had a small restaurant and the beginnings of a history museum. That would be interesting, indeed, thought Peter. He could probably add a chapter to their story. In the center of Bärnau they found a rather lively community. Shops were open, people were scurrying about and drivers were giving the typical "crazy" sign to other drivers by pointing to their head with their index finger, scowling and mumbling something unintelligible. Peter chuckled when Willie commented that things were returning to normalcy since his last visit. *Bahnhofstrasse*—with no useable *Bahnhof*—was one of the busier streets in Bärnau. Peter could envision the day when trainloads of expellees from Tachau passed through the then useable train station on this street. He wondered if his parents had been among them. Was it possible that they were living somewhere in West Germany? They would be in their fifties now—still in the prime of their lives.

Back on the south perimeter of Bärnau they spotted another US Forces vehicle being allowed passage into the area marked *Sprengstoff*. The vehicle was marked with a transportation battalion identification. Could this be an ammunition storage area? If so, why hadn't they been informed? The perimeter security personnel were all German, which would be normal for a US Forces ammunition dump. This was a puzzling situation, but answers would have to wait. They had more work to do after a lunch break.

The *Gasthaus Blei* was a short drive back in the direction of Altglashütte but they agreed that the chances of overhearing useful information were better there than in Bärnau. The *Gasthaus Blei* had only a few tables. The bartender / waiter was working alone since it was afternoon and only one other patron was present. As usual, the patron acted very surprised to see a black man. He showed his interest immediately with constant glances at their table. Willie noticed that the man had crutches leaning against the wall near his table. They ordered a *Bier* and were informed that because it was between meals the only warm food was *Wiener Wurst* with *Kartoffel Salat* (potato salad), if desired.

The patron told them the *Wiener* was very good and asked if they were Americans working in the depot, as he called it. Sensing a potential information source Willie asked him to join them with his self-taught German and a few explanatory hand signs.

"No, we're just tourists," Peter answered in English for Willie's benefit and because the man preferred to test his English skills. The man needed the crutches to cross the room. He was an amputee below the knee of his right leg. He introduced himself as "Christian."

"American tourists in a border village are unusual," he replied suspiciously. "Most Americans that come through here are working in, or visiting the depot."

"We saw American vehicles entering the depot. What kind of place is it?"

"I thought you could tell me. Nobody in Bärnau knows. The guards don't know any more than we know. All we really know is that loaded heavy cargo trucks come out of there almost every day. We know they are loaded because we can hear them gearing down to get up the hill."

"That is interesting," said Peter. He suppressed the urge to comment about more intrigue along the border.

"How long have you lived in the village?" Willie was entering the conversation.

"I was born here. In 1939, I was conscripted into the *Wehrmacht* (German Army), but was only gone about a year when I had a training accident. That's how I lost my leg. They couldn't find a job for me so I got lucky and they sent me home."

"What was in the restricted area during the war," Willie asked?

"It was just an open wooded area, until the Nazis took control. We never knew what they were doing there, but they sure brought in a lot of heavy equipment. Now the rumor is that prisoners from the camp at Flossenburg were working there. There was no border because the Sudetenland was already a part of Germany. Nonetheless, the area was marked for military use only."

These revelations were astounding to the team. What could the Nazis have been doing that encouraged the Americans to take it over and keep its use classified? Why they weren't informed during briefings bothered them more and more with each new discovery..

Christian—still suspicious—asked if it was an ammunition storage area.

"We have no idea . . . what do you think?"

"All we know is that there is some digging going on. The Nazis dug and now the Americans continue to dig."

"How do you know that," Willie asked?

"Because I and other village people have seen the trucks haul debris and rocks away from there for many years. The truck cargo beds are always covered now, but I've retrieved some large pieces of granite rock that fell off a truck."

This one-legged ex-soldier's story was becoming more and more credible as he continued his account. Willie and Peter were having difficulty containing their excitement. They didn't want to stray from the "tourist" cover, but one last question needed an answer to satisfy them.

"Where could they dispose of the rock cargo if it really is rock?"

"We were so curious that one night my friend Jacob and I followed a truck in Jacob's car all the way to Grafenwoehr. The truck went into the American training range. We didn't try to follow, but assumed there was plenty of space to unload their cargo without being observed by inquisitive eyes and raising the question of what it was and where it came from."

They finished their *Wiener Wurst* with *Kartoffel Salat* and graciously excused themselves. Their heads were spinning with questions evolving from the encounter. It was time to find lodging for the evening.

TWENTY SIX

FINDING TRUDI

In need of a little relaxation the team chose the *Gasthof Zur Post* in central Bärnau for their overnight. It appeared to be a popular destination for the locals with advertisement of live music that evening. Rooms were upstairs above the restaurant which could make sleeping rather difficult until the music stopped. Surprisingly, there was a raised, but still low, stage-like area for the musicians. The *Silbermond* was slated to perform that night. Featuring a guitarist, drummer, a bass player and a female singer, it looked interesting to the team. The *Silbermond,* or Silver Moon, was scheduled to begin performing at 2000 hours. Willie and Peter settled in their room which they found equipped with two beds, two wooden chairs, a clothes closet and a wash basin. Toilet and shower were "down the hall." Lighting was dim from small lamps at each bedside. A steam radiator under the lone window was out of operation for the summer months. The top of the window could be slanted inward toward the room for ventilation or opened conventionally by turning the prominent window handle. A simple room, but adequate for an overnight.

At 1930 hours they went downstairs to get a table and order a meal. The *Fräulein* who tended their table had a typical reaction to the presence of Willie. Willie was accustomed to this reaction as normal after his months of experience in West Germany and Peter was beginning to expect the reaction to Willie as quite normal. Many of the tables near the bandstand were already occupied so they had chosen one toward the back of the room. They relaxed with a *Bier* and an excellent hot meal. The band was setting up and people were coming and going. Some families with children departed when they finished their meal, while others appeared to be there to enjoy the music for the rest of the evening.

The *Fräulein* waitress was very attentive to their table and seemed very pleased when they ordered a second *Bier*. In the best German he could manage, Willie asked her name.

She smiled and answered, "Gisela."

Willie was quite relaxed now and pleased that she understood him. West Germans had begun to study English routinely in school, but not all cared about English because they had little chance to use it in their daily lives. This was especially true where Americans and other English-speakers were not commonly found.

The *Gasthof* was filling with people who had come for the entertainment. As dinner-only groups departed, entertainment seekers filled the empty tables. To the Americans, people-watching was part of the fun. Willie recognized one of the first songs the *Silbermond* performed. He didn't know all the words, but sang along as he heard the group singing, "*Marina, Marina, Marina . . . wunderbar das Mädchen.*"

Peter thought Willie's singing was funny. He asked what the

words meant in a teasing manner. Willie smiled and stopped Gisela as she passed by. He said something to her that Peter couldn't understand. When she smiled again and answered, Willie thanked her, turned to Peter and said, "It means, Marina, the wonderful girl."

Peter laughed, and said, "Willie you are a hoot. When we get back to Bad Tölz we will have to go out and find a Marina or two."

They were relaxing and bonding beyond that required by mission responsibility. Peter had been people watching as the evening progressed. These people were his people whose recent life experiences had been dramatically different than his. One *Fräulein,* accompanied by an older lady, especially interested Peter. That *Fräulein* seemed vaguely familiar. She was obviously looking after the old lady and treating her to a night out. They had found a table very close to the low stage and were thoroughly enjoying the music and food. They both appeared to be drinking wine.

Peter noticed that the older lady had turned to see what everyone was looking at near their table. A black man in Bärnau was unusual indeed. When the *Fräulein* turned to look, Peter got a better view. This *Fräulein* is beautiful, thought Peter. He couldn't take his eyes off of her. The *Fräulein's* eyes caught his, their gazes locked momentarily, then she looked away. She said something to the older lady before letting her head sag slightly as if in deep thought.

She made several surreptitious glances at their table as Peter began to conceptualize the possibilities. He didn't know anyone in this village and hadn't been in West Germany long enough for this to be a chance meeting of a recent contact. The possibilities were dwindling. He was tensing up with thoughts of the only possibilities remaining. It could be a case of mistaken identity or, as unlikely as the possibility was, it could be someone who had been in his life a long time ago.

As the band returned after their break, the mysterious *Fräulein* stepped forward from her table and talked briefly with the songstress. The lady nodded her head in agreement and said something to the band leader. The band leader then seemed to notify the other band members what the next song would be.

As strains of *"Lili Marlene"* were heard softly in the background, the songstress seductively dedicated the song to the man in the back of the room and gave credit to the pretty requesting *Fräulein*. Peter realized then, that this was a test. He hardly heard the words in his excitement. *"Vor der Kaserne, vor dem Grossem Tor."*

Peter stood up. Willie called to him as he moved quickly toward the *Fräuleins* table: *"Wie eins, Lili Marlene."* The song continued; Peter ignored Willie.

The beautiful *Fräulein* saw him coming and stood to face him. "Trudi!" He thought he was whispering, but his excitement made it a shout. The diners, sensing something special, were watching curiously.

"Peter! I wasn't sure it was you. It has been twelve years since you left Tachau."

Almost as soon as she uttered the words she realized they shouldn't have acknowledged each other so publicly because she sensed this chance meeting could arouse more than casual curiosity if she was being watched. She didn't understand the reason for Peter's presence in the *Gasthof*. Her astonishment had temporarily blinded her normally coherent thinking.

It was confusing and could have been chaotic had quick

thinking and cooler heads not prevailed. This was a chance meeting of old friends with new and dangerous implications. They moved outside as discreetly as possible. Trudi's *Oma* followed, then a confused Sgt Kyles. Out of hearing range of anybody nearby, they stopped.

"How did you get here, Peter? Where have you been for twelve years?"

Peter thought it was safe to offer an explanation, but warned that *Oma* shouldn't be told anything. "I live in America now, Trudi. I am in the US Army stationed in Bad Tölz. I am on assignment here."

Trudi realized this wasn't the time or place for details, so she skipped to the immediate basics." I understand. I know American soldiers are not supposed to be in what they call the 5K zone. You must be on border patrol or your assignment must be very important. I still live in Tachau, but I have an authorized pass to visit my grandmother who lives in the nearby village of Thanhausen. I must be back at the border crossing point by 1300 tomorrow." Trudi was trying to relate all the important information quickly with short choppy sentences.

"Where can we safely talk?" Peter was torn between security and the desire to continue this conversation. They were both nervous about the chance encounter because both had reasons to not be seen together.

"Meet me at the *Geschichtspark* tomorrow at 0800. Follow the *Waldpfad Bich*l path to the first bench. I run there quite often, so it won't be unusual for me to be seen there. The Czechs used to follow me with their agents in Bärnau, but it should be safe tomorrow. I know places near the path where we can talk in private."

The picture was clearing now. It was evident that they both needed security and time to evaluate their chance meeting. They said good-bye for the evening so that Trudi and *Oma* could get a ride to Thanhausen with a neighbor who had accompanied them. Willie was as dumbfounded as was Peter.

"Can this be real . . . ? This changes everything. I can hardly wait to hear what transpires at your meeting tomorrow. We need another *Bier* before we turn in."

And Peter agreed; a *Bier* was in order!

Thursday, June 19, 1958 . . . Trudi approached on the *Waldpfad Bichl* right on time. Peter remembered that she was always on time if not early. Dressed in her running clothes, she still appeared to be the stereotypical superwoman. Lithe and strong, but not muscle-bound, her presence made him slightly nervous because of her beauty and bearing combined with the surprising events of the past twelve hours. They embraced briefly before Trudi began to speak. Very seriously she warned that she had to be careful who she met or talked to because she was occasionally followed.

"We are alone right now, though, because I picked a place to meet where I go often. They know I am serious about my conditioning. My boss is a Russian sports enthusiast and has plans for me. I train for me and to keep him happy. That is why I have authority to visit my grandmother in Thanhausen. But first, tell me what happened to you after you left Tachau? How did you get away? It was two years after you left before I could get back to the *Blitzbaum* to read your letter."

"Do you know where my parents are?"

Trudi's expression soured somewhat as she replied, "Not really, Peter, but I suspect it isn't good. I believe they were shipped to the Russian zone of Germany. Things got even worse after you left. I was happy for you when you disappeared because I knew you were strong and capable enough to take care of yourself. Your parents were gone within weeks after you left, and your house was occupied by a Czech family."

Peter had held out hope for many years that his parents were safe, but was prepared for the worst. There was still hope, which he never abandoned, but this information was not entirely unexpected. Trudi didn't tell the stories of the inhumanity of the expulsions, opting to break those circumstances to him slowly.

"But Peter, tell me your story. What have you been doing and why are you here now?"

Peter gave the details of his escape, his time with both the US Army in Altglashütte and the resettlement camp in Weiden. He spoke glowingly of the Waldbaus in Nandlstadt and the entire trip to Snoqualmish. He told of his student days at the University of Washington and subsequent enlistment in the US Army.

"I structured my life to get back here. I am on assignment and it has to do with Tachau."

Trudi was nervously checking for any persons that might be visible, but saw none. "You know you can't cross the border. Even if you could, it's not safe for former German residents to be there. The Czechs would be afraid of claims on their property or that they might be identified as assailants during the expulsions."

"That we met and are here talking is a complete curve-ball.

I'm not sure what I can tell you. I have to talk to my boss. I know you have to go back to Tachau today, but when will you be here again?" Peter couldn't get information fast enough.

"A curve-ball is American slang, I'm sure, but yes, we met very unexpectedly. Is that black man your boss? Where is he?"

"He's in our room. He is one of my bosses, but I have others in Mähring I have to talk to."

Trudi continued, "I get an overnight every two weeks. My mother gets the same at times when I'm not here. They never let us come together because they really don't trust Germans loyalty. They are afraid we won't come back, but they want to appear to be compassionate at the same time. Since my mother's husband died, she and I have talked a lot about coming over permanently, but have never found a way to do it. That's why they don't let us come together."

"Trudi, my mind is racing right now. We have to meet again after I talk to my bosses so we can make further plans. Right now, I can tell you I want to find a way in and out of the Tachau area. You and your mother want out. There are some possibilities for mutual assistance. Have you been to the *Blitzbaum* lately?"

"Yes, your packet is still there in good condition." I still run to the Studánka hill often, so they seldom follow me there."

Peter was fantasizing about the safety of his parents, the accomplishment of his military mission and helping Trudi and her mother get out. "Do you ever see military equipment around Tachau?"

"Yes! Russian and Czech. I have been warned not to talk about that in West Germany."

"I understand! When we meet again we may want to give

each other lots of information. It will be very helpful to me for my military mission if you would develop an estimate of the number of Russian and Czech military personnel and the types of equipment they have in Tachau. I feel confident my bosses will authorize me to work with you. It's possible even to get you out of Czechoslovakia!"

Trudi seemed to simply glow when she heard those words—accentuating her natural beauty. Peter hoped he wasn't letting his emotions commandeer his good sense, as his training had warned him. But Trudi wasn't a female spy seductress. They had a history that transcended any relationship he had ever experienced or of which he was aware.

"I work for a Russian Colonel named Vladimir Gochenko. I am an administrative assistant. He's the one that wants me to keep training. I met him at the athletic club when he was training for a marathon. He said he got extra consideration for promotion if he could run a complete marathon under the designated time for military officers. We used to train together with all the other distance runners. When I won the Bohemian women's ten-thousand meter race he was there. Shortly after that he offered me a job. It has been a useful job for the favors I get or I wouldn't be here today. He signs the border passes for my mother and me."

Listening to Trudi, Peter reflected on the phrase he heard often in America. "The truth can be stranger than fiction."

"According to Colonel Gochenko, they may add the 5,000 meter race to the women's competition in the 1960 Rome Olympics. He asked me to compete for the Russian team, but I told him my mother would never leave Czechoslovakia and I couldn't leave her alone. So now I'm training to run for

Czechoslovakia." She smiled and continued, "Now I'm his pro-tégé and mother and I get border passes to visit *Oma* in West Germany."

Peter smiled to himself and thought about the definition of pragmatism. "Whatever enables a person to achieve an objective."

"I have to go now so that I'm at the border by 1300. Can we meet again in two weeks? Hopefully you will be able to give more details and I will try to get some information for you."

"Yes, that will be great. Same spot, same time—in two weeks."

Trudi jogged back toward the *Geschichtspark* café and disappeared. Peter waited five minutes and walked back to meet Willie.

Thursday-Friday, June 19-20, 1958 . . . Peter was energized. Meeting Trudi was totally unexpected good fortune. That she was alive and doing well was a dream come true, even if she and her mother weren't happy. On the negative side the news about his parents did little to raise his spirits. He sensed that Trudi was sugarcoating what she knew; if she knew anything at all. Positive expectations for the welfare of his parents were a fading hope. The lack of news dampened his spirit until his mind was distracted by the business at hand. He would never give up seeking the truth as long as he was able.

Willie was digesting the new discoveries with Trudi, the culvert and with the mysterious Bärnau depot-compound. Willie was an excellent evaluator and planner. His skill would be needed in presenting this information to Major Taylor and suggesting where to go with it. Willie wasn't sure how Trudi could help them with their mission, but his curiosity led to discussion as they drove north toward Mähring.

"Is there more than just a past friendship with Trudi that I should know about, sergeant?"

Peter knew Willie was assuming a serious professional posture when he addressed him as "sergeant." The time has come, Peter thought, to reveal his secret agenda. He might never have a better leverage position than now. Trudi could, and he felt would, help with intelligence on the ground. She would help in any way she could to get Peter into the Tachau area and possibly provide cover and assistance while he was there. In short, she could be extremely valuable to the mission and the US Forces in general. His bargaining point, in order to secure his "packet" and enable the mother and daughter escape from Tachau, was Trudi's assistance. Peter had only scratched the surface of the ways she could help. What he knew now was huge. What he might learn from her in two weeks could be even bigger. She had access to a Russian Colonel, crossed the border routinely every two weeks and had an enviable physical and mental capability.

Peter told the entire story. He covered the pertinent details of his parents, the film packet, his relationship with Trudi and his previous efforts to find a means of returning to Tachau.

Willie absorbed and contemplated. He was completing a difficult puzzle in his mind.

"Peter, I knew something was boiling below the surface. I could never put my finger on it, but I never worried because you never showed any weakness in our pursuit of and planning of the assigned mission."

Peter thought this conversation might go his way.

Willie continued, "I understand. You've been succinct and truthful with me. I will support you when we talk to Major Taylor."

This was a huge relief for Peter. He knew the major and his superiors had confidence in es corial. Willie's support would be invaluable in his position as the team leader. Nobody knew Peter and the mission's principal contributors better than he. The meeting could clear Peter's last barrier to the near life-long endeavor of doing everything he possibly could to find his parents and expose further proof of the inhumane expulsion of the Sudeten Germans from Czechoslovakia. He relaxed as they drove the short distance to their home station in Mähring. At this time es corial knew nothing of the surprises that would soon materialize.

TWENTY SEVEN

FINAL PUZZLE PIECES

June 23, 1958 . . . Precisely at 0900 es corial was standing before Major Taylor in his office. The team's after action report had been prepared and submitted to Sgt Martinez the day before. It was classified Top Secret by es corial pending verification of the security level by higher authority. Both Sgt Martinez and Major Taylor had reviewed the report.

"I'm impressed with your work and with the preparation of the report." Major Taylor was opening the conference with an acknowledgement that he was informed and pleased.

"Of course we were aware of the border conditions in general, but your discovery of the culvert was the type of information we had hoped your reconnaissance would uncover."

Both Willie and Peter were anxious to hear what he had to say about the depot-compound as well as the chance meeting with Trudi.

"I have plenty of questions about *Fräulein* Kehle, but first I want to brief you on the restricted area you found in Bärnau. You weren't informed until now because that site is a work in progress in which you have had no need-to-know."

Peter felt relief in the fact that the site wasn't going to be some sort of obstacle to their mission. Apparently they would have to work around or with that site.

The major went into his explanation after stating it was indeed a top secret site. Near the end of the war the Nazis were in a panic. The underground sites they had built for construction and launch of their V-2 rockets were being destroyed by British and Allied bombing raids. *Mittelbau Dora* had been the primary site for building rockets that were then transported to other bunkers, or to mobile launch vehicles when too many Nazi bunkers were destroyed. The Bärnau site had been a last-ditch effort by the Nazis to build another site which might escape allied bombs. The site had extensive excavation work completed using prisoner labor from the nearby Flossenburg Concentration Camp. Fortunately, the Americans arrived there at war's end, before the Russians, and occupied the abandoned site before the Russians even knew it existed.

The Major then continued into the interesting part. "We Americans did nothing with the site pending determination of borders at the end of the war. It remained classified and guarded for many years with little significant activity. As the Cold War developed the site gained more attention from US Forces until in 1953 a potential intelligence use was found for the site. Because it nearly undercut the newly restored border it was viewed as a potential clandestine entry point into Czechoslovakia. Underground surveying and construction has taken place periodically ever since that determination. We now have an entry point 350 meters under the Czech border. Our intelligence tells us that the entry point is clear of barbed wire, lights, raked sandy areas and watch towers."

Team es corial was stunned by this revelation. They understood immediately why they were there. This was the alternate
plan that had been referenced so often in the past.

Willie had the first question. "Why weren't we told about
this plan before?"

Major Taylor answered that it was because the plan still
hadn't been given final approval, but he now had authorization
to take the team into what he called Site Yankee.

"Before I take you into Yankee, I want to know more about
Trudi. Give me the history, Sgt Ackerman—everything! Every
contact you ever had with that woman."

Peter was offended by the major's reference to Trudi as
"that woman," but he realized that his job was to discuss un-
emotional logical business. Peter narrated the complete relationship timeline. It was the optimal opportunity to integrate
the story about his parents, the packet and his systematic program to return to Tachau. This was the worrisome part for
Peter. Would the major see Peter's involvement in es corial as
secondary to his personal agenda? He had to take the chance
to satisfy his own need for integrity. There were other options
at a later point in time if his personal mission was aborted. He
didn't want to wait until he was discharged from the army, but
it was a distinct possibility.

Major Taylor listened attentively and was pensive when
Peter finished. He was absorbing and contemplating what he
had just heard. There were pros and cons of this development
in the major's mind.

"Do you realize, sergeant, that Trudi fits the classic description of a spy? She remained in Czechoslovakia when most other Germans were expelled. She works for a Russian colonel.

She has authorized movement between Tachau and the Bärnau area. You haven't had contact with her for twelve years. This is just a few of the obvious red flags. I don't know what else we will find."

Peter had a sinking feeling throughout his body. He had to admit to himself that he hadn't considered these possibilities. He realized that the major, as an experienced, impartial overseer of the planned mission, was looking at Trudi from a different perspective. It was his job to be the objective devil's advocate.

"Sir, I want to follow up with Trudi. Can we give her a chance, but proceed with caution? We met by chance at the *Gasthof Zur Post*. She had no time to make up a cover story if she is a spy. Her words and actions have caused no doubts for me. I do understand that the emotional connection with her could cloud my reasoning, but I see an enormous opportunity to gain information if we proceed with caution."

The major responded, "You've given me a lot to think about. I don't know if I can justify integrating her into the plan. It will be a hard sell in Heidelberg with USAREUR. Your personal agenda would have to fit seamlessly into the plan."

Peter was encouraged by this quick reversal of perspective by the major. He thought he might have his foot in the door.

"She has already answered the question about my parents. There is nothing more I can do here and now about that. My packet is hidden in a location that I was planning on using for observation of troop activities anyway. I would be well concealed and with caution I will have movement over the highest point near Tachau."

"What do you have to say about this situation, Sgt Kyles?"

"Sir, I'm leaning toward pursuing the use of Trudi. Her intelligence information about present and past Warsaw Pact capabilities and operations could be an overwhelming intelligence windfall. We do need to check her out in depth, however, before we proceed. If she does prove to be for real we would have to extract her and her mother if they are in danger. An end-of-mission extraction is a given."

Willie's words were music to Peter's ears. He couldn't have been any more tactfully supportive. Those comments deserve a pat on the back, a handshake and at least two *Bier* at the NCO club in Tölz.

"OK, men. You guys are right on top of it. I think we understand each other. What I'm going to do is have Trudi's and her mother's border crossing record checked. I'll find out how often they have entered West Germany, how long they stayed and if they were engaged in any unusual activity. The record will give a more complete picture of their time spent in West Germany. We will find out if the story she has given you is consistent with her border crossings. Sgt Ackerman, you need to take the emotion out of your relationship with Trudi until I get her cleared. I will get some input from my superiors as to how we should proceed. If all goes well, we will visit Yankee soon. I want you to keep your scheduled appointment with Trudi. If she has a Czech tail that day, she might well have two tails after we add one!"

The major smiled for the first time since the meeting began. Peter was mostly relieved, but realized there were some hurdles to overcome in order to get Trudi cleared. Willie was in awe of the circumstances arising in this ongoing saga. He wondered if it was possible to make up a story like what was developing right before his eyes!

TWENTY EIGHT

SITE YANKEE

Tuesday, June 24, 1958 . . . Peter thought of the old army adage, "Hurry up and wait." Guidance on how Trudi would be handled would come from USAREUR Headquarters. He was confident the green light would be given to rendez-vous with her on July 3. This was a coincidence of American Independence Day occurring the day after such an important meeting with Trudi. Peter couldn't find much parallel between what he was doing and American independence, but it was a coincidence nonetheless.

The team busied itself with map study of the area between Bärnau and Tachau primarily because there were more and more indications that this would be the final choice of access route. Terrain and vegetation were important as well as remaining buildings, roads, streams and how the land was being used. Peter wanted to find the best way for him to get to Studánka, where he would be more familiar with his surroundings. Using the non-linear location of forested patches the distance to Studánka, for him, could be fifteen kilometers. At night, this would be no easy task. They plotted route markers on the map as a means of checking accurate progress and locations during the intrusion. Progressing one marker at a time would keep Peter on the correct route. Peter would be equipped with a map light and a wet-weather poncho which could be used to shield the light if a map reference became necessary.

They discussed their meeting with Major Taylor and the probable future course of action.

"I can't thank you enough for your support on the Trudi issue," offered Peter.

"I was giving my honest opinion, Peter. I wouldn't be granting favors because you are a good guy. Our mission is far too important and dangerous. I gave an objective professional opinion. From your account of your relationship with Trudi and from having learned of her current situation, my good sense tells me she is genuine and can be a tremendous asset to our intelligence-gathering effort. I'm glad you were fortunate enough to find her."

"Thanks, Willie. Your support means everything to me. How do you think this will go over in Heidelberg?"

"That's a tough call. We're dealing with some serious stuff here. The army can't afford a mistake that might lead to an incident or worse—a provocation. We're asking for intelligence from Trudi, and an extraction for Trudi and her mother. Seems like a fair exchange to me—just keep your fingers crossed."

"You are correct, Willie," Peter seemed to be deep in thought. "Do you ever think about why we are here? I mean . . . not just the here and now . . . but, historically."

Willie was puzzled by the change in direction of the conversation and asked, "Where are you going with thoughts like that?"

"It's easy to say the Nazis started all this. There is no doubt that what they did is beyond cruel and barbaric . . . We haven't even digested the full extent of their atrocities, nor have we captured and brought to justice all the worst offenders. We probably never will, but, speaking of barbarians, let's just go back in European history a few thousand years. There was a time when you were either a part of the Roman Empire or you were a barbarian. They killed each other at the slightest provocation. The killing and inhumanity started a long time before those days and has never stopped. We never learn. That's what I think about why we are here—we never learn."

"That's very perceptive, Peter. You and I have come to similar conclusions from different life experiences. Slave owners killed some blacks, also; the same as African tribesmen killed rival tribesmen or sold them to slave traders. So, which of the three groups were the worst? I think the answer depends on where you stand in life, unless you realize that they were all cruel and inhumane."

"We do try to make everybody accountable for their actions, though, don't we?"

"Of course not. Our justice system is highly selective."

"What do you mean?" asked Peter in surprise.

"Take a look at the Wernher von Braun case. A German who was born in Poland and was the brains behind the V2 rockets that killed thousands of people in England and other parts of Europe during the war. But, when Germany's surrender was imminent in 1945, he defected to the Americans in order to avoid capture by the Russians. Both sides coveted his brain power. He wasn't exactly accepted in the United States with open arms, but he became the primary scientist in our space program. He was never held accountable for the deaths he indirectly caused in Europe. Where is the justice in that?"

"You are correct. There hasn't been any justice for Josef Mengele or Adolph Eichmann, either. Makes you wonder if anyone other than the Israeli's is even looking for them. Well, anyway, here we are in the middle of another political powder keg. But now, we both have documents that say we are Americans. But, are we really Americans in the eyes of white native-born nationalists? I was born in Czechoslovakia to German parents whose fate only the Russians know. You were born in America but haven't been accepted by all. What are we doing here?"

"We're dreamers, Peter. We believe we can help make it right. And we can't just drift through life like gypsies. We have to believe in something and put down roots that we are willing to defend. You and I are very different, but also very much alike."

"That brings me back to my favorite word . . . pragmatism. In this case, it's pragmatism with a conscience."

This conversation was serving to enhance their already solid bond. It was the type of conversation that gets stored in the deepest recesses of your mind for perpetuity. You don't walk away with a superficial handshake and a pat on the back, but you do walk away with a certain resolve and respect. Bonding, loyalty and respect aren't strong enough words.

They reviewed the latest reports from Hoherbogen, Schneeberg and the local listening post in Mähring. They noted plenty of routine military electronic traffic in both Czech and

Russian languages. It was categorized as normal volume. Visual sightings were infrequent over the last few weeks, but some military wheeled vehicles were in evidence. It was anticipated that a Warsaw Pact training exercise would occur sometime during the summer. A summer exercise was unusual in the eyes of the American intelligence community because the American philosophy had always been to train in the winter when the weather challenges were formidable. No doubt the intelligence brain trust would make something out of the summer exercises. There must be a reason—right?

Most of the methods of entry into Czechoslovakia had been discounted by this time. The problem of exit was always the most difficult to overcome. For that reason the culvert and the possible entry through Yankee seemed most likely. They had considered that a trained dog might be used to explore the culvert. Sgt Martinez had promised to follow that up with the dog training school in Lenggries. This approach to the problem had a remote chance of acceptance, but in retrospect Peter was thankful for a mistake he had made in his haste when inspecting the downhill end of the culvert so many years ago. He had left the screening door open. Now, it turns out that if they were to send a trained dog into the culvert, the dog could exit and make a round trip. They had briefly toyed with parachuting, gliders and the hand-held mine detector idea which wasn't very popular with Peter. All the bridges they had seen were heavily guarded. Trains and water passageways were deemed unlikely. It looked to the team that the original idea for an entry and escape had not given enough weight to the return phase. They wanted to interview or get information about successful escapes from defectors, but hadn't yet been able to do so. There was no doubt that border security had been improved significantly by the Warsaw Pact military element since Peter's escape in 1946.

Occasionally they found time to explore the local area and partake of a local hot meal and a *Bier*. When they relaxed and talked mostly non-business they laughed about being "9 to 5" spooks. But, it was good that they maintained some semblance of a normal life. It could be months before their real action started. They didn't want to become disinterested and start making mistakes. Willie was a Grambling State University football fan. It would be several years before major football powers like Notre Dame and Michigan State would utilize black players—even longer for teams in the Southeastern Conference. When Peter mentioned that it looked like Brazil was going to win the World Cup after West Germany lost to Sweden, Willie asked, "What's soccer? That game puts me to sleep."

"Hush, Willie, you won't have a friend in West Germany if you talk bad about soccer. By the way it's called *"Fussball."*

"Sorry, sergeant. I guess I should stanch the comments about *'Fussball'* players not being true athletes. I still remember how you blitzed me in your first run with the forces in Tölz."

"Touche, sergeant. Let's have another *Bier* and go to our billet."

Thursday, June 26, 1958 . . . Sgt Martinez brought the welcome news that the major wanted to see team es cori-al at 1300. Peter and Willie were more than happy that the expected news about the disposition of the Trudi question was forthcoming. USAREUR's reaction to Peter's personal agenda was also expected. Circumstances had made the army mission and his personal agenda mutually inclusive. It appeared to be a win-win situation for everybody involved. The army would receive intelligence from an unexpected inside source, while Peter integrated *Blitzbaum* access with the original army objective. That Trudi and her mother might be rewarded with an authorized extraction was a bonus.

Major Taylor was stone-faced as they reported. "I have some news for you, men. I have consulted with USAREUR G-2 about es corial plans and the possible addition of Trudi to the plan. This was a difficult discussion for me. It's always difficult asking superiors for changes in plans when the superiors aren't close enough to the planning. That's true at all levels of the chain of command as you are undoubtedly aware. The first consideration is always to accomplish the mission . . . and I might add, by whatever means possible!"

Peter thought he was hearing a rehash of his Special Forces training. He realized that this is the military way of maintaining focus on the job at hand. Define the objective and ensure that all actions contribute to realizing that objective. OK, I agree, thought Peter. Pragmatism lives! Now let's get on with the details.

"G-2 (Intelligence) has approved the changes with caveats." The major let a slight smile creep into his explanation. "We found nothing negative or suspicious about Trudi at the border-crossing station or in her background check. Not much background to check since she has lived in Tachau all her life, but we do have classified methods of checking some individuals across the border. Anyway, she's clean. You can meet her on July 3 as scheduled. The caveat is that she has to be above reproach. She must give an honest attempt to help us and to help you in your border intrusion. This doesn't mean that she has to provide any earthshaking information, but it does mean she has to be honest and to be helpful to you."

"I understand, sir. We haven't made promises to each other at this point, but we have a mutual understanding of the possibilities. I can proceed with caution at our next meeting. It will be interesting to see if she has any information for me. I will let her know exactly what the conditions of her family extraction will be. I will tell her we expect any information she can obtain without endangering herself. I might add I see no reason to alert her mother at the present."

Willie felt like a stand-by afterthought, but understood that this part of the operation was Peter's ball game.

"Good! Mother doesn't need to know—yet. The next step is the tour of Site Yankee."

The history of Site Yankee was a curiosity of its own. The site was a very large bunker occupied by the American 3rd Infantry Division in the waning days of the war. It was abandoned by the Nazis as they tried to escape the inevitable. The Nazis had used prisoners from nearby Flossenburg Concentration Camp to perform the physical labor needed in the construction of the bunker. Conditions, in what the American forces have named Site Yankee, were equally as depressing as in the camp at Flossenburg. Hundreds of laborers worded at Site Yankee until they died. There were no sleeping facilities and little food. The guards and work supervisors were cruel, unfeeling and relentless in their discipline.

The site's intended usage by the Nazis had not been determined. It was known that Hitler made extensive use of bunkers for many purposes. The V2 and other rocket types were constructed and launched from massive bunkers along the French coast until the Allies found them and bombed them into ineffectiveness. Other bunkers were used for storage, defensive positions, as work sites or as clandestine hiding places. Site Yankee was likely intended to be some sort of work site.

There was a scramble at war's end between the Russians and the Americans to secure the spoils of war assets. A decision was made to take control of and secure Site Yankee for inspection and possible future use. Because the two Allied forces were coming together triumphantly in the Sudetenland, it was important for each side to quickly claim anything of potential value wherever the American and Russian forces met on common ground. The Americans claimed the site and called it Yankee. That it could one day be used for intelligence purposes was not a factor at that time. It was a case not unlike the blind squirrel who finally found a nut. The decision to occupy Site Yankee was America's good fortune on which es corial hoped to capitalize. The picture was clearing. It might be possible to tunnel into Czechoslovakia through Site Yankee.

TWENTY NINE

THE THREE-TOED SLOTH

Sunday, June 29, 1958 . . . Sgt Martinez was driving the major's US Army sedan. En route to Yankee his passengers were team es corial and Major Taylor.

"The site has been under tight US control since 1945. At first it was just a matter of possession pending disposition. It wasn't known what we might find there. Evidence of how it was built, and by whom, was important for understanding Nazi war conduct. Anything left behind, from an empty food container to documents or art treasures, would have received close inspection. Because of Nazi secrecy during construction and the subsequent rapid takeover by the American Third Infantry Division, there was little chance of locals gaining knowledge of what was going on inside. I'm positive no one except the personnel involved in its recent work or administration have knowledge of the intended use of the site. We make it look like an ammunition storage area for nearby live-fire training ranges. To enhance the deception the German outside-perimeter guards have been briefed on emergency procedures in case of a munitions accident."

Willie was curious and asked, "How close is the site to the border?"

"From the outside main entrance to the bunker it is about one kilometer. From where the Nazis had excavated, it's about two-hundred meters. We already have access tunnels that our surveyors tell us are well into Czechoslovakia. Work now is concerned with finding the safest and most secure exit points. We want to be sure we clear all the border barriers and find spots out of the sight lines of the tower guards."

Peter felt an adrenaline rush as the major's briefing continued. They entered a nondescript side road, passing a "*Sprengstoff, Eintritt Verboten*" sign which was meant to forbid civilians from entering. Past the sign they were met by two civilian German guards who flagged them down and asked for identification. After checking the ID's with their access roster they saluted and allowed the sedan to pass. Out of the corner of his eye, Willie saw the guard turning the crank on a field phone, ostensibly to alert the inner US Forces guards of the sedan's presence.

The wide road was rather well constructed with corrugated concrete bricks embedded firmly and evenly in the ground as it dropped slightly in elevation. European white-birch trees shaded the road and concealed it from overhead observation. At the US checkpoint they were met by a team of guards under the supervision of a sergeant first class. The bunker was not yet in sight, but a guard with a large unleashed German shepherd security dog was visible on a path outside a perimeter barbed-wire fence. The terrain was hilly with abundant vegetation, mostly grasses and ferns. It was obvious that until the occupants of the sedan were granted access the guards were in control. The major alone was ordered out of the car. The security sergeant took the major to the rear of the sedan, while the remaining guards closely observed the passengers and driver. When the major was cleared, the sergeant saluted and stated in his best military command voice, "You may enter, Sir!"

Peter asked what that was all about.

Sgt Martinez answered that it was to ensure that the major, who the security sergeant recognized, was not being brought to the facility under duress by unknown passengers.

"Just an added layer of security," offered Sgt Martinez."

The entrance to the bunker was reinforced by thick wooden support beams. Peter thought the opening was high enough to get a five-ton vehicle under it with no problem. They parked inside, as directed, and were met by Lieutenant Edelman. Es corial had been briefed that the personnel working at the site were not privy to any plan for its use. They could only surmise and talk, which they did privately—and in groups—when it wasn't a breach of security to do so.

The lieutenant first briefed the visitors on what the Third Division had found in 1945. It was a very large cavern blasted out of the granite and sandstone. The ceiling was roughly fifteen meters high and the rounded walls were over thirty meters apart at their broadest point. The ceiling was reinforced with concrete and steel. The walls were jagged, uneven shards of rock. Wooden gangways had been laid for vehicles and workers ease of movement.

The engineers had installed a lighting system powered by generators located outside the inner bunker. The Nazis had created an excellent ventilation system which only had to be reworked when the US Forces moved in. There was little dust or other irritants in the air that the visitors could notice.

Several soldiers were working in the area with forklifts, bucket-loaders and other construction equipment. These men were all engineers by military occupation specialty (MOS), supervised by the engineer-trained lieutenant.

The lieutenant told them that the men were on two week shifts at the site. They were rotated with similar groups from their units in Grafenwoehr and other parts of West Germany. Mess, hygiene and sleeping facilities were outside the bunker in buildings which were concealed from air observation. The OIC was a Captain Lokar, who also had quarters and an office outside the bunker. His responsibility was to ensure the daily operation of the work force and to care for the welfare of the men. Captain Lokar was an active part of the escorial mission. They were to meet with the captain after their tour.

Most of the work activity was taking place on the east side of the bunker. The lieutenant explained that they had excavated two-hundred meters into the bedrock and then branched out at thirty degree angles to the left and right as well as continuing straight ahead as if they were constructing a giant three-toed sloth's foot. He estimated that they had an additional hundred meters remaining on each toe. At that point he was charged with drilling toward the surface until they broke through the bedrock and reached soft soil. The work crews were to wait for further instructions when they reached that point. The lieutenant gave no indication that he knew the purpose of the work, but it was obvious to all working there what they were trying to accomplish.

The tunnel ceilings allowed passage without fear of

bumping heads and the tunnels were wide enough for all to pass through easily, but could be intimidating for a person who might be claustrophobic. Portable lights and large flashlights were being used by two-man drilling teams.

"How much longer will it take before you finish this project, lieutenant?" Willie was asking from the rear of the single-file group.

"Oh . . . if it goes well, it will be two weeks until we wait for further instructions."

"Do you know what is on the surface above us?"

The lieutenant suppressed a slight smile and answered, "Czechoslovakia! The captain has the exact location. He will be the one to direct us once we reach soft soil."

Captain Lokar brought the Yankee site preparation effort into focus. He knew Willie and Peter were the designated intruders and that his site team was responsible for providing an exit and re-entry point. He was also responsible for ensuring camouflage of the exit-entry hole to reduce the chance of accidental discovery. Re-entry would be requested using short range, low-output, portable radio. According to the captain, one of his men would be waiting with a radio inside the exit point at all times after the intrusion was under way. One of the es corial team would also be waiting at the pre-designated return time. The outside radio could be concealed in the re-entry area by the intruder until he returned and the radio was used to request re-entry.

The captain was confident that his area of responsibility was progressing well. "We will be prepared to climb out with weapons if that becomes necessary. I will have my best men at the ready here in the bunker and at the release point. Any questions?"

Willie had a question, "Sir, will the inside person have light and will he be comfortable for long stretches of time at the release point?"

"Yes, sergeant, we will be blasting out sufficient room and providing light, radios, weapons and even a place to sit. I'll have a telephone wire line laid for communication between the central bunker location and all the potential release points."

"Water . . . first aid?"

"Good point, sergeant. I'll have medics and a doctor standing by in the bunker."

"Can you give us the exact coordinates of the three potential release points so we can plot them on our maps?"

"Affirmative . . . the surveyors will give me that information when we choose the spots. Only one release point will be used. We cleared three because we're not sure what we will find on the surface. We want to be away from tree roots in a dry, concealed area."

"How far beyond the guard towers?"

"We believe one hundred meters at the least. The towers will be behind you, but you will need to be aware of their location. I assume this will occur at night, which should help. Czech civilians are not allowed in your release point area as a deterrent to defection attempts, but that's both good and bad news. Civilians won't be there to interfere, but, at the same time, if the military sees you, you will be challenged. If that happens, it could be a fight or flight situation for you."

"Not me, sir! Sgt Ackerman is the man for that job," Willie clarified.

An easy calm enveloped Peter as more plan details were discussed. Fleeting thoughts flashed through his mind: I'm going home; I have a job to do; I could get killed; this is what I signed up for; I owe it to *Muti* and *Vati*—and Trudi. It was all a natural fear, like the oft-told tale of a dying man's life flashing before his eyes. Peter was numb, but confident.

Subdued conversation filled the air in the sedan on the return trip to Mähring. At one point Sgt Martinez told the team to take a few days off before the meeting with Trudi. Willie talked about map study and preliminary plan development, but thanked the sergeant for the option.

"We aren't going anywhere. We have a lot to think about. Just give us a shout if anything comes up!" Willie was establishing the seriousness and attitude of team es corial from his position of team leadership.

THIRTY

MAKING PLANS

Thursday, July 3, 1958 . . . *"Guten Morgen, Fräulein Kehle."* Peter greeted a rather anxious-looking Trudi.

"Guten Morgen, Peter. Follow me. I want to go to a more private place."

They followed the trail further up a slight rise until finding a path that took them to a tree-shaded bench. Small talk followed a brief embrace. They knew they had serious business to discuss in a limited amount of time.

"I have information for you, Peter, but I'm not sure how important it is."

"Anything you have will be helpful, Trudi. We always deal with bits and pieces of information that our intelligence units use to connect the dots."

"OK . . . first about my job. Colonel Gochenko's official title is liaison officer. As far as I know, he is the senior Russian officer in Tachau. He has more Russian visitors than he has Czech. He appears to be the commander of the permanent Russian troops in Tachau. Three administrative assistants work in my office. Yelena, the Russian lady, handles all the Russian-language correspondence and speaks only Russian. Božena is a Czech lady, who also speaks Russian. I assist her with Czech-language documents and I handle the few German-language documents that come to the attention of the colonel. Most of my work has to do with the authorized border-crossing station. I also translate the *Tagesblatt* newspaper which is delivered at the crossing point."

Trudi was recalling everything from memory. Peter assumed she was searched on every movement into or out of Czechoslovakia and couldn't possess suspicious items. He was taking notes based on her verbal information.

Trudi continued, "There are three *Kaserne* in the Tachau area with both Russian and Czech soldiers on each one. All have some tank-like vehicles with big guns on them."

"Do you ever see them outside the *Kaserne?*"

"Seldom, except for last summer. The soldiers are in town often at night drinking and acting aggressively. My friends stay away from them because of their boisterous behavior and because they speak a language my friends don't understand. Last summer there were many soldiers and tanks all around the area. They have a big training area over by Mýto. This is about all the information I could accumulate without becoming suspiciously nosy."

"Understand! Your security is the most important thing. Don't do anything out of the ordinary. Just keep your eyes open and your memory sharp. Never write anything that might make the Colonel suspicious if he found it."

When it appeared that Trudi had finished, Peter began to relate to her the new information that he had developed.

"My access route into Tachau is almost finalized. I now

have authority to include you in my entry plans with the possibility of eventually getting you and your mother out of Tachau and into West Germany permanently!"

This is what Trudi had hoped to hear. Since meeting Peter at the *Gasthof Zur Post,* the anticipation of the future was overwhelming her with excitement. She was finding it hard to sleep or concentrate on her job. She knew she had to maintain an aura of normalcy in her daily activities, but it was difficult.

"When everything is ready, I want you to meet me at the *Blitzbaum.* On the designated day, whoever gets there first will wait in the tree, or in a safe area near the tree, and have the packet secured and ready to go. That should be before the summer is over, but I can't give you a date yet."

"What about *Muti?*"

"It will happen when she is in Bärnau with your *Oma.* On that day you will say good bye to Tachau forever. No more friends . . . no more job . . . nothing except the clothes on your back and what you can easily carry with you."

"Is it safe, Peter? I trust you, but I'm afraid. This is happening so fast."

"I'm afraid, too, Trudi, but if you want a life of freedom to be your own person, you will take the chance. I've lived in Tachau and I've lived in America. There is no comparison. Hopefully, I can get authorization to have you admitted to America; but, if not, West Germany is a wonderful place to live, also. The West Germans are recovering quickly from the war."

"I understand, but it doesn't stop me from being afraid. I have something else to tell you. Remember Anton from our school? You were on the *Fussball* team together."

"Aaahh . . . Anton Schwarz, the goalkeeper."

"Yes, that's the one . . . he has a plan."

"What kind of plan? Are you involved in coming across?"

"He is planning an escape, but I'm not involved. He asked me, but I can't just leave my mother."

"Can you tell me his plan?"

"I only know it involves two Czech border guards who will cross with him."

"This is unreal. How did he ever get that close to Czech border guards?"

"One of them is from our school also. They were childhood friends before Anton's family had to move to Prague. They met by chance when Anton came back. The plan developed when they started talking. That's all he would tell me."

"How did Anton get to move to Prague instead of being expelled from the Sudetenland?"

"His father had a skill the Czechs needed. He made a deal with them. He agreed to move to Prague for the new job if they would compensate him for his family's Tachau property and give the family a cover Czech identity."

"That's amazing! We didn't know those types of deals were being made secretly. Our parents probably knew something about that."

"*Muti* says she didn't know. Anyway, Anton now has a Czech name. His papers say he is Jaroslav Hruby. He can move freely in Tachau with a minimum of suspicion."

Peter was becoming less and less surprised at the facts of what transpired in the Sudetenland after the Czechs assumed control. Anton's father was pragmatic—there's that word again—in caring for his family. Success in life can sometimes be a matter of being in the right place at the right time along with a liberal dose of cleverness. He thought he himself had benefitted from that principle.

"I've been thinking about your plan, Peter, and now with the Anton situation there are other possibilities."

"Such as?"

"Anton is your age and the physical resemblance is similar. He isn't well known in Tachau now, because he was a young boy when he left and now he is posing as a Czech. If he makes it across you could use his identification, and even clothing, to safely move around Tachau—at least for a short time."

Again, Trudi had come up with an interesting idea. Peter was momentarily stunned by this revelation. Was it preposterous or would it actually work? In order to be useful, this idea would depend on Anton actually making a successful escape without being identified.

"Where and when, Trudi? I need some details."

"Soon . . . in the Broumov/Mähring area. That's all I know."

Peter was trying to make something out of this information as his brain's processing mechanism scanned millions of nerve synapses. "Tell Anton I can help if he makes it across. He should seek out the *Bundesgrenzschutz* or an American border patrol unit immediately after crossing. He should tell the patrol contact that they are looking for 'Brigitte Berg' and that Major Taylor knows where she is. That will get them to my boss who will process them as part of my plan. They can come across when they will, Trudi, but my entry into Tachau depends on my bosses. I know some work has to be completed first. I believe they want to schedule my crossing to coincide with the predicted Warsaw Pact maneuvers. Scheduling your

extraction concurrent with your mother's visit and the maneuvers will be chancy. Nothing is set in stone at this point,
but I do have some influence in the decision. Next week is too
early. I'll see you again on the seventeenth. At that time I will
try to have everything in order for your extraction as early as
the twenty-fourth; your mother will be in Thanhausen on that
date. If it can't be done that soon I will try for either two or
four weeks after that. Is there any chance your mother could
change her schedule?"

"I think that's possible if she can find a plausible reason."

"Would it be safe to meet with her here next week?"

"It's probably safe enough. I'm not sure she will want to
do it though. Why don't you check here a week from now. I'll
give her the plan and persuade her to assist in our communication. I'm fairly certain she will want to get involved. She has
wanted out of Czechoslovakia ever since Rudi died."

Trudi and Peter finally had some time to just visit. The at-
traction and friendship was as strong as ever. They were aware
of the adult presence they had each achieved even though their
meetings were all business. They had fleeting thoughts of better times in a safer environment. They both had hopes the day
would come.

When she asked about the crossing, Peter only offered that
they would be together; she wouldn't have to worry about
landmines or barbed wire, and that her athleticism would be
an important part of the escape.

"Be prepared for running, climbing and crawling." Peter
said this was the best advice he could give.

Then she was gone. The carrot was dangled before
her for a few short hours; now he had the stick. Peter had

difficulty containing his excitement about his plans and the reward he sought for the army and for his personal goals. Trudi and her mother now made it a triple reward. The stakes were getting higher.

THIRTY ONE

DEFECTORS

Sunday, July 6, 1958 . . . Peter and Willie were awakened by an insistent tapping at the door of their room in the Mähring compound. The charge of quarters (CQ) had been notified by the BGS that they had three defectors. Because they had used the code words Brigitte Berg, Major Taylor had directed the CQ to summon es corial to meet him in his office when he arrived. It was 0700 hours.

"BGS has three Czech defectors in their custody. One speaks perfect German, used the Brigitte Berg code word and says he is German. It's very likely the contact you made through Trudi."The major was animated and nearly lost his composure momentarily as he related the information to es corial.

Major Taylor had been briefed about the Anton Schwarz situation by es corial during their weekly meeting. The major recognized this contact as potentially very valuable, but had no idea it would be so soon or such a seamless defection.

Peter recognized Anton immediately as Anton stepped out of the BGS van. Matured physically, but with the same posture; he appeared fatigued but still had his identifiable cocky look on his face. All three of the defectors appeared to be frightened and tired. They had been sleepless the entire night as they awaited their 0400 escape attempt.

The defectors were being held under apprehension procedure. All the documents confiscated by the BGS were turned over to the sixty-sixth MI personnel. The interpreters questioned them in order to verify their intentions. When the preliminary processing was complete, Peter approached Anton. Although he recognized Anton, he was cautious. Anton's German was flawless and he related information about Peter's years in Tachau that only a boy that had been there could have known.

"Your identification papers say you are Jaroslav Hruby. What is your real name?"

"I am Anton Schwarz."

"Anton, my friend . . . I am Peter Ackerman."

"I know, Peter, I recognize you. Trudi told me I would find you if I used the Brigitte Berg code word."

Everybody in the room noticeably relaxed at the obvious familiarity of the two men. Willie was stoic, the major observant, the MI assistants and interpreters business-like; the Czech defectors appeared to be gaining confidence. One of the Czech men, named Miloslav, was familiar to Peter. It could only have been from the school so many years ago. The other man was named Josef.

Immediately Peter asked, "Does anyone in Tachau know that you had contact with Trudi or her mother?"

"No, Peter. . . I am sure of that. We always met secretly after our first chance meeting at the post office. I had to be sure she wouldn't expose me as a German. Then we started talking about getting out. She says that she and her mother desperately want out. I invited her to come with us, but she declined. We are all very grateful for her help. I trust her as a dear friend and as the true Germans that we are."

The three defectors were being handled with minimum security because Peter had assisted their escape and was aware of some detailed background on two of them. They were assured they would be safe in their current location while awaiting their formal interrogation the next morning. After they had received food, showered and had rested, the MI knew from experience that the defectors would be more likely to answer questions and talk freely about their experiences.

Monday, July 7, 1958 . . . Es corial was allowed to observe the questioning from outside the secure interrogation room. Sgt Martinez was present for the interrogation observation. The trained MI interrogation team was thorough. The questions ranged from how they knew each other, to their backgrounds and to the actual escape method. More intelligence-oriented questions followed. Anton couldn't add any intelligence information that Trudi hadn't already provided, although his answers did serve as a crosscheck confirmation of previously obtained data. The two Czech guards were not involved with the military combat forces of which they knew little. They offered what was often heard from defectors about the reasons for defecting. The slow, subtle foothold of communism, loss of freedom and the stagnant economy were not to their liking. Es corial had no doubt about the sincerity of the defectors. In time, the Czechs would probably be released to West German authorities for resettlement. Sgt Martinez was certain that Anton would be useful for further assistance to the es corial team.

Major Taylor wanted to discuss the results of the interrogation along with the use of Anton's Czech identification as part of Peter's intrusion plan. Peter seized the opportunity to ask permission to extract Trudi when he returned. He was surprised at the quick affirmative response. Obviously the major had considered this possibility and received approval from USAREUR G-2.

The major explained, "We couldn't have been happier with the quality of information and with the assistance we received from Trudi. She can add even more when she is safely under our control. Your fake identity idea and your plan for extracting Trudi and her mother are a go."

Peter had expected that his plan would eventually gain approval. He was relieved and somewhat surprised that it happened so fast.

"We have encountered no red flags while studying this plan. Anton's identification is authentic. Hopefully you will never need to use his ID but it does provide a layer of security and could provide you with ease of movement in Tachau. That will be your call when you get there."

"How soon, sir? When can I go?"

"It looks like the three tunnel fingers at Yankee will be finished this week. The crews have named them 'Larry, Curly and Moe.' " Curly, which is the center finger will be the exit tunnel. They have found a clear exit point surrounded by large broadleaf-tree roots. You should be well concealed when exiting the tunnel."

Team es corial felt a high degree of satisfaction and relief that they had come this far.

"But, you have work to do before then. You have a potential rendezvous with Trudi's mom——*Frau* Jelinek, correct?"

"Yes sir . . . on Thursday."

"And then you will need to meet with Anton to discuss Tachau. You will need to avoid people that know him and places that he frequented. You need to avoid situations where there is a chance of recognition. Your hair colors and styles are similar, but you might need a tint job. There may be other considerations before you attempt to imitate Anton . . . er, should I say Jaroslav? The point is, you have work to do!"

Willie asked the major, "Sir, can you give us the map coordinates of the Curly exit point? We will also need the date and title of the map sheet to ensure compatibility."

"Good point, sergeant, I'll get that to you later today."

"Good, then we can plot and record compass azimuths and estimate distances that can be checked with a pedometer as Peter progresses from checkpoint to checkpoint. Hopefully, he can use a series of back azimuths on the return route."

Thursday, July 10, 1958 . . . Peter sat on the first bench found on the walking trail *Waldpfad Bichl* waiting for his rendezvous with *Frau* Jelinek. He remembered Trudi had called her Hannelore; as youngsters they were never on a first-name basis with adults. Soon, Peter saw a woman walking in his direction pretending to visually scan the surroundings. As she neared his bench, he stood in respect from force of habit.

"Pardon me, young man, have you been to the *Blitzbaum?*"

The question caught him by surprise even though it was

the perfect word to establish their contact. Thinking quickly, he answered, "Yes, many years ago I saw it in Tachau."

She paused momentarily, then replied, "You must be Gertrude's friend."

"Athletic Trudi . . . Yes, we are friends from long ago. You must be *Frau* Jelinek."

"Little Peter . . . you have grown and have become a handsome man. Things have changed since you were a boy in Tachau . . . and, I prefer the name Hannelore Kehle when I am in West Germany. I think Trudi told you my husband died; so now we are Germans—alienated and stranded in Czechoslovakia."

Peter appreciated, but ignored the flattering remark, preferring to seek answers and information quickly.

"What do you know of my parents?"

Hannelore's expression noticeably saddened as she seemed to search for words.

"It was horrifying, Peter. I never told Trudi because I was afraid it would devastate her at such a young age. As time went by, she saw how the Germans were treated, so I didn't have to burden her with specifics."

"What did happen?" Peter was aware that the details probably wouldn't be good, but Hannelore's story almost brought him to his knees.

"It was another tumultuous and noisy expulsion morning. I could hear the soldiers shouting and firing their weapons over by the river, so I found my way to the wall where I could see what was going on. I wasn't required to wear the white armband so nobody stopped me. I saw everything with binoculars."

"And?"

It was difficult for Hannelore to continue, but felt she had to tell the truth. "I saw Isabella and Armin being forced along the bridge with many other German families. A little girl fell and was crying. A soldier yelled at her and kicked her. Armin stopped and tried to comfort the girl."

"What happened?"

Hannelore's limp body was holding back tears, but she continued, "The soldier used his rifle butt to hit Armin with a vicious blow to his head. He fell to the surface of the bridge and didn't move. Isabella was screaming and crying while she tried to fight the soldiers."

Peter was visibly shaken. He sat down.

"The soldiers yelled at Armin to get up, but he didn't respond. They picked him up and threw him over the side of the bridge. Isabella didn't hesitate . . . she climbed up on the bridge railing and jumped. You know the bridge; it was forty meters or so above the water. Nobody went after them."

Hannelore tried to comfort Peter in his obvious state of shock. They both cried while Hannelore held him tightly.

"I'm so sorry, Peter. You might have looked for them the rest of your life if I hadn't told you. There may be a few Germans still living in the East who knew what happened, but it's doubtful. There are hundreds of murder stories to tell from the days of the expulsions."

Peter recovered quickly. He had always known that something like this was a possibility. The reality was a severe shock, but he knew he had to regain his composure and carry on.

"That's one reason I am here, Hannelore. I wanted to know what happened to them. Now I have eyewitness proof of the atrocities and I have photographic proof hidden away in the *Blitzbaum*."

"Trudi mentioned that. We want out, but I can't just stay in Germany and leave her behind in Tachau."

"Tell her the plan is set for the twenty-fourth or for August seventh. You will both be leaving Czechoslovakia permanently. By the time I see her next week, I should have the date set. You will be with your mother in Thanhausen and I will meet Trudi at the *Blitzbaum*. She should work until late afternoon on escape day and then tell the colonel she is going for a training run. She won't be missed until the next morning. By that time she will be with you in West Germany!"

"How will you get in and both of you get out?"

"I can't tell you that. It's security in case something goes wrong. Hannelore, I know you are afraid. I'm afraid, also. But let me tell you what I have done to create this opportunity and what has motivated me since I was eleven years old. My parents were good people, like you, and any number of other Germans. They helped Czechs and treated them fairly. My parents were not Nazis. They didn't deserve their fate. I'm determined to expose what happened in the Sudetenland, whether the world wants to hear it or not. I spent my life preparing for this opportunity. It's going to work and I'm very happy that you and Trudi will be a part of it. The beginning of a new life for all of us is the prize. We can once again live like free people to pursue what we will in life . . . and beside that . . . I love Trudi! There, I've said it out loud for the first time."

"I trust you, Peter, as does Trudi. I know she never forgot you in all those years. We will do what we have to do. You can count on us. I am pleased that you have such feelings for Trudi."

When it was time for Hannelore to go to the border-crossing

site, each had teary eyes as they embraced physically and emotionally.

"I'm so sorry, Peter."

"Thank you, Hannelore. The rage I feel is tempered by your understanding and truthfulness. I needed the closure on that part of my life."

As Peter watched her walk away quickly with bowed head, he knew they were both looking to the future with a silent resolve.

THIRTY TWO

WHO PETER IS

Monday, July 14, 1958 . . . On Monday, Sgt Martinez informed the team that Larry, Curly and Moe were finished and that Curly was the designated exit finger. When the team returned to Site Yankee for a final inspection, they found everything in order: lighting, air, water, first aid, radios, weapons and landline telephone. A crude rock bench had been carved out of the granite and there was a short step ladder to facilitate Peter's exit and prevent caving in the edges of what was being called the "window." The plywood window of the exit had been fitted with a frame to reinforce and prevent a cave-in and minimize the possibility of detection. The three tunnel exit areas were located within the forbidden zone that was off-limits to local residents; homes within a kilometer of the border had been involuntarily condemned or completely destroyed. No farming, logging or recreation was allowed in the restricted area without border patrol supervision. The immediate exit area from Curly was expected to be isolated from any activity, which was an enormous advantage for Peter. For further preparation and study in their compound work-area, they had obtained: maps, compass, backpack bag, camera, binoculars, Czech *Koruna*, flashlight with filtered lens and the Jaroslav Hruby identification documents.

Peter would meet with Trudi on Thursday to confirm the escape for the following Thursday. Intelligence from Hoherbogen and Mt Schneeberg led the sixty-sixth MI to believe that the Warsaw Pact maneuver would not be conducted until November. No increase in radio traffic was noted as of the July 13 *Bohemia Status of Warsaw Pact* report, which was generated in-part with intelligence received from the three observation outposts. The es corial mission was authorized to go because valuable information had already been delivered by the team and more could be added with minimal risk, if immediate action was taken. Supervisors at all levels, to include USAREUR, wanted to reward Trudi and Hannelore, who they considered agents deserving of protection.

A secondary, but extremely important consideration was to accomplish the intrusion with entry-exit means undetectable upon completion of the mission. If the circumstances of Trudi's disappearance were never discovered, Larry, Curly and Moe could be used in November or whenever deemed necessary by USAREUR G2. For Peter Ackerman—the man—the entry into Tachau was another high-risk, high-reward situation, just like the high-risk, high-reward circumstance of Peter Ackerman—the boy—twelve years earlier.

Thursday, July 17, 1958 . . . Trudi was on-time as usual. The concerned look on her face gave Peter reason to worry momentarily, but it soon became clear.

"*Muti* told me about your parents, Peter. I am so sorry."

"Thanks for the concern, Trudi. I will never forget them. I only wish I had a way to vent personally. I'd like to hurt someone for what happened to them."

"No you don't, Peter. That's not who you are. You'll try to bring all the guilty Czechs and Russians to justice. That's what your plan has been since you left Tachau. Nothing changes except the hope you held out for them. I was a girl when my *Vati* died. It's all so useless. We have to continue to live and do what we can to bring criminals to justice and make life better for everyone."

"Of course, you are correct. That's why we are here. I'm glad I have you to help me focus on the job at hand. Next week we will meet at the *Blitzbaum*."

Peter gave her all the details of the plan that concerned her. He warned her to not approach him in the event she saw him anywhere other than the *Blitzbaum*. It wasn't likely to happen, but they had to prepare for every eventuality. Their meeting would be Thursday evening, but his military intelligence-seeking mission necessitated his entry into Czechoslovakia on Tuesday night. He suggested taking comfortable hiking-type shoes and rugged clothing to the *Blitzbaum* before Thursday evening, if possible. He also asked her to leave a blanket there because he might sleep there when he got a chance, and July evenings were usually rather cool in this part of Europe. Water might be important, as well as some sausage and bread—fresh or stale. Weather-wise, only fog might be a deterrent. Peter had hoped to go in cloudless weather for more light. Part of the reason the next Thursday was chosen was because the weather forecast was good. He had to identify checkpoints and needed some light to do so. Light was risky, but necessary for this mission.

"Be prepared to walk and run quickly for as many as ten kilometers. We may have to hide and wait at times. We will be taking the same route out that brought me in if it's safe. Good weather will be important for us to move rapidly, but we will not sacrifice caution for speed. In addition to route familiarity, I will have my compass and I have memorized an old hiking trail map. For our purposes that map is even better than the military topographic maps. Trails, roads, streams and other bodies of water will be important. Buildings and trail-marking and other signs will be less important if they are new because they may not appear on maps. I can tell you, now, so you won't worry; we will be exiting Czechoslovakia by means of a tunnel constructed by the US Army."

"I thought it would be a tunnel. If you get in, I won't worry about us getting out. Do you know about the aircraft beacon near the *Blitzbaum?*"

"No! Is that something new? There was never a beacon there when we were youngsters. Willie did mention a light when we were doing a night reconnaissance near Bärnau, but he could never pinpoint where or what it was."

"The Russians constructed that back in the late forties. It was so long ago I had almost forgotten about it. I think they use it to warn about the elevation of the hill and guide their helicopters to the airstrip at Mýto."

"That's valuable information for me, Trudi. I may be able to use that as a guide to the *Blitzbaum*. When we return safely to West Germany, I must remember to send Colonel Gochenko a thank-you note for the helpful beacon."

With a slight giggle, Trudi commented, "You are so thoughtful, Peter!"

"Remember the black guy from the *Gasthof Zur Post?*"

"Yes."

"That's my partner and boss . . . Sgt Willie Kyles. The next time you see him, we will be safe. He may be the first American you see after we enter the tunnel."

"I'm afraid, Peter, but there is no turning back now. If it wasn't for you, I wouldn't do this. M*uti* is anxious and afraid also. She will worry until she sees me in West Germany. We've never been together in West Germany."

"The plan is to get you, *Muti* and *Oma* to a safe house in Mähring. We need to get all of you out of Thanhausen just in case somebody has been following you and reporting your activities. Mähring is temporary until the army can provide you with a new location. I may have some input in that decision."

"I want to be near you, Peter."

"And I want to be near you. I think that is going to happen."

For a moment they became pensive, reflecting on their mostly chaotic lives. Their days of carefree running through Studánka were a distant memory. Trudi barely remembered the good times in Tachau. Her life had been turned upside down by the Nazis, who set events in motion that caused a downward spiral in the lives of her family members. Peter had endured the beginning of the Sudetenland disaster, and now realized that his parents had made a good decision in encouraging and enabling his escape from Tachau. Soon the culmination of his plan to return to Tachau would come to fruition. For better or for worse—the time had arrived.

Before Trudi departed, she stopped Peter in his tracks. "I

want you to know that I love you. Never forget that no matter what happens in the next week!"

"And I love you, Trudi Kehle. We will see better times if we stay strong and smart! I will see you Thursday evening before it gets dark."

THIRTY THREE

SHOW TIME

July 18-22, 1958 . . . Team es corial worked on the intrusion plan to be submitted to Major Taylor in time to have it reviewed and forwarded to USAREUR for approval. Every conceivable detail was put in writing: equipment, false ID, projected route, approximate exit and reentry times, possible sites to be observed in Tachau, behavior if detained and the fact that Gertrude Kehle would return with Sgt Ackerman.

The plan was detailed to the point that Peter would carry much-coveted West German HB cigarettes as bargaining items, and a moderate amount of *Koruna* currency and coins.

Willie had done most of the map work and route planning. He instructed Peter to proceed on an azimuth of 87 degrees after reaching the tree line near his exit point. The pedometer would be helpful for estimations of distance traveled between checkpoints, but because of the unknown zigzag nature of the route it couldn't be used as a definitive gauge of distance. They had discussed Trudi's revelation of the probable purpose and location of the beacon light near the *Blitzbaum*. Following the tree line would enable Peter to negotiate the entire four kilometer distance with only one short open space to cross before reaching the wooded *Blitzbaum* area. Peter would rest at the *Blitzbaum* and use it as a base of operations until Trudi arrived late on Thursday. Three suspected military sites had been identified based on: intelligence information from Hoherbogen, Mt Schneeberg, from Trudi and information gained from the three defectors. He would carry necessary equipment: a camera, binoculars, water and a few dehydrated food items to sustain him for two days in the event Trudi was unable to leave sufficient food.

A primary consideration of the intrusion, which had been emphasized by Major Taylor, was that he would make every effort to prevent detention from becoming an East-West "incident." In the event of a detention, Peter's story would be that he was a defector from the US Army trying to escape a courts-martial and, if he was unable to dispose of the Czech ID, his story would be that he had purchased the ID on the Mähring black market. Protection from Warsaw Pact aggression was one NATO objective, provoking an "incident" was to be avoided. For this reason Peter would not carry a weapon and would eschew a military confrontation at all cost.

The plan was in place. Every detail the team could think of had been addressed. Trudi and Hannelore knew what to do. Site Yankee's main cavern was ready as was Larry, Moe and the primary tunnel, Curly. Captain Lokar and Sgt Kyles would be on-site for the duration of the mission. Security teams and tunnel operators would be rotated on twelve hour shifts with a sergeant first class in charge of each. Tuesday night couldn't come soon enough for Peter.

Tuesday evening, July 22, 1958 . . . The team was checking equipment and reviewing the plan before entering Curly. It was almost time to go.

"It's show time, Peter. I don't know another person I would have more confidence in than you. You are my inspiration and my hero. If you don't return by 0300 Friday morning, I'm coming after you."

Peter recognized the attempts at *Atta boy*, but felt comforted by hearing Willie's words. He was numb, but self-confident—afraid, but brave.

"I know the route as well as you. I'll find you if I have to come out—now let's get it on."

At the Curly exit door, the light was extinguished and moonlight shined in from the cloudless night. The tunnel operator peeked out carefully and declared it clear after scanning visually in all directions. Peter used the stepladder to climb out without caving in the sides of the opening. He knew this was a dangerous phase of the operation, but it was going well. He reached down to receive the low-range radio and other items of needed equipment. When the door was replaced, Peter immediately looked for a secure location to conceal the radio that would be easy for him to find when he and Trudi returned. When he found an adequate hiding place he sat down on a tree trunk and turned on the radio to test and report its location, as planned.

In his best Czech accent he said three words. *"dva-vlevo sedm."*

Willie acknowledged the transmission with a return, "*dva-vlevo sedm*."

This coded transmission was to report safe exit from the tunnel and the concealment of the low-range FM radio two steps straight ahead of the tunnel opening and seven steps to the left. This would narrow the search area in the event Willie had to retrieve the radio for whatever reason. A primary concern was to remove the radio, which might lead to the discovery of the tunnel, if Peter didn't return.

Peter concealed the radio and thought to himself how happy he would be to see it again. He took a few minutes to let his eyes fully adjust to the ambient light and to imprint the picture of this location in his memory. He walked back to the sod door and covered it with a few small fallen tree branches that he was able to move quietly. The engineers had done a good job of fitting the displaced sod on a frame which fit the tunnel exit door perfectly. He doubted that anyone would be in this area since it was in the no-entry zone for Czech residents; the disturbed sod wouldn't be noticed unless someone was looking specifically for evidence of human activity, Peter assured himself. He could not see the border guard tower, but he knew it was there. It would have been helpful for orientation if he could see it, but the forest floor was dark and the foliage thick. He could see the tree line, however, as he had hoped. He walked on an azimuth of ten degrees for thirty-two steps to reach the edge of the tree line. He would need to find this exact location on the tree line when he returned. That would enable him to walk thirty-two steps on a back azimuth of one-hundred-ninety degrees in order to reach the radio and the sod door entrance to Curly. But how would he find this exact tree line spot? As he surveyed the open field ahead of him, he noticed a tall rounded object about twenty-five meters away. It looked like a haystack in the poor light, but he reasoned it probably wasn't because of the prohibition of work in this area without border-guard supervision. Must be a glacial erratic left over from an ice-age that Dr Philip Swanson had first brought to his attention, but why worry about what it is, he thought, as long as it didn't move before he returned. He could easily follow along this tree line until the azimuth to the haystack look-alike object was fifteen degrees, as it was at the present. At the tree line he checked his compass again, utilizing its illuminating backlight, for an azimuth of eighty-seven degrees. It was 0130 hours. He wanted to be at the *Blitzbaum* by daylight, which would be about 0430 hours. Following the tree line he saw no one and heard only tree branches rustled about by the soft, cool breeze. He slowly and cautiously moved along the tree line for about fifteen minutes. The tree line seemed to be trending north, which was consistent with his memory of map study, so he checked his compass again. Eighty-seven degrees would be the desired route, when possible, so now he needed to leave the tree line and enter the forested area for about one kilometer. He felt safer and more relaxed with cover all around, but the darkness made his progress slow. He knew this stealthy journey would not have been possible on a cloudy or foggy night.

He made periodic checks for signs marking paths and for the beacon light near the *Blitzbaum*. He stopped at frequent intervals to listen for unnatural noises. He heard nothing! Everything was going as planned. The time was 0209 when he reached a farming area stretching to the north. Here he saw a sign marking the area he had just departed as the beginning of the Czech citizen no-entry zone. He felt relieved that now he had a chance of talking his way out of an accidental meeting with a farmer or other civilian. Military personnel he didn't want to see this night under any circumstances.

Although the open area was on his left, to the north, an azimuth of 89 degrees still took him along a more desired southerly tree line. Suddenly he heard the sound of leaves and underbrush being disturbed. Instinctively he fell and hugged the earth while trying to see what was making the noise. He heard animal noises which sounded like a pig. Then he saw the outline of a huge wild boar about ten meters away in the darkened forest. He could see the two eyes staring at him threateningly. He slowly scooted away on his stomach. When he sensed that the boar was not going to attack, he slowly stood and backed away. The wild boar turned and disappeared in the darkness. The wild animal had given its warning—"Stay away!" He got its message. They communicated well! In his silliness he congratulated himself on understanding the animals "pig Latin." He remembered the research and planning session with Willie when they discussed single nocturnal male wild boars in the central European countryside. They would eat almost anything except humans! Still, he was thankful he hadn't received a boar tusk in his leg.

A close call for Peter, but on the positive side, he reasoned that the wild boar must feel safe here, which could mean humans are not frequently seen in his territory. Peter continued along the tree line cautiously. The new route took him off his desired azimuth slightly, but he felt comfortable with the general easterly direction. Now he was in the interior Czech area away from the border; at nearly 0300 in the morning, hikers would be a curiosity indeed. The restricted area warning sign he had found would serve as a return checkpoint. He wanted to play it very safe until at least daylight, when he could consider posing as Jaroslav Hruby. He had purposely avoided roads for fear of meeting up with a military patrol. He was sure they were out here, he just didn't know where and when. Explaining his presence to a farmer would be much easier than explaining his presence to a Czech or Russian patrol.

The red beacon light caught his eye. Trudi was correct! The light is there and it could be near the *Blitzbaum* area. He checked his compass. The azimuth was almost exactly correct. Now, at the end of this tree line, he only needed to cross an open farming area in order to access the Studánka forest. He relaxed momentarily and sat to take a short rest.

Wednesday, July 23, 1958 . . . 0330 hours. Following the tree line had taken him a little further to the southeast than he intended. What he gained was a shorter route to the Studánka forested hill by way of a hiking trail his memory told him he would find. Crossing the open farming field would have meant difficult passage through deep plowed rows of soil, which was not only difficult walking, but could also leave evidence of something with two legs having crossed. The trail was shorter and smoother, but more likely to encounter civilians or border patrols. But not at 0330! After studying the surrounding area for a few minutes, he quickly started up the slightly rising trail. The night was windless and on the cool side when sitting. He heard and saw nothing except the flashing red airport guidance beacon as he moved rapidly along the trail. He could make out the tree line where the trail appeared to enter the forest. The relative safety of the wooded area, with which he was somewhat familiar from twelve years earlier, was reassuring. As he paused at the forest's edge, his pedometer had registered the number of steps roughly equivalent to five hundred meters. This information might be useful when he returned with Trudi.

The trail through the rising hillside took him to an area he recognized. He quickly found his old friend—the *Blitzbaum*. The nostalgic element of once again standing before his personal childhood icon gave him momentary pause. It was a fleeting moment of his memories return to more pleasant days, but he quickly dismissed the distraction from his current mission. The light from the beacon was coming from about two hundred meters to the north. Peter was aware that maintenance or security personnel might be near the beacon, but reasoned that Trudi would have mentioned that if it was going to be a problem for him. Whatever the circumstance, he would be especially alert for military vehicles when he later ventured into Tachau.

Trudi had replaced the thin clothesline rope with a much sturdier rope. Peter smiled at her thoughtfulness. Neither of them weighed forty to fifty kilograms (eighty-eight to one hundred-ten pounds), since their physical maturity. The shop plug/weight was attached to one end of the rope. He tossed the weight over a large branch, shook the rope until the weight notched itself, and he climbed into the familiar bowl above the tree's huge bole. He pulled the rope up in order to conceal it. Trudi had been there! There was a blanket enclosed in a plastic cover to keep it dry, a large bottle of *Sinalco* lemon drink, an apple and a neatly wrapped package of assorted sandwich meats. She also left a short note that read: "*Wie eins,*"and was signed "*Lili Marlene.*" The message was a reminder of her thoughtfulness and of her ability to connect with him. She had obviously never forgotten their spirit of camaraderie even in this most dangerous of times. He checked and found that his packet was present and had not been disturbed. He felt secure for the first time since leaving Site Yankee. It was after 0430 as the first light appeared in the east. He was relaxed and exhausted. The blanket kept the chill off while he slept.

THIRTY FOUR

THE RUSSIAN SOLDIERS

Wednesday, July 23, 1958 . . . 0730 hours. Peter awoke to bright light and the chattering of a red squirrel whose territory he had encroached. Even squirrels get upset and belligerent when strangers violate their space. "Calm down, Mr Red Squirrel, I'm not after your nuts . . . or whatever it is you eat." Talking to himself had a soothing effect on his inner soul. His mind needed a break from the pressure he felt for the dangerous exploration ahead. "Not much has changed for you, has it Mr Red Squirrel? You know nothing of the suffering caused by human politics here in your space. When a human fells your tree, you just move to the next tree if another still exists. OK, OK, so it is tough for you, too!" It's crazy how the human brain works when it is not challenged by human interaction.

Solitude and danger trigger thoughts hidden away in the recesses of the human mind. The squirrel and his situation triggered some of those thoughts in Peter's mind. The fact that he was a spy moved to the first position of his thought process. He knew what the Russians did with spies. It wasn't a pleasant thought, but it was reality. He suppressed that thought and began his preparation for the day.

Peter had heard a helicopter overhead during the night. From several locations on the hill he could view specific landmarks in Tachau and the vicinity. The airfield at Mýto was clearly visible with his binoculars. He saw five helicopters and two fixed-wing aircraft tethered outside two hangars. There was also a refueling tanker and several maintenance-type vehicles visible. Construction work appeared to be in progress with road-clearing and support vehicles. It appeared to be a runway-lengthening project. Peter estimated the current runway at about one-thousand meters with lengthening to extend another three to four hundred meters. The added length might provide sufficient surface to land troops or equipment-bearing aircraft safely. He mentally reminded himself that his job was to collect information   not to make evaluations—but it was his nature to try to put two and two together.

From other locations on the Studánka hilltop he could make out what appeared to be military installations in areas that Trudi had brought to his attention. He would have to get closer to these installations to better determine what equipment and manpower was present at those bases. That was his primary duty agenda.

As he moved around the hilltop he didn't see anyone until he neared the trail that he and Trudi had frequented so often in their youth. The trail was no longer in good condition. Vegetation was threatening to overtake the main walkway and there was evidence that heavy vehicles had recently caused ruts in the soft shoulders. A lady on a bicycle was straining to overcome the steepness of the trail. There was an empty plastic and metal bottle-carrying container strapped to the frame of the bicycle, which Peter remembered as an everyday sight of his young life in Tachau. Built as a case for bottles, it was sometimes a permanent fixture on the bicycle to be used to transport any number of items.

"*Dobrý den*,"greeted Peter as he spoke his first Czech words to a native since exiting the tunnel. He wondered what she was doing on the hill so early in the morning. She was probably searching for firewood or maybe even mushroom hunting, although it was early in the year for mushrooms.

She ignored him with a scowl. Peter was momentarily taken aback, but remembered that the locals were not especially friendly with strangers even when he lived here. Unhappy people seldom smile. They often lash out at the slightest provocation, except of course, when dealing with persons of more stature or power.

So be it, he thought, this is the attitude I must be comfortable with until I can meet Trudi tomorrow evening and take her to West Germany. To gain confidence, it would be good to make a few non-threatening contacts before he got into more dangerous situations. He had decided to try to blend in with the current everyday conduct of Tachau life unless it was obvious he was arousing suspicion. Several times he rehearsed his story of purchasing the fake identification and being a defector from the US Army. He knew if he ever had to use that story he was in deep trouble. The Russians were not going to release him until they felt they had gleaned every bit of intelligence information that they felt he might possess, and probably not even then. American defectors, deemed no longer useful for intelligence or any other purpose, were thought to be prisoners spirited away in the remoteness of Siberia.

His first task, as he entered Tachau proper was to test how to become an almost invisible body attempting to survive in the depressed economy. He was surprised at how closely he resembled the young men he saw on the streets of Tachau. For the most part, they were loners in tattered clothing with sad looks on their faces. Good, thought Peter. He had dressed appropriately for the party. Nobody paid attention to him in his Jaroslav Hruby disguise. Social interaction was minimal which pleased Peter. He could easily play a down-and-out loner. A few commercial outlets were open for business if you wanted to stand in line until your entrance was allowed. An employee accompanied the customers in non-food stores. When the customer selected an item for purchase the employee took the item to the cash register, where the transaction was completed. In the food stores it was more complicated. First, you stood in line to gain access to the enclosed shelves where limited selections were available. Then you gave the number of the item to be purchased to the employee, who gave the customer a written list of selected items. Another line was for payment and yet another for actually gaining possession of the item(s). Although *Muti* was the provisions shopper in his family when he lived in Tachau, he had no recollection of shortages of goods or these complicated purchasing procedures. West Germans, who had lost the war, already enjoyed more availability of food and consumer goods than what he observed in Tachau.

This was interesting, if not depressing, but Peter had work to do. Uniformed soldiers were visible: some Russian, some Czech. Peter made a mental note of the insignia on the uniforms because they might identify the type of unit they were assigned to. He was nervous about possessing the camera tucked away in his bag and decided against taking pictures at this time. At this point he wasn't sure what the reaction would be if he provoked one of the soldiers.

Peter's plan was to return to the *Blitzbaum* as darkness approached. Today he would go to the area of Bilitin/Lom and tomorrow to Ctibor. These areas had been identified by Trudi as sites that she knew were used by the military. To get to Bilitin he could walk about four kilometers or he could find a bus going in that direction. He had seen several old rusty, faded-red busses with some dirty, broken windows, but hadn't noticed destination signs. He walked a few hundred meters to the central bus station that he remembered and found that it was still in use. Movable sandwich-board type signs were placed at obvious bus loading locations. One of the signs read Lom and had a listing of departure times. At 1115 hours the bus arrived fifteen minutes late.

He rode past the stop for Bilitin reasoning that he could go to Lom and walk back toward Bilitin. The military facility would be somewhere in the area, hopefully. From his dirty, broken window, he saw the facility to the southeast. He got off at the next stop and searched for high ground that provided cover. He expected only to determine the size of the facility, which military occupied the facility and the types of vehicles moving in and out. He found the high spot he needed and got his camera ready. He could see large vehicles with tubes capable of firing high explosives, but couldn't determine if they were Czech or Russian, or if they were tanks or artillery. He took some photos and made a mental note that his security was even more important with the photos in his possession. After he had a number of photos and for the reason of security, he decided to move on for the day. He found a trail leading in the direction of Tachau. It might take an hour to get back to Tachau, but afforded time for general observation and was safer since the camera contents now required extreme protection. In town, he found a kiosk with bottled drinks and meat sandwiches. It didn't matter what the meat was . . . he was famished.

Peter was curious about his former home that had been confiscated by the Czechs. He carefully walked by in case residents from his childhood recognized him. He couldn't do anything, he just wanted to have a look in order to satisfy a somewhat depressing curiosity. It brought back memories of his childhood and his family. The house appeared to be poorly maintained and the garden was grown over with weeds. The lawn chairs he had relaxed in so often were no longer present. Sadness overcame him, but he didn't linger.

He walked past one of the seventeen Tachau wall-towers, which had been restored and maintained, and through the Church of St Wenceslas wall gate where he had so often met Trudi for their training runs and trips to the *Blitzbaum*. In the direction of the Mže River he heard loud male voices talking and laughing which he thought had to be something very unusual. As he approached the noisy area, he saw that it was a group of Russian soldiers drinking at an outdoor *zahrádka*. This was a case of unexpected situations appearing suddenly which require quick thinking. He wasn't quite sure whether to avoid the beer garden altogether, or get closer to see what might develop. He was aware of the sensitivity of his pack containing camera, film and binoculars. The soldiers were drunk, loud and boisterous; and they might also have loose tongues! He didn't understand the Russian language, but sign language had a way of overcoming some communication problems. He had seen the American soldiers in Bad Tölz do quite well with non-English-speaking *Fräuleins* and other Germans using only their crude hand signals and body language. One of the Russian soldiers looked his way, stood, and motioned for him to come to their table. Hesitantly, he moved toward the group.

In heavily accented Russian, the soldier spoke some Czech and invited him to sit with them. Peter was hoping the group just wanted to tell him how good they were. The soldier asked Peter's name and drunkenly shook his hand. His Czech language was barely understandable, but Peter did his best to pretend to understand. He didn't want to pass on this unexpected target of opportunity. The Russian introduced himself as Dmitri. His friends were Josef, Vladimir and Boris. They bought Peter a beer, which they called *piva*. Good, Peter thought: a place to start. Beer in Czech is *pivo*—in Russian, *piva*. He smiled, shook hands and tried to relax. Obviously the soldiers wanted to show a friendship toward Peter, who appeared to them to be a local Czech peasant. He played along.

Dmitri soon got into the bragging mode, which Peter had hoped for. He didn't even have to ask questions. All he did was listen, smile and offer his kindest words about Russia and the local Russian soldiers. Soldiers in all armies have a tendency to talk about how important they are to their country and how good they are at their jobs. Dmitri was no different. His insignia identified him as a non-commissioned-officer in the artillery. His loud talk varied from how Russia loved the Czechs to how much better the artillery was than the infantry units stationed with him in Lom. Peter listened and smiled. He couldn't believe his intelligence windfall. The more he stoked their egos the more Dmitri talked. He only hoped he could remember all this without suspiciously asking for repeats when Dmitri's Czech language mumblings became drunkenly unintelligible.

As darkness approached Peter looked for a way out. He knew he had to get back to the *Blitzbaum* and didn't want to drink too much more beer. He made up an excuse, shook everybody's hand, and turned to go.

"Wait, Jaroslav!"

Peter held his breath as he turned to face Dmitri.

"You forgot your bag."

"Peter, you better get some sleep." He was talking to himself again after the near compromising blunder. Getting the windfall information was one thing, but nearly compromising the mission and everything he was currently living for was something else. He had nearly made a disastrous blunder, but still, a certain feeling of security enabled him to hike the path to the *Blitzbaum* rather casually. When he was secure at the "place," he made some notes about the day's activities as his memory was quickly becoming oversaturated with potentially important information. He was rather surprised that he had not encountered any acknowledgement of the recent defection of the Czech border guards, but dismissed that thought as being because they didn't want to publicize the fact that any Czech could be unhappy with the new communist Czechoslovakia. Dmitri had bragged about the November live-fire phase of a joint Czech-Russian training maneuver north of Tachau and into East Germany. That meant it would be conducted in the area the US Military called the Fulda Gap. Peter was well aware of the concern the intelligence people had about the potential for invasion through the Fulda Gap. An apparent training exercise would be an opportunity to mobilize and amass a formidable fighting force under conditions NATO forces would consider a threat and would monitor closely.

Sleep was fitful at best for Peter. Not only was he excited about the mission and the meeting with Trudi scheduled for the next evening, but the night was very chilly and the hard tree branch was hardly a comfortable mattress. Peter had rejected an offer to stay at Trudi's house as too dangerous for both of them. She had Czech neighbors who would be suspicious of strangers sneaking into the house after hours. Some might even recognize Peter. Life had always been unpredictable for those Germans remaining in Tachau after the expulsions, and even more so for Hannelore Jelinek and her daughter after the death of Hannelore's Czech husband. He shrugged off all the inconveniences as he remembered that this was what Special Forces troopers do. Sleep overcame Peter despite thoughts of recent and future events associated with his entry into Czechoslovakia.

THIRTY FIVE

AUF WIEDERSEHEN, TACHAU

Thursday, July 24, 1958 . . . Trudi was relieved when she awoke early Thursday morning. Relieved that she had been able to get some restful sleep even with the anticipation of what she hoped was her last day in Czechoslovakia forever. Hannelore was already busy preparing for her last day under the current communist doctrine after a lifetime of ever-changing, unstable government entities in Tachau. It was a nervous time for both Trudi and her mother as thoughts of the danger and the potential reward flashed through their minds. They were experiencing a controlled nervousness that results from making dangerous life-changing decisions which are resolute and from which there can be no reversal.

"What will you take with you, *Muti?* I know they always inspect your belongings just like they always do mine."

Trudi was referring to the border crossing procedure that her mother would endure en route to *Oma's* residence in Thanhausen.

"That's the sad part of leaving as an escapee, Trudi. I can't take anything but identification, the clothes on my back, a few

Koruna and a gift for *Oma*. We will be homeless and penniless, but if it wasn't for the promise of a brighter future, we wouldn't be doing this."

They both readied themselves as if it were a normal day. They planned to leave no indication that there had been an escape plan. When the authorities came searching for the missing women, they would find nothing but an empty lived-in house. That Hannelore didn't return would be explainable, but Trudi smiled at how the mystery of her whereabouts would perplex the local authorities. She felt sure that her disappearance and the failure of her mother to return from Thanhausen would eventually lead to the conclusion that she had defected. Colonel Gochenko would stand with egg on his face before his superiors because he had vouched for, and granted special favors to his athletic protégé. Trudi had always appreciated the good intentions of the colonel for the reason of her own interests. That his country's politics left much to be desired didn't make him a bad man. She felt a twinge of regret for the position she would leave him in, but she realized that life was more than winning races to satisfy his vicarious appetite.

When she had an athletic uniform and running shoes packed, she stood by the door trying to find comforting and reassuring words for her mother. Their next meeting would be in West Germany. Peter had assured her that her mother and grandmother would be moved or protected as soon as Hannelore reached Thanhausen and that they would all be together again as soon as Trudi had made a successful escape. Everything seemed to be in order.

"Auf wiedersehen, Muti, bis Morgen."

Trudi bid her mother good-bye until tomorrow. It was the

most difficult good-bye of her life. They both realized that this could be the beginning of a better life or the end of any life at all. They embraced until Trudi pulled back, looked her mother in her eyes and conveyed, without speaking, the love and understanding she had for her. Their eyes held the visual embrace until Trudi turned and walked out the door. They understood they had to be very clever and especially strong for the next twenty-four hours. They were both confident they were up to the challenge as the controlled nervousness returned. Trudi hurried along to her workplace office.

Peter had another job to do. He wanted to verify what Dmitri had so willfully bragged about the night before at the *zahrádka*. Dmitri had been more than willing to talk about all the local military installations even though he was stationed at Lom. Ctibor was three kilometers away just northeast of Mýto, where the airstrip was being lengthened. It was convenient, thought Peter, that they would have a facility with infantry and artillery units so close to an airstrip capable of landing troop and cargo-carrying transport planes. This isn't the Fulda Gap, but its close enough for these Warsaw Pact units to reach in a few hours.

He was confident enough to walk via a trail he found on his trail map. In forty-five minutes he was close enough to see the military compound. He had passed only a few disinterested Czechs along the mostly flat trail. The flat trail was good for rapid walking, but bad for getting enough elevation to see inside the compound. The entire area was flat, but the compound was enclosed in only a chain-link fence which afforded him partial vision. It was true! Dmitri had given him accurate information

about the units stationed here. He could see self-propelled how-
itzers and armored personnel carriers. He made sure he wasn't
being observed before he took some pictures. He moved from
one location to another to get better views and insure that he
wasn't too obvious by working too long out of a single location.
He could see guards with dogs walking inside the perimeter
fence. The soldiers were doing maintenance on the tracked vehicles with what appeared to be five or six-man crews. He would
record all this information when he returned to the *Blitzbaum* as
a backup to the photographic evidence. Risky, of course, and not
a part of the standard operating procedure (SOP) for this mission, but the potential loss of valuable information outweighed
the minimal risk of compromise in this case. This thought reminded him that the mission was far from complete. It had been
a smooth, unencumbered mission to this point, but he understood the risk of getting careless.

Peter again made a quick survey of his surroundings to be
sure he wasn't under observation before he started back to
the Studánka hill. Along the way he found a crude bench a few
meters off the trail which looked like a good, shady place to
rest and snack on some hard salami. A young Czech man soon
came from the trail and engaged Peter in conversation. Peter
was hesitant and guarded with this stranger, but it appeared
he was also just resting and passing time. After a few words
of mutual acknowledgement, the conversation turned to the
recent defectors. It seems the Russians had made it very clear
in the Tachau newspaper that this defection was an inexcus-
able act by some Czech traitors, and that all border guards
would be replaced by Russian military personnel in the near
future. The warning also alluded to the fact that additional

mines would be placed between the raked sandy ground cover and the vehicle patrol path. Peter doubted the accuracy of the stated locations, but had no doubt that many mines were out there. Why would border security tell the populace exactly where the mines were being installed?

Peter recognized this as an opportunity to get some input about the morale of the typical Czech, now that Soviet policies had been fully implemented.

"Some people just want out, it seems," said Peter.

"Can you blame them," the stranger asked? "After three different phases of economic reform, we are just as poor as ever. I still don't have a job. They keep telling me I will be assigned a job soon, but it never happens. Do you have a job?"

"No, and I don't think I'll apply to be a border guard now, either."

They both chuckled over the joke. Peter wanted to maintain the levity of the conversation so he continued with another joke. "Do you know why the Russians will always have three guards in the towers at one time?"

Sensing something humorous to follow, the young man smiled and answered, "No! Why?"

"Because one knows how to operate the radio, one can read a map and the other is there to keep an eye on the two intellectuals!"

The stranger laughed loudly while Peter smiled and chuckled along with him. The stranger realized it wasn't a good idea to get too far into civil unrest with someone he didn't know, but the truth was that there was an underground resistance group, of which he had knowledge, that was growing in numbers and degree of discontent.

This encounter would also be reported by Peter because he knew that Major Taylor and the American MI liked to pore over any and all intelligence from the East. Soon Peter said good-bye and started on his way. It wouldn't be long until he met with Trudi and they could be on their way to Site Yankee.

Trudi arrived at work before Yelena and Božena. The Russian guard at the building entrance checked her ID like he had so many times in the past. The *Tagesblatt* newspaper had arrived. Scanning the *Tagesblatt* would be her first task for the day. Political and economic articles of general interest to West Germans were also interesting to the colonel. West German societal progress seemed to be a sore point for the colonel. He never talked about that, but Trudi could detect the jealousy when she translated an article favorable to the welfare of the general West German population. He was also interested in sports news if it included track and field.

The colonel wasn't in a particularly good mood when he arrived. Trudi hoped she could contribute toward the continuation of that mood all the way until tomorrow when she didn't arrive for work. This morning he complained about the tea and then about the news stories. Trudi wanted to remind him that if it wasn't for German goldsmith Johannes Gutenberg inventing the printing press over four hundred years ago, he wouldn't even have a newspaper to read. She had learned since the colonel's arrival that subtle digs like this usually shut him up for a while.

Good man, bad politics: from a country historically poor and oppressive. But, she couldn't argue with his pragmatism.

He did what he had to do, in order to achieve his desired lifestyle, with whatever structured opportunities existed. She, on
the other hand, would soon be where she could achieve her
lifestyle of choice according to her personal ability and degree
of motivation. At least that was what Peter implied, and what
she believed.

It was a rather routine day for Trudi fraught with an anxiety she fought to conceal. The colonel was always interested in
her training so he granted her request to leave for the sports
club a few minutes early. This always made the other ladies in
the office angry, but, at this point, she didn't care what they
thought. Božena was easy to get along with but she had never
been fond of Yelena. Good-bye girls, good-bye colonel, good-
bye working for the evil empire and *Auf wiedersehen* Tachau. I'm
out of here! She waved at the Russian guard, suppressing the
urge to express her nefarious thoughts about the local Russian
soldiers, as she confidently moved along toward the athletic
club.

After changing clothes and securing her bag she departed
the club. She had left her work clothing behind so whoever was
looking for her might think she was accosted somewhere along
one of her many cross-country running trails. Any confusion
she could create about her disappearance might be helpful. She
knew she had time. Peter had instructed her to meet him "in
the evening." She assumed the escape would be well after dark.
Peter had told her about the symbolism of using the Tachau
westerly-directed street called Americká for his escape. Peter
now lived in America where she hoped she would someday
live. The symbolism might seem meaningless, but to her, it
was an expression of the finality of her decision to defect. She

could feel the adrenaline rush and the morale boost just by thinking about West Germany and America. She had no fear as she jogged through the streets toward the Americká better-life route to the West.

THIRTY SIX

HALLO, DEUTSCHLAND

1900 hours . . . Peter waited in the park away from the *Blitzbaum* where he could see the Tachau-Studánka trail. A few disinterested seniors walked by on their evening exercise routes. It was secure for him alone, but together they would need to move to the tree hideout. He saw her in the distance, jogging up the hill as she had in her youth. That Trudi was jogging in Studánka would be nothing unusual for the casual observer; the exercising seniors might not even remember seeing a jogger if they were later questioned.

When she saw him, she smiled broadly. He went to the tree and waited in the seclusion of the nearby thick overhanging vegetation. When she arrived, they embraced until she whispered in his ear, "It's going to happen!"

Peter squeezed her affectionately and whispered in return, "Yes! Let's go up . . . we have to think as one if we want to leave Czechoslovakia tonight. West Germany and your family are waiting for us."

Peter outlined the entire plan for her, complete with map route and numerous danger points.

"It will be very dark, but with some moonlight to be especially aware of in the open spaces. Fortunately the weather is favorable for us. We will leave here about midnight if everything is quiet. The airport beacon will give us some light and provide somewhat of a distraction for anyone in the area. We should avoid looking directly at the light in order to preserve our maximum night vision"

"How far to the tunnel, Peter?"

"Three or four kilometers the way we will go. We will have to cross one open area, but mostly we will be in the tree line. Whisper only!"

"What about your packet?"

"I'll carry that in my bag along with the notes I made and the equipment I brought with me. I can't discard anything because the equipment was all made in America. I don't want to leave any evidence that we were here. All our trash gets deposited in the park containers as long as it has no US markings."

"*Muti* is with *Oma* now. I left her this morning when I went to work."

"Yes . . . nobody will miss her until tomorrow when she doesn't make her return appearance at the border-crossing point. By that time the colonel will be wondering where you are. Their search will begin."

"You're sure *Muti* and *Oma* will be safe in Thanhausen?"

"It's like I told you . . . they will be taken to Mähring before you or your mother are missed. You did tell your mother that, did you not?"

"Yes, I'm just worried."

"Understand . . . I'm worried, too, but not about that part.

I have full confidence that those two ladies will be well cared for."

"What shall we do with this blanket?"

"We're going down to our escape trail in a minute. I want you to see the open area we have to cross later, while vision is still good. We can dispose of the blanket then. Somebody will take it as soon as they see it."

"Can we do that now?"

"No."

"Why not?"

"I heard a dog bark."

"Silly . . . dogs can't talk."

"No, but their owners can."

"Peter, you think of everything!"

"That's why we are going to be in West Germany in a few hours."

At midnight they lowered themselves from the *Blitzbaum*. No evidence that they had ever been there was left behind. Peter shook the rope and weight loose. The rope went in the trash and the weight was thrown into the underbrush.

The tree-lined trail through the park escape route was dark. Trudi could understand the wisdom of checking this area earlier. They could see the light at the end of the trail where the open space began. Peter smiled nervously when he thought about the light at the end of the tunnel really being a freight train. Strange thoughts again crossed his stress-encumbered mind. Apparently mirth and silliness was his way of dealing with pressure. Peter was sure that the stress he felt was probably less than that felt by Trudi. She was risking her life for a chance at a better life with a man she hadn't known for over twelve years. Peter was in awe of her mental and emotional strength as well as the strength of her resolve. Peter felt sure that their collective strength was enhanced by their individual strengths and mutual trust.

At the clearing they waited. They listened and looked. No train, thought Peter, being silly again.

In a whisper, Peter told Trudi to move quickly and quietly on the trail to the next tree line. He told her to bend at the waist so she would look like a wild boar, or other animal, if anyone saw her. She ran in a crouch. It was no problem for the athletic Trudi. When she reached the distant tree line she waited for Peter, who arrived noiselessly a few minutes later. They looked and listened. Still no train and little light where they were going. After resting, they proceeded carefully along the tree line until Peter pointed to the airport beacon light to signify that it would soon not be visible as he had briefed her. Trudi found the earth rough and difficult to negotiate. She hadn't been able to take boots and hiking clothes to the *Blitzbaum*, and now she wished she had them. She had to be careful to not stumble or injure herself with only her running shoes on the rugged terrain. A twisted ankle could be a disaster.

They paused momentarily while Peter checked his compass to find an azimuth of two hundred sixty-three degrees. That took them through a forested area where it was nearly pitch-black and progress was even more difficult. Peter signaled for her to grasp his pack and follow closely. It was dark enough to cause a separation if they lost physical contact. A separation could make a noiseless reunion impossible. Making their way through this wooded area silently was slow and time-consuming. She didn't know that Peter was also worried about that single nocturnal wild boar he had encountered two nights earlier.

Eventually they reached the distant edge of the tree line where Peter checked the azimuth and started looking for the haystack reference point. Alternating between inside and outside the tree line made progress a little faster. Outside the tree line vision was considerably better with the help of the occasional splashes of bright moonlight. Walking on the cleared edge of the tree line wasn't the safest thing to do, but the dark canopied forest was almost an impossibility to make good time noiselessly. Trudi's legs were becoming dotted with scratch marks and her feet were sore from the often twisted, uneven footing on the forest floor. They stopped while Peter checked his watch in the moonlight. It was 0214. Peter wanted to get back by Willie's deadline of 0300. Willie may not have been serious about coming after him if he didn't make the deadline, but he didn't want to take the chance. That reason, in addition to gaining the safety of Curly, made the deadline important.

Peter was relieved when he could make out the haystack-looking object in the distance. After finding the exact spot on the tree line that displayed an azimuth of fifteen degrees to the haystack, he turned toward the tree line and found an azimuth of one hundred ninety degrees. It would be thirty-two steps to the Curly window. In order to reassure Trudi, he whispered that they were close. She followed closely as he counted off the steps and ensured that he was on the correct azimuth. After twenty-four steps he encountered broken branches, leaves and other debris on the forest floor that he didn't remember placing there.

"What? This isn't right!" He was whispering to himself. Almost in a panic, he rechecked the compass, turned to verify the haystack location, and quickly walked around the debris which was covering the door. He knew he was in the right place.

"Somebody's been here, Trudi. We have a problem."

Trudi sensed his confusion and distress. She told herself to stay calm and not add panic to the problem. At that moment she had no idea what was happening and what she should do.

Peter searched for the radio he had hidden in a nearby tree trunk. It was gone! His heart was racing as thoughts of failure crossed his mind. He began to formulate a logical course of action when suddenly he heard a voice whispering nearby.

"Who's there?" Peter asked instinctively.

"Brigitte Berg," was the answer.

" . . . Willie!" Peter was shocked.

Willie approached them, held a finger in front of his lips, and pointed in the direction of the border guard tower. It still wasn't visible, but Willie probably knew where it was. He motioned for them to follow him. Quietly they made their way deeper into the forest and up a rather steep incline. The underbrush was thick and tall. They could see several tall trees encircling an open space. Willie held his hand up to signal a stop. He searched the ground with his hand and then stood, bringing the radio near his lips. He turned it on and whispered "Hotel."

Peter could hear a reply in the headset close to Willie's ear. It sounded like a repeat of "Hotel."

Willie motioned for them to back off the open space. The earth moved as a door similar to the window on Curly opened.

Willie motioned for Trudi to enter first. A hand reached out to assist her as she slid into the tunnel entrance. Two other tunnel assistants guided her out of the way to make room for Peter and Willie. When all were safely in the tunnel, the tunnel door was replaced. A light came on to illuminate a tunnel similar to Curly. A tunnel assistant turned the signaling handle on a field telephone.

"Three people are in and safe. Sgt Kyles, Sgt Ackerman and I assume——Trudi Kehle."

Peter nodded in the affirmative.

"Welcome to Moe . . . both of you!" Willie had a huge grin on his face.

"What happened to Curly?"

"We had a cave-in on Curly. We worked all night to overcome that setback. I'll explain later. Right now you have to follow me to the main cavern."

It did not escape Peter's attention that, when the pressure was on and the mission was in jeopardy, Willie had made good on his promise to come to his rescue.

Peter reassured Trudi that they were safely under American jurisdiction. She relaxed as she read the positive expressions on everybody's face. Peter noticed her limp slightly as they moved toward the cavern. Peter wanted to scream with joy; Trudi was confused, but happy. The first thing they saw when they entered the cavern was a huge banner that read: *WILLKOMMEN IN DEUTSCHLAND*: Trudi Kehle *und* Sgt Peter Ackerman.

Major Taylor stood before them; he was stoic, standing with military bearing. Peter reported to him with all the pride and confidence of a man who knew he had done well and accomplished an extremely difficult mission.

"Sir, Sgt Ackerman reporting. Mission accomplished, sir! I am accompanied by *Fräulein* Gertrude Kehle. She is responsible for much of the success of this mission."

"At ease, sergeant," He smiled broadly as he shook the hands of both Peter and Trudi. "I want to congratulate you both on a job well done. Now get looked after by the doctor and enjoy your homecoming. You have some friends and family waiting for you. When you are ready, Sgt Martinez will escort you to Mähring."

"Thank you, sir . . . I have a packet of intelligence information to turn over to you. It also contains photographic evidence of life during the post-war expulsions. My family valuables are also in the packet."

"You safeguard that packet until we can establish a formal chain of custody. For now, just enjoy yourself a few moments."

Standing behind the major in the primary cavern area near a table with sandwiches, snacks and champagne was Hannelore Kehle. When the military formalities were completed, Trudi saw her mother for the first time. They greeted one another with huge smiles and hugs. Tears rolled down the cheeks of both. Unintelligible words of relief were exchanged. Hannelore said *Oma* was safe in Mähring with a German-speaking MI agent.

Peter joined them and gave Hannelore a big hug. "We did it," he said. "This is the first day of your new life!"

"Yes, Peter, and I am so grateful. This is the first day Trudi and I have ever been in West Germany together. We are Germans who have never been out of the Bärnau/Thanhausen area. Everything will be new to us except the language."

"You will love it. Right now Trudi and I need water and something to eat and then she has to see the doctor about her legs and feet."

"I brought her some clothes and comfortable shoes. They said she might have a very difficult journey if she had only running shoes and an athletic uniform. I can see the scratches on both of your faces and I can see Trudi's torn clothing."

"OK, *Muti,* if I can call you that, you have a sandwich and a glass of champagne. I'll go with Trudi to see the doctor."

"I am honored that you want to call me *Muti.* Trudi gave me her ID that she had strapped to her waist and a few worthless *Koruna.*"

The doctor quickly determined there was no serious problems, cleaned and disinfected their wounds and pronounced them tired, but fit as fiddles. Trudi was shown to a makeshift restroom that the engineers had used during construction and was able to wash up and change clothes. When she returned to the snack table, Trudi couldn't contain her joy. She kissed Peter, hugged everybody in sight and jumped for joy. Her joy was contagious. Everybody was happy. Major Taylor was there, Captain Lokar, Sgt Martinez, tunnel engineers and assistants were all there. Trudi personally thanked Willie in her best English/German mix. They made a toast and gave a loud exclamation of "hip-hip-hooray, hip-hip-hooray."

Sgt Martinez reported that *Oma* was safe in Mähring at the MI compound and had already been notified by a military telephone link that Trudi and Peter were safely in West Germany. A German agent had cleared *Oma's* residence in Thanhausen. There would be no indication of where *Oma* was if anybody ever inquired. *Oma,* Hannelore and Trudi were temporarily under the care and control of the US Army. There would be weeks, if not months, of debriefing and resettlement in Mähring for them and for es corial.

Sgt Martinez had orders to move the team and the Kehle family to Mähring for lodging and reuniting with *Oma*. When the euphoria surrounding the escape began to abate, loading the sedan commenced. Peter protected the bag full of film and valuables by keeping it with him in the back seat of the sedan. Willie sat in the front "shot gun" seat. The Sgt was hoping they could get past the American guards, up the access hill, through the German guard station and onto a public road without attracting unexpected attention. He felt they were still somewhat vulnerable until they got far away from Yankee.

That was not to be the case. Peter spoke excitedly, "Willie . . . Look! It's Christian from the Gasthaus Blei. He is the ex-German soldier who was so curious about Yankee."

Christian, the one-legged man, was sitting in a leisure chair, staring at the sedan with a perplexed, mystified look on his face.

"It looks like he recognizes you," said Peter.

"No, to the Germans we all look alike." Willie was trying to be funny, but he understood the potential problem of the team's lies about their presence in the 5K zone and now being seen departing Site Yankee with two women in the sedan.

Nobody laughed, so Willie continued, "Be sure Christian gets emphasis in our after-action report, sergeant."

The women didn't understand, so Peter gave them a short explanation in order to ease their confusion. Peter was well aware that this circumstance would have to be reported. Even if Christian had no ill intent, it wasn't good that he could talk in the community about his observations and suspicions.

The es corial team had completed its mission. Peter was satisfied that there was no more he could do about his personal agenda. He was sure that *Oma,* Hannelore and Trudi could be resettled near him in Bad Tölz after debriefing in Mähring. The passengers in the van were relaxing and being overcome with the fatigue of the tense twenty-four hour they had endured.

Trudi leaned her head on Peter's shoulder. The last thing he heard before sleep overcame him was Sgt Martinez talking about the ongoing Cold War and the need for good people like team es corial and the Kehle family to help protect western Europe.

Epilogue

The intelligence gathered from Trudi and Hannelore during debriefing was a windfall for NATO forces. As a reward, Trudi's family was provided with the means to begin a new life in West Germany and to be relocated to the village of Gaissach near Peter's home station in Bad Tölz. All were issued ID cards which allowed them access to US and NATO facilities. To their neighbors in Gaissach they appeared to be dependents of Peter. Peter stayed with the family when duty allowed, but was not granted family benefits without legal matrimony.

The photographic evidence of the expulsions was reviewed and sent through military and political channels for further disposition. That there would be hand-wringing and uncertainty by interested governments was not surprising to Peter—he had done what he could. The family valuables were important to the resettlement of Trudi and family. He no longer had a family of his own, but wanted to give another family a solid foundation upon which to start anew.

Peter and Willie introduced Trudi to Colonel Watts and Captain Wilcox, who were in awe of her contributions to the es corial team mission. They had reviewed the complete report of the conduct of the mission and Colonel Watts had commented, jokingly, that he wished he and his men could be as strong as Trudi and Hannelore.

On the very serious side, he assumed a father-figure persona and hinted about how good the youngsters would be for a new unit the army was activating. The LRRPs (pronounced lurps) were under activation with projected missions very much like that which es corial had just completed. The Long Range Reconnaissance Patrol would breach borders, gather information and give timely reports via portable continuous wave (CW, also known as Morse code) radio systems. There was already a mission in which a mentally and physically tough German-speaking female would be utilized.

Neither Trudi, Hannelore, nor Peter commented; the seed had been planted. Each had a different first reaction. Trudi had an overwhelming sense of debt to the Americans, which needed repayment; Hannelore immediately understood the baited statements and worried about her daughter's safety; Peter understood his unique qualification for missions like this. All three were consumed by thoughts of exposing the Warsaw Pact for what it was and exacting a "pound of flesh" for deeds which could not be undone. Peter and Trudi were aware that, after resettlement, their futures could involve more danger and intrigue. Peter still felt the need to repay supporting friends since his escape from Tachau. Anything he could do to help neutralize the threat from the Warsaw Pact would be his repayment: to Sgt Grimes, Corporal Mays, the Waldbaus, the Swansons, his allegiance to his country of birth and to America.

Das ist Alles!